City of Lies

R. J. ELLORY

An Orion paperback

First published in Great Britain in 2006
by Orion
This paperback edition published in 2007
by Orion Books Ltd,
Orion House, 5 Upper Saint Martin's Lane
London, WC2H 9EA

An Hachette Livre UK company

Reissued 2008

Typeset by Deltatype Limited, Birkenhead, Merseyside

Printed in Great Britain by Clays Ltd, St Ives plc

The Orion Publishing Group's policy is to use papers
that are natural, renewable and recyclable products and
made from wood grown in sustainable forests. The logging
and manufacturing processes are expected to conform to
the environmental regulations of the country of origin.

A QUIET BELIEF IN ANGELS

'*A Quiet Belief in Angels* is a beautiful and haunting book.
This is a tour de force from R. J. Ellory'
Michael Connelly

'This is compelling, unputdownable thriller writing of the
very highest order'   *Guardian*

'Once again R. J. Ellory shows off his special talents . . . it
confirms his place in the top flight of crime writing'
Sunday Telegraph

R. J. Ellory is the author of five other novels: *Candlemoth,
Ghostheart, A Quiet Vendetta, A Quiet Belief in Angels* and
A Simple Act of Violence. Twice shortlisted for the Crime
Writers' Association Steel Dagger for Best Thriller, Ellory's
books have been translated into Italian, German, Dutch
and Swedish. Having originally studied graphics and
photography, he intended to pursue a career in photo-
journalism, but for many reasons this never came to
fruition. He started writing more than ten years ago and
hasn't stopped since. He is married with one son, and
currently resides in England. Visit his website at
www.rjellory.com.

By R. J. Ellory

Candlemoth
Ghostheart
A Quiet Vendetta
City of Lies
A Quiet Belief in Angels
A Simple Act of Violence

Dedicated to

Jimmy the Saint
Frank White
Cody Jarrett
Johnny Rocco
Tom Reagan
Jimmy Conway

ACKNOWLEDGEMENTS

To Jon: editor extraordinaire, partner-in-crime.
To Genevieve and Juliet; everyone at Orion.
To Euan: challenging my prose, preserving my humour.
To Robyn: incisive, endlessly patient.
To my brother, Guy; my son, Ryan.
To my wife: the only woman who told me how to behave and got away with it.

A hundred times have I thought New York is a catastrophe, and fifty times: It is a beautiful catastrophe.

Le Corbusier

Always you must play yourself. But it will be an infinite variety.

Constantin Stanislavski – *An Actor Prepares*

ONE

Old man crawled out of the doorway on his hands and knees. Crawled out like a dog.

Sound from his mouth almost inhuman, face all twisted, like someone had taken hold of his hair and screwed his features a few inches backwards.

Blood on his hands, on the sidewalk. Blood on his knees. Made it to the kerb and then collapsed forward.

Smell in the air like snow, cool and crisp.

Later, people would be asked what they remembered most clearly, and all of them – one for one and without exception – would speak about the blood.

Snow didn't come. Not that night. Would come a few days later perhaps, maybe in time for Christmas.

Had it come there would have been blood in that snow, spooling around the old man as he lay there, twitching and mouthing while cabs flew by and people went from one part of their lives to yet another; while New York made it safely out of one long day and hoped the next would be somehow better.

Such is the way of the world some would say, grateful for the fact that it had not been them, had not in fact been anyone they knew – and that, if nothing else, was some small saving grace.

People were stabbed and shot, strangled, burned, drowned and hung; people were killed in automobile accidents, in freak twists of nature; people walked from their houses every day believing that it would be a day no different from any other. But it was.

The old man lay on the sidewalk until someone called the police. An ambulance came; police helped the medics put the old man on a stretcher and lift him in back of the vehicle.

'He try to stop the guy with the gun,' a Korean man told the officer after the ambulance had peeled away, cherry-bar flashing,

1

lights ablaze. It was a Sunday evening; the traffic was as quiet as it would get.

'Who the hell are you?' the officer said.

'I own liquor store.'

'Liquor store? What liquor store?'

'Liquor store down there.' The man pointed. 'Some guy robbing the store . . . some guy with a gun, and the old man went for him—'

'The old man tried to stop a guy robbing your store?' the officer asked.

'He did . . . guy was trying to rob the store. He had gun. He was pointing gun at my wife, and then old man come down the aisle and went for the guy. Guy got real scared and shot the old man. Don't think he mean to shoot anyone, but old man scared him and the guy lost it.'

'And where did the guy go?'

'Took off down the street.'

The officer looked down the street as if such a thing would serve a purpose. 'He went that way?'

The man nodded. 'Yes, that way.'

'You better come with me then . . . you better come to the precinct and make a statement. You could look at some pictures and see if you recognize him.'

'Who?'

'The one with the gun . . . the one who tried to rob you.'

'Oh,' the store owner said. 'I thought you mean old man.'

The officer shook his head. Sometimes he wondered about people, how they managed to make it through each day.

The owner's wife came down from the liquor store later, maybe half an hour or so. She carried a bucket, hot soapy water inside, in her hand a mop. She cleaned down the sidewalk, sluiced the blood into the gutter, and she too thought *such is the way of the world*, perhaps those words exactly, perhaps something close. She was Korean. She had a short name, more consonants than vowels, which folks kept mispronouncing, so she called herself Kim. Kim was easy to remember, easier to say. She had come to America with every intention of being nothing but herself. Eleven years on and she was called Kim and standing on the sidewalk washing blood into the street from some old man who came to buy his wine each Sunday, an old man who'd tried to help them.

And then it was kind of forgotten, because in and of itself such an event was of no great moment.

This was New York after all. Used to be Sinatra's town. Now it belonged to *Sex and the City* and Woody Allen. Shit like this went down each and every day, each and every way. People wrote about this place – people like Roth and Auster, Selby and Styron. This was the center of the world, a microcosm that represented all that was senseless and beautiful about the world.

A place where someone could get shot for no reason; where a woman called Kim could wash blood into the gutter with no greater ceremony than if it were spilled diesel wine; where the reasons to live – love and money, perhaps the hope of something better – were indiscernible from the reasons to die. Blessed and brave, impassioned, afflicted, forever believing in fortune, a million lives crossing a million lives more, and all of them interwoven until the seams that lay between them could no longer be defined.

Sunday evening, mid-December; they rushed the old man to St Vincent's and, despite knowing nothing of his life, not even his name, they all – the liquor store owner, his wife, the police officer, the medics in the Blue Cross ambulance . . . all of them hoped and prayed and willed that he would live.

Such was human nature; such was the way of the world.

An hour later, maybe less. Middle-aged man – greying hair, white shirt, woven silk tie, features made of character and muscular tension – stands in front of a desk. Replaces the phone in its cradle. Looks away towards the window of the room, a window that overlooks the street from where the sound of traffic, making its way from wherever to someplace else, is like staggered breathing.

Middle-aged man turns and looks across the desk at a younger woman – dark hair, beautiful yes, no doubt about it, but a ghost within her features that speaks of some internal disquiet.

'They shot Edward,' the man says. His voice is matter-of-fact and businesslike, almost as if such news has been expected.

Sharp intake of breath. 'Who? Who shot him? Is he okay?' The woman, name of Cathy Hollander, starts to rise from her chair.

3

The man raises his hand and she pauses. 'We don't know anything,' he says. 'Maybe something direct, maybe simple bad luck. Go get Charlie Beck and Joe Koenig. I have to make some calls. I have to get someone here—'

'Someone?' the woman asks.

'I have to get his son from Miami—'

She frowns, shakes her head. 'His son? What the fuck are you talking about? Edward has a son?'

The man, goes by the name of Walt Freiberg, nods his head slowly and closes his eyes. 'Yes,' he says, his voice almost a whisper, 'he has a son.'

'I didn't know—' Cathy starts.

Freiberg lifts the receiver and dials a number. 'You didn't know he had a son? I wouldn't feel left out sweetheart . . . neither did the rest of the world.'

The phone connects at the other end of the line.

Walt Freiberg smiles. 'Evelyn? It's Walter . . . long time, no see. Calling because I need you to do something for me.'

TWO

So this – amongst so many other things – was the real deal, the hard-bitten truth: when he was drunk he believed in God.

But these days John Harper didn't drink so often, and thus his moments of faith were few and far between. Harper was one of the very fortunate who'd experienced the moment of special revelation: sleep off the drunk and the debt was still owed; the girlfriend still pregnant; the wife knew you'd walked out on her for a twenty-two-year-old Thai girl with universal joints for hips. The fan was still spinning, the crap still airborne six ways to Christmas. Life turns a corner, and all of a sudden your soundtrack plays in a minor key.

And so John Harper stopped drinking, and therefore stopped believing in God.

But before that: raw-faced and noisy; thundering migraines surrendering to nothing but a combination of Jack Daniels and Darvon Complex; fits of anger, more often than not directed towards himself; a frustrated man; a man of words bound within the limits of a stunted imagination. Ate too little – corn-dogs and cinnamon cake and sometimes a cheeseburger from Wendy's or Sambo's; late-night shuffles through the kitchen searching out Ring-Dings and handfuls of dry Froot Loops, making inhuman sounds, hands shaking, wondering when the muse would come back.

Because John Harper wrote a book one time; called it *Depth of Fingerprints*; sold it for twelve thousand dollars up-front to a smalltime publishing house in Miami. Optioned for film; film was never made. Helluva story, even posted a squib in the *Herald Tribune* which told him he had a future if he kept his narrative dry and his prose succinct. That had been eight years before. Started a dozen things since; finished nothing.

Lived in Miami now. Had headed south from New York in the

hope of inspiration and wound up staying, and like someone once said: Miami was a noise, a perpetual thundering noise trapped against the coast of Florida between Biscayne Bay and Hialeah; beneath it Coral Gables, above it Fort Lauderdale; everywhere the smell of the Everglades – rank, swollen and fetid in summer, cracked and featureless and unforgiving in winter.

Miami was a promise and an automatic betrayal; a catastrophe by the sea; perched there upon a finger of land that pointed accusingly at something that was altogether not to blame. And never had been. And never would be.

Miami was a punctuation mark of dirt on a peninsula of misfortune; an appendage.

But home is where the heart is.

John Harper's heart was taken in Miami, and to date – as far as he knew – it had never been returned.

Pushed his pen nevertheless; wrote inches for the *Herald*, and sometimes those inches were pressed out once more for the *Key West Citizen*, *The Keynoter*, *Island Life* and *The Navigator*. John Harper wrote human interest squibs about poisonwood and pigeon plum and strangler fig and gumbo limbo in Lignumvitae Key State Botanical; about shark sightings and shark tournaments; about the homes of Tennessee Williams and Papa Hemingway on Key West; about all manner of minutiae that swallowed the attention for a heartbeat and was just as soon forgotten.

Greyhound Bus made eight stops between Miami and Key West. Down through Islamorada, Key Largo, Marathon and Grassy Key; two routes – one from the Florida Turnpike which wound up in Homestead, the other along 1-95 which became US 1 at the southern end of Miami. Both roads hit the Overseas Highway. Both roads he had travelled. And there was something about the islands – all thirty-one punctuations of limestone and the eight hundred uninhabited islands that surrounded them – that forever gripped his imagination. Here, on this awkward peninsula of hope, he believed himself a million miles from the disappointment of New York. South and east was the Atlantic, west was the Gulf of Mexico; forty-two bridges, dozens of causeways; New England and Caribbean architecture – gingerbread verandas, widow's walks, wrought-iron balconies, population of twenty-five thousand, a million tourists a year.

John Pennekamp Coral Reef State Park with its starfish and lobsters, its sponges and sea cucumbers, its stingrays, barracuda, crabs and angel fish. And then there was Key Largo Dry Rocks, the Bronze Christ of the Deep Statue, shoals of blackfin tuna, the waves of frigate birds overhead that would tell you when the fish were running. And the smell, the once-in-a-lifetime smell of salt, seaweed, fish and marsh, mangrove swamps and rocks; the memory of pirates and Ponce de Leon, the Dry Tortugas, the footprints of turtles, the reefs, the clear water, the citrus, the coconut.

All these things a hundred and fifty miles from where he sat in his small backroom office in the *Miami Herald* complex.

John Harper: journalist, one-time novelist, one-time New Yorker; thirty-six years old, muddy-blond hair, good jawline, clear grey eyes. Single now, single and without options; small address book, maybe a dozen girls in all, but each one – right to the last – had been ousted from the Harper camp by the necessity to do something more with their lives than wait for the bitter and sardonic humor to lighten up. Last got laid a handful of weeks before. Sweet girl, olive complexion, emerald eyes. Called him 'Johnnie' which irritated him, but not for long. Lasted a couple of months; she found someone else – boat captain called Gil Gibson running tourist trips out of Bayside around HMS *Bounty*. She took another little piece of that heart, the one that belonged to Miami, and she stole it away silently, walking on eggshells, for she knew John Harper was a man of too many words, and some of those words could be hurled with a raised voice and clenched fists. He let her go; she would have gone anyway; told her it was better for both of them if she walked out into life and found what she really wanted. To her, to himself, he had lied, but he had lied like a professional.

And Harper believed, *had* to believe, that one day the muse would come home, and then he would find his dry narrative and his succinct prose, and he would pen a prizewinner that would give him enough money to leave Miami and head south along Overseas until he reached the end. And he'd walk out to the beach come nightfall and know that Hemingway and Williams, John Hersey, James Merrill, Tom McGuane and Phil Caputo . . . know that all of them had once stood right where he would be standing, and they too had looked out towards the Keys of Fish

Hawk, Sugarloaf, Halfmoon and Little Truman. He would stand in the footprints of giants, and there – at the southernmost point of the continental United States – John Michael Harper, he of the dry and bitter humor, he of the lost loves and lonely nights, he of clenched fists and silent typewriter, of burgeoning promise and unfulfilled potential, would know that he had come home.

Home, perhaps, is not where the heart is, but where – at last – you found it.

But that was all so much of so many different things. That sort of thing was dreams and wishes and other stuff related.

Reality was less complex.

Simple job. Showed up Monday morning.

'John?'

Standing in the doorway was Harry. Harry made most doorways look too small. Harry – a.k.a. Harry Ivens, Assistant Editor-In-Chief, *Miami Herald* – smiled like he'd just got the joke, a joke pretty much everyone else had gotten three-quarters of an hour before.

'Harry . . . good morning,' John Harper replied.

Harry nodded. 'Shark tournament, Blackwater Sound into Florida Bay, all the way out and round Sandy, come home south-west into Marathon . . . you know the routine, you love it, you know you do . . . get your shit together.' Harry smiled again.

'Today?'

'Today.'

'Thought it was next Monday.'

Harry tilted his head to one side as if considering the significance of Harper's comment. He looked at Harper again. 'It's December, John, same trip every year, same time. We'll soon have Christmas, if you didn't know. Get a diary, write this stuff down. Hell, get a computer, a laptop maybe . . . you could be better organized. We're not asking you to cover Watergate. Time for coffee now, little more than that, and you better be away or the boats will be sailing without you aboard. Camera, remember? Pictures are good . . . get some pictures and we can put your piece in all the Keys papers three times over.' Harry nodded. 'I've got to go now, but I envy you. Sun and fun and fish, right?'

'Right, Harry.'

Harper watched him leave the room and head through the maze of partitions to his office in the far corner, then he turned

8

his chair until his back was to the door. He made-believe he was looking out through a window. Behind him, there on the wall, he'd hung a calendar, a calendar with pictures of Molasses Reef, Mallory Pier, Fort Zachary Taylor and the gulls at Higgs Beach. Made-believe he was looking out through a window at these things and, sometimes when he did this, he would close his eyes and imagine the tradewind breeze through his hair, would find the smell, would hear the shrill echoes of birds and the sound of the surf against the shore.

Minutes would dissolve away silently, and then someone would say, 'Where the fuck is Harper?' and Harper would turn and wait for the someone to come through the door, and hear them say, 'John, I need four and a half inches split three ways. Pages six, nine, eleven. Any old crap will do. Need it within the hour, okay?'

And John Harper would nod and smile, and spend twenty-five minutes writing four and a half inches of any old crap, and they would use it like mortar between the bricks, fill in the gaps between one real story and the next, and even as he was doing it he would smell the tradewind breeze, would hear the gulls, feel a sense of warmth on the back of his neck.

And that – fundamentally – was what he did. Rented a comfortable, simple apartment on N.W. Twelfth between Gibson Park and the North-South Expressway, not so far from his workplace; couple of bars he frequented, not because he needed to drink but because he liked the sound of real people with real enough lives, and bars were where he would find them when evening came and Miami slowed down; five days a week in a small office writing fill-ins and bylines, more than not without credit, and the only reason he got the job in the first place was because of *Depth of Fingerprints*, which – all in all – wasn't so much a bad book as a good start that never went anyplace.

John Harper was a man without a purpose, and he knew – above all else – that a man without a purpose was destined for unhappiness whichever way he walked.

What he *told* himself he wanted was the tradewind and the blackfin tuna, the pigeon plum and the poisonwood, the eight hundred punctuations of limestone and the smell that haunted the spaces in between. The truth was perhaps different. What he

9

wanted was something to drive him forward, much the way he'd been driven to write *Depth of Fingerprints*.

But that December Monday morning – late December, but still so warm you felt punch-drunk before reaching the car – he left his office and the complex and headed home. Mid-morning he was packed and prepped for a two-day jaunt out of Blackwater Sound; a flotilla of boats captained by seasoned and veteran drunks, men with faces like storm-hammered rocks, hands like dried-up leather gloves, their passengers business types – from Miami and Hialeah, Coral Gables and Kendall; men who split their time between the office, the Key Biscayne Golf Course, the mistress, and three times a year this wild two-day fishing jag after barracuda and shark, staggering close to blind near the edge of the deck, loaded to the gunnels with cold beer and warm sun. This was as real as life got for guys like this, and John Harper was there to see it all, to tell the tales, to take the pictures, to write another byline or fill-in that would grace the pages of *The Key West Citizen* or *Island Life*.

Took him an hour to get down there, all the way to Key Largo, and already he sensed, perhaps with something preternatural and intuitive, that these couple of days ahead would see a storm out of the Gulf of Mexico. He parked his car, a Pontiac 6.6 that had seen so many better days, off of the highway between Newport and Rock Harbor, and then he hitched a ride back towards the mouth of the Sound with one of the many pickups that were headed that way.

All jeans and tee-shirts, lumberjack checks with the sleeves torn off, unshaven since Friday morning in preparation for this; belts with hunting knives in hand-tooled leather sheaths, strong boots with sealed soles, weatherproofs and all-in-ones packed in holdalls; men shouting, laughing, already drinking, not even discreet despite the hour of the day, and thumping shoulders and real-life honest-to-God man-hugs, and *Shit, you old fuck . . . you look like you gained forty fucking pounds since a year ago! And You hear about Marv? Hell, if his missus didn't catch him bangin' some Filipino chick. Took him for half his fucking company, poor son-of-a-bitch.*

And amidst this vast throng of noisy humanity – amidst these real people, their lives put on hold for forty-eight hours –

John Harper stood, watching the jetties bear up beneath the strain, and down along the wharf there were twenty-five or thirty boats hitched and waiting to carry them out, a thousand bucks a man, with fiberglass rods and high-tensile lines, and carbon-steel hooks and hats bedecked with flies that were hand-wound and hand-tied and a work of art in themselves, and all of this on a Monday morning while regular folk were filling out requisition dockets for insurance claims, or ferrying kids to band practice or hairdressers or football or drama class.

There were some regulars down there, faces he had seen before, and every once in a while he would nod and smile or grip someone's hand, and look at their face, and think *You were here last time around, and for the life of me I cannot remember your name*, and get a look back that meant exactly the same thing, but they were all too polite to say so, and it didn't matter a goddamn anyway because they would more than likely lose one another in this vast mêlée, and wouldn't see one another again until next time they did this thing.

Harper walked down the wharf until he found the Press vessel, the *Mary McGregor*, her name freshly painted on the stern.

He smiled to himself, and wondered what in hell's name he was doing there. Hadn't it been a year ago that he'd told himself he would never do this trip again? The story was always the same; the pictures would be syndicated on the web for anyone who wanted to use them; it would be the same faces, the same tales, the same fisherman's lies.

Harper reached the stern of the boat and, with his kitbag over his shoulder, hauled himself up and over the railing. He stood there for a moment and then turned and looked out towards the sea. Turquoise and cerulean, the sky clear, giving a view all the way west to Joe Bay, the smell of salt clearing the nostrils, the warmth of the sun overhead.

Back and behind Harper was Key Largo. Down along Overseas Highway and the first mile marker would appear – MM126, one hundred and twenty-six miles north of Key West – and a little way beyond that you would cross the Jewfish Creek bridge. Once upon a time it was called Rock Harbor, but Bogart and Bacall changed all that in 1948. Here was the Caribbean Club, a coquina rock facade and a tin roof, old movie posters on the walls and the redolent haunt of rum and bourbon, as if the very

11

structure of the place was imbued with it. Often times Harper would drive down there Sundays just to eat at Mrs Mac's Kitchen, and then head out to the Wild Bird Center, across wooden walkways that meandered through mangrove wetlands crowded with saffron plum trees, pine bromeliads and prickly pear cacti. One time he'd gone out to the reefs: White Banks Dry Rocks and Carysfort, the French Reef and Molasses, and then Conch where the sunken wrecks of the *Capitana*, the *El Infante* and the *San Jose* lay sleeping. He'd never been back, not because he couldn't dive, not because he didn't want to see them again, but because he knew that the more he went the more dissatisfied he would become with the life he had chosen. The same way he'd felt when he'd left New York so many years before.

And it was then that the call came. The defining moment perhaps. His cellphone jangling awkwardly, and Harper thinking, *This is some other unwanted aspect of an unwanted life.*

He looked at the number on the face of the phone – the *Herald*, and for a moment he was tempted not to take the call. Protocol and the threat of unemployment censored his thoughts. He pressed the green button.

'Hi.'

John . . . it's Carol at the desk. Harry asked me to call you. You out with the boats?

'Yes . . . just got here, why?'

He asked me to tell you to come back.

'Come back . . . what have I got to come back for?'

There's been a call for you.

'A call? What call?'

Your aunt called the paper . . . said there was something urgent, something to do with your family.

Harper frowned. 'Carol, believe me, the woman is crazy, absolutely fucking crazy . . . don't worry about it. Just get someone to tell her I'm out, won't be back for a while, okay?'

John . . . don't give me a hard time. Harry told me to get you back here, whatever you said. Just come back, alright?

'Is he there?'

Harry? Of course he's here.

'Put him on the phone, Carol.'

A moment's pause.

John?

'Jesus Harry . . . what the hell is going on over there?'

People after you, John . . . had two calls from your aunt in New York, and then a further three calls from some girl called Nancy Young.

'What?'

Just get your ass back here, John . . . I'm sending someone down to cover the trip, okay? Whatever's going on with your family seems like a big deal and I can't have your friends and relatives calling the paper and upsetting people. Come back and sort this shit out, will you?

'Right, Harry . . . right, sure thing.'

Puzzled as hell, John Harper finished the call.

It cost him fifty bucks to get someone to drive him back to where he'd parked his car. Annoyed, irritated, wanting to be out there on the deck of a boat making his way towards the limestone punctuations. Life had a habit of interrupting pretty much everything these days.

By the time he reached the *Herald* it was gone eleven. Walked in just as Carol rose from behind her desk. She pointed towards Ivens' office.

Harper frowned, shook his head, couldn't believe that such a fuss was being made about a call from one crazy relative, a relative he hadn't spoken to for as long as he could remember.

'So what the fuck is going on here?' was the question with which he was greeted. Harry Ivens – big man that he was – came out from behind his wide desk.

'Going on?' Harper asked. 'I haven't a clue, Harry . . . you said my aunt had called, and Nancy Young.'

'Who the hell is Nancy Young?' Ivens asked.

'Girl I used to date.'

'So what the hell was she doing calling David?'

Harper frowned. 'David? David Leonhardt?'

Harry nodded, pointing to one of the cubicles ten yards or so from his office. Harper could see the back of Leonhardt's head.

'David!' Ivens hollered.

Leonhardt turned, rose from his chair, and even as he reached the office door his phone started ringing again. Leonhardt glanced at it and looked at Harper.

'It's Nancy,' he said, and then he paused awkwardly.

Harper's eyes widened.

Leonhardt shrugged. He handed his phone to Harper.

Harper held it up and peered at the name that flashed on the screen. *NANCY ... NANCY ... NANCY ...*

He was confused. He hit the button, and then passed the phone back to Leonhardt.

'Nancy?' Leonhardt paused, silent, looked embarrassed. He nodded his head, looked at John Harper, and then said, 'You ... she wants to speak to you ... says she's called you but couldn't get a signal.'

John took the phone, held it to his ear.

John?

'Nancy ... what is it?'

Hadn't spoken to her for the better part of a year. Bitter and acrimonious relationship breakdown. Hurling vases down the stairs, old 45s, a couple of signed and framed pictures he'd had for years. Had to clean up the hallway below, sweeping shards of glass from along the baseboard. Sour taste in his mouth. Harsh words echoing in his head even as he heard her voice.

John ... I've been trying to get hold of you ... your aunt called me earlier, an hour ago, I don't remember ...

She sounded worried, fretting, anxious, uptight. Sounded like a woman on the edge of an episode.

She didn't have your cellphone number ... not that it would've done any good ... your phone's off—

'I've changed my number.'

Right ... anyway, I couldn't reach you—

'You called David's phone,' Harper interrupted.

He looked up at David Leonhardt who glanced away like he wasn't listening, like he didn't hear the last thing said. Tension in the air. Awkwardness.

Yes.

John shook his head. 'You called David's phone ... David Leonhardt ... from the paper?'

Yes, I called David's phone ... I called him because I thought he might know where you were. You guys have done a lot of work together ...

'But how do you have his number, Nancy?'

John looked at Leonhardt again, Frowned like he was trying to see if it worked as a useful expression. 'David?' he asked, and for a moment it wasn't clear whether he was speaking directly to his

14

colleague, or if he was talking on the cell. 'I don't understand . . .
how does Nancy have your phone number?'

Leonhardt shrugged, mouth turned down at the edges, trying
to appear nonchalant.

John?

Back on the phone.

*John . . . shut up for a goddamned minute will you? I've been
calling you because your aunt didn't know how to get hold of you . . .
she needs to speak to you.*

There was silence for a moment, a tight pocket of silence, like
Nancy was going to say something else and then she cut it short,
pulled in the reins, didn't know what words to use.

'What?' Harper asked. 'What is it?'

I don't know, John . . . it doesn't make sense.

'Whaddya mean, it doesn't make sense? *What* doesn't make
sense, Nancy?' His tone one of irritation. He could hear it, clear
as a bell at daybreak, and he knew this was some overspill from
way back when; something tied up tight inside, tied up with
whipcord, something vindictive and vengeful towards the girl
who seemed to have effortlessly broken his heart.

*Don't get nasty, John . . . I'm just calling you because your aunt
couldn't get hold of you so she called me. I'm here at work, John, still
at work, and she called me here and I've been trying to find you. I did
meet her, John, remember? She must have remembered where I worked.*

'So what's so important, Nancy? What's so important that she
needs to call my ex-girlfriend?' Emphasized *ex*, like he wanted to
say something to get back at her.

Like I said, it doesn't make any sense to me—

Nancy paused, and then, *She said it was about your family John.
She said she needed to speak to you about your family.*

'She what?'

*John, will you stop asking me questions I can't answer. You have
any idea how stupid you sound?*

A heartbeat of hesitation, then, 'I'll call her, okay?'

Okay . . . that's all I wanted. Now let me speak to David.

Harper opened his mouth to say something else. He felt
awkward, disjointed; his thoughts present, half-formed, but
seemingly disconnected from speech.

He held out the phone. Leonhardt took it, turned and walked
back to his desk, speaking as he went.

'So what the fuck is going on?' Harry Ivens asked.

Harper looked blank. 'My aunt—'

'You need to call her, right?'

'Yes . . . call her . . . yes . . .'

Harry took a step forward. 'So go call her, John. Go call the woman and find out what's going on.'

'Yes,' Harper said. 'I'll call her.'

Harper backed up and started towards his office at the far end of the corridor. He glanced left at Leonhardt. Leonhardt had his back to him but sensed that he was being watched. He shifted his chair a few inches forward in an effort to disappear. Harper would have said something, would have asked him how the hell Nancy Young had his cellphone number. He didn't. Kept on walking. Stepped into his office and sat down at the desk. Picked up the phone. Dialled a number he remembered by heart.

She answered the call within three rings. 'John,' she said, and Harper knew from her tone that something serious had happened.

THREE

An hour later. Sky had bruised, color of blood washed out but still visible. Atmosphere was punch-drunk kind of hot, moody and solid, humidity up around the barely tolerable. Traffic gridlocked on the North-South Expressway. Windows down, people shouting and cussing and losing their language amidst expletives – F-words and sometimes worse. Pounding rap: Eminem thundering from the back of a jacked 4x4. Emotions tilting towards the regrettable edge of anger where things are said in the heat of the moment, things that are best forgotten and if – somehow – memory serves to float them back, they are viewed with shame and a sense of awkwardness that makes folks wonder if they really knew themselves.

They didn't; truth was what truth was; people didn't know a great deal about much of anything and – guaranteed – they knew least of all about themselves.

It had rained for fifteen or twenty minutes; hot-top damp, steam rising now, and though this should have served to lighten the atmosphere it did not. All closed up inside a fist of sky, oppressive and swollen with pressure and tension.

Now there was a cool breeze from the Atlantic, tradewinds from the Gulf of Mexico, and John Harper stood near his inched-open bathroom window, closing his eyes and imagining the rumble of traffic along the Expressway was something else altogether. Frustration perhaps, or some other awkward emotion he could not identify. Hadn't taken a holiday for as long as he could recall. *Life is like this sometimes*, he thought, and then tried not to travel the line that ran an indefinite course between what he'd hoped would be, and what he found he had. But the line was there somewhere back of his forehead, and even as he crossed it he wondered if he would feel this way in a year's time, or two, or five. Come June of the following year he would be

17

thirty-seven, more than likely single, more than likely standing in the same bathroom listening to the same sounds, pretending those sounds were something else altogether. *Life need not always be this way*, he added. *Life need not always be sharp corners and rough edges. Life could be cool and spacious, uncomplicated, profound but possessing humor. Life could be a great many things besides what we have here . . .*

He stepped back, back and to the left. Looked sideways in the mirror as he exited the bathroom.

'What the fuck went wrong?' he asked himself, and turned out the light.

The call had been brief.

'You need to come back to New York, John.'

'Come back to New York?' He'd laughed briefly. 'That is the last thing in the world I need to do, Evelyn—'

'Don't argue with me, John. You need to come back.'

'Why? What on earth could be so important—'

Interrupted him again. 'I'm not going to get into it on the telephone. This is not a matter of negotiation dear, it's just one of those things. I need you to get on a plane and come back home right now.'

'But Ev—'

'John, I might not be the most important person in your life, and after all these years I don't necessarily consider that I have any right to tell you what to do, but *this time*, I want you to listen to me. After your mother died we took you in against Garrett's wishes, and we never had children of our own as a result . . . I think that you owe me something for that John, I really do.'

Not again, Harper had thought. *Don't do this stuff to me again.*

But she did. Did it again. Truth or otherwise, his maternal aunt, Evelyn Sawyer, had taken him in when his mother died. All of seven years old and moving across the river into Manhattan; Greenwich Village, small apartment, not the sort of place for a little kid, but Evelyn and her sister had been close, and when she died there was a burden of responsibility that she'd felt duty-bound to carry. Garrett Sawyer had been a different story. Tough man, hard-edged, laconic, unreachable at the best of times. Committed suicide 2 August 1980, once again another story. Harper's own father, a man called Edward

18

Bernstein, had left Harper's mother when Harper was two, had died sometime in the early seventies. Harper knew very little of the details of their lives, and Evelyn had never been willing to speak of such things. So, all in all, it had been John Harper and Evelyn Sawyer, a strange and unwilling co-operation, and when Harper had reached nineteen he'd left New York and gone south to find his own way.

So when Evelyn talked of 'owing' and 'emotional debt' Harper felt the twist of obligation. He listened to her, he didn't argue, and though he pressed her for further details she said nothing.

'Just come home,' she told him.

'New York isn't my home, Evelyn.'

She'd laughed drily. 'Born in New York, John Harper . . . once you're born in New York there's nowhere else that can be called home. You might have run away but everything you ever were is here.'

Harper folded quietly inside. He felt tension in his lower gut. 'Evelyn, I have work here . . . I can't just up and leave—'

'I'm not going to argue with you, John.'

'We're not arguing. What makes you think we're arguing. All I'm saying is that there's things I have to do here.'

'There's things here too, important things, and I need you to come back.'

'Give me a reason why Evelyn, for Christ's sake. Give me one good reason why I should just drop everything and fly up there.'

'I can't John, not on the phone. It's too difficult to speak about on the phone. You *need* to come back. That's all I'm going to say right now. Just come back and I'll talk to you when you get here.'

'Evelyn—'

'Listen to me, John. It's real simple. You need to deal with whatever you have to deal with and come back.'

Harper could hear the emotion in her voice. She sounded strained and exhausted.

Conversation lasted a handful of minutes more before he acquiesced resentfully, then spoke to Harry Ivens.

'How long?' Ivens asked. Always businesslike, always to the point.

'Not sure. Few days, perhaps a week.'

'Holiday or unpaid leave.'

'Either which way, doesn't really matter. Figured I might swing a compassionate—'

Ivens laughed. 'Swing your fucking dick more like. Take half holiday, half unpaid. Have to understand that such a departure at short notice leaves me in the crap.'

'Harry, you've got more miles of my fill-ins and bylines than Miami has freeways. You'll cope. Pull some stuff from archives.'

'I'm not happy, John. Don't like to be caught short on such things.'

'I'll owe you, Harry.'

'Trouble?'

Harper paused, thought for a moment. 'No idea, Harry. She didn't say a great deal. She was insistent, and when she gets her mind set on something she won't give way.'

'I hope it's not bad news.'

'Thanks, Harry. If it's nothing I'll get a return flight in a day or so, okay?'

'Let me know, John. Take the time you need . . . I'll handle things here.'

'Appreciated.'

The negotiation ended.

Harper stood for a moment at the window of his apartment. Looked out over Gibson Park, north-west to the Expressway. Tried to think of nothing, to read nothing of significance into the conversation with Evelyn. Evelyn had her moments, her episodes, and this was more than likely no different. Something had spooked her, spooked her enough to call him, to insist that he come. There was no-one else for her to call. That was the simple truth. Maybe it was time he saw her. Last visited the better part of four years before, Christmas time, and it had been hard; not only Evelyn but everything that New York represented.

Harper picked up the phone and called Miami International. Flight departure for Newark in two and a half hours. Booked a seat, paid by credit card, left it open for return. Half an hour to put a few clothes in a bag and get himself ready. Stood in the doorway looking at his empty apartment, nodded as if acknowledging the presence of someone unseen. Said his goodbyes as if he somehow knew that things wouldn't be the same when he returned. Things were never the same when you left and then returned. Something always changed, often internal, often profound. Such was living.

Banking high and steep, evening casting sequins across Florida as the setting sun reflected off a hundred thousand mangrove swamps and tributaries. Window seat, no-one beside him, Harlan Coben book in his lap which he couldn't find the concentration to read. Stewardess asked if he wanted something to drink and he declined, changed his mind, asked for a Jack Daniels with a single ice cube. Ice melted before he drank, and it didn't taste so good.

New York beckoned like a half-forgotten dream, a dream he'd had before and recalled with a feeling of tight anxiety. Altogether unsettled, angular distractions that sat between duty and resistance, emotions bound one to the other – anger, resentment, sympathy for Evelyn and her all-too-evident loneliness. Harper smiled to himself, a smile that did not reflect in his eyes, leaned his head back and exhaled deeply.

He drifted away and did not wake until the stewardess leaned across him, smiled like an angel, asked him to buckle up for landing. She smelled of something one could breathe in forever and never be satiated.

Newark Airport, New Jersey. Took a cab through the Holland Tunnel. Evening; the swollen hum of the city pressing against the windows as he went. Everything he remembered, nothing had changed, and all of this crowding up against his eyes like it had a wish to burn itself indelibly into his mind. *Home is where the heart is*, he thought, but the heart that lived in New York was a dark and shadowed version of his own. He realized that only in his mind was this the same city. Notwithstanding his Christmas visit four years before, he had been gone since 1987. This was New York post-Bush Snr, post-Clinton, post the fiasco that saw Al Gore take the popular vote by 540,000 but lose at the Electoral in 2000. This was New York after the first attack against the homeland by foreign aggressors since the War of 1812, the ghost of 9/11 inclusive and encompassing despite the passing of three years. Harper could still recall a news headline that had stopped him in his tracks – 'Vacant Rooms, Empty Tables and Scared Tourists'. *I've come back*, he thought, *but what have I come back to?*

21

Detoured on Sixth, headed for West Third on foot. Diverted by the Blue Note Jazz Club where he paused and drank a soda. Evelyn would have smelled alcohol and bitched at him, called him a deadbeat, a bum. Garrett had been a drinker and had fallen by the wayside. By the time Harper left it was gone eight. Yellow medallion cabs, New York buses, cars crowding fender to fender, smell of diesel and cigarette smoke, the sweat and frustration of several million lives, each of them intersecting, each of them lost and yet still looking for something in their own quiet and special way. Back out into Greenwich Village, bohemians and skateboarders, freethinkers and hopheads; sharp darts from the past, like edges of things he didn't want to recall, but he did recall them, and somehow they hurt. This was all a hundred thousand years before, and yet – with each step towards Evelyn's three-storey walk-up on Carmine between the Cherry Lane Theater and Sheridan Square – John Harper felt the past rolling up towards him, inexorable and relentless. The past did not tire, the past did not disappear, it merely waited for you to come home. *Home?* Harper stopped right there on the sidewalk. Was that what he believed, even after all these years – that he was really coming home?

He remembered this same walk as a child; a particular day, an unforgettable Wednesday.

He shrugged off such thoughts; they scurried away like trick-or-treat children, catcalls and snickering and curse words.

Harper started walking again, crossed West Fourth towards Bleecker and angled left. Thought back to the moment on the *Mary McGregor*, the defining moment. After that the call from Nancy Young, the question asked but never answered of David Leonhardt. Why did Nancy have his number? She'd met Leonhardt a couple of times – *Herald* functions, such things as that. Had there been something between them? Had they started something, and had starting something with Leonhardt given her cause to end what she had with him? He wouldn't know, not until he returned to Miami, and even then Harper felt sure he would find only a slim impostor of the truth. Wished he was back in his own apartment and not a block and a half from the junction of Carmine, a junction that came back all too familiar.

Harper paused and looked at the house, sensing tension and unwanted premonition inside of him; oblivious to the car across the road, a dark sedan, in the front two people – a middle-aged man, a younger woman. Unaware of their conversation.

He stepped up to the riser and felt his heart have second thoughts.

'That's him? That's John Harper?' Cathy Hollander asked.

'Sure as hell is,' Walt Freiberg replied.

'He looks like him . . . he really looks like Edward.'

Walt Freiberg nodded.

'And this woman is his aunt?'

'Right, Evelyn Sawyer. Her sister was John's mother. Evelyn Sawyer is a hard-hearted bitch . . . a dangerous woman. A really dangerous woman.'

'Dangerous . . . why? What did she do?'

Walt Freiberg smiled. 'Do? She didn't *do* anything. It's what she knows . . . woman is dangerous because of what she knows.'

'They're going to come around here, the police?'

'They'll be round. They'll come and ask her about Edward, about what she knows, about why she thinks he might have been shot.'

'And she could say things? She could tell them what she knows?' Cathy Hollander asked.

'Not any more,' Freiberg replied. 'Not now John Harper's here.'

'Late,' she said. 'Why'd you have to be so late?'

'Hi, Aunt Ev . . . good to see you, you know?'

'Figured you'd be here hours ago. What you been doin'?'

'Having a life. Organizing myself to come up here. Catching a flight . . . the usual shit.'

'No need to badmouth me young man . . . always had an answer for everything didn't you? Always had a sharp tongue in your head.'

'Can I come in, Ev?'

'Yes, you can come in, but wipe your shoes . . . in fact, take your shoes off at the door and leave them in the hallway. Come on through to the kitchen.'

Sixty-four years old; hair silver-grey, eyes as sharp as pins; whiplash in her voice, a little edgy, easily irritated. House hadn't changed – smelled of cinnamon, violets, camomile, a robust undercurrent of oil of bergamot from the constant supply of Earl

23

Grey tea that fuelled Evelyn Sawyer. Stairwell to the right of the lower hall, kitchen to the left, ceramic-tiled floor, window over the sink that looked into the yard. Nothing had changed, and though Harper believed he himself had changed he still felt the same emotions, considered the same thoughts as he always did when he came back here. The Carmine house was not so much a representation of his own past, but a representation of everything that he'd never wanted to be, never wanted to become. The house was silence and tension, tight emotions and anxiety; it was Evelyn's crying jags and Garrett's drunken stupors; it was the awkward transition from child to man to departure . . . it was the memory of a family that never really existed at all, a family that Harper had prayed for so many times, and a family that had never returned.

'Tea?' Evelyn asked.

Harper shook his head. He set his bag down just inside the kitchen door and took a seat at the plain deal table. Twelve years, two meals a day, many of those times seated alone, Garrett out, Evelyn bustling around the kitchen making her existence seem busy. Eating in silence, nothing much of anything to say; wondering if the kids from his school went to homes just like his, or if there was another kind of life out there somewhere. He'd believed he'd heard rumor of such a thing, but wasn't sure.

'You want a scotch or something?' Evelyn asked.

'Do I need one?' Harper asked.

'Depends if you need to have your nerve steadied before I say what I have to say.'

'Sounds foreboding, Ev . . . what's going on?'

Evelyn stood with her back to him, stood looking out through the window above the sink. Almost without thought she retrieved a packet of cigarettes from her apron pocket. She lit one, turned and offered one to Harper.

Harper shook his head. 'I'm trying to quit,' he said.

Evelyn laughed awkwardly. '*Trying* to quit. What does that mean? You've either quit or you haven't.'

Harper smiled to himself. She was as sharp-edged as ever. Evelyn Sawyer would go to her grave in a bad mood. He clenched his fists out of sight. He was no longer a child. She would not bully him.

'So?' he asked, his tone almost aggressive. 'What's so damned important it flies me all the way from Miami?'

Evelyn took a drag of her cigarette. Her hand was shaking. Harper could see her reflection in the window.

'Ev?'

She turned. She seemed colorless, almost transparent. 'Some things were said way back when,' she started.

Harper opened his mouth.

Ev raised her hand. 'Don't say anything, John Harper. I'm going to say what I'm going to say, and if I think about it too long I'm not going to say it and then you an' I are going to get into one helluva fight.' She paused, took another drag of her cigarette. 'Some things were said way back when . . . back when you were a child, and some of them were true and some of them weren't. I told you things because I believed it was better that you figured something one way instead of another. I told you things . . . I told you things that weren't entirely accurate, like some of the details were changed—'

She paused, closed her eyes for a second.

'Sometimes you consider that you do something for the best, you know? You say something because you think it's going to be less hurtful or something, but I don't know that there can ever be a way to be sure if what you're saying is right or wrong. I mean . . . like you mean well, you want the best thing, but somehow things get turned inside out and back to front—'

'Evelyn. What the hell are you talking about?'

She looked dead-set at Harper. He thought there were tears in her eyes.

'Your father,' she said matter-of-factly.

Harper frowned.

'Your father, John . . . about your father.'

'What about my father? I know about my father. He left when I was . . . what? Two years old? He died, right?'

Evelyn was shaking her head.

Harper wanted a cigarette, wouldn't have dared ask for one. Somewhere the specter of a withdrawn child attempted to surface. He wanted to know why Evelyn was shaking her head.

'Your father is—'

Harper felt nauseous. He wanted to stand up but there was insufficient strength in his legs.

'Your father is . . . hell, John, he's in hospital. Someone shot him and he's in St Vincent's.'

'Hospital?' Harper asked. 'Up on West Twelfth?' The sick feeling seemed to radiate from his lower gut, up into his chest, his trachea, and then out through the remainder of his body. Once again he thought to stand. He pressed his hand against the surface of the table, but the sweat on his palm prevented any traction. He felt the color in his face drain away.

'Up on West Twelfth,' Evelyn said. 'He's seventy years old John . . . seventy years old and he tried to stop someone robbing a liquor store, and he got shot . . . someone shot him and they've got him up there right now—'

Harper felt his spirit leave; felt as if a vacuum had opened up inside him.

She lost it then, lost it much the same way she had when Garrett went for the big hereafter. She leaned back against the sink, head down, eyes swollen with tears, and though Harper's father had never earned anything but curses in this house, though Evelyn couldn't have uttered his name more than a dozen times in all the years Harper had lived there, she nevertheless folded quietly beneath the weight of emotion.

Harper rose to his feet. He felt the walls bending around him.

'I don't understand—' he started, and then realized that there wasn't a great deal *to* understand.

'Your father . . . he's seventy years old and he's going to die, John.' Evelyn lifted her hand to her face.

John Harper took the still-smouldering cigarette from her other hand. He took a drag, inhaled the smoke and held it in his chest. There were tears in his eyes also, and though he could never have explained what emotion he felt he still felt it.

'I have to go out,' he said, and his voice was strained and unnatural. He sounded like someone else. Sounded like someone lost. 'I have to go out for a little while Ev, okay? I just have to go out and take a walk . . . just take a walk around the block, you know? Just take a walk around and get some fresh air . . .' He started to shake his head. 'I don't think I understand what's happening here, Ev. I don't understand . . .' His voice trailed away into nothing.

Evelyn didn't speak. She was silent, her shoulders moving as she fought whatever was inside herself. She raised her hand and waved him away.

Harper felt like he should reach out, take her hand, pull her close, rest her head against his shoulder. He couldn't, wasn't able to. He took a step towards the kitchen door, hesitated, and then went through and down the hallway. He struggled to get his shoes on, leaning against the wall, dizzy, disoriented, and then he looked back towards the lighted kitchen, at the lower risers of the stairwell, remembered what he'd felt that night when the thing had happened with Garrett. He shuddered. He couldn't believe what was taking place in his mind. He opened the front door and went down into the street. He stood for a moment on the sidewalk. He looked down at the cigarette in his hand and then flicked it out into the road. He looked right, and then turned one hundred and eighty degrees. The tears in his eyes were now large enough to break their own surface tension and roll lazily down his cheeks.

John Michael Harper started walking; didn't look back at all for a while. Eventually he glanced over his shoulder and, try as he might, he couldn't stop that awful Wednesday coming right back at him like a tidal wave.

That December evening in Greenwich Village, in and amongst its sights and sounds, its rhythms and recollections, John Harper paused at the junction of Carmine Street, no more than thirty yards from the steps of Evelyn Sawyer's house. The house where he'd spent all of twelve years of his life, the house where Evelyn had wrenched every godforsaken bitter, twisted, awkward emotion out of herself and shared it with him. Where she had told him of his father, a man believed to be dead for the last thirty years or more. His mind felt like a balloon at bursting point.

All of it was here; here in this place.

Home is where the heart is.

'Go,' Walt Freiberg said.

Cathy Hollander reached forward, turned on the ignition.

'He'll walk to the hospital,' Freiberg said. 'Follow him . . . don't get too close. Let him walk there and we'll go in after him.'

Cathy Hollander nodded, pulled the car away from the edge of the sidewalk and started down the street.

FOUR

Early evening Manhattan, south-west of Greenwich Village.

Sky like washed-out watercolor smoke. Traffic still swollen and gridlocked, everyone pushing west along Beach and Vestry and Watts, trucks and taxicabs choking up the Holland Tunnel, leaning on their horns like such a thing would make a difference, like New Jersey was all-of-a-sudden the Promised Land and the gates closed at seven. *Make it through the Turnpike and you're free forever boys!*

Sixth Avenue – Avenue of the Americas – east corner of Tribeca; narrow-fronted, blink-and-miss-it restaurant: Cantonese, a little exclusive. Ambience within – warm, like a wood-burning Newfoundland fireplace; anachronistic, like this place should have been five blocks the other side of Broadway, down there in Chinatown between Columbus Park and Chatham Square.

A dozen or so customers, mostly in pairs: one or two illicit rendezvous – people there when they were believed to be somewhere else, hushed words, repressed emotions, hidden agendas, ankles out-of-sight and touching beneath the table; middle-aged married couple, obvious even as she orders for him 'cause she knows what agrees with him and what doesn't, possessing that comfortable blanket of familiarity that has soundlessly replaced what they once possessed, the awkward rush of desire and discovery that marked the early years of their confederacy.

Back in the right-hand corner, a table against the wall. Two men seated, their meal almost finished. Late thirties, early forties perhaps, one of them smart in dark suit, tie, spit-shine shoes, the other less so: a heavy cotton suit that has seen better days, and a face marked and lined and patterned and crossed with a hundred years of living. A worn face; a face with a story, a narrative, a journey around it; a face like a suitcase that has travelled the world; shoulders hunched as he leans forward, listening, hands folded together, fingers interwoven; fair-haired, eyes blue-grey-greenish, like a smudge of unnameable color at the edge of a palette.

Smart-suit is talking, animated, smiling, cheeks reddened with beer and sake, saying, 'So it's . . . I don't know, '74, maybe '75, and he's down in Vegas for whatever reason. Elvis is down in Vegas—'

Suitcase-face interrupts. 'He pretty much lived down there . . . don't think he sang anywhere else during the last years of his life.'

Smart-suit nods, waves aside the interjection. The reason that Elvis was in Vegas is irrelevant, a distraction. 'So he's down in Vegas . . . down there in Vegas, and he hears about some Elvis impersonation contest—'

'An Elvis impersonation contest.'

'Yes, sure . . . you know the kind of thing? Whole bunch of fat saddos all dressed in this sequinned cabaret shit, big sideburns, three cans of hairspray to fix their hair, right?'

'Right.'

'You know the deal, yeah?'

'I know the deal.'

'So, like I was saying, the King . . . he hears about this contest, and just for the hell of it he figures he's going to enter this thing—'

'Elvis? Like the *real* Elvis Presley . . . he's going to enter an Elvis impersonator contest?'

'Right,' Smart-suit says, and he's starting to laugh, like one of those times when the teller knows the punch-line, and maybe he's told it a hundred times before, but there's still something godawful funny about this story and there's nothing that can be done about it. 'So he figures he's going to enter this contest.'

'And he does?'

Smart-suit nods. 'He enters it. He comes along all dressed up in the real deal costume, all the sequins and rhinestone, the heavyweight boxing belt, the cape, the whole charabanc, you know? He gets up there, he belts out a classic, gives it his best freakin' shot just to see what will happen.'

Suitcase-face is smiling, nodding, like he knows what's coming, and if you asked him he would've sat there 'til Tuesday and never figured it out, but there's a quiet tension to how the story goes that gives it a certain magic.

'And you never guess what happens?'

'What? What happens?'

'He comes fourth.' And Smart-suit loses it, and he starts laughing, and Suitcase-face sits there for a moment, and then he starts laughing too, and the pair of them just come apart at the seams, and heads are turning, and those with uptight repressions and guilt complexes, the kind of things you share with a two-hundred-bucks-an-hour shrink, feel awkward and embarrassed and a little on-edge, and those with adulterous thoughts behind their eyes feel somehow illuminated by the harsh sound of humor, and they know they could never really laugh like that, not here, not now, because they're living a lie. And despite all else the two men at the wall table are breaking up like there's no tomorrow and all the laughing has to be used up good and proper before everything comes to an end . . .

Like that. Just like that. A true and simple story.

'You're shittin' me?' Suitcase-face asks, and then he starts laughing again.

'As God is my witness . . . as God is my fucking witness it's the truth—' and then he starts up again, starts up like a fire siren, and if there was anyone upstairs trying to get some sleep they wouldn't have done, at least not for a while, and perhaps if they'd heard the story they wouldn't have cared.

Later – a handful and a half of minutes – and things are back to battery.

'So where do we go from here? You up for hitting a bar or somethin'?' Smart-suit asks.

The guy with the well-travelled face – his name is Frank, Frank Duchaunak, and people spend their time asking him what kind of name that is, and he spends his time shrugging and shaking his head and saying, 'Well hell, I don't know . . . as good a name as any other I suppose.' Stands in queues sometimes, like for a passport or in a waiting room, and receptionists and officials double-take and squint, sometimes frowning, and then call out 'Dutch-nark' or 'Doosh-nak', and he smiles to himself and walks towards them, and then explains how you say it.

'De-show-nak,' he enunciates quietly, and they smile and nod, and invariably ask, 'What kind of a name is that?'

'Just a name,' he replies. 'As good as any other name you care to mention.'

Frank winds up his laughing, and the Smart-suit guy – whose name is Don Faulkner – reminds him 'As God is my fucking witness that's the truth, Frank . . .', and then repeats his question: 'So where are we going from here?'

Frank shrugs, and then a phone rings, and both of them instinctively reach into coat pockets for cells, and Frank remembers he turned his off when he came in from the street.

Don Faulkner – without thinking perhaps, or perhaps thinking in slow-motion through alcohol and good humor – holds up the phone and frowns. 'The precinct,' he says. 'You want to know what it is, or do we have them find someone else?'

'Fuck 'em,' Duchaunak says.

The phone keeps on ringing. Faulkner looks at it. It hums and buzzes on the table. It edges excitedly towards a plate of gelatinous lemon-honey chicken pieces.

'Fuck,' he says quietly, so quietly Duchaunak barely hears it, and then Faulkner lifts the phone, pushes the button, answers up.

'Faulkner,' he says, like he's confessing to a misdemeanor. He nods. 'Yes,' he says. 'He's here with me.' And then the caller is saying other things, and Faulkner's face is changing as he listens, and Duchaunak is creasing his brow with a frown, and feels like he wants to take the phone away from his partner and hear whatever's being said.

'You're shitting me,' Faulkner says, and then he looks at Duchaunak and his eyes are wide – surprised, kind of amazed.

What? Duchaunak mouths, and Faulkner does that irritating thing of shaking his head and half-raising his hand.

'What the fuck is it?' Duchaunak says.

'Okay,' Faulkner says. 'Okay, yes . . . on our way.' He hangs up. He holds the phone in his hand, holds it like he's fixing on hitting someone with it. He looks away towards the front of the restaurant, and then back at Duchaunak.

'What? Tell me what the fuck is going on?'

'Lenny,' Faulkner says. 'Lenny is up in St Vincent's—'

31

'What the fuck's he doing there?' Duchaunak says, and he's rising from his chair.

'Sit down a minute will you?' Faulkner says.

Duchaunak stands awkwardly for a moment, and then sits down heavily. Looks, just for a moment, like a short man who needs a long drink.

'He was shot last night, early evening . . . some liquor store up near Washington Square Park.'

'Shot?'

Faulkner nods. 'Chest wound . . . pretty bad they say. He's in intensive care, hooked up to everything they've got and then some. Not sure he'll make it, his age an' all, you know?'

'Jesus,' Duchaunak sighs. 'What happened? Was it Marcus? Did Ben Marcus do this?'

Faulkner sort of half smiles, like he feels awkward relaying what he's been told. He shrugs. 'Well, no . . .'

'Well, no what?' Duchaunak asks.

'What they said was that he tried to stop someone robbing a liquor store—'

Duchaunak starts to laugh, a nervous sound, the sound of someone told something they cannot quite comprehend, or perhaps something that so obviously contradicts what they know to be the truth. Was this what it would come to? After all this time, was this how it would end? 'He tried to stop someone robbing a liquor store?' he asks, and though it sounds like a question it's one of those questions that isn't really a question at all; still he sounds like a nervous man, a man unsettled by something profound and significant.

''S what I was told,' Faulkner says. 'You want to go see him?'

Duchaunak is nodding his head, rising from the chair again. 'Of course I want to go see him . . . just to make sure he dies for real this time.'

Faulkner smiles. 'You have issues, Frank Duchaunak . . . maybe your daddy didn't hug you enough when you were a kid.'

Duchaunak doesn't reply. He's walking towards the door.

Faulkner shakes his head and sighs. He goes to the counter to pay for the meal. It is his birthday. Duchaunak had been the one to suggest the meal. Duchaunak had promised to pay. *Such is the way of the world*, Faulkner thinks, and then wonders if that really was the case, if it really *was* the way of the world, or if he was on the rough end of something awkward with little chance of reprieve.

Ten minutes later Frank Duchaunak pulls the car out onto Varick, doubles back towards West Broadway, and takes a route towards St Vincent's that would avoid the gridlock on Sixth and Seventh. At some point he mumbles something.

'You what?' Faulkner asks.

Duchaunak shakes his head.

'What did you say?'

'I said that I take back what I said earlier.'

'About what?'

'About going to make sure Lenny dies for real this time.'

'Eh?' Faulkner frowns, one of those concerned frowns that indicate a degree of anxiety about another's mental state.

'It wouldn't be right.'

'What?' Faulkner says, surprise evident in his tone. 'But—'

'I know, I know, I know,' Duchaunak interjects. 'I know it might not make sense, but I really don't think it would be right for a man like him to die like this.'

Faulkner hesitates for a second, and then says, 'I know what you mean, Frank . . . know exactly what you mean.' He is quiet for a moment, and then, 'You reckon the thing is still going to go ahead? You reckon they're still going to do this thing if Lenny's out of the picture?'

Duchaunak shrugs. 'Aah, Christ only knows, Don. I still haven't got my head around how these people think. Let's just go up there and see what happened, okay?'

'Okay,' Faulkner says. 'We go see what happened.'

Neither of them speaks again until they reach the lot behind St Vincent's Hospital on West Twelfth and Seventh. Duchaunak parks the car, sits there for a moment without uttering a word, and then he opens the door and steps out.

'You go,' Faulkner says, almost as an afterthought. 'It doesn't need both of us.'

Duchaunak doesn't reply. He slams the door shut and starts walking towards the hospital.

FIVE

'A bold Sumatra,' the coffee guy said. 'Which is kind of earthy and aromatic. Or we have arabica, Colombian . . . the Colombian's very good, freshly ground just an hour or so ago, kind of rich and chocolaty with a hazelnut undertone—'

Harper cut in. He felt sick, a little dizzy. 'Just a cup of coffee,' he told the guy, and wanted to add *What in God's name is a hazelnut fucking undertone? Are you people on drugs or what?* But he didn't say a word.

The coffee guy kind of sneered condescendingly, and said 'Well, alright, if it's *just* a cup of coffee you want then *just* a cup of coffee you'll get.'

A handful of minutes later, coffee in his hand still too hot to drink, the smell of it almost turning his stomach, John Harper stood on the corner of Seventh and Greenwich and looked at the impressive facade of St Vincent's Hospital. Christmas lights hung in some of the windows on the upper floors, and a lone pine tree stood sentinel at the top of the front steps. He had walked all the way from Evelyn's, had considered going back but felt he couldn't face her. Not yet; not until he'd come out here and seen for himself.

There was a smell in the air like snow. Cool and crisp. Harper clutched his jacket around his throat with his free hand and looked up at the sky. Clouds, pale and thin, scudded awkwardly towards a yellowed harvest moon. God, how he wanted a cigarette. Cursed himself for leaving Evelyn's house without an overcoat.

Didn't know what to feel. Thirty-six years old, and the father that had left when he was two – a father he'd never spoken to, a father he'd believed dead – was up ahead of him in the hospital, dying of a gunshot wound.

He took a step, now resolved that he would go up there and

see. One foot forward, hit the edge of the kerb, and then stopped dead in his tracks. He closed his eyes for a moment. He raised the coffee cup to his lips, caught the aroma and decided against drinking it. He popped the lid, leaned to pour the contents into the gutter, and then backed up a step to put the cup in a trash bin. He folded his arms and stamped his feet. He *really* wanted a cigarette, just a couple of drags, just to feel that rush of sensation in his throat, his chest. Something to help him feel grounded.

He walked down the sidewalk. He went no more than three or four yards, and then turned suddenly and hurried across the road to the front of the building.

By the time he realized what he was doing he was standing beside the pine tree inside the front entrance. A small paper angel sat on the uppermost branch. A slight breeze caused its tissue-thin wings to flutter, but the angel hung on relentlessly. A man came out of the revolving glass doors and looked at Harper. The man nodded, sort of half-smiled, like there was a sense of fellow-feeling and camaraderie that naturally existed between all those who came to such places. *You're here because someone died*, it said. *Or maybe someone is going to die and you want to make sure you settle things with them before they go.* Something such as this. Harper smiled back and went in through the doors. He stood for a moment and then located the reception desk to the right.

The duty administrator possessed the face of someone who spent their life sympathizing.

'I'm here—' Harper started, his voice faltering.

'You are indeed, sir,' the woman replied.

Harper looked at the badge on her jacket. *Nancy Cooper*, it read, and Harper thought of Nancy Young and David Leonhardt and the question that was neither asked nor answered.

'I'm here to see someone,' Harper went on. 'To ask if I can see someone who was admitted.'

'Name?' Nancy Cooper asked.

'Mine?'

'The person admitted.'

'Edward . . . Edward Bernstein.'

Nancy rattled her fingernails on the computer keyboard. 'And you are?'

Harper looked at her, his eyes wide.

'Sir?'

'His son,' a voice said from behind Harper.

Harper emitted a strange sound from the back of his throat, something both of fear and surprise.

'Hello there Sonny,' the voice said.

Harper swallowed awkwardly. He turned.

'How've you been keeping?'

Older, much older, but the voice, the face, the smile – everything was unmistakable.

For a while, a handful of years after Garrett died, there was a family friend, a man called Walt Freiberg. He came every once in a while; he gave Evelyn money, brought gifts for John, called him 'Sonny'. A drinking man, always smelled of liquor; thick neck, dark eyes, fingers swollen and red at the tips as if cauterized to stop them fraying. Laughed like an express train through a smoky tunnel. Visited infrequently until Harper reached his teens, and then he too disappeared into the maw of living that was New York.

Now Walt Freiberg stood right behind him, and as Harper turned Freiberg raised his arms and put his hands on Harper's shoulders.

'You're here,' Freiberg said.

Harper didn't move. There were no words to express what he felt. There was too much emotion, too much feeling altogether – memories flooding back, a sense of anger, something akin to loss, something else that threatened the very structure of his body as he stood shaking and sweating and trying to keep it all together.

'I was so hoping you'd come,' Freiberg said. 'I called Evelyn and told her to get you here. She was surprised to hear from me after all these years, but considering the circumstances I felt it was the right thing to do.'

'I . . . I don't know—'

Freiberg smiled. He pulled Harper close and hugged him. The prodigal son returned. 'It's okay, Sonny,' he said, and Harper felt like a child, all of nine or ten years old, standing in the bay window of the Carmine Street house as Uncle Walt came out the back of a yellow cab with flowers for Evelyn and birthday gifts for himself.

'He's here,' Freiberg said. 'He tried to stop someone robbing a liquor store—'

Freiberg released Harper and stepped back. 'Christ almighty . . . you look like him, John, you *really* do look so much like him. It's good to see you, so very good to see you after all these years . . . such a terrible thing, such a terrible reason for you to see him, but . . .'

Freiberg's voice trailed away. He closed his eyes for a moment. He sighed and shook his head. 'We'll go up now.'

Harper nodded involuntarily.

Freiberg stepped in front of the desk and smiled at Nancy Cooper. 'We'd like to go on up and see Mr Bernstein if that's okay?'

Nancy shook her head. 'He's in Intensive Care right now. You won't be able to go in and actually see him, but they might let you into the ante-room. Third floor, turn right as you come out of the elevator. Speak to one of the orderlies and they'll find you a duty doctor.'

Freiberg thanked the woman and then, with his hand on Harper's shoulder, guided him to the elevator.

At one point Harper slowed and stopped. He turned, eyes wide, his face pale and drawn, every muscle in his body tense and jagged.

'It's okay,' Freiberg said. 'Just go with it Sonny . . . just go with it.'

Third floor, heading right as they came out of the elevator just like Nancy told them. Long corridor, sound of shoes on the linoleum, sound of shoes echoing back from above and beside, heart beating in Harper's chest. Felt like a kid. Uncle Walt's hand on his elbow, guiding him, being there for him. Like when he was little. Uncle Walt coming with presents from the back of the car, and small Harper never really understanding why Aunt Ev made him feel so unwelcome. Tension in the house between them, tension you could feel.

And then, suddenly, Walt Freiberg slowed down as they neared the end of the corridor. To their right was a wide window, must have been eight or ten feet, and through it Harper saw a man in a suit talking to a doctor.

'What the fu—' Uncle Walt started, and then he said 'Stay here, John . . . just stay right here a minute.'

Harper was rooted to the spot. Couldn't have moved without external motivation had he even known where to move. A

37

thought: after his break-up, the one with Nancy Young, he felt hollow. Just that; nothing more; just hollow. Felt like a shell of flesh with nothing inside. Felt like that now. Felt like he'd woken suddenly from a bad nightmare, a real bad nightmare, and realized that he hadn't been sleeping at all. Understood that everything he'd imagined was real.

He turned slightly, just his neck because he was incapable of moving much more than that, and he saw Walt Freiberg saying something venomous to the man in the suit. The doctor had taken a couple of steps backward; he looked almost threatened, and the man in the suit stood there listening to whatever Walt was saying, and every once in a while he sort of side-glanced towards Harper. He frowned, just a fleeting shift in his expression, but Harper registered nothing. Because there was nothing to register. Because he was hollow.

Walt kept on talking. He even raised his hand and pointed his finger. The man in the suit looked away, and then he looked down, and then he held a momentary expression like he'd been caught doing something bad. He looked like a man ashamed.

Walt stopped talking. The man in the suit said something – not very much at all, but something – and then he started towards the door at the end of the wide window. He came out. He walked towards Harper. He stared at him, didn't avert his gaze. He frowned, tilted his head to one side, and he opened his mouth to speak. 'You look like—'

Suddenly Walt Freiberg was beside Harper.

'Don't say anything,' Freiberg said, and Harper didn't know who he was talking to. Wouldn't have mattered much anyhow: Harper had nothing to say.

'Go do your job,' Walt said. 'Jesus man, can't you have just a little compassion. Go find out who did this thing, huh? Isn't that what you're paid for?'

The man in the suit looked over his shoulder at Freiberg. He didn't respond. He turned and walked past Harper without a word.

Freiberg walked after him, just two or three steps, but Harper sensed the territorial thing. Freiberg was seeing the man away, making sure he didn't get halfway down the corridor and turn back.

'Come on,' he told Harper, and then he was guiding him once

more, walking him through the doorway at the end of the window.

The doctor still looked unnerved and ill-at-ease. 'I'm sorry sir—' he began. 'I didn't—'

Walt Freiberg raised his hand. 'It's okay doctor. No harm done. You were doing your job . . . which is more than can be said for that asshole.'

The doctor seemed simultaneously concerned and relieved. 'I'm actually unable to let you into the room,' he said. 'There's a window to the side. You can see him from there, but in his present condition I am maintaining a strict policy of no visitors. His vital signs are too weak for any non-medical contact at all.'

Freiberg nodded. 'It's okay doctor, I understand. It will be fine if you just let us through to see him, right John?'

He smiled as he looked at Harper. Harper smiled back without awareness of what he was doing, what he was smiling at.

The doctor seemed satisfied. He stepped past them and opened another door.

Freiberg led Harper through and down a narrow corridor to the end. To the left was another window, smaller than the first, and as Harper drew to a stop, as he stood beside Uncle Walt and looked through the glass, as he saw the old man lying right there before him, tubes in his nose, his mouth, wires and lines and machinery humming and buzzing and making green jagged lines across black screens, he realized that the man before him was a father he had never known, had never really been aware that he didn't know . . . Everything that had happened in the last thirty-six years came back to him, everything he had experienced alone and yet now felt he'd been meant to experience with this dying stranger. As all of these things crowded up against him, pushing the walls of the corridor into him claustrophobically, he believed he was actually feeling nothing at all.

The machines hummed and buzzed and clicked. They drew their jagged green lines across black glass screens.

Harper felt the tension in his own chest rising and falling.

It was the only thing that told him he was still breathing.

*

Standing half a block down the street, looking back towards St Vincent's, Frank Duchaunak buried his hands in his pockets and exhaled. Condensation issued from his mouth.

A few feet to his left Don Faulkner sat in the car, engine idling, window down.

'Get in the freakin' car, Frank . . . it's goddamned cold.'

Duchaunak turned and looked at him. 'Freiberg was in there.'

'Walt Freiberg?'

Duchaunak nodded. 'The very same . . . and someone was with him, someone who looked like Lenny.'

'You think he'll die?'

'Fuck knows, Don,' Duchaunak said.

'Frank?'

Duchaunak looked at his partner.

'Get in the car, will you?'

'I don't want him to die like this,' Duchaunak said. 'Not after all this time . . . after everything we've gone through to get here. It can't end like this . . . it wouldn't be right.'

Faulkner didn't reply. He wound the window up, sat watching as Duchaunak stood there for a further two or three minutes. Faulkner couldn't see clearly, his own breath was misting the glass, but it seemed like Frank Duchaunak was talking to himself.

'Jesus,' he whispered eventually to no-one but himself. 'Jesus Christ almighty. What the fuck do we do now?'

Evelyn Sawyer stands at the top of the stairs. Her house is silent.

'You heard him?' she asks, as if to no-one, and does not wait for a reply.

'He was here. You heard him, right? You should have seen him . . . looked so much like Edward you'd have figured him for a ghost. I wanted you to hear him . . . hear his voice, you know? Wanted you to know who he was so you'd understand why we made this agreement. If anything happens to him . . .'

Her voice fades. She lowers her head and closes her eyes. 'Well, if anything happens to him . . .'

She never finishes what she planned to say. She turns and makes her way back down the upper hallway to the head of the stairwell.

The house on Carmine is silent once more.

SIX

Harsh wind. Walking down the back steps of the hospital, leaning against Walt Freiberg. Wind almost blew him over. Uncertain steps. Tears in his eyes. Difficult to see. Nearly lost his footing on the last riser, but Walt was there, Walt was there to hold him up. Said nothing, just felt Walt's hand hold him tighter, and regained his balance.

Passenger door of the car opened as Harper and Freiberg approached it. Someone came out and started towards them. A woman. Long hair, dark, blowing wild in the wind. Hard to see her face clearly through his tears. And then she was there beside Harper, there on the other side, and she and Freiberg led him like a lost soul to the back of the vehicle. The girl opened the rear door. Harper climbed in. Didn't say a word; couldn't find any. Had been looking for half an hour but there were none inside.

Girl came in beside him and he shuffled along the seat. Walt climbed in on the driver's side up front, and then all the doors were closed and the wind had stopped blowing and for a brief moment there was silence.

'This,' Walt Freiberg said, glancing over his shoulder and smiling at the girl, 'is Cathy Hollander. Cathy is a good friend of your father's. She came over with me.'

Harper turned as Cathy brushed the windswept hair from her face. His heart missed a beat. Whatever he might have said died a quiet death somewhere between his mind and his mouth. He felt his eyes widen. His mouth was dry.

Cathy frowned, tilted her head, kind of half-smiled.

Harper continued to stare. A knot of emotions, tied so tight it could never be unravelled. Would take a sharp blade to sever it cleanly and release him. Harper blinked twice, blinked in slow-motion like a lizard. Almost heard the sound of his eyelids closing, opening once again. Cathy Hollander. *Cathy Hollander.*

41

Harper felt as if he'd taken a swift roundhouse to the solar plexus. Nothing much left of him but wishful thinking and absent words.

'It's unnerving,' she said. She looked at Freiberg. 'Jesus . . . this is a little freaky, Walt.'

Harper shook his head. He had difficulty taking his eyes off her. He frowned. It was pretty much the only change of expression he could manage.

'You look so much like him,' Cathy said. 'You look so much like him it's actually quite unsettling.'

Harper looked at Walt, did so simply to change the direction of his gaze. Walt smiled. 'We're going to go eat . . . it's good to eat at a time like this. We're also going to call Evelyn and tell her you're okay, that you're with us and we're going to take care of you tonight.'

Cathy shifted in the seat and looked more closely at Harper. Harper looked back. He still felt unable to speak.

'So – no more staring at each other,' Walt said. 'Eyes front and center. We're driving now, all eyes on the road, okay?'

'You sound like a schoolteacher,' Cathy said.

'Good enough,' Walt said. He started to laugh. 'We should sing a song, a school song, right? The kind of song kids sing when they go on a trip.'

'Forget it, Walt,' Cathy replied. 'You sing if you want to, but you're on your own.'

'Radio then,' Walt said, and leaned forward to switch it on. 'Tell Her Tonight' by Franz Ferdinand rushed from the speakers behind Harper. He looked to his left and out of the window. His heart thundered. The engine gunned into life and drowned everything but the tension in his chest. He wanted to look at Cathy Hollander again; wanted to look at her and nothing else.

Walt turned out of the lot and headed onto West Eleventh. Harper looked at the lights of New York, the shops, the pedestrians. He saw someone stringing a line of Christmas bulbs across the front of a delicatessen. He saw himself as a child, walking streets just like this one. He remembered everything that had happened with Garrett Sawyer. He remembered the rank smell of drying blood – coppery, earthy, immediately identifiable. He remembered the way Evelyn fell apart, the way the seams that kept her together just unravelled. He remembered

42

all these things with a child's perspective. Remembered them like they were yesterday. Realized he was concentrating on anything he could, anything to take his mind off the mess of feelings that had swamped him.

'You alright?' Cathy asked.

Harper turned and looked at her. Her hair was past her shoulders, her features clear and perfectly proportioned, her eyes a kind of hazel color, bright and inquisitive. She had long fingers, Harper noticed, as she once again reached up to fingertip a stray lock of hair away from her cheek and tuck it neatly behind her ear. A pianist's fingers. He thought to ask her if she played but let it go. He thought to ask her if there was someone she loved, someone who loved her in return. His heart was now twice its natural size, and the blood it pumped was molasses.

He shrugged his shoulders. He felt like such a fool.

She reached out with her long fingers and took his right hand. She closed her other hand over it. He felt the warmth of her skin. Felt the unmistakable security and assurance of female contact. A rush of electricity invaded his entire body. He wanted to slip sideways, wanted to just slip sideways and lean his head against her shoulder. He wanted to close his eyes and sleep with his head on her shoulder, feel her hair on his face, smell her perfume, smell the leather upholstery – anything but the smell of drying blood which he now seemed unable to forget.

He didn't say a word. His heart continued to beat in two-four time. His mind continued to wander.

They drove in silence for a long time. They must have been heading south because at one point they passed the Fire Museum. Harper hadn't been there for the better part of thirty years, but still recalled it vividly. Perhaps he drifted away at some point, because it seemed that, as they drew to a halt, he opened his eyes. He couldn't remember closing them.

'You hang in there, John,' Cathy said, and squeezed his hand with her pianist's fingers, and John Harper sort of half smiled and closed his eyes in slow-motion like a sunbathing lizard on a New Mexico rock, and then the back door of the car was open and Cathy was leading him out and across the sidewalk, and Uncle Walt Freiberg was standing there smiling, but there was something in his eyes that said everything that needed to be said about the real reason for their long-overdue reunion.

43

The old guy – the one that was both a friend and a thirty-year-absent father, well he was laid up in St Vincent's connected to everything they possessed and then some, and he was going to die.

'Who was the man?' Harper asked eventually, and the words slurred from his lips like the memory of an unpleasant taste.

'Man?' Freiberg asked. He frowned and shook his head. 'What man Sonny?'

Don't call me Sonny, Harper thought. *I'm thirty-six years old. I was Sonny when I was a little kid*. Thought it, but didn't say it. What he did say was, 'The one in the hospital. The one that was there when we went up in the elevator.'

Freiberg snorted contemptuously. 'Asshole cop!' he snapped, and then he laughed again. 'It was nothing John, absolutely nothing . . . now let's get inside here, it's cold.'

Harper followed Cathy. She walked beside Freiberg and they entered a narrow-fronted Cantonese restaurant. Harper glanced over Cathy's shoulder. They were down near the east corner of Tribeca, on Sixth. Inside it was warm, welcoming almost, and Harper realized how hungry he was.

'We sit, we talk, we eat,' Freiberg said. He started to remove his overcoat. The maitre d' approached them, smiling, hand out to greet Freiberg like a long-lost.

'Mr Fleeberg,' he cooed, and Uncle Walt was talking, laughing, walking with the guy to a small table at the back of the room, and before Harper knew it he was up tight and close beside Cathy, the pressure of her leg against his, the smell of her perfume, the awareness that there now seemed to be an altogether different reason for being in New York. She turned and put a glass of sake in his hand. Uncle Walt was laughing louder and telling some anecdote he'd heard about Elvis in Las Vegas and an impersonation contest.

Surreal, disconnected from anything even remotely close to reality, John Harper sat and listened, and every once in a while he talked, but in all honesty he felt he didn't really have a great deal of anything to say. Felt like the world had closed in on him, a world he never chose to belong to, a world that just came rushing right at him without respite.

He thought of Miami, catastrophe by the sea; of the islands, of the shoals of blackfin tuna, of the waves of frigate birds, and the smell – the once-in-a-lifetime smell of salt, seaweed, fish and mangrove swamps. He thought of pirates and Ponce de Leon, the Dry Tortugas, the footprints of turtles, the reefs, the clear water, the citrus, the coconut . . .

Such things as these, a hundred million miles from the dark streets of New York just before Christmas.

Later, how much later he didn't know, Walt came from somewhere and sat down facing him.

'I called Evelyn,' he said, and he smiled. He smiled like when Harper was a kid and he came visiting with gifts. 'I called her and said we'd be taking care of you tonight. You have money John?'

Harper merely looked back at Walt Freiberg with a blank expression.

Freiberg nodded, buried his hand inside his jacket, and was then pushing a wad of notes into Harper's shirt pocket.

'We'll have you stay in a hotel near here,' he said. 'Should get some rest, eh? Long day for you, Sonny . . . long old day for you . . .'

And then his voice faded, and maybe it was exhaustion, or the sake, or perhaps nothing more than the tidal wave of emotion that seemed to sweep over him and carry him away.

Later he couldn't even remember leaving the restaurant.

SEVEN

Ben Marcus: simple name, simple man. Ancestors were Polish Jews, perhaps even further back they were people who came out of the Carpathians with names built from too many consonants and too few vowels. Ben Marcus's grandfather on his mother's side, hard-edged bastard, all angles and corners – he came to 'Hamereeca' with a vision of something that was a world apart from what he found. Man makes shoes in Lodz; comes to the States and dies of emphysema after eleven years of clearing storm drains and sewage junctions for the New York Metropolitan Sanitation Department at one dollar eighty-five cents an hour.

Ben Marcus's father made different decisions; wouldn't bow to The Man, so he figured the angles and sidelines, made a handful of dollars on the racetracks, bought himself into a warehouse crew ferrying liquor during Volstead. Volstead was repealed in '33; Marcus Senior ran lines in silk stockings and cigarettes, and a protection gig for bookies' runners, and everything went fine and dandy until May of '55 when he was shot in the throat by a man called Fraschetti, a man with psoriasis and bad teeth. Ben Marcus was ten years old when he buried his father, celebrated his twelfth birthday in a South Brooklyn Juvy, and by the time he was twenty-seven he'd done nine years all told between Fulton Correctional, Sing Sing and Altona. Then he got smart. He got other people to do the wet-work and running. Benjamin Marcus, hard head like a clenched fist, collection of features that seemed to argue about who owned center stage, kind of man who stated the obvious and everyone agreed such a thing was a very new idea. Crew he ran was a mixed bag of stealers and blood-letters. People like Sol Neumann, Raymond Dietz, Albert Reiff. Neumann was the right hand, the one who translated the nods and frowns into words and actions. Marcus would say,

'That thing Sol . . . that thing with the Williamsburg fuck-up. I don't think we should leave that behind without an example being made.' Neumann would say, 'I'll take care of it Ben, I'll take care of it,' and three, maybe four days later, New York's finest would find some poor bastard hanging from a fire escape back of a derelict building, his tongue cut out perhaps, his balls in his overcoat pocket. But it was business, always business; never personal with such people. Such people never got close enough to anyone to consider anything personal.

Monday, 15 December, Ben Marcus sat in a wicker-backed colonial chair in a smoke-filled room. The window behind him overlooked La Guardia Place and Bleecker. Sol Neumann sat to his right, and ahead of him a man called Henry Kossoff who carried a bruised and beaten look about him, as if he'd been tied tight, hands and feet, and dragged across rocky unforgiving ground. Kossoff was saying something, something about 'The asshole didn't show Ben . . . McCaffrey didn't fucking show.'

Marcus sighed and shook his head. He glanced towards Neumann. Neumann kept his gaze fixed on Kossoff.

'Maybe he got himself fucked up,' Kossoff said. 'These guys . . . hell these blacks are running their own gangs. They've got a different view of things. They shoot people they don't even know. Maybe he was into something and got himself into trouble,' and there was something in his tone that suggested he hoped to hell that was the case. There was also something that said he knew it wasn't.

'He did a runner, Henry, plain and simple,' Neumann said. 'It's not your fault . . . don't sweat it.' He turned slightly and nodded at Ben Marcus. Marcus nodded back, an almost imperceptible shift in expression, and yet it seemed to grant Papal indulgence to whatever Neumann was thinking. 'See to it Henry,' Neumann said. 'Send some people out and bring McCaffrey in. We can't have this asshole running around all over the city, okay?'

Kossoff nodded, didn't speak.

'The other thing,' Marcus said matter-of-factly, the first words he'd spoken since the meeting began.

'I don't know if it was something. Maybe it was something, maybe it was nothing. I had Karl Merrett over at St Vincent's keeping an eye on the show. Freiberg was there with the girl, and they had some other guy with them—'

Sol Neumann uncrossed his legs and leaned forward slightly. 'What other guy?'

Kossoff shook his head. 'Fuck knows, Sol . . . never seen him before. Karl said he looked just like Lenny—'

Neumann laughed drily. 'Don't pay any mind to what Karl Merrett has to say. I know Merrett better than anyone . . . I was down in Five Points with the guy for more than a year. He has his uses, but reliability of information isn't fuckin' one of them.'

Marcus raised his hand. Neumann fell silent. 'Find out who he is,' he told Kossoff. 'Find out who he is, and have some people on this McCaffrey as well. I need McCaffrey as a priority. Find out if he has family. Go speak to them. Go shake some favors up and see if we can't get this matter tidied up in the next twenty-four hours. We got a busy time ahead of us and I don't want things interfering. I also don't want any grievances with the blacks.' Marcus shook his head. 'The whole thing is falling apart, what with the blacks and the Eastern Europeans. These are things I don't want to get involved in. When I'm gone I'll be pleased to leave what's left of New York to these people.'

'Yes, Mr Marcus. It will be taken care of.' Kossoff rose from the chair. He buttoned his jacket and started towards the door. He was on edge, evidently nervous.

'And Henry?' Sol Neumann called after him.

Kossoff turned.

'Call Reiff and tell him Mr Marcus needs him over at the warehouse in the morning. Tell him ten a.m.'

Kossoff nodded and made his way out the door.

There was silence for some while.

Eventually Ben Marcus turned towards Sol Neumann. He smiled, but without humor; a smile befitting Cesare Borgia. 'He will not lie down.'

Neumann raised an eyebrow.

'Freiberg . . . he will not stand by and watch the territory taken from Bernstein. Seems to me we may have a bloodier fight on our hands.'

Neumann shrugged his shoulders. He reached for a cigarette and lit it. 'Whatever,' he said, his voice almost a whisper. He drew on the cigarette and exhaled smoke from his nostrils. The grey cloud half-obscured his face. Everything was flat-toned and chiaroscuro, almost monochromatic. 'He wants a fight he's going to get one.'

'We change nothing . . . we run it the way we agreed. There will be ample opportunity to take these things apart either on the day or soon afterwards.'

'Makes sense,' Neumann replied. 'Seems to me we miss the chance for some good returns if we just go to war . . . and like you said, we start a war and we have no idea who's going to get involved.'

Marcus acknowledged the comment without speaking; stayed silent for a time. He rose from his chair after a few minutes. 'I have made my decision,' he said, almost to himself. He turned to Neumann. 'You come tomorrow as well . . . we will go through some of the details again with Reiff. With Lenny Bernstein laid up in St Vincent's we have to make busy. I believe the kingmaker intends to become the king.'

'Of course, Ben. Sure thing.'

Ben Marcus left the room. Sol Neumann, close behind him, turned out the light as he left, and through the window the faint indigo-blue pulse of the external neon sign haunted the glass and made faces on the wall.

EIGHT

A little after five a.m. New York hadn't woken. John Harper stood at the window of a room on the tenth floor of the American Regent on the corner of Hudson and West Broadway. Room was cold. Raised his hand and pressed his palm against the glass. Spread his fingers, watched the lights from beyond appear in the spaces. Tried to count them. Too many.

He tried to focus on a single thought; just anything at all. He found something, and then it was gone. Like the past he believed he had. There, then gone. You have no father John Harper . . . oh fuck, yes you do, and by the way, he's seventy years old and laid up in St Vincent's 'cause someone shot him. Nothing. Then something. What the fuck was that?

Harper walked back and sat on the edge of the bed. He felt chill, the hairs raised on his arms, and he reached for his shirt. As he tugged it around his shoulders dollar bills spilled from the breast pocket. Harper gathered them up – fifties, all of them, and in counting them he remembered that Walt had leaned across the restaurant table and tucked them inside. Seven hundred dollars, the better part of half a month's salary.

Harper looked at the money, fanned the notes out between his fingers and held his arm up.

'Seven hundred dollars,' he said to no-one but himself.

He folded them and set them on the edge of the bedside table. He wondered how much the room would cost – three, four hundred dollars a night, and that was without the mini-bar and the pay-per-view cable movies.

And then he thought about the old man he'd seen through the window at St Vincent's Hospital.

He wanted to call Evelyn and scream at her down the phone. *What the fuck were you thinking, you stupid fucking bitch! Did you think this didn't matter? Did you think you could just leave me the whole of my life without telling me the truth?*

John Harper didn't call Evelyn Sawyer. He had a shower instead, and then he spoke to room service and asked who was paying the bill.

'The room is booked in the name of a Miss Cathy Hollander, sir,' the room guy said, and Harper told him *Thank you* and ordered a breakfast trolley sent up.

While he ate slender crisps of smoked bacon and eggs Benedict, while he sipped fresh-squeezed orange juice and drank coffee that tasted like good Colombian with a hazelnut under-tone, he wondered what he should do. He needed to go back to Evelyn's and collect his bag, but the impulse to return to the hospital was strong, very strong indeed. His father lay in a bed in the ICU. His own father, seventy years old, and someone had shot him for trying to prevent a liquor store robbery. Harper wondered who the shooter was: how old, what he looked like, whether he actually went away with any money, where he was now . . . was he scared or stoned or drunk, or maybe between the legs of a thirty-dollar hooker in a cheap room in a cheaper hotel somewhere on the Lower East Side . . . ?

Wondered all of these things. Had an answer for none of them.

Finished eating. Wanted a cigarette real bad. Thought to call room service and have them send some up. They would've done that in a hotel like the American Regent. Couldn't risk it. Smoke one and he'd smoke the whole pack, and then where the hell would he be? Right back where he started. He possessed more willpower than that; he exercised it and didn't call.

Thought he should leave New York. Make a call, book the flight, go home. Wasn't the first time he'd have such a thought. Second time it would be stronger.

Dressed in the same clothes as the previous day. Everything else he'd brought was in his bag at Evelyn's. Picked up the money Walt had given him, figured he would give it back; couldn't accept such an amount from a relative stranger. Sure the man had been there however many years before, but Harper had been a kid, a kid all of seven, eight, nine years old. Hell, he was thirty-six now. He had his own money, not a great deal for sure, but he wasn't one to be accepting unsolicited charity.

51

Harper glanced at the clock on the table near the window. Ten after seven. Before the point of decision arrived the phone rang, right there on the nightstand beside the bed.

Harper frowned; picked it up. 'Hi,' he said.

'Hi.' A woman's voice.

A moment as Harper put a name to it. 'Miss Hollander.'

She laughed. 'Jesus, no-one calls me Miss Hollander except the police and the IRS.'

Harper smiled. Sharp sense of humor.

'You're up,' Cathy Hollander stated matter-of-factly.

'I am,' Harper replied. Remembered the way she looked, the way he'd felt the entire time he'd been with her. Strong feeling, like a dull ache after a hard smack.

'I checked with room service that you'd called for breakfast . . . they told me you had so I figured you were up and about. How're you feeling?'

Harper didn't say anything for a moment, then, 'Tired maybe . . . a little confused. This has been some twenty-four hours.'

'I can imagine,' Cathy replied, but Harper – knowing nothing about her – figured that she couldn't have known a great deal about how he felt. She was being polite: uttering such words of empathy was basic human nature.

'The room—' Harper started.

'Don't worry about it,' she interjected. 'Walt is taking care of everything.'

'It's in your name.'

'It doesn't matter,' Cathy said. 'Walt isn't one to go writing his name down and signing things, you know what I mean?'

'Sure I do,' Harper said, and wondered if he actually had any real idea what she meant.

'So what do you want to do now?' she asked.

'Was thinking to go to my aunt's and get my bag, and then maybe go back to the hospital. After that . . . after that I figured I'd go home.'

'I can come pick you up and drive you,' she said, and there was something in her tone that told him she was ignoring his last statement.

Harper smiled and shook his head. 'It's okay Miss . . . it's okay Cathy, I can handle it.'

Cathy laughed. 'Walt says I'm to take care of you. I'll come get you in half an hour. I'll take you over to your aunt's and then I'll drop you at St Vincent's, okay?'

Harper shrugged. 'Whatever,' he said. 'As long as it's no hassle for you.'

'No hassle,' she said. 'See you in a half hour or so.'

She hung up before Harper had a chance to respond. He stood there with the receiver in his hand, and then he set it in its cradle and sat on the edge of the bed. He wondered what the deal was between the Hollander woman and Uncle Walt, perhaps more relevantly the deal between her and his own father.

His *own* father.

Harper closed his eyes, took a few deep breaths. He couldn't stretch his mind enough to make this thing fit inside. After a short while he stopped trying. He'd learned from times past that to push at such a thing only served to slide everything else out of whack.

Cathy Hollander arrived before Harper had had a chance to collect himself together. When she knocked on the door it was a minute or so before he got to opening it.

'You alright?' was the first thing she asked.

'Compared to what?' he asked back, which perhaps wasn't such a polite thing to say to a visitor.

Cathy nodded her head like she understood something about what he was feeling, and for the first time – there in daylight – Harper noticed that she looked rough around the edges, like she herself had endured her own hardships. Nevertheless there was something. The same something as the night before. Perhaps nothing more than his own emptiness, the absence of any anchors, but she was beautiful. There was no denying that simple, honest fact.

'Sit down,' he told her. 'I have to get some shoes on.'

She took a chair, lit a cigarette, looked around for an ashtray.

Harper wanted to ask her not to smoke, but he didn't. She looked like she needed it as much as he did. He found it difficult not to stare at her, difficult not to think of how she might look beside him – in the street, at a restaurant table, close up against him.

53

'So, what are you going to do?'

Harper sat in the chair near the window. He worked his right foot into his shoe without untying the laces. 'Do?' he asked. 'What d'you mean?'

She shook her head. 'I don't know what I mean . . . this is awkward.' She closed her eyes for a moment, and then she turned towards the window. 'It's very strange—'

'What is?' Harper reached for the left shoe.

'You.'

He frowned. 'Me?'

'You look too much like him . . . I mean, of course he's older, a lot older than you, but I can imagine that he looked exactly the same as you when he was your age.'

'I wouldn't know,' Harper said. His right foot found its home inside the shoe and he looked at her.

Cathy Hollander had ground the cigarette into the ashtray. She had a Kleenex in her hand; she was holding it against her face. The movement in her chest and shoulders told Harper she was stifling tears.

He thought of the *Mary McGregor* easing away from the jetty and making its graceful way towards Blackwater Sound. He knew if he concentrated for a second he would recall the smell of saltwater, the earthy swell of mangrove beneath it. He wished he was there, wished he was anywhere but here. His second thought about leaving New York.

'I'm sorry,' she said, and balled the Kleenex in her fist, her knuckles whitening. The mascara around her eyes had smeared. She looked like someone had kicked her six ways to Sunday and then some.

'I don't have anything to tell you,' Harper said, trying to dispel the thought of how she would feel up close against him. His voice was edged with irritation. 'I'm thirty-six years old. My father, a man I knew nothing about, left when I was two years old. My mother died when I was seven. My aunt and uncle raised me. My uncle shot himself in the head when I was twelve. That's my life story. I left New York when I was nineteen, and aside from one or two visits I have stayed away. Last time I lived here Ed Koch was mayor. You guys have had seven years of Giuliani and a couple of Bloomberg since. My aunt called me and told me to come back, and here I am. After thirty-four years

54

I find out I have a father, a father I thought was dead, and I get to see him in a hospital bed because someone figured he deserved to get shot. With people like me you get what you see. It isn't complicated, and I'm not trying to make it so. I don't know anything about you, and I know just as little about Walt Freiberg. How you figure in this is your business and I'm not asking—'

'Don't you *want* to know?' she asked. She sounded surprised, like Harper's reaction was exactly the opposite of what she'd expected.

'Know what?' he asked. He leaned back in the chair. The window was behind him. To Cathy Hollander he was nothing more than a silhouette.

'About your father? About how I know him? About Walt?'

Harper shook his head. 'I figure I'll get to know as much as I need to if I stay here—'

'*If* you stay here?'

Harper leaned forward. 'What do you want from me?'

Cathy frowned. 'I didn't mean to come here and upset you John—'

Harper opened his mouth to speak.

'I can leave if you like. I can go back and tell Walt that you don't want to be here and that you're going to go home.'

'You're putting words in my mouth, Miss Hollander—'

'Don't call me that.'

'Why the hell not? It's your name, isn't it?'

'Jesus Christ! I'm sorry, I really am very fucking sorry for intruding in your life.' She gathered her purse, her cigarettes. She stood up, straightened her skirt. 'I'll go,' she said coldly. 'I'll go see Walt now. I'll tell him that you're going back to Miami—'

'Who said I was going back to Miami?'

Cathy Hollander stood there for a moment. She looked like she would break down right where she was.

Harper figured he'd shaken her up enough. He felt sorry for her. Why, he couldn't have said, but there was something about her – despite the apparently tough exterior – that aroused not only desire but sympathy. 'I'm sorry,' he said, but he knew it didn't come out sincere. He tried again, once more with feeling. 'I am sorry,' he said. 'Sit down. Sit down for a minute. I've got a lot of shit going round in my head and you're trying to fly right

55

through it. Give me a minute or two, okay? Just gimme a minute or two to get myself together and then we'll go get my stuff from Evelyn's.'

Cathy sat down. She set her purse on the bed. She retrieved her cigarettes and lit another one.

'You a religious man?' she asked after a while. Her voice was softer, like she'd settled something within herself and it was showing on the outside.

'You what?'

'Religious . . . you know, like do you believe in God?'

Harper shook his head and smiled. 'What was that Pacino movie . . . the one where he was the Devil?'

'*Devil's Advocate*?'

'Right,' he said. 'What did he say about God? An absentee landlord? Something like that. No, I can't say that I am a religious man, Miss Hollander.'

'Do you have to call me that?'

'Just for a while,' Harper replied, believing that maintaining some semblance of distance would serve to quieten the sense of attraction he felt towards her. 'Until I know how you figure in my father's life, and how you connect to Walt Freiberg, and whether or not you and I are going to be anything close to friends, I'm going to call you, Miss Hollander. Until you're something more than an acquaintance.'

'Whatever you say, Mr Harper.'

'So why the religious question?'

She shook her head. 'I pray sometimes,' she said quietly.

'You what?'

'I *pray* sometimes.'

'What the fuck for?' Harper looked around the room for his jacket.

'Whatever I feel I would like to have happen, you know?'

'Why don't you just go get it instead of praying for it?'

'Because sometimes you want things that aren't so easy to just go get.'

'Such as?'

'Such as your father getting better, something like that.'

'Well, that's understandable, Miss Hollander.'

'Why do you say that?'

Harper shrugged. He located his jacket on the chair behind the

56

door. 'Because you're his friend I s'pose, and when your friends get shot it seems common sense that you'd want them to get better, right?'

'I don't want him to get better just because of me,' she said.

Harper looked across at her. There was that expression again, the one that begged sympathy.

'I want him to get better so you can find out what kind of a man your father is.'

Harper sat staring at her for more than a minute. She didn't look away. Neither did he. It was then that he wondered if he should stay.

They shared no more than a dozen words on the way to Evelyn's. She'd come in the car that Walt had driven the night before. She knew her way around New York, knew the back streets that took them from Hudson and West Broadway to Carmine.

When they pulled over in front of the walk-up she turned and asked him a question. Right out of left field it came, like a curve ball from a greased glove.

'You wrote a book, right?' she asked, and the tone in her voice made it feel like an accusation.

Harper didn't reply.

'Something about fingerprints.'

'I did.'

'Takes some kind of person to put that many words together and have them make sense.'

He laughed suddenly, abruptly. Why it was so funny he didn't know, but it was.

'What's funny?'

He shook his head. 'Hell of a way to describe a book.'

'Was it really about fingerprints?'

He smiled. 'The title was an analogy.'

'You can still buy it?'

'I s'pose so,' Harper replied. He didn't know. For months after its publication he'd searched through the book lists, even gone to libraries to see whether people were checking it out. After a while it hadn't seemed so important anymore, so he'd stopped. When the royalty checks dried up to nothing he'd pretended to himself it didn't matter. Nothing, in all honesty, could have

57

been further from the truth. His predominant thought, right there a couple of inches back of his forehead, had been the wish to feel that rush again, the sense of personal achievement that came with seeing his own name on a book cover right there in Walden's or some such store.

'I'm going to get one,' Cathy Hollander said. 'I'm going to read it and tell you what I think, okay?'

'Sure,' Harper replied, and felt a sense of interest he hadn't experienced for as long as he could recall.

'You go in and get your bag,' she said. 'I'll wait here.'

'I might be a little while.'

'I'm not doing anything else.'

Harper climbed out of the car. He hesitated on the sidewalk for a moment and looked back at her. The fact she'd chosen to wait for him gave him a distinct sense of reassurance.

'Not a good idea,' Evelyn said.

'Like not telling me my father was alive for the past God knows how many years?' he retorted. 'Like *that* was a good idea.'

'Had my reasons, John Harper.'

He stood there staring at her, stood there in the kitchen doorway with his bag in his hand. He felt like cussing, shouting at her, but he gritted his teeth and kept his tongue in his head.

'I had my reasons and, right or wrong, they *were* reasons,' she went on. 'I never did anything in my life that didn't have some kind of reason behind it, and even now, even with this thing happening, I've not changed my mind.'

'I'm not arguing with you, Ev,' he said. He tried to make his voice gentle.

'Who's arguing,' she came back. 'You want an argument I'll give you a run for your money.'

'Jesus, Ev, this is crazy talk. What the hell has happened to you?'

She frowned, looked askance at him. She raised one eyebrow and peered at him with eyes like small river-washed stones. 'Happened to me? Happened to me? You want to know what happened to me? I'll tell you what happened to me, John Harper. I lost my sister, your mother, and out of the goodness of my heart I took you in despite what my own husband wanted, and then he died and I kept right on going even though I knew you didn't possess a respectful or grateful bone in your body, and then as soon as you got it in your mind that there was something better out there for you ... well, as soon as you figured you were old enough, you took off out of here. How long ago was that? Sixteen, seventeen years ago, and in all those years I saw you what, three or four times? You called maybe twice?'

'A little more than twice—'

She raised her hand defensively. 'I don't want to hear explanations. Don't want to hear anything, John Harper. You're a grown man now, and I have to take some degree of responsibility for the way you turned out. The fact that you're an ungrateful, self-centered—' Evelyn took a step forward and sat down awkwardly at the kitchen table. 'You're here. You're here now, and that's all that matters. Your father got himself shot because he's a fool more than likely, and I can't say that I feel a great deal of sympathy for what's happened. Goes around comes around, you know?'

Harper shook his head. 'What d'you mean?'

'He treated your mother like she didn't matter, John. He got her pregnant, and then as soon as you were born he disappeared.' She laughed, a bitter and caustic sound. 'Like father like son, right? He took off the moment there was anything even remotely resembling responsibility showing its face. He ran away just like you did, and left everyone behind holding the baby.'

'I didn't leave any baby behind, Ev—'

'It's an expression!' she snapped. 'You should know that, what with your writing books and being all self-important and having no goddamned time for the people who raised you. I did everything I could for you, and then you left me here on my own and never had the decency to even mail me a copy of your stupid goddamned book. For Christ's sake I had to go into town and buy one for myself. A boy I raised as my own son and he never even sent me a copy of the book he wrote.'

She looked up at him. There was a threat of tears in her eyes. 'I read your book, John. I read your book and I recognized things that were said in this house, things I said to you, things you said back. I was in there, right? I saw myself in there and you made me out to be some wicked stepmother ... a hard and bitter person who never had a good word for anyone.'

Harper felt his blood rushing, his pulse quickening. 'You read whatever you wanted to read, Evelyn, plain and simple. You want to talk about not having a good word for anyone then I suggest you take a good, hard look at yourself. You called me back here. I came. Seems to me that there's one helluva lot of questions that have not been answered, and I figure you owe me some answers—'

She shook her head. She had a way of doing it that made it clear nothing was going to get through. 'Questions? Answers? The past is the past. Let it go, John. What you did and didn't mean is all water under the bridge now. I read the book, and I have to tell you it made me mad. But that was a long time ago, and time has a way of drawing everything up inside itself and making you feel it wasn't so bad. I figured I deserved at least one good word, you know? Just one good word amongst all the blackness you painted around me. I'm not a crazy person, whatever you might think.'

'I don't think you're crazy, Ev,' Harper started. He felt like someone had taken his mind and heart and smashed them together. Somewhere inside the wreckage he was peering out and trying to remember where he was and what his life meant. There were no clues. It was all too much, too much by far.

'You don't?' she said. 'Well, is that so? Well, if I'm not crazy then you can hear me on one thing. Agreed?'

Harper waited for it.

'Agreed?' she repeated.

'Agree what? What are you asking me to agree to?'

'Just that you'll hear what I have to say now and don't immediately put it down to the ramblings of some crazy lonely evil stepmother with a stone for a heart and a head full of black thoughts.'

'I never said you were anything like that Ev, and if you read it that way—'

'Whatever,' she interjected. 'Whatever you think and whatever you say is your own business. Right now, all I'm asking is you listen to me one time, even if you never step foot inside this house again. At least I'll know I said this one thing and you listened to me.'

Harper smiled as best he could. 'I'm listening.'

'Go home,' she said.

'What?'

'You've seen him. He's an old man. He's not going to make it I understand. Too old. Too much damage. He wasn't part of your life before yesterday and he doesn't have to be part of your life now.'

'So what the hell did you call me for, Ev? Why did you call the newspaper? Why did you call Nancy Young?'

'Because of your mother,' she said.

'You what?'

'Because of your mother, John. She told me a while before she died that if anything ever happened to her I should wait until your father was dead and then I should tell you who he was.'

'She told you that?'

'She did.'

'So why didn't you wait until he was dead?'

Evelyn didn't reply.

'Why, Ev? Why didn't you wait until he was dead?'

'Because of Walt Freiberg.'

'Eh?'

'He heard about your father. He called me. He came over here. He told me that if I didn't call you and bring you up to New York he was going to call you himself. I didn't want him to call you . . . I didn't want you to have anything to do with these people—'

'*These* people? What d'you mean, *these* people?'

Evelyn lowered her head. She rested her elbows on the edge of the table and buried her face in her hands.

'Evelyn? What do you mean?'

'I want you to go,' she said quietly. 'I want you to turn around and go right back to Miami.'

'I'm not going to do that, Ev . . . I only just got here.' Harper realized, even as he spoke, that he was saying such a thing only to be contrary. 'You're saying things that don't make sense. I want to know what you're talking about.'

She laughed drily. 'Always the stubborn one. I can say what I think, I can tell you what's right, but it doesn't mean you're going to listen to me does it? Do whatever you're going to do John. You're here and you might as well find out for yourself. You're a grown man . . . more than likely you can take care of yourself. I'm telling you to go. Telling you for your own

61

goddamned good. Whatever the hell happens here don't come back and tell me I didn't warn you.'

Harper put his bag down and walked towards her. He stood over her for a second. She didn't move, didn't look up. He stepped to the side and put his hand on her shoulder. He felt the tension as the muscles twitched beneath his fingers. Evelyn moved her left hand and closed it over Harper's.

'Just go,' she said. 'I can't speak any more . . . go find out about your father, John. I won't be able to stop you, I know that, and it's probably best that you find out for yourself. You always were a single-minded child, always the one to put his hand on the stove just to prove to yourself that it was hot, eh?' She tried to laugh. It came out strained and uncomfortable. 'You remember I'm here, you remember who looked after you when they all disappeared.' Evelyn's hand tightened over his. 'And when you've seen him, then take a good look at whether there's any reason to stay here. Seems to me you won't find one, and if you don't, then get on the first flight you can and go home.'

Harper closed his eyes. Felt like he'd walked through a wall of emotion, an entire life's-worth collapsed into forty-eight hours.

'I didn't mean to hurt you, Ev,' he said. 'But you brought me here and I need to understand what's happening. I want to know about my mother—'

'I know, John, I know.' She was silent for a few moments. 'I will tell you, but not now. Go see your father, eh? Go see how he's doing.'

Harper withdrew his hand. He leaned down and kissed the top of Evelyn's head. He walked to the door, picked up his bag, and made his way quietly down the front hallway.

He glanced back once again, up the stairs. He was struck with the sudden and inexplicable feeling that they were not alone in the house; the feeling that someone was up there. He shuddered. The hairs rose at the nape of his neck. He tried to see around the corner at the top, up towards Garrett's room, the room where he'd consigned himself to the hereafter in the belief that whatever waited there for him was better than what he had. The house was full of ghosts. The house on Carmine was a repository for the dead.

Crazy family, all of them, and in such a light Harper believed he was perhaps a little crazy himself. He reached for the door, opened it, stepped out into the street.

'Hard,' he said. 'She's taken it real hard.'

Cathy Hollander whistled through her teeth. 'Don't know what the fuck to say about that.'

'Not a great deal you can say.'

'You knew about it?'

Harper nodded. 'I found him.'

'You what?'

Harper turned and looked at her. He could see over her shoulder and through the driver's-side window of the car. There wasn't a single person on the street. 'I found him. Went upstairs and found him in his room. Shot himself in the head.'

'Christ, John . . . I can't even begin to understand how that must feel.'

'Don't worry, Miss Hollander, you don't have to.' Harper looked around and up at the Carmine Street house. It felt as if the life he'd once lived had been someone else's all along. He could not connect the child he'd been, the child who'd walked along this very street, with the man he'd become. Truth be known, they were not the same person.

'We can go?' he asked.

Cathy snapped to. 'Sorry,' she blurted. 'Sorry, I was miles away. Yes – yes, of course we can go.' She leaned forward and turned the key in the ignition.

As they pulled away Harper closed his eyes and exhaled. Rock and a hard place. Stay or leave. Miami or New York.

Inside he shuddered. Didn't let it show, didn't want Cathy Hollander to think he was anything but strong.

NINE

The same doctor – the one from the day before – came running towards him as he turned at the end of the corridor. Harper expected him to go flying by towards some emergency, but in a moment it became obvious that the doctor was gesticulating at him, waving his arm and beckoning him. Harper was both surprised and puzzled.

'Come!' the doctor urged as Harper came with earshot. 'Come quickly. He's awake!'

Harper started walking rapidly, and then he was running, catching up with the doctor as the two of them reached the door at the end of the corridor and went through it into the ICU ante-room.

'A few minutes ago,' the doctor said breathlessly. 'Just a few minutes ago he started to move, and then he opened his eyes . . . he didn't say anything.'

Harper reached the window, and there – right there behind the glass – the old man who was his father looked back at him through narrow, pained eyes. There was a split-second of recognition, recognition that came from how unmistakably similar they were, and then something close to fear seemed to permeate the old man's expression. It was as if he was both shocked and frightened to see Harper standing there.

Harper couldn't breathe. For a moment he was completely disoriented and took a step backwards. The doctor was behind him, held his arm to prevent him losing his balance, and then he stepped forward again and reached out to steady himself against the glass.

The second defining moment: then, with his hand against the window. The old man, weak and frail, tubes running from his nose, one at the side of his mouth, his eyes screwed up into tight knots of pain, lifted his hand, inch-by-inch, excruciatingly slowly, until it was level with Harper's. They connected, like convict and visitor through the armored glass of a booth, their hands matching one another, their fingertips connecting.

'Huuuh,' Harper exhaled, and instinctively jerked his hand away. Once again he stepped backwards, a sensation of reeling confusion rushing up into his chest, his head, and that sound from his throat – *Huuuuh* – like he was ready to burst at the seams, ready to collapse to his knees and release every pent-up emotion in one almighty strangled sob.

The doctor held him up, taking his weight as his knees buckled, and then Harper was looking again, watching as his father – *his* father – lowered his hand, closed his eyes, and turned his head away. It was like watching someone disappear, watching someone become a ghost.

The doctor, still holding Harper, edged around and opened the door that separated the rooms. 'It's okay,' he whispered. 'It's okay.'

Harper went with it, one foot ahead of the other. Without thought, without understanding what was happening to him, and then he was there at the foot of the bed. He could see his father's face. The age, the lines, the imprint of pain and loss that clung to him. He lifted his hand once more, a hand that seemed to possess no strength at all, and the fingers moved slightly, almost unnoticeably.

'He wants you to come closer,' the doctor said. 'Closer.'

Harper moved with assistance, and before he could resist he was right there, right there beside his father, and his father was trying to speak.

Harper leaned down, his ear merely inches away from the old man's face, and the word that came from his parched mouth – awkward and stuttering – was nevertheless unmistakable.

Leee-ave.

Albert Reiff – graduate of Edgecombe and Attica; two strikes, third one will take him for life – sat facing Ben Marcus and Sol Neumann at a plain deal table, kind with a baize surface to play cards. It was a little after ten in the morning. Marcus had a thing for punctuality; Reiff was fifteen minutes early, had sat outside in a car smoking and listening to big band music on the radio, feeling inside like he'd drunk a pint of Pepto-Bismol and done three circuits of the park. Low building on the corner of West and Bloomfield near Pier 53 and the Fire Boat Station – two-storey, ground level catering to a launderette, a 7–11, some kind of key cutting shop; upper floor belonged to Ben Marcus. Like an open-plan storage facility, it was a meeting place; boxes of cigarettes and bottles of liquor, a pool table, a secure room at the end where things needing a safehouse could be placed short-term. It was into this building that Reiff had gone when his watch said three minutes to ten. Punctuality meant not only never late, it also meant not being too early.

'Things have gone and upset themselves,' Sol Neumann said after they'd shook hands, greeted Reiff, indicated where he should sit. 'This thing with Lenny, the fact that he's in Vincent's and he isn't dead . . . I don't even know what to think about that. We made an agreement with Lenny Bernstein, and now this.' Neumann shook his head and sighed. 'It isn't right, this isn't fucking justice, you know what I mean?'

Reiff nodded. 'Justice?' he said. 'That and hope have to be the most overrated commodities on the face of the fucking earth.'

'So what are we going to do now?' Neumann asked: a rhetorical question. 'Smartest thing we can, that's what. What we do is go ahead and work out these things we agreed with Lenny.' He glanced to his left at Ben Marcus. Marcus was implacable. 'We work these things out, just like Lenny was still here with us. That's what I believe we should do.'

Reiff didn't respond; he was waiting for instructions.

'We've had Victor Klein working on some sites,' Neumann said. He spoke quietly, almost a whisper. Reiff leaned forward to better hear him. 'We've had him working on a few things which seem good. These things take time, and that's another commodity that is scarce right now. We have to work fast; where we usually have weeks, this time we have days.'

'And there's the other thing,' Marcus said.

'Right. The other thing,' Neumann said. He looked down at the floor, and then up at Reiff. 'I want you to speak to Ray Dietz. I want you and him to go check on the runaway's family, this guy McCaffrey. Word came this morning that the guy has a sister and a brother. Make some calls, share a few words, go see some people, find out where this kid has gotten to. You can do that for me?'

Reiff nodded, started up out of his chair.

'This is going to be a mess whichever way it goes down,' Neumann added.

Reiff smiled; shrugged his shoulders. "S why we have cleaners, right?'

Neumann smiled. 'Sure it is,' he said. He turned towards Marcus and laughed. 'That's why we have cleaners.'

Once Reiff had left, Marcus rose to his feet and walked to the window. He stayed motionless for some time, his hands behind his back. 'Any news of this phantom who looks like Lenny Bernstein?'

'No, nothing yet,' Neumann replied. 'It's Merrett,' he added. 'Kid's a fucking whacko. Like I said before, I did time with him at Five Points. He gets an idea in his head he won't let it go. He was mistaken. It was nothing. Don't sweat it.'

Marcus shook his head. 'Way things are right now I have to sweat it Sol. Merrett says there was someone at St Vincent's with Freiberg and the girl. Doesn't make a difference who he looked like. Fact that they had someone there means something. I want to know who he is and what he's doing.' Marcus turned slowly and pinned Neumann with his gaze. 'Good to know how many people I gotta kill.'

'Sure, Ben, sure.'

'I mean it, Sol. I don't want to hear some bad news the day before we go to work. We already have additional factors to handle—'

'I'll handle it, Ben. I'll find out who he is.'

'Okay. We're done then. Go see Victor Klein, make sure he's organizing the people we need. And speak to Henry Kossoff . . . tell him we need hardware and cars. You know the routine.'

They left the upper floor together, made their way down a narrow iron fire escape to the car lot at the rear of the building.

'Call me later,' Ben Marcus said. He glanced at his watch. 'Call me before one and let me know what's happening.'

Later, much later, seated on a bench along the third floor corridor, Harper questioned what he'd heard.

Leave?

The doctor was by the door. He merely saw the old man's lips move. He did not hear anything.

'You must have,' Harper insisted, but he knew he was merely wishing for the doctor to agree with him so he could try and make some sense of it, so he could attempt to find its relevance and meaning.

'I'm sorry,' the doctor said. 'I really am sorry, Mr Harper, I was too far away.'

The single word was uttered, if it had *been* a word at all, and then Edward Bernstein – absentee father, gunshot victim, dying man – had slipped into unconsciousness once more.

John Harper had knelt by the side of the bed, his hand closed over his father's, and he'd tried to feel something personal for the man.

Finally – ten, perhaps fifteen minutes – and the doctor called for an orderly to help him take Harper out. Bernstein's vitals were growing even weaker and he needed attention. The doctor told Harper to come back the following day. Harper did not protest or argue. He tried to leave. He made it as far as the bench situated ten yards down the hallway, and there he sat until Frank Duchaunak found him.

'Mr Harper?'

Harper looked up.

'I thought it was you,' Duchaunak said. 'I asked for your name downstairs. I am a police officer. My name is Frank Duchaunak, Detective Frank Duchaunak.' He waited for Harper to speak, and when he said nothing Duchaunak nodded at the seat beside him. 'May I?'

Harper shrugged.

Duchaunak sat down. He leaned back and sighed. 'I understand Edward Bernstein regained consciousness.'

Harper neither spoke nor made any indication of having heard the question.

'Mr Harper?'

Harper looked down at the grey-green tiles beneath his feet. The hexagonal tessellation ran both ways, as far as he could see. Tiny scuffs of black were scattered along them, marking the hurrying feet of attendant nurses and doctors; the fingerprints of an emergency, of a life surfacing, a life slipping away.

'I don't want to intrude at a time like this, Mr Harper, but I came as soon as I heard.'

Harper frowned. 'Heard what?'

'That Mr Bernstein had regained consciousness.'

'Who told you?'

'The duty nurse called me.'

'Why would she do that?' Harper asked.

'Because I am the investigating officer, Mr Harper. I am in charge of the investigation into Mr Bernstein's – into your father's – shooting.'

'Right,' Harper said. 'Of course.'

'Did you see him?'

'Yes, I saw him.'

'And did he speak?'

Harper shook his head. He turned and looked at Duchaunak. He realized it was same cop, the one from the previous day, the one Uncle Walt had called an asshole. He was older than Harper, perhaps by half a dozen years or so, but he carried the world-weary beaten look of someone who'd crammed the contents of two lives into half as many years.

'Are you an asshole?' Harper asked.

Duchaunak frowned, then started laughing. 'Am I an asshole?' he asked. 'Sure I'm an asshole, a real professional asshole. I'm one of those assholes who isn't only born an asshole, I get up early in the morning to practise.'

Harper smiled.

'Who said that?' Duchaunak asked. 'Walt?'

'Walt? You know Walt Freiberg?'

'A little,' Duchaunak said.

'He didn't want you here yesterday . . . and then when you went he called you an asshole cop.'

'An asshole cop . . . that's what he said? I'm not sure what one of those is, but hell, if that's what Walt thinks then fair enough. Man has a right to an opinion.'

Harper didn't reply. He wanted the man to go away.

'So this is a real surprise for me, the fact that Edward Bernstein has a son.' Duchaunak just looked at Harper for a few moments.

Harper wanted to tell Duchaunak that it had been a greater surprise for himself, but felt that such a comment would serve no purpose.

'Did he speak?' Duchaunak asked.

'I think so.'

'He said something?'

'I'm not sure,' Harper replied.

'Did it seem like he said something?'

'I think he told me to leave.' Harper closed his eyes, ran his right hand through his hair. His hand stopped at the back of his neck and he appeared to massage the tense knot of muscles at the top of his spine. He wanted a drink, perhaps three, but he still felt no motivation to move.

'To leave?' Duchaunak asked.

'I don't know, Detective. I don't know that he even spoke, to tell you the truth. It sounded like one word . . . one word from a dying man I've never met before, and I think I wanted it to be a real word, a word that had some meaning, a word that perhaps had some relevance to the fact that he's about to die and I'm his son—' Harper stopped and looked directly at Duchaunak. 'For Christ's sake, I don't even know that I *am* his son. I'm going on the word of my crazy aunt and a guy called Walt Freiberg who I haven't seen for the better part of thirty years.'

'If he told you to leave . . . well, if he told you to leave, then I figure he gave you the best advice he could.'

Harper smiled and shook his head. 'I only just arrived Detective.'

Duchaunak nodded. 'Sure you did, sure you did. Doesn't change the fact that it's possibly the best advice you were ever given, regardless of who it came from.'

There was silence between them for a moment.

'You look like him,' Duchaunak said eventually.

'So?' Harper replied. 'A lot of people look like a whole lot of other people, doesn't mean they're related.'

'It wasn't an accusation, Mr Harper.'

'I'm sorry,' Harper said. 'This has been a difficult couple of days, still is difficult. I don't know what the hell I'm doing here.'

'Who told you about this?'

'You mean who told me that he was here in the hospital?'

'Yes, who told you?'

'My aunt. My mother's sister. She raised me after my mother died.'

'She lives here in New York?'

'Yes, over on Carmine Street off of Seventh.'

'And you live where?' Duchaunak asked.

Harper shook his head. 'Miami. I'm a reporter for the *Herald*.'

'Long time away from New York?'

'Left here when I was nineteen. Went to Florida to get away from all of this.'

'All of what?'

'New York, everything it represented for me.'

'The death of your mother, right?'

'That, and my uncle's suicide.'

'Suicide?'

'Yes,' Harper said. 'My aunt's husband, name was Garrett Sawyer. He killed himself when I was twelve.'

'Difficult childhood.'

Harper smiled. 'Difficult life, Detective.'

'You married?'

'No. No wife, no kids, crappy job . . . and now this.'

'And your relationship with Walter Freiberg?'

'Relationship?' Harper asked. 'What relationship would that be?'

'You tell me.'

'Walt . . . Uncle Walt. He used to be around a little after Garrett died. He was a friend of the family so to speak.'

'Involved with your aunt?'

Harper turned and looked at Duchaunak; he frowned, felt irritated. 'Why the third degree? I didn't have anything to do with the shooting.'

'I know you didn't, Mr Harper. I have a curious nature. Did you know Walt Freiberg and Edward Bernstein were business partners . . . have been for many years?'

'I don't know anything, Detective. I got a call from my aunt. She told me to come back to New York. When I got here she told me that a father I thought was dead was actually alive . . . well, nearly alive. She told me he'd been shot. I came here to see him yesterday and Walt Freiberg was here at the same time. I haven't seen Walt for about twenty-five years. He was here when I arrived at the hospital, and then we left and had something to eat. I stayed in a hotel last night, and then when I got up I came back here. Now you show up and ask me all manner of questions like I know a great deal more about what's going on than you do. I'm tired, stressed, confused, overwhelmed, the last thing I can deal with right now is the third degree from you.'

Duchaunak was silent for a time. He looked the other way

down the corridor. When he turned back he looked exhausted, as overwhelmed as Harper felt. 'I don't mean to bust your balls, Mr Harper. I got a headache the size of Michigan and then some. I haven't slept all night. I don't know who you are, except that you might be Lenny . . . Edward Bernstein's son. I don't know much of anything at all to tell you the truth, probably as little as you. I just have to find out who shot your father, and anything that might lead me in the right direction is something I have to follow. That's all.' Duchaunak rose from the bench. He looked down at Harper. 'I'm sorry for harassing you at a time like this, but you have to understand that this is my job—'

Harper raised his hand. He didn't think he could tolerate any more words from anyone. 'It's okay,' he said. 'No harm done. I'm going to stay here a while if it's okay with you. I just need some time to figure all of this out.'

'Sure thing,' Duchaunak said. He held out his hand. Harper reached up and took it. 'Take care, Mr Harper. Maybe we'll speak again sometime.'

'Maybe we will, Detective.'

Duchaunak started to walk away. He slowed, turned, and Harper looked up.

'Still think you should go back home,' Duchaunak said.

'I know, you told me once already. You and Evelyn both.'

Duchaunak nodded, looked like he was going to say something else, but he merely shook his head.

Harper listened to the sound of Duchaunak's shoes echoing down the corridor, could still hear him walking even when he turned left at the end.

Harper leaned forward and buried his face in his hands. He felt as if the world and all its troubles had settled on his shoulders.

Across the street, half a block down, Duchaunak and Faulkner seated in the car.

'Didn't see anything.'

'Nothing at all?'

'Nope, not a thing. Kid seemed wired up tight. Don't think he has a clue who these people are.'

Faulkner put the lid on his styrofoam cup and slotted it in the cup-rest beside his seat. He turned the key in the ignition and the engine kicked into life.

'Hang fire,' Duchaunak said.

Faulkner killed the engine.

'That's her,' Duchaunak said.

'Where?'

'Over there in the black Merc.'

Faulkner leaned forward and peered through the windscreen. 'You sure?'

'Sure as can be.'

'She waiting for Harper?'

'Fuck knows. Maybe she's waiting for Freiberg.'

'You're sure it was the aunt who called Harper, not Walt?'

''S what the kid said. Said his aunt called him, told him to come back to New York, and it was only when he got here that she told him about Lenny. Said that Freiberg was here when he came to the hospital yesterday, and when they were done visiting they went for something to eat and then he stayed overnight in a hotel.'

'Wonder why he didn't stay with his aunt.'

'Christ only knows—' Duchaunak started, and then 'Lookee here . . . look who's come to town.'

A second car, a midnight-blue sedan, pulled up behind the Merc. It drew to a stop, the driver's door opened and Walt Freiberg stepped out.

Within a moment Cathy Hollander emerged from the Merc.

'Told you it was her,' Duchaunak said.

'I'll get you a Kewpie doll.'

Duchaunak and Faulkner watched as Walt Freiberg and Cathy Hollander exchanged a few words on the sidewalk, and then the pair of them crossed the street and started up the steps of St Vincent's.

'I want to know what the deal is with this, John Harper,' Duchaunak said quietly. 'Either he's in this and he's a really fucking good actor, or he's walking around the edges of something he knows nothing about.'

'And if it has anything to do with Marcus then there's a good chance he won't get back to Miami.'

Duchaunak nodded slowly, said nothing.

Faulkner started the engine a second time. 'Precinct?' he asked.

Duchaunak nodded. 'Precinct.'

TEN

'Cathy called me,' Freiberg said, when he was five or six feet from where Harper sat on the bench. 'She called me and told me that Frank Duchaunak was here.'

'Walt,' Harper said. He stood up and shook Freiberg's hand. 'Hi there. How are you?'

Freiberg placed his hand on Harper's shoulder and sat him down. Freiberg sat on one side, Cathy Hollander on the other. 'I'm fine John, just fine. Did he speak with you?'

'Who?'

'Duchaunak . . . the cop.'

Harper nodded. He was quiet for a moment. 'He said something to me Uncle Walt.'

Freiberg nodded. 'I know, John, you just told me.'

'No, Edward, my father . . . he said something to me.'

Freiberg started to rise. 'He's awake? He's conscious? Jesus, John, why didn't you say so? Christ almighty, what the hell are we doing sat here?'

'He's not conscious any more, Uncle Walt. He came round for just a second or two, and I don't know that he actually did say something, but it sounded like he was telling me to leave.'

'To leave?'

'That's what it sounded like. Sounded like he said the word "leave". That was all. I could have been mistaken, but—' Harper exhaled deeply and shook his head. He looked at Cathy Hollander. She smiled sympathetically. 'Hello, Miss Hollander.'

'Hello, Mr Harper.'

'You okay?'

'As can be.'

'Thanks for waiting for me.'

'No problem, no problem at all.'

'Let's get out of here,' Freiberg said.

'Walt?'

'Yes, John?'

'Who is Lenny?'

Freiberg smiled and frowned simultaneously. 'Lenny? Who's been talking about Lenny?'

'Detective Duchaunak. He spoke of my father, and when he went to say his name he called him Lenny and then he corrected himself. Why did he call him Lenny?'

'It's nothing, John, just a nickname, like a joke kind of thing.'

'A nickname? What does he have a nickname for?'

'Your father, Edward, he is a ... businessman, quite an influential and important businessman. He manages a lot of things, co-ordinates stuff, gets everybody working together. They call him Lenny after Leonard Bernstein, the composer, the music guy you know? Your father makes sure everyone's playing the same tune ... that's why they call him Lenny. Lenny Bernstein. You get it?'

Harper nodded. 'But why a police detective, Uncle Walt? Why would a police detective know him well enough to use his nickname?'

Freiberg laughed. 'Enough questions, John, enough questions for now.' He put his hand beneath Harper's arm and helped him to his feet. 'Let's get out of here. We'll tell whoever's on the desk downstairs to have the doctor call us if something happens with your father. Let's go have some lunch, okay? Let's go somewhere real nice and have some lunch.'

Harper didn't speak again. He walked down the corridor, Uncle Walt on one side, Cathy Hollander on the other. He felt as if he'd escaped an auto smash, a bad one, the kind where they close the road and the emergency services have to hose the blood off the hot-top. The kind where folks with kids and house payments and their whole lives to look forward to have just lost it all. Just like that – a fingersnap, a single heartbeat – and everything's gone to hell. And he, John Harper – the one with nothing, the one with no-one at all to remember him – had somehow managed to survive.

'Torchon of Foie Gras, lemongrass-scented Gulf shrimp with cilantro and mango, and then we'll be having a black truffle cavatelli, grilled filet of beef and braised short rib, or turbot stuffed with Maine lobster with a ragout of corn, leeks and chanterelles in a caviar sauce.' The maître d' smiled effusively. 'Finally there will be a selection of Artisanal cheese served with fig jam and raisin-walnut bread. And you know Bruce Springsteen?'

Walt Freiberg smiled and said he did, not personally of course, but he had heard of him.

'Well, Soozie Tyrell of the E Street Band will be performing live. There will be dancing until three a.m., and once your table is booked it's yours for the night. That, Mr Freiberg, will be our New Year's Eve extravaganza, and we would be honored to have you and your guests celebrate with us.'

Walt smiled. He reached out and took the man's hand. 'Anton, you are a gentleman, a true gentleman. I am sorry, I have absolutely no idea what we will be doing on New Year's Eve, but I can guarantee that if I find myself without arrangements I will be here in a flash.'

'Of course, Mr Freiberg, of course. You are here for luncheon?'

'Yes, Anton, just the three of us.'

'This way, Mr Freiberg,' Anton said, and circumvented the tables of the Tribeca Grill on Greenwich Street as if he was performing a graceful *pas-de-deux*.

Walt Freiberg, John Harper and Cathy Hollander were seated within moments, and Anton glided away to despatch their waiter.

'This,' Walt said as he leaned closer to Harper, 'is the Tribeca Film Center. This is Bobby De Niro's place. Here you got Tribeca Film and Miramax, and if you sit here long enough you get to see all kinds of people. One time I seen Bill Murray here, another time Christopher Walken. Hell of a place, you know? Won all sorts of awards. I love to come here.' Walt grinned. He reached out, closed his hand over Harper's and squeezed it firmly. 'Me and your father, we love to come and eat here. They got some great food . . . really great food. Right, Cathy?'

Cathy smiled. She shifted a few inches closer to Harper. Once again he felt the pressure and warmth of her thigh against his own, sensed the friction created by the taut silk of her stocking against his jeans. Seemed that whenever she appeared the distress and unreality of his situation was somehow diminished.

The waiter came. He greeted Walt as if they were long-lost. Walt didn't want to see the menu.

'Go with my choices, okay boys and girls?' he asked.

Cathy smiled. Harper merely grunted. Food was the last thing on his mind.

'Okay,' Walt said. 'We'll go with a plate . . . you have a plate today?'

'Indeed Mr Freiberg. We have a veal and foie gras ballotine, serrano ham and chicken liver mousse.'

'Good. On the side we'll have butternut squash and apple mousse and some sautéed chanterelles.'

The waiter nodded, smiled, scribbled furiously.

'We can be medieval and share entrees,' Walt said. He looked up at the waiter. 'Don't tell Anton I said that, eh?' Walt laughed. The waiter laughed too. Harper stared at the huge mahogany bar that centered the room.

'So, we'll go with the garganelli pasta, Atlantic salmon . . . that comes with the bacon and onion stew, right?'

'It does, Mr Freiberg, yes.'

'Good, we go with that, and we'll have the sea scallops as well.'

'Very good, Mr Freiberg – and to drink?'

Walt glanced first at Cathy Hollander and then at Harper.

'You easy?' he asked.

'Whatever you like, Walt,' Cathy replied.

'Châteauneuf du Pape, an early one . . . whatever you recommend.'

'Of course Mr Freiberg . . . and I must say it is a pleasure having you here again. Might I ask as to the whereabouts of Mr Bernstein?' The waiter glanced at Harper. Harper didn't see it, but Walt Freiberg was on it like flypaper.

'You see the resemblance, yes?' he asked the waiter.

The waiter smiled. 'I couldn't help it, Mr Freiberg. I did, of course I did, but I didn't wish to be rude.'

'This,' Walt Freiberg said proudly, 'is Mr Bernstein's son, John.'

The waiter nodded deferentially. 'A pleasure sir, a great pleasure.'

Harper looked up at him with a blank expression on his face.

'And Mr Bernstein himself?'

Walt shook his head. 'Unfortunately, Mr Bernstein has been taken ill.'

'Oh my goodness. Not too serious I trust?'

Freiberg shook his head. 'Not too serious, no.'

The waiter seemed relieved. 'I can speak for everyone here in wishing him a very rapid recovery.'

'Thank you,' Walt said. 'That is most kind.'

'I shall collect your wine.'

The waiter smiled at each of them in turn, and then he hurried away.

'So you had a run-in with Frank Duchaunak?' Walt Freiberg asked Harper.

Harper perceived a thought at the back of his mind, something he'd been trying to remember since Walt had appeared at St Vincent's. 'A run-in? I wouldn't say I had a run-in. He asked me a few questions, that was all.'

'Questions? Questions about what?'

Harper shrugged. 'Nothing specific . . . how long I'd been away from New York, where I was living. Nothing important.'

'And he said nothing about your father? About his interest in him?'

'No, nothing like that. He said that you and Edward Bernstein were business partners. He called him Lenny, like I said. He asked about my relationship with you—'

'With me?'

Harper nodded. 'Yes, with you. He asked what my relationship was with you.'

'And what did you tell him, John?' Walt smiled, smiled like he was being nonchalant and relaxed.

Harper was aware of a cool tension in that moment, as if it could have been possible to say the wrong thing. 'I said you were a friend of the family, that you had been there after Garrett's death—'

'Garrett? He asked about Garrett?'

'He didn't know who Garrett was.'

'So how did he know to ask about Garrett? You told him about Garrett?'

Harper shook his head. 'No, not directly.' He turned and looked at Cathy Hollander. All of a sudden he felt nervous, like there was something for him to be afraid of. Cathy looked back at him without changing her expression.

'He asked who called me. I told him Evelyn called me. He asked who Evelyn was and I told him. I happened to mention Garrett in passing, that was all.'

The waiter appeared as if from nowhere. He smiled broadly. He held a bottle in his hand and showed the label to Walt.

Walt little more than glanced, said, 'Yes, that's fine,' and waited patiently while the bottle was uncorked. The wine was poured, tasted, complimented, and then Walt said he would take care of its service.

The waiter vanished as effortlessly as he had appeared.

'So . . . anything else he asked you?'

Harper was silent for a while. He remembered the thought. He put his hand in his pocket and took out the money Walt had given him in the Cantonese restaurant. 'I don't need this money,' he said. 'I brought this back for you.'

Walt laughed suddenly. 'Jesus, John, what the hell is this? Keep the money for Christ's sake. You need some money . . . everybody needs some money, right Cathy?'

Cathy was smiling. She reached out her hand, closed it over Harper's. Harper felt the notes crumple within his fist. More than that he felt the pressure of her fingers, the closeness and promise he wished they represented. 'Put the money in your pocket, John. One thing you're going to learn about Walt is his generosity.'

Harper planned to repeat himself, to tell Walt that he *really* didn't need the money, but Walt was asking questions again.

'So that was all he asked about? Nothing more specific, just passing the time of day right?'

'Right, like he was interested in who I was and how I'd heard about my father—' Harper stopped. It felt so strange, so out-of-place to be saying such a thing. *My father*. He repeated it over in his mind – *My father . . . My father . . . My father* – but still felt awkward and unsettled. 'I think he was trying to find out anything that might give him a lead on who did the shooting.'

Walt smiled. He seemed more settled, less angular in his manner, as if Harper's words had satisfied what he wished to know.

The waiter appeared bearing dishes. Even as he was serving Walt was distracted by someone entering the restaurant.

'Jesus, Mary and Joseph,' Freiberg exclaimed. 'Well I never—'

Walt stood up and started waving his hand in the direction of a man who'd entered. Heavy-set, shorter than Harper, hair dark and thick, greying at the temples. He possessed an air of great confidence, certain and assured in his movements. He saw Walt and laughed out loud.

'Well, fuck me!' he exclaimed.

Walt waved him over, and as the man started towards their table Walt leaned down and whispered to Harper: 'Don't say anything about Edward, don't mention his name, okay?'

Harper looked confused.

'It's okay . . . trust me,' Walt said. 'Don't say anything specific, right?'

Harper glanced at Cathy.

She nodded, raised her hand and pressed her index finger to her lips.

Harper didn't have time to speak, to ask what was going on. The man had arrived at the table and was standing over them.

Walt reached out and shook his hand. 'Jesus, Sol, how ya doin'?'

'Good, good, good,' Sol said, and then he glanced at Harper, double-took, frowned and shook his head. 'What the fu—'

Freiberg laughed. 'Sol . . . want you to meet someone. This is Edward's son, John.'

'Well, Jesus Christ Walter, what the hell is this all about, eh?'

Walt was laughing, and Sol was leaning across the table and reaching out his hand.

Harper took it without thinking, felt his hand almost crushed with enthusiasm by the man ahead of him.

'John,' Walt said. 'This is Sol Neumann, a friend of your father's.'

Neumann smiled broadly. He continued punishing Harper's hand with his relentless grip. 'Friend? An acquaintance really, not so much a friend. It is a pleasure to meet you, John . . . may I call you John?'

Harper nodded. He needed his hand back before he lost all circulation in his fingers.

'Join us,' Walt said. 'We're having some lunch. You are welcome to join us, Sol.'

Neumann released Harper's hand. 'Most kind, most kind,' he said. 'I was looking for someone. I am attending to something for Mr Marcus. I don't wish to offend Walt, I would love to eat with you, but—'

Walt raised his hand. 'Say no more Sol, business is business. If you are busy we shall eat together another day, yes?'

Neumann grinned enthusiastically. 'Yes, another day, another day.'

He shook hands with Walt, again with Harper. He nodded politely at Cathy, and then he made his farewell. 'Respects to your father,' he said to Harper as he backed away from the table. He continued walking backwards until he reached the bar, and then he raised his hand once more, turned, and was gone.

The waiter, silent, almost motionless during the entire exchange, stepped forward once again and served starters.

'Asshole!' Walt hissed once the waiter had disappeared. 'Like that asshole Duchaunak . . . fucking Marilyn Monroe freakin' weirdo motherfucker,' and then he sat back and raised both his hands, palms forward in a conciliatory gesture. 'I shouldn't say such things,' he said. 'I apologize, John, there was no need for such an outburst.'

Harper was taken aback, wondered what the hell was happening. 'He seemed friendly enough,' he said, and even as he said it realized how utterly naïve he sounded.

'They're all friendly,' Walt said. 'Smiles and shaking hands, all of them, people like Neumann and Duchaunak—'

'Sol Neumann is a cop as well?' Harper asked.

Walt laughed, Cathy also. 'Sol Neumann a cop?' Walt said. 'No, John. Sol Neumann is about as far from a cop as you could get.'

'He knows my father,' Harper said.

Walt raised his hand and gripped Harper's shoulder. 'Eat, John, eat. Don't worry yourself with any of this.'

'What was this thing you said about Duchaunak, the thing about Marilyn Monroe?'

Walt smiled and shook his head. 'Frank Duchaunak is a haunted man, John. He has a thing about Marilyn Monroe.'

'A thing? Whaddya mean?'

Walt glanced at Cathy.

Cathy leaned towards Harper. He could smell her perfume. 'Frank Duchaunak was born on August fifth 1962,' she said.

Harper frowned. He didn't understand.

'The day Marilyn Monroe died,' Cathy explained. 'He figures this has some meaning and significance in his life, and he is a little obsessed with the woman.'

'Obsessed?' Harper asked.

'Books, posters, videos of every film she made . . . and that doesn't even get close to the Di Maggio baseball.'

'What baseball?'

'Apparently Frank Duchaunak paid five thousand dollars for a baseball signed by Joe Di Maggio because he believed Marilyn Monroe might have held it for him when he signed it.'

'You're kidding?' Harper said.

'No word of a lie,' Walt said. 'It is what it is . . . and hey, I don't have a problem with a guy having an interest, you know? Some guys like racing cars, others like to collect stamps or shot glasses or whatever, but you get a guy like Duchaunak with this Marilyn thing, and hey, this goes a little out into left field, if you know what I mean.'

Harper – about to ask another question, a question about Sol Neumann and Mr Marcus – was interrupted by Walt Freiberg's cellphone.

'Ah, for Christ's sake,' Walt said under his breath, and retrieved the phone from his jacket pocket. He looked at the screen, and then edging his chair back he stood slowly, his expression changing as he rose.

'You have to excuse me,' he said. 'I have to take this call.'

Harper smiled, nodded.

Walt Freiberg started walking, and as he did so he took the call. 'Tell me all about it,' he started. 'I want to know what the fuck went wrong—'

Harper strained to hear what he was saying but Walt walked out of earshot and made his way towards the exit.

'You don't try and listen,' Cathy Hollander said.

'Eh?'

She smiled, glanced towards Walt Freiberg as he vanished through the doorway.

'To the conversations, the phone calls, whatever. You don't try and listen.'

Harper shrugged his shoulders.

'For real,' Cathy said. 'There are certain things Walt is very conscious of, and one of them is his work. His work is his own business, no-one else's, and he makes it a very definite rule that nothing interferes with it.'

'Hey,' Harper said. 'I'm neither one way nor the other on this thing. I'm the new kid on the block. I'm here and I don't even know what the hell I'm doing here. Walt Freiberg is a distant memory from my childhood who happens to have surfaced. This cop guy, this Duchaunak, he tells me that Walt and my father are business partners, that they've been partners for many years, right?'

Cathy shook her head. 'Whatever you say.'

'It's not what *I* say, Miss Hollander, it's what the Marilyn Monroe-obsessed cop told me, that Walt and my father have been business partners for many years.'

'Okay, so what?'

'So what?' Harper asked. 'Well, I don't know what kind of business and I don't s'pose it matters what kind of business, but it seems to me that if Walt has been around my father for as long as I think then it seems awful strange that he's so calm.'

'So calm? What d'you mean, so calm?'

'Your partner, your friend, whatever . . . they get shot, shot in a liquor store robbery. They're laid up in hospital and there's a very good possibility that they're going to die, and you spend your time out and about having lunch in some fancy fucking restaurant—'

'What would you have him do, Mr Harper?'

Harper looked at Cathy, his expression one of surprise. He sensed that his outburst had alienated her. He wished he could wind it back and start over.

'Walt Freiberg has lost a lot of people,' Cathy said.

Harper shook his head. He had no idea what she meant.

'I can't tell you a great deal from personal experience,' she went on. 'I haven't been around for an awful long time, and to tell you the truth I don't know a great deal more about Walt Freiberg and your father than you do, but I know that Walt has had a pretty interesting life, and when it comes to losing people

83

Walt has done a good deal of that. Walt has made losing people something of a secondary career.'

'I don't understand,' Harper said.

Cathy smiled. 'And you're not going to . . . here comes the man himself.'

Harper turned and saw Walt walking across towards them. He was grinning broadly. He took his seat. Harper could tell he'd been outside from the coolness he exuded.

'Sorry kids,' he said. 'Just a little matter that needed sorting. Now where were we? Oh yeah, we were talking about Frank Duchaunak and his Marilyn Monroe fixation. Freakin' whackjob if you ask me,' and Walt Freiberg was talking, and Harper was listening, and there was something about the manner in which he spoke, the way he seemed to make everything he was saying the most important thing to be said, and there were jokes, another reference to Duchaunak thinking with his dick instead of his head—

'Guy's put so much trust in his dick he's the only person I know who washes his hands *before* he takes a leak!'

And Harper, caught somewhere within the overlapping emotions of everything that had happened – anxiety, confusion, grief, loss, a fear of the unknown perhaps – forgot to ask about Sol Neumann and Mr Marcus, and even if he had remembered perhaps would not have possessed the nerve to ask, because everything except that which Walt Freiberg was speaking of seemed insignificant. When Walt was there it was Walt's life, Walt's words, Walt's moment. Walt Freiberg possessed the ability to sweep everyone around him into the whirlwind of his own reality, and there was little that could be done to avoid its magnetism. Walt seemed to make the idea of being excluded something awkward and potentially unpleasant. John Harper, a man with little bearing and few reference points, went with the flow. He ate the food, he drank the wine, and at the end of the meal he smoked two of Cathy Hollander's cigarettes, didn't even try to remind himself that he'd quit.

She seemed animated, more alive, and Harper considered an odd thought: that the more time he spent with someone, the more he got to know them, the more attractive they became. It was as if the real personality shone through the exterior facade. In that moment, and those that followed as he watched her, listened to her, he believed she was the only real reason he had for staying in New York.

And when they were done; when the check was paid, coats gathered, farewells uttered and hands shaken; when fifty-dollar bills were discreetly pressed into receptive palms, John Harper went out of the Tribeca Grill onto Greenwich Street feeling as if he'd touched the edges of a world he could never hope to occupy. Walt Freiberg – a man who'd made losing people a secondary career – told Harper that it had been good to eat together, that they should do it again the following day, and then explained that he had some affairs to deal with and Cathy would drive him back to his hotel. He would call Harper later, perhaps in the morning, because there was someone he wanted Harper to meet.

And then he was gone. Like that. Just gone.

Harper stood there, Cathy Hollander to his right, ahead of them the black Merc that she'd driven over that morning, and he wondered where the rest of his life had disappeared to.

He thought of Harry Ivens, figured he should call him, and then realized that he'd been in New York less than twenty-four hours.

'What?' Cathy asked him.

Harper shook his head. 'I arrived here yesterday,' he said quietly. 'I feel like I've been here days.'

Cathy smiled knowingly. 'That's New York,' she said. 'Well, half of it's New York and half of it's Walt.'

'And you?' Harper asked. 'How much of it is you?'

Cathy laughed. 'I'm just the eye candy sweetheart,' she said, and then she put her hand through and beneath Harper's arm and pulled him close. 'There aren't a hundred ways to say this, and maybe there isn't even one way to say it pretty, but I sort of come with the territory.'

Harper once again recognized his own naivete. He wanted to ask more but couldn't.

'I'll drive you to your hotel,' she said. 'Unless there's somewhere else you want to go.'

Harper watched her carefully, tried to read some deeper meaning into her comment. He perceived nothing and was disappointed. He smiled and shook his head. 'I'm tired Cathy, real tired. Feel like I could sleep for a month.' It was only after he'd spoken that he realized he'd called her by her first name.

'Well, seems to me the greatest difficulty people have in life is not doing the thing they feel they should do. You want to go sleep for a month I'm sure Walt will settle the tab at the Regent.'

Harper started laughing. He realized he was a little drunk. He didn't care.

'Get in the car,' she said. 'I'll drop you off.'

Harper did as he was told.

Cathy pulled away, turned the CD player on – Peggy Lee, radio broadcast recording, *a cappella* version of 'Fever'. It felt like the woman's voice was seducing him. He leaned back against the headrest, closed his eyes, could smell Cathy Hollander's perfume once again. Maybe it was neither Peggy Lee nor Cathy Hollander; maybe it *was* New York. New York wasn't America, never had been, never would be. It was as far from America as one could hope to get. The city owned itself, and no-one owned the city, except maybe Frank Sinatra and he was dead.

Harper smiled to himself. Wondered why he'd resisted coming back all this time. Because of Garrett? Because of what had happened back then? *Back then* was all the way back then. Didn't seem like it was following him, didn't seem like he'd find it around the corner or waiting on the junction when he took a walk.

'Can I have a cigarette?' he asked.

'Help yourself,' Cathy said, and nodded towards the glove-box. Harper flipped the catch, searched through the CD cases and traffic citations and found a pack of Winstons.

'You can keep those,' she said. 'I'm actually trying to quit.'

Harper smiled. 'That's what I was telling myself yesterday.'

'Hell of a thing eh? I've known people quit coke and heroin and pills, but never able to quit smoking.'

'Hell of a thing,' he echoed, and put the cigarette in his mouth. Cathy passed him a lighter from her coat pocket.

It was only minutes, but minutes stretched at their seams, and then they were pulling up outside the American Regent. Harper opened the door, and before he stepped out he paused and turned to look at her.

'Feels like a dream,' he said quietly.

'Better than a nightmare,' she replied.

86

He smiled. 'I don't know what to think about Walt Freiberg.'

'Don't try and think anything.'

'He worked with my father for a long time?'

She shrugged. 'Far as I can tell . . . haven't been around that long myself.'

'And where do you go now?'

'Home . . . until he calls me, and then I'll go meet him. Perhaps he won't call me and I'll stay in my apartment and watch TV or something.'

'You want to come up?' Harper asked.

'Like a date or something?'

Harper laughed, felt awkward, but pleasantly so. For a moment he believed he didn't care what she thought of him. 'A date? No,' he said. 'Just for company.'

'If it isn't a date I'm not coming,' she said, and smiled almost coyly.

'I'd like you to come up,' Harper repeated, even though he was aware of how foolish he sounded. 'Really.'

She paused for a moment, reached out and touched his hand. 'I don't think that's such a good idea. I think it'd be better if you went and got some sleep, Mr Harper—'

'John.'

'My turn to be difficult, *Mr Harper,*' she repeated.

Harper eased out and stood on the sidewalk. He leaned down and smiled like the fool he was.

'Go,' she said, 'before you say something you don't mean and will regret tomorrow.'

Harper stood up straight and closed the car door. She drove away. She didn't look back, didn't glance over her shoulder.

In a small kind of way Harper was disappointed.

ELEVEN

Up on Fifty-first, right there between Eight and Ninth, there's a church building, St Paul's something-or-other. High up on the wall overhanging the street there's a neon cross, like a Jesus kind of cross. Words on it read *SIN WILL FIND YOU OUT*. Glows bright at night, like a warning, a halfway house for the soul; there to remind the folks of New York that God is watching, that God sees everything.

Frank Duchaunak stands on the facing sidewalk. He believes what the cross says. He believes that sin will find you out.

He knows nothing about John Harper, except that he wrote a book called *Depth of Fingerprints*. He tried to order it on the internet but didn't succeed. He sent Faulkner out to find one at a library, to call him when he had it, and in the meantime he took a drive, just took a drive for no other reason than to be outside of the precinct house.

He will get a call in a little while and he will go back. Faulkner will have found a copy, and Duchaunak will sign out and go home. He'll read the thing in one sitting, and he will enjoy the book despite its darker aspects and narrow shades, but it will not serve to answer the question that has plagued him since Lenny Bernstein's shooting: Who is John Harper, and why is he here?

He feels that the answer to that question may provide the answers to so many others. Was Lenny's shooting an inside thing, perhaps carried out by Ben Marcus, or was it the random consequence of an opportunist hold-up? Tomorrow he will retrieve the CCTV footage from the store and see if something can be gleaned from it.

He stays there for a little while, there on the sidewalk looking at the neon sign. He doesn't want Lenny to die. Doesn't want him to die until the scales have been balanced.

He buries his hands in his overcoat pockets.

The evening smells cool and crisp; smells like snow.

'He said that?' Marcus asked. 'Those were his words exactly?'

Neumann nods. 'Hell, Ben, you should've seen the guy. It was like Lenny twenty, thirty years ago. He introduced him, said that it was Lenny's son, called him John. I followed them, followed Freiberg and the girl. They took him over to Bobby De Niro's place in Tribeca, you know? He even had the nerve to ask me to eat with them.'

'You should've stayed,' Marcus said. 'You should've stayed and found out whatever you could about this John Bernstein.'

Neumann raised his hands, palms upwards. 'Ben ... after what happened with Lenny I figured—'

'It's okay,' Marcus said. 'It's okay, Sol.'

Marcus sat almost motionless, his back to the window. Neumann could hear him breathing, and felt on edge.

Eventually Marcus broke the awkward silence: 'Any news from Reiff or Dietz on this McCaffrey runaway?'

Neumann shook his head.

Marcus nodded slowly. 'Okay ... arrange a sit-down. I want everyone there. Reiff, Dietz, Victor Klein, Karl Merrett, everyone who's going to be involved in this thing.'

'We're going ahead with the action?' Neumann asked.

Marcus smiled. 'Going to do more than one,' he said. 'We're going to carry through with what was agreed with Lenny, but it's going to be a little bigger than we thought, you know?'

'Bigger?' Neumann asked. 'How d'you mean, bigger?'

'Tomorrow,' Marcus said. 'Tomorrow morning. Everyone at the warehouse, and then we talk.'

Harper took a shower. Dried his hair, made some coffee with the complimentary provisions beside his bed. Stood at the tenth floor window smoking another of Cathy Hollander's Winstons. Could see out across the Hudson, right over the West Side Highway and Battery Park City. Hell of a view, all the way to New Jersey.

Was this his city? Was this really where he would find himself? Had he merely divorced himself from all recognition because of the things that had happened here?

Like that Wednesday?

Harper shivered. There was no breeze. He was not cold. He drank his coffee, smoked his cigarette, willed himself not to remember.

The past came anyway, came like it had always intended to, right from the moment he'd boarded the plane in Florida with the knowledge he was coming here. Here to New York; returning to the past.

Before he had another chance to stop it, the past had found him, rolling up against him and pressing in from all sides. Something like a shadow perhaps; maybe more like a ghost.

Back a while; back some considerable time before. 1980, beginning of August. Twelve years old, standing beside the window looking out into the street.

Evelyn was worried, like a wound-up kind of worried, and her anxiety seemed to seep into everything like color through water.

'Where is he, John? Where'd Garrett go to this time?'

Small John shook his head. 'I don't know Aunt Ev. Just said he needed some time to himself, and off he went.'

'He took the car?'

'No, he didn't take the car . . . just walked right out the front door.'

Evelyn nodded. Couldn't feel anything now, just nothing at all. Tears had come and gone; inner sense of guilt and pain and heartbreaking anger; all that shit backed up inside her like a reservoir waiting to burst the dam, and once upon a while ago she would have let it all run out of her, but now – now that she knew . . .

Garrett Sawyer was going to die sometime soon. Evelyn, strangely enough, kind of felt nothing much at all. He was going to drink a hole right through his guts, and his entire life would just pass right on out. Sometimes she wondered what made him the way he was, whether it was her, something she had done or said. Sometimes she remembered that wondering served no purpose and thus tried to think nothing at all.

Twelve-year-old John Harper, unwanted nephew, knew more than both Ev and Garrett put together. Garrett Sawyer was drinking himself into forgetfulness for the bad shit he'd done. What it was John Harper couldn't tell, but he could see the shadows the man carried, and they were heavy shadows, dark and forbidding. Such things had a way of taking over some part

90

of your mind and catching you unawares. Just when you figured you'd got it licked there it went again. This one was the deep six, the Holy Roller, that *Come and meetcha Maker* kind of deal.

'We'll go out and look for him,' Ev said, like such a thing made sense. Greenwich Village, late afternoon, middle of Manhattan. *We'll go out and look for him.*

Harper agreed because there was no point in disagreeing. Disagreeing would make her mad and bitter and *I took you in, and this is the way you respect me you little—*

John Harper put on his coat and followed her out into the street.

An hour later, maybe a little more, Evelyn Sawyer stood on the corner of West Houston and Seventh. 'I'll stand here,' she said. 'I'll stand here and see if he comes by.' She smiled weakly, nodded her head up and down in a vague attempt to make herself believe that what she was saying possessed some slight degree of rationality. 'You run back to the house and see if he hasn't come home, okay?'

Harper stood there for a moment, didn't move a muscle.

'Go!' she said, and shooed him away like a hungry rag-taggle dog.

John Harper turned and started walking.

Garrett Sawyer scared him. One time he'd heard him shouting at the top of his gravelly voice from the bedroom. One time he smashed something and things went silent for a godawful long time.

Wedding photos. That was what he'd hurled against the wall.

He was screaming at God. Believed in God when he was drunk: something John Harper would ultimately inherit from the ancestral line.

August second 1980. A little after eight in the evening. John Harper walking down the street where he'd lived for the better part of his memory.

Everything had a cold blue light that time in the evening, and it didn't come from the fluorescent street-lamps, nor from the moon. Came from the collective lights of the world reflecting back from the heavens; something such as that. God was up there, and God was smiling, because he knew the joke and the punch-line and he wasn't saying. *Here 'til Friday folks . . . don't forget to tip your waitress. Hardest working girls in the U.S. of A!*

Sounds were dead, like darkness could swallow most of what those sounds had to say, and what they had to say wasn't a great deal of very much at all at that time in the evening.

Stood on the steps in front of the house for a while. John Harper wondered how long this would all go on; how much longer he could take his uncle being some crazy guy he didn't even recognize. Not for long he reckoned, and then guilt kicked in like adrenaline and he remembered that you weren't s'posed to think such things about your own flesh and blood.

Went up the steps and pushed open the front door. House was silent like a church. Kicked off his shoes and padded through to the kitchen in his socks. Stood there breathless and kind of frightened for a while, and then turned and made his way back to the bottom of the stairwell.

Thought: *Scared. I'm scared. Can feel my heart beating, rushing inside my chest like . . . like something in a real damned hurry . . .*

And then: *This is no life for a twelve-year-old kid.*

Smiled to himself because he knew he wasn't serious.

Moved slowly then, like the body wanted to stay right where it was; went one step at a time, slow-motion, hand on the banister, sweat on his palms.

Sensed his uncle was in the house; *knew* he was, though had he been asked why he knew he couldn't have said.

At the top he turned left towards his own room, and then – almost as an afterthought – he turned back towards Garrett's room, figured he should at least take the bottle off the bed, cover him with a blanket and put out the light. Nothing more than the decent thing to do before he went back to get Evelyn and told her that her husband was home. At least he was home, right?

Garrett Sawyer was losing his mind down the neck of a bottle, but he was still one half of the only family Harper had. Whatever went down, he was still family.

For a moment John Harper pressed his ear against his uncle's door. Not a sound. Old guy must have drunk himself into a stupor, insufficient energy to even raise a snore. Garrett had always been a hard man, a man of little communication and rigid views. Garrett Sawyer had never gotten in touch with his feminine side, and would've landed you a five-fingered thunderbolt if you'd suggested such a thing.

John Harper reached for the door-handle. He held his breath and eased it anti-clockwise. He smelled the liquor even as the door inched open. Ripe, like sour watermelon, heady and intoxicating.

Hell, he thought. *Old man's going to punch a hole right through his middle.*

Wondered if he should take his heart in his hands and talk to him, try to help him, and then thought: *I'm a twelve-year-old kid. What do I know?*

Pushed the door wide, because John Harper knew that if the room smelled that bad then Garrett must have drunk two quarts of rye all by himself and would be unconscious.

Garrett Sawyer was more than that.

Garrett Sawyer was sat in the chair by the right-hand wall. Head was lolled right back and most of his brains were up the wall.

John Harper's first thought was: *How in hell did he get a gun?* Second thought was: *Oh my fucking Christ almighty.*

Garrett Lewis Sawyer had blown the back of his own head off.

Image was like a hotwire into the small Harper's brain. Vivid, surreal, beyond description.

Image that came back to him as he stood looking out from the tenth floor of the American Regent. Twenty-four years older, perhaps twenty-four years wiser, no less troubled by the memory of that evening and how things had been from that point on.

Evelyn came down like a house of cards. An emotional whirlwind tore up her foundations and scattered what was left of her to the four corners. Blamed herself, blamed the Harper boy, blamed everyone but Garrett who had drunk himself insensate and gotten the idea salvation lay somewhere through a hole in his cranium. Took the better part of six months to gather the loose ends and unravelled threads of her senses together, and then – finally – she took John Harper aside and admitted that Garrett had been the one to kill himself. She had somehow managed to forgive herself for whatever part she'd played in his demise, and thus – in forgiving herself – had also tried to forgive the world.

John Harper did not scar. John Harper believed himself built of taut steel and whipcord, perhaps a heart made of kevlar. John Harper became a teenager regardless of everything else, and angled through those teens with an element of precarious grace. He walked a tightrope that ran a straight line between familial allegiance and a thin hope for the future, and when he turned nineteen he left New York behind. That had been both the beginning and end of his growing up. He aged quickly, perhaps too quickly, and it was out of these things that *Depth of Fingerprints* was written. Perhaps an element of autobiography, perhaps not. These days it didn't matter. Believed nevertheless that one day, one day sometime whenever, he would find the muse, the words she carried, and he'd write another book.

Wondered in that moment if such a belief was nothing more than fantasy. Now there were so many other things. Now there was a father. A dying father.

Harper reached forward and pressed his hand against the glass. Eight millimeters of transparency between himself and a hundred-foot drop. Between his fingers there was New York – home from home, home of his heart: a place he wanted to leave, wanted desperately to leave, and yet somehow believed he could not.

He closed his eyes. He exhaled. Seemed like the end of an era.

TWELVE

Cellphone rings, an awkward and fractured sound in the cool silence of early morning.

Cathy Hollander leans over and fumbles for it. She retrieves it before it slides off her bedside table, answers it.

'Hey,' she says, recognizing the number. 'How goes it?'

She pauses.

'How the fuck would I know?' she replies. Frowns. Eases herself up into a sitting position, tugs down her tee-shirt.

'Hey, that was not the deal . . . that was not the fucking deal here. You set rules so you keep them—'

Interrupted, looks angry, looks like she's going to let fly with something she might regret tomorrow.

'Well, on your head be it. You want to risk screwing everything up then on your head be it. You tell them what I said. Harper is here. You have to get the word out, you understand? You fuck this up and he's a dead man, and you can tell whoever the fuck wants to listen that I—'

Turns the phone to look at it. Back to her ear. 'Got another call coming.'

She jabs the button, smiles. 'Walt,' she says. Her voice is calm and gathered. 'Sure. What time?'

She nods, raises her left hand and tucks her hair over her ear. 'Sure thing . . . meet you there about ten.'

She ends the call, returns the phone to the table, collapses back on the bed.

'Fuck,' she says to no-one but herself. 'Fuck, fuck, fuck.'

'Visitor?' Harper asked. 'Who is it?'

He nodded. He should have known. 'Tell her to come on up.'

He put the phone down and walked through to the bathroom. He stood looking at his own reflection. He looked like a hundred and fifty pounds of crap tied tight in the middle. Hadn't slept well. Carried the look effortlessly, like a condemned man the night before the cookhouse. Had woken sometime in the small hours and smoked some more. Had finished the pack, vowed never to smoke again, wished he could go out and buy another carton.

Minutes, and Cathy Hollander was knocking at the door.

She looked great. Better than ever. Looked like she'd slept enough for both of them. Asked her to come in and sit down.

'A little adventure,' she said.

'Walt?' he asked unnecessarily.

She smiled, sat on the edge of the bed. Crossed her legs and leaned to the side, one hand on the mattress, the other on her knee. Looked like she was practising an invitation.

She laughed. It was a good sound, an alive sort of sound. Harper felt she was the embodiment of temptation; in that moment she looked better than any woman he'd ever seen.

'So what is the deal with you?' he asked. 'How do you fit into all of this?'

'All of what?'

'My father, Walt Freiberg.'

'Fit in?' she said. 'I don't know that I've ever fitted into anything.'

'You don't want to answer the question just say so,' Harper challenged.

'You're in a bad mood.'

He paused in the bathroom doorway. He was buttoning his shirt, shirt that hadn't seen an iron for forty-eight hours. 'Bad mood? I'm not in a bad mood. I'm confused. Simple as that, just confused. You could help me out by giving me something to stick a label on.'

'You always talk like that?'

'Like what?'

'Like Raymond Chandler wrote the screenplay of your life?'

Harper grinned. He'd been trying to sound tough, trying to sound like he had corners and edges. Truth be known the corners and edges that made up John Harper had long since worn smooth. Life did that. Wasn't complicated. Life was tougher than any human being, and the more you fought it the more it wore you down. Emotional attrition was the penalty for possessing a heart.

'Now you look plain stupid,' she said, challenging him back.

'Going to insult me you can leave.'

'No insult intended. You ask me a question I'll answer it.'

'Truth?'

'Sure the truth.'

'Where are you from?'

'Right here in New York.' She sat up straight, reached for her cigarettes. She offered him one and he declined.

'How old are you?'

'Thirty-four in January.'

'Ever married?'

She shook a negative.

'Ever nearly married?'

'Like a long-term relationship thing?'

Harper nodded.

'Longest relationship I ever had lasted maybe two years, a little more.'

'You canned him or vice versa?'

She laughed. 'There you go again.'

He frowned. 'What?'

'That. You canned him or vice versa. Who the fuck talks like that, 'cept maybe James Cagney or Humphrey Bogart?'

'*I* talk like that,' Harper said.

'And it isn't an act?'

'An act? Why the hell would it be an act?'

'People play life like it's theater.'

'They do, do they?'

She nodded. 'Sure they do. Everyone carries a suitcase full of faces for the world. Face for the parents, face for the boss, one for the wife, another for the mistress, you know?'

He nodded. He knew. 'It's not an act. I don't have an act. I am who I am. I talk how I talk because that's the way I talk.'

'Like a writer.'

'Eh?' He was caught off-guard.

'Like a writer. You talk like that 'cause you're a writer, a novelist.'

'*Was* a novelist.'

She laughed again. 'No-one *was* a novelist John Harper. That's like saying you *were* a human being. Something like that is inside you. Something like that is inside everyone, it just takes a particular type of person, maybe even a particular type of situation to make them bring it out and share it with the world.'

'Interesting perspective.'

'Don't know about interesting. Real, perhaps?'

'So what *is* the deal with you and Walt?'

'What makes you think there's a *deal*?'

'It's an expression . . . you know what I mean.'

'I know what you mean, John. You just use the word like it's an accusation.'

'Apologies.'

'Accepted.' Her manner, her body language, everything about her told Harper she wasn't only there because of Freiberg. He read in her words and expressions that she had also come for herself. He wanted to believe that, wanted to believe it very much.

'So?' he prompted.

'We've known each other a little while.'

'And my father?'

'A little while too.'

'How did you meet?' Harper took a few steps forward and sat down in the chair. He crossed his legs, mimicking her perhaps.

'Just in the general run of things.'

'The general run of things?' Harper asked. He smiled. 'What the hell does that mean?'

'Just out and about—'

'You said something yesterday,' he interjected. 'Something about coming with the territory, that you were just the eye candy.'

'It was a joke.'

'Never a truer word, right?'

'It was a joke, John. Nothing more than a joke.'

'So tell me the truth.'

Cathy Hollander looked away, glanced back towards the window, the skyline of New York. 'You don't know anything at all about these people, do you?'

'My father? Walt?' Harper shook his head. 'Walt I last saw about twenty-five years ago, and as far as my father is concerned

I've spent thirty years thinking I didn't have one. What I know about them is what you've told me.'

'I haven't told you anything.'

'Exactly.'

Cathy looked down at her shoe, turned her foot slightly as if she was inspecting it. 'If you had some idea of who they were and what they did then you'd have some idea of what I'm here for.'

'So why don't you tell me?'

She shrugged. 'Figure it's one of those things you should find out for yourself.'

Harper shook his head and sighed. 'This is a circular conversation. I was hoping for too much, wasn't I?'

Cathy nodded. 'Aren't we all?' she said drily. She seemed to have cooled. Harper wondered if he'd read her wrong.

'So what's the adventure?' he asked.

Cathy stood up, straightened her skirt. 'We're going to go see Walt. There's someone he wants you to meet.'

'We go now?'

Cathy glanced at her watch. 'There's no frantic hurry, but we should leave in ten minutes or so. Walt appreciates punctuality.'

'He does, does he?' Harper rose and walked towards the small bathroom. He finished buttoning his shirt. As he walked through he gently kicked the door to behind him.

'I'm going to go down and wait in the car,' Cathy called through from the bedroom.

Harper didn't reply. He waited until he heard the door close and then he leaned forward, hands on the edge of the sink, face mere inches from the surface of the mirror.

'What the fuck,' he said quietly.

'Like what kind of book?'

Duchaunak made a face, a kind of mouth-turned-down-at-the-corners face. He leaned forward and took his coffee cup from the desk. 'I don't know . . . like a thriller maybe? No, not a thriller . . . Christ, I don't know. How the hell d'you describe a book like that?'

'Genre-defying,' Faulkner said.

Duchaunak frowned. 'You what?'

'Genre-defying.'

'Whatever you say.'

'Is it good though? That's always the point isn't it, always the acid test. Is the book any good?'

Duchaunak paused, smiled. 'Yeah, it was good, good enough to keep me reading to the end.'

'So what the hell is a guy like that doing in New York with these people?'

'I'm going to go see the aunt and find out,' Duchaunak said.

'You're just going to show up?'

'Sure, nothing official. Don't want to upset her.'

'And Harper said that it was the aunt who called him, not Freiberg?' Faulkner asked.

Duchaunak nodded.

'Bet you Freiberg got to her, told her to get the guy up here from Florida.'

'Who the hell knows, eh?'

'Freiberg does,' Faulkner said.

'You figure he has a place for this John Harper?' Duchaunak asked, more rhetoric than a real question.

Faulkner laughed, a dry and brittle sound. 'Freiberg is into everything. Freiberg is a fucking genius—'

'Genius is not a gift, but the way a person invents in desperate circumstances.'

'Eh?'

'Jean-Paul Sartre,' Duchaunak said.

'Don't care what the fuck he had to say about it. Freiberg is as sharp as a needle, more the player than Bernstein ever was.'

'He's not dead yet,' Duchaunak said.

'Well, either he will be very soon, or he's going to be out for a few scenes yet.'

'And Freiberg will run the company while he's gone.'

'Sure as shit he will,' Faulkner said, 'which makes me think that there must be an exceptionally good reason for Freiberg letting this guy hang around.'

'I'll go see the aunt. She can give me some of the back story. See what turns up, eh?'

'And what d'you want me to do?'

'Read Harper's book if you want . . . call it research.' Duchaunak picked up the book from his desk. He turned it over. *An exciting new literary talent*, the blurb read. *A testament to the indomitability of the human spirit in the face of adversity. Harper has created a model for our times in a challenging and difficult hero.* He tossed it to Faulkner who caught it with his left hand. 'I'll call you,' Duchaunak said.

Faulkner said nothing; watched him go. He leaned back in his chair, turned Harper's book over and scanned the back. He flicked through it, read a paragraph or two, smiled, turned to the front and started reading.

THIRTEEN

An unholy bag of smashers. Scars and bullet-wounds; clenched fists, white-knuckled knots of trouble; wide necks, short hair; ill-fitting two-thousand dollar suits, itself an art, itself a contradiction; small room heavy with smoke, cheap cigars with fake Montecristo and Cohiba labels; bottles of sourmash, Coors chasers, mismatched glasses; see-your-own-reflection shoe-shined wingtip cordovans, light-colored socks; wafer-thin platinum watches on eighteen-carat gold bracelets; all of it expensive, yet all of it made to look somehow cheap and used and pointless.

This was the Marcus crew: Victor Klein, Attica and Green Haven; Sol Neumann, Queensboro and Five Points; Henry Kossoff, Altona and Sing Sing, their tours of penitentiary duty reading like a high school graduation list. Alongside them were Raymond Dietz, Karl Merrett, Lester McKee, Maurice Rydell and Albert Reiff. Something in the region of three hundred years of collective criminal experience, maybe a century of hard time in the Big House.

The warehouse near Pier 53, Ben Marcus sitting up front near the window overlooking West and Bloomfield. The hubbub of voices, the cacophony of laughter, the sound of familiarity amongst men who were only ever gathered in one place if there was trouble or the promise of money.

'Enough!' Sol Neumann shouted. 'Enough of this. We got business!'

The voices quietened, the sound within the room staggered to a halt, and each of the seated men turned his attention towards Neumann, to Ben Marcus also, seated behind Neumann and to the right.

'We have a situation,' Neumann started. 'Some of you may

102

know, some of you may not, but we have a situation with our friend Lenny Bernstein—'

Neumann was interrupted by a rush of noise, catcalls and badmouthing.

'Enough!' he shouted once more, and the rabble fell silent.

'So, like I said, we have a situation with Lenny Bernstein in that he's been hit—'

''Bout fucking time,' Albert Reiff said.

'Okay, differences aside,' Neumann continued, 'there is a matter to discuss and a question to resolve regarding an agreement that was made with Lenny before he got himself shot.'

Puzzled faces, men frowning, wondering what agreement might have been made with such an adversary as Bernstein.

'As we all are all too aware, things have changed. Can't turn the corner without discovering some part of the neighborhood has been taken by the blacks, the Hispanics, the Puerto Ricans. Everything is hookers and crack houses. These people have no scruples, they have no ethics. They have mules buying and selling this stuff in schoolyards for God's sake. And then there's the Eastern Europeans.' Neumann shook his head resignedly, glanced over his shoulder at Ben Marcus. Marcus was implacable, immobile. 'Cheap guns,' Neumann continued. 'Connections into Bosnia and the Czech Republic. Used to be that you'd pay two hundred bucks for a .38. Now these people can get you Glocks and Uzis and Berettas for half of that.' Neumann glanced at Reiff. 'What was that stuff you got? C4?'

Reiff nodded. 'Anything I wanted. C4, Semtex . . . crazy prices. Prices we could never compete with.'

'So that's what we're dealing with, and let's face it—' Neumann smiled and looked at the men gathered before him. 'None of us are getting any younger, right?'

Reiff laughed, the others were waiting for the punch-line.

'So, here's the thing,' Neumann went on. 'Lenny was going to retire.' He waited for questions; there were none. 'Lenny came to speak with Mr Marcus and myself. He told us he was thinking of taking his retirement from the business. He proposed a resolution of past differences and a settlement between himself and Mr Marcus that would give us his ground, several little things he had in the pipeline, other stuff. We were going to speak again,

103

going to talk about some ideas we had, but then this thing happened with him getting shot and he was taken out of the picture.'

'So no deal?' Merrett asked.

'Maybe, maybe not,' Neumann said. 'That's what we're here to discuss.'

'What's there to discuss?' Klein asked. 'Seems to me we're in a situation where we just take what we want and fuck Lenny Bernstein—'

Ben Marcus raised his hand. The gathering fell quiet. He leaned forward slightly, and as he did his face seemed to emerge from the half-light. The effect, perhaps not intended, was nevertheless unnerving. 'It isn't that simple Victor,' he said quietly. 'It never is just as simple as taking what we want. Fact of the matter is that I made an agreement with Lenny Bernstein. The fact that he was shot puts us in an awkward position. Now this is something I've thought long and hard about, something that I have talked about with Sol, something that Albert knew a little about . . . I just need you to understand the bigger picture here and take a vote on something.'

Marcus paused, looked at the faces ahead of him, glanced at Neumann. Neumann nodded. Ben Marcus leaned back and his face disappeared.

'So here it is,' Neumann said. 'We're dealing with Walt Freiberg now. Walt Freiberg is a different kind of man. He's a business type guy. He doesn't do the talking and negotiating like Lenny does. He's a straight lines kind of guy, all action, no bullshit. He doesn't go for the sit down stuff. He knew about our meeting with Lenny. He knew what we discussed. For us to now go back to him and say we don't want to go through with the deal lays us wide open to suspicion that we did the hit on Lenny.'

'And the problem with that?' Klein asked.

'The problem Victor, is that Walt Freiberg is not a man to stand back. He's right in there already if I know Walt. He's right in there figurin' out every angle on this thing, and if he believes for a moment that we had anything to do with Lenny's hit then I guarantee there's going to be a war.'

There was silence amongst the gathering.

'A war we don't want,' Neumann continued. 'Bernstein may

be in a vulnerable position, but right now we cannot deal with a war. We are not set up to deal with the costs and losses of such a thing. And there is another factor.' Neumann paused and looked at Marcus.

Marcus nodded.

'Lenny's son has come into the picture.'

'You what?' Klein asked. 'Lenny's son? Who the fuck is that?'

Neumann leaned forward and placed his hands flat on the desk. 'We don't know. Right now all we know is that Lenny's son has come to New York, and from some inside track we think he's come up from Miami. We don't know who he is, we know nothing about his history or connections. For all we know he could have his own crew down south who are set to come and clean the slate for his father if a wrong step is taken. With Lenny's shooting there appears to be a power vacuum. Freiberg could have stepped in, may very well have done so, but we now have this unpredictable factor to contend with.'

There was silence from the gathered men.

'Which leaves us in a situation of making a decision,' Neumann said. He cleared his throat, reached for a glass of water on the desk ahead of him and took a sip. 'We have to decide whether to go with the plan Lenny Bernstein was proposing.'

'Which was?' Henry Kossoff asked.

'Four actions, simultaneous—' Neumann stated.

'The hits I was working on?' Victor Klein asked.

'The very same,' Neumann said.

'And what do we get from this?' Ray Dietz asked.

Neumann nodded his head. 'It's real simple. We go through with this thing then we minimize any suspicion Walt Freiberg may have about our involvement in the shooting of Lenny Bernstein. We avoid any possibility of Lenny's son bringing people from Miami into a war we don't want. We all make some money and we wind up with Lenny's territory.'

'Seems a good deal to me,' Dietz said.

'Okay, there it is,' Neumann said. 'We need a majority on this, whichever way it goes.' He scanned the faces. 'Okay . . . yes for the Bernstein deal, no for anything else.'

The vote was unanimous. All of them – Ray Dietz, Victor Klein, Karl Merrett, Lester McKee, Maurice Rydell, Henry Kossoff, Albert Reiff – all of them voted for the Bernstein deal.

'So there we have it,' Neumann said. 'Victor is going to get some details together on some places we've been looking at, and myself and Mr Marcus are going to have a meeting with Walt Freiberg and straighten out any changes as a result of what has happened with Lenny. Then we're going to get with Bernstein's people and go through this thing until we got it nailed down tight. We have days, not weeks, but we've done this kind of shit before and we're all still here to tell the tale, right?'

A chorus of agreements.

'So get the fuck out of here,' Neumann said. 'Go kiss your wives and fuck your girlfriends, buy presents for the kids. Get whatever shit together you need to 'cause we've got a busy Christmas ahead of us.'

The men rose from their chairs, talking amongst themselves, draining glasses, laughing once more, and in twos and threes they filed out of the warehouse and started down the fire escape to the car lot below.

Neumann walked across the room just as Ray Dietz was leaving and touched his arm. He indicated back towards Ben Marcus. Ray Dietz turned.

'Ray,' Marcus said. 'Come and speak with me.'

Ray Dietz walked towards the desk and sat down.

Sol Neumann sat beside him, almost between him and Ben Marcus. Dietz was struck with the impression that it was always Sol's words, but somehow they were generated and driven by Ben Marcus.

'So here's where we stand on this,' Neumann started. 'Only people who know about the thing that happened to Lenny are me, Mr Marcus, Henry Kossoff and yourself. Only thing Henry knows is that you were s'posed to pay this McCaffrey guy off, he didn't know any details. I'm lost on this one Ray, I really am. Tell me exactly what happened.'

'We went to the meeting,' Dietz said. He glanced nervously at Ben Marcus. He found it disturbing talking to Neumann, knowing that really he was speaking to Ben Marcus. 'We went to pay McCaffrey the balance and he wasn't there. He didn't show. Nothing more than that.'

'Someone would have to have a pretty good reason not to show up and collect fifty grand, don'tcha think?'

'Fuck knows, Sol. I don't know what the hell happened.'

'You knew him from where?'

'From Attica a few years back. We shared a cell together.'

'And you rated him?' Neumann asked.

'Sure I did. McCaffrey and I were close. You spend that much time in a room with someone you either kill each other or wind up like brothers. I wouldn't have suggested him for this thing if I didn't figure he could do it.'

'He did it, no question about that,' Neumann said. 'Didn't do all that was needed, but we don't know exactly what happened in that liquor store . . . we can't make a judgement. Only thing we know for sure is that he's done a runner.'

'He has family,' Marcus said, the second time he'd spoken since the others had left the room.

'A brother and a sister here in New York,' Dietz replied.

'You know where they live?'

'Can find them easy enough.'

'So go find them,' Marcus said. 'See if they can't help you find out where this guy is. I cannot have him running around New York with a .38 all spooked and upset. I need him found and I need him dead.'

Dietz nodded. 'I think I should have gone to the pay-off alone. I think he must have seen Henry with me and got frightened.'

'Sure as shit he was frightened . . . bastard probably knew Henry was going to kill him,' Neumann said.

Marcus raised his hand. 'Now it doesn't matter. Turning this thing back and forth serves no purpose. I need him found Ray . . . take Albert, Karl, whoever you want. Victor needs a little time to work on some things with these sites. I need a day or two to sort things out with Freiberg before we have a full meeting of both crews. Get these people found, this brother and sister, see if they know where your guy is hiding. I need him found Ray, I need McCaffrey found and dead within twenty-four hours, okay?'

'I'll sort it out,' Dietz said, and started to rise.

'One other thing,' Neumann added.

Dietz sat down again, looked at Ben Marcus, back to Sol Neumann.

'You probably know more about Bernstein's people than anyone here.'

'Jesus, that was twenty, thirty years ago Sol. I knew Garrett

107

Sawyer, met his wife a couple of times. Think she had a sister that went out with Lenny. You're talking history, real history.'

'Lenny have a son you were aware of?' Neumann asked.

Dietz shook his head. 'Maybe he did, I don't know. Maybe he had a son with this girl, Evelyn Sawyer's sister; Garrett never spoke to me about it. Jesus, I did a couple of things with the guy. We used to go out drinking every once in a while. Later, when the territories separated we went different ways. He killed himself more than twenty years ago.'

Sol Neumann nodded, was silent for a moment. 'And Walt Freiberg?' he asked. 'You know much about Walt Freiberg?'

Dietz shrugged. 'By reputation, nothing else.'

'You think he's a talker?'

Dietz shook his head and smiled. 'Freiberg? Christ, no. From what I've heard Lenny had Walt Freiberg on a short leash 'cause the guy was so fucking dangerous.'

'So you think the right decision was made today?'

Dietz nodded. 'No question about it. Irrespective of whether or not Lenny has a son from Miami, and whether or not he has a crew he can bring here, I sure as fuck wouldn't want to go to war with Walt Freiberg.'

Sol Neumann smiled. 'Okay . . . so you have to sort this thing out with your boy McCaffrey. He came to us on your recommendation Ray. You said he could do the hit on Lenny, and he was reliable. Well, he's done a runner, and *you* have to find him and kill him, okay?'

'I'll find him,' Dietz said.

'I know you will Ray, I know you will. Stay in touch, let us know what's happening – and get it straightened out because shit is going to happen fast once we've met with Freiberg.'

Dietz rose from the chair and straightened his jacket. 'I'll take care of everything,' he said. He glanced across at Marcus, smiled nervously, nodded his head deferentially. 'I'll find him and straighten everything out.'

Ben Marcus raised his hand in acknowledgement.

Ray Dietz turned and crossed the room to the stairs.

FOURTEEN

'Sonny!' Walt exclaimed from ten yards down the sidewalk.

Harper felt cold and loose inside. What could he say? How do you ask someone not to do something like that? He smiled, stood there as Walt Freiberg hurried towards him. Cathy stood patiently, her hand through Harper's arm. To an observer they perhaps looked like a young couple awaiting a family friend, a shopping trip, perhaps a theater matinee.

Cathy stepped forward and greeted Walt. She kissed him on the cheek.

Walt reached out and took both of Harper's hands. He gripped tightly, looked directly at him, said, 'Good to see you, John, really good to see you. You look better today, a little less ragged around the edges.'

Harper smiled. Looked better yes, felt better no. He said nothing.

Freiberg released Harper's hands. 'I checked on Edward,' he said. 'His vital signs are a little stronger . . . they feel optimistic that he might make a fight of this. He's a tough man, your father, a very tough man. If anyone can make it through such a thing it will be him.'

Harper, once again, said nothing. Walt Freiberg was speaking of someone that was as much a stranger as Cathy Hollander, more so in fact. Cathy he had spoken to, held at least two or three conversations with – awkward, ever present his awareness of how *charged* he felt around her – but nevertheless they had exchanged words. Edward Bernstein was a dying man in St Vincent's Hospital, a man who'd shared only one word with him in his life, the one word he could remember, if in fact he'd said anything at all.

Leave.

Harper looked away. A knot of unidentifiable emotion constricted his throat. Anger, confusion, grief, emptiness? He didn't know. Safer not to know perhaps.

'So we are out together,' Walt said. 'I figured we should get some things for John, seeing as how he may be here for a little while—'

Harper frowned. 'A little while? What d'you mean?'

'A few days perhaps.' Walt looked concerned. 'To see how he is doing, John. To stay a little while and make sure that he has all the support he needs.'

Harper laughed. It sounded remarkably incongruous. He was amazed that anyone could speak of being there to support a father who had left a child alone, disappeared for more than thirty years, turned up seventy years old and shot, turned up in such a manner as to wreak havoc in other peoples' lives, people he had evidently cared little for. 'I don't know that I'm going to stay, Walt. More I think about it the more it makes sense to go back to Miami.'

'No,' Cathy Hollander said. 'You can't go back to Miami.'

Walt was shaking his head. 'You should stay here, John, seriously you should, at least until we have a better idea of how Edward is doing.'

Cathy stepped closer and touched Harper's arm. 'We want you to stay,' she said. 'Me and Walt, we really want you to stay, at least a few days more.'

Harper shook his head. 'I don't know . . . I just don't know . . .'

'I understand,' Walt said. He raised his hands, palms facing Harper. 'I understand something, I think, at least something of how you might be feeling.'

'Do you, Walt? Do you think you have even the faintest clue about what might be going on in my head?'

'No confrontations, John, no confrontations. We don't do confrontations here. This is all for another time, another day. I had Cathy come over and get you simply because I wanted to get a few things for you, that was all. I don't want you to read anything into this. It's not complicated. Your father and I have been friends and business partners all these years. Evelyn told you Edward was dead. I've carried that lie for thirty years or more. After your mother died I wanted to make sure you were okay. I felt a sense of duty.' Walt smiled, shook his head. 'Don't ask me why, John. Maybe because I never had kids of my own. I wanted to make sure you were okay, so for a little while I kept an eye on you the only way I could. I couldn't tell Evelyn what to say to you. Who the hell was I? I was just another of Edward's no-good friends.'

Walt stepped forward and took Harper's arm. He led him to the edge of the sidewalk away from the road, out of the path of other people who were walking back and forth.

'I was never your father,' he went on. 'I never tried to be anything other than a friend to you. Evelyn didn't want me coming around, and after a while it seemed pointless. I didn't want to see you get caught in the middle of some imagined upset she had with me. I never did anything to harm her. I never said anything that was designed to be anything other than helpful, but she had her reasons, and who was I to question them? When you were old enough to recognize that everything she said wasn't the gospel truth I left. I didn't want to, it made me feel bad, but I left. I had a life to get on with as well. I was young then, younger than you are now, and there were things I needed to do, people I had to deal with. I did what I felt was the right thing, and when I felt you could deal with things yourself I let it all go.'

Walt Freiberg paused to catch his breath. It was bitterly cold.

'So it is what it is. She told you your father was dead. I didn't agree with her, but Evelyn Sawyer was never a woman to wait for anyone's agreement, right?' Walt smiled, squeezed Harper's arm. 'Right, John?'

Harper nodded.

'So it went the way it went. And then when Edward was shot and I figured he might not make it I felt the very least I could do was make her call you. Whether that was right or wrong I don't know, and now it's too late to make a judgement. The call was made. I insisted she tell you. If she'd had her way you'd still be in Florida none the wiser. Tell me I made the wrong decision. What can I do?'

'It's okay Walt,' Harper said resignedly, perhaps for no other reason than he couldn't listen to any more. 'It's okay. It's been one helluva couple of days, that's all I can say, and I haven't had a chance to figure out what I'm going to do.'

'Do?' Walt asked. 'What makes you think you have to *do*

111

anything?' He smiled, laughed almost. 'You don't have to do a goddamned thing, John. Just stick around for a few days, have Cathy and me keep you company. We'll go out, have dinner, maybe see a show or something.'

Harper shook his head. He couldn't really comprehend what he was hearing. Have dinner? See a show? He possessed no context within which to place any of this.

'John?'

Harper looked up at Walt Freiberg.

'It *won't* make sense, none of it. He was shot. He was in a liquor store Sunday night and someone shot him. He's going to make it or he isn't, it's no more complicated than that. He's in the hospital, and those people know what they're doing. Everything that can be done is being done, and there isn't anything we can do apart from be here. The doctor is going to call me if he comes round, you know? And if he does we go see him, okay?'

Harper nodded. Walt was right. There was nothing any of them could do.

'So we go see someone,' Walt said. 'That's what we were going to do today, go meet someone and get some things organized for yourself.'

'What things?' Harper asked.

Walt smiled. 'It isn't a big deal, John, just a little sartorial influence. If you're going to play the game then you have to look the part, right?'

Cathy smiled. She took Harper's arm. 'Come on,' she said. 'Let's go see Mr Benedict.'

Harper walked with them to Walt's car. He didn't enquire where they were going or who Mr Benedict was. Truth be known he was past the point of challenging any of it. The questions he asked never seemed to realize answers. A little while longer, a few days, surely no more, and regardless of what happened he would be out of New York and on the way home. Had to be. There they were again, the rock and the hard place – Evelyn and Frank Duchaunak on one side, Cathy and Walt on the other. Perhaps the easiest thing was not to try and make a choice. Go with it, go with the flow, deal with whatever might come when it came.

Harper sat in the back of the car, Cathy Hollander right beside him, and he was intensely aware of her closeness. At one point she reached out and closed her hand over his, gave it a reassuring squeeze, and then let go. He looked at her but she did not look back. He wanted to feel her hand again, wanted to touch her once more, but he dared not. The woman was a confusion of messages, or perhaps not. Maybe it was him, him and him alone. Maybe he just wanted something to be there, wanted it so much that he justified his wishful thinking with everything Cathy said and did. His life in Miami, however narrow it might have been, was neverthless under control. This was the opposite, a complete dichotomy, and dealing with it did not come easy.

Walt Freiberg drove, silently for a little while, and then he started to tell Harper a story about Edward Bernstein, his friend and partner, and Harper listened with a sense of detached interest. But within moments his attention was distracted by the city beyond the window. It started to rain, lightly at first, and then Walt had to put the wipers on to facilitate a clear view of the road ahead.

Harper leaned back. He closed his eyes. He felt the warmth of Cathy Hollander beside him, the ghost of her perfume, not only that which she had applied, but also that which she possessed.

Walt's voice was something that belonged to a distant past. Try as he might to associate and identify with all that it represented, everything within John Harper urged him to leave that past alone. What was done was done.

And if his father lived? Well, if he lived, that would be another bridge to burn or build when the time came.

Harper listened to the sound of the rain, the sound of the engine, the wheels on the road, the breathing of New York City as it swallowed him. Here he possessed no real identity, and perhaps never had. Surely without awareness and recognition of the past there could neither be present nor future. A tree without roots is not a tree.

John Harper opened his eyes as the car drew to a halt.

'Where did you go?' Cathy asked.

Harper turned and looked at her. She was smiling.

'Nowhere special,' he said quietly, and then a gust of rain unexpectedly caught him as Walt Freiberg opened the door.

FIFTEEN

'Who said that? That New York becomes a small town when it rains?'

Duchaunak shook his head.

Evelyn was silent for a moment, and then, 'Gunther, John Gunther, I believe.'

She reached into her apron pocket and took out a pack of cigarettes. She opened it and offered one to Duchaunak.

He raised his hand, shook his head, smiled. 'Trying to quit,' he said.

Evelyn laughed.

Duchaunak frowned, watched her as she lit her cigarette. 'So you were saying?' he prompted.

'I was saying that Walt Freiberg called me the night Edward was shot. He told me that it was what Anne would have wanted now, that she would want John to know he had a father, that I should call him and tell him to come to New York.'

'And if Walt Freiberg hadn't called you?'

'I would've left it all well alone, Detective. I have to admit there was an element of self-preservation in there somewhere.'

'Self-preservation?'

Evelyn nodded. 'I was the one who told John that his father had died. I've kept that up for thirty years or more. That's what Anne wanted me to do right from Edward's departure, and it went on after her death . . . went on until the day before yesterday.'

'It came as a shock to him,' Duchaunak said.

'What do you think, Detective?'

'I think it came as a shock to him, Mrs Sawyer.'

'A thunderbolt.'

'And now?'

Evelyn shook her head. 'I've told him to leave, to go home,

114

but knowing John he will please himself. John is a single-minded and independent man, was that way even as a child. He stayed here long enough to save enough money to move out, and then he left, went all the way down to Florida. We didn't keep in touch, not the way a family's supposed to, and that was how he wanted it. We had a difficult time. He lost his mother, I lost my husband, and yet we somehow made the best of it despite everything. There is a certain irony, however, in how things have turned out, don't you think?'

Duchaunak said nothing. His expression was quizzical.

'That the one man we decided to have disappear from our lives is the one man who brought us back together.'

'Edward Bernstein,' Duchaunak stated matter-of-factly.

Evelyn smiled resignedly. 'Edward Bernstein.'

'You don't like him . . . never did like him, did you?'

'You ever read Stanislavski?'

Duchaunak shook his head.

'You know who he is, right?'

Duchaunak shrugged. 'Some Russian guy?'

'Constantin Stanislavski. He developed a school of acting, a philosophy if you like. He wrote things, you know? One of them was about the phenomenon of an actor being entirely alone despite the audience. He called it 'solitude in public'. He suggested that even though an actor is presenting himself to an audience of thousands he could still remain in a circle of light, like a snail in a shell, and he could carry that shell with him wherever he went and whatever he did—'

'I don't understand—' Duchaunak started.

Evelyn scowled at him. 'Let me finish what I was going to say and you might.'

'I'm sorry. Please, continue.'

'This was Edward Bernstein, you see? This was the point I was making. He possessed this ability to be anywhere he chose without ever being there at all.'

Duchaunak leaned forward. The smell of cigarette smoke was both irritating and exceptionally appealing.

'Edward led his own life. He possessed people—'

'What d'you mean?'

Evelyn Sawyer looked at Duchaunak. 'Where the hell did you grow up?' she asked.

'Eh?'

'You grow up someplace where people have no manners at all? What is it with this interrupting me every other word? You come here and ask if I have time to answer some questions for you. Did I tell you to go to hell? No, I didn't. I said sure I can answer some questions, come on in and sit down. Have some coffee. I offered you some coffee, right? Fact you didn't want any doesn't change the fact that I asked. This is manners, you see? This is what we call manners, Detective, and now you've asked a question and I'm answering it, and the way it works in this house is I talk until I'm finished talking, and then you ask me something else. We understand one another?'

'Yes, ma'am,' Duchaunak said.

'Well, good. Now don't interrupt me. You have a question that you want to ask, well you make a mental note of it and ask it when I'm done.'

Evelyn took a drag of her cigarette and looked at Duchaunak. Her gaze was sharp and unflinching. 'Okay?'

'Okay.'

'Right, good . . . so where were we?'

'Edward Bernstein possessing people.'

'Oh yes, the Stanislavski philosophy. He did that. He would be there, right beside you, and yet you'd feel as though his mind was always three or four steps to the left. It was a very strange feeling. And like I said, he seemed to have the capacity to possess people, and that's what he did with Anne, my sister. She was all of twenty-three or twenty-four, nothing more than a child really, and Edward was quite a bit older. He must have been – oh, I don't know – he was nine or ten years older than she was. He was an extraordinarily charming man, Detective . . .' Evelyn paused. She smiled to herself as if remembering some particular moment. 'It was Trilby and Svengali,' she went on. 'He possessed a manner quite unlike anyone we had ever met before. Edward Bernstein took a shine to my sister—' Evelyn stopped mid-sentence and looked directly at Duchaunak. 'She looked a lot like Marilyn Monroe, the real Marilyn, Norma Jean Baker, you know?'

Duchaunak nodded.

'We saw her one time, me and Anne, right here in New York City.'

'No,' Duchaunak said, in his voice an element of surprise and incredulity.

'Sure as you're sitting there, Detective, we saw her. I cannot even begin to describe how beautiful she was.' Evelyn smiled, closed her eyes for a moment.

Duchaunak edged forward on his seat. 'Where?' he asked. 'Where did you see her?'

'Not far away from where we are right now . . . the old New York Picture House on Broadway.'

'What was she doing here?'

'She was promoting a film called *Bus Stop*—'

'1956,' Duchaunak interjected.

'You know it?'

Duchaunak nodded.

'There was a scene when Marilyn has her first upset with the lead man—'

Duchaunak smiled. 'Bo and Cherie in the Blue Dragon Cafe. He tries to grab her costume and the train comes off the back.'

Evelyn laughed. 'You've seen it then?'

'A couple of times, yes.'

'Anyway, she has this expression, feisty, independent, a real firecracker . . . and when we saw her, me and Anne, you could tell that she had that kind of character inside of her. Anne had that too, that kind of fiery attractiveness, the kind of thing that drew men to her like moths to a flame.' Evelyn paused and shook her head slowly. 'Edward Bernstein broke that down. She became dependent on him, like she was nothing unless he was around. It made me mad, but Anne couldn't see any of it. She was blind to what he was really like.'

Duchaunak watched the woman as she remembered her sister; he saw the way her hands seemed to clench and unclench into white-knuckled fists as she spoke; he saw the way she took a cigarette from the packet, the lighter flame stuttering, evidence that she was nervous, perhaps angry. She would not hold his gaze, and when she was done talking and he asked about Walt Freiberg she seemed to tense up completely.

'Walt Freiberg?' she asked. 'What about Walt Freiberg?'

Duchaunak leaned back, tried to give the impression of nonchalance. 'He was around, I understand, for a little while after the death of your husband.'

117

Evelyn looked back at Duchaunak, and the agitation vanished as rapidly as it appeared. 'Why are you here, Detective?'

'Why am I here?'

'I don't need you to repeat the question, I need you to answer it.'

'I'm sorry, Mrs Sawyer. Why I'm here . . . well . . . I'm here because someone shot Edward Bernstein, and now his son has appeared out of nowhere, a son I wasn't even aware he had—'

'There was no reason for you to be aware of him,' Evelyn said. 'You're talking the better part of forty years ago, and however liberal and forgiving the society might be today it was not the same then. Unmarried people did not live together, they didn't admit to sleeping together, and they sure as hell didn't have children. John Harper was an accidental child, and as soon as Anne was pregnant Edward Bernstein figured he should take his business elsewhere.'

'Didn't he stick around for a while?'

'You ever seen someone someplace who wasn't really there at all?'

Duchaunak frowned.

'That's what Edward Bernstein was like from the moment he found out she was pregnant. He left by inches, little by little but, from the moment she told him, he was never the same person to her. That's what broke her, Detective. She loved him more than anything, more than life itself, and after he left I just watched her slip away into nothing at all. When Edward left he took the very best of what made Anne so special, and with that gone there was so little left she couldn't survive.'

'How did she die?' Duchaunak asked.

Evelyn tilted her head to the side. She smiled ruefully. 'You don't know?'

'No, I don't know.'

'She took an overdose, Detective . . . just like Marilyn Monroe.'

SIXTEEN

'A Chesterfield Regent in black,' Mr Benedict said. 'Three button, double vent, a deep cuff on the trouser, and I have another Aquascutum in navy with a pinstripe.' He smiled, walked back and forth, left and right, looking John Harper up and down as if considering a purchase.

Harper was stuck for words.

The three of them – himself, Walt Freiberg and Cathy Hollander – had exited the car, crossed the sidewalk, and walked through a shopfront doorway. Beyond the doorway Harper found an empty room – empty but for the odd item of dusty furniture – and without a word Walt had led him and Cathy to the right and through another doorway into a corridor beyond. At the end of the corridor a second entrance. Here Walt knocked twice, the door was inched open, and then – almost with a flourish, something from vaudeville – the man behind had opened the door wide and welcomed them effusively. They had arrived with Mr Benedict.

Referring to Walt as 'Mister Walt', to Cathy as 'Miss Cathy', he seemed completely at ease. And then he turned to Harper, and Harper saw it once again, that momentary flash of awkwardness as yet someone else recognized a younger version of Edward Bernstein.

'Good Lord almighty,' Mr Benedict had whispered, and then he'd stepped forward and taken Harper's hand, introduced himself, and told Harper what a pleasure it was to meet Mr Bernstein's son.

'A great pleasure, a great pleasure indeed. I heard about your father—' Benedict paused, looked towards Walt. Walt smiled, nodded understandingly. 'My very best wishes for his swift recovery, Mr Bernstein.'

Harper smiled. 'My name is Harper,' he said. 'John Harper.'

'But—'

'Edward's son,' Walt interjected. 'You are right, Mr Benedict, this *is* Edward's son.'

Benedict smiled. 'Another story for another day, and none of my business I'm sure.'

'It's not important,' Walt said. 'We're here for some things for John. He'll be staying a little while, we'll be going out you know? Dinner, visiting some people, and he has little more than he stands up in. I need you to take care of him, three or four suits, some shirts, shoes, ties . . . the usual, Mr Benedict.'

'Of course, Mr Walt.'

'I have some calls to make, some things to finalize. I can use your office?'

'Of course, yes indeed. Let me—'

'It's alright, I know the way.' Walt turned and smiled at Harper. 'I'll leave you in Mr Benedict's very capable hands . . . and Cathy can tell you how good you look, right Cathy?'

Cathy nodded, raised her hand.

'Wait a minute,' Harper said. 'What's happening here?'

Benedict stepped forward. He smiled enthusiastically. 'It's quite alright, Mr Bernstein—'

'Harper. My name is *John Harper*, not Bernstein or anything else.' He looked at Cathy, then at Walt Freiberg. 'What the hell's happening here, Walt? What am I doing here?'

Benedict seemed a little awkward. He stepped back as Walt Freiberg approached.

'It's nothing, John, nothing at all. Me and Cathy . . . hell, John, we just want you to stay a little while, that's all. Call it nostalgia, call it something like guilt for all the years I never did anything to help you. Don't make something out of nothing, John. Mr Benedict here . . . he's your father's tailor. You don't have any clothes with you. You came for one night, maybe two. Least we can do is get you some things to wear, right?'

Harper looked at Mr Benedict. Benedict nodded, raised his hands as if demonstrating he had nothing to hide.

'Some clothes,' Harper said matter-of-factly.

'Not just some clothes,' Mr Benedict said. 'Some *real* clothes, Mr Harper.'

'Some clothes, John,' Freiberg echoed. 'A suit or two, something you can wear if you and Cathy go out for a meal, if we have lunch together tomorrow. That's all there is to it, nothing else.'

Harper looked at Cathy. She smiled, and her smile was so warm, her expression so guileless and sincere that he couldn't help but smile back. 'It's okay,' she said. '*Really*.'

Harper nodded.

'We're all okay here,' Walt said. 'We're all just fine now.'

Harper looked at Cathy once more. Her expression told him nothing. *Go with the flow*, he thought, and wondered if there was anything he could lose by playing their game. Hell, maybe if he played it right there might be something in it for him.

'Okay,' he said quietly, and let his defences down.

Walt smiled, nodded at Mr Benedict, and then turned to leave the room. He backed up and passed through another door behind them.

'So Mr Harper . . . is the English or European cut to your preference?'

Harper frowned.

'In a suit?'

Harper shrugged.

'Aha,' Mr Benedict pronounced. 'We have a newcomer to the joys of tailoring. Come, come . . . step forward, stand straight, let me see what we have here.'

Harper did as he was told, stood tall, shoulders back, and Mr Benedict fussed around him with a tape measure.

The room was well-furnished, almost as Harper felt a gentleman's dressing room would be, but it did not explain why the entrance from the street had appeared as if no business operated from there at all. He glanced at Cathy. She sat in a chair to the left, in her hand an unlit cigarette, a knowing smile playing across her lips like a child caught somewhere she shouldn't be. He felt as if he was being silently teased, that she was flirting with him, but in considering such a thing he wondered if it was his imagination. He hoped it was not.

And then Mr Benedict started speaking a language Harper barely understood, a language exclusive to tailors and outfitters it seemed.

'So the English prefer a broader cut, a sense of strength if you like. Think Sean Connery in the early Bond films. The Europeans go for something a little slimmer, a narrower leg, a cut in at the waist. With your build I suggest we stay with the English, except perhaps the Victor/Victoria which is Italian, and quite different from, say . . . say a Lubiam or an Armani. I think we should go with Aquascutum, Daks perhaps, the Signature line . . . and shirts, shirts from Gieves & Hawkes, T.M. Lewin I think. We have some Canali shirts, a very good cotton. French cuffs, Prince of Wales collars . . . say with white, pale blue, perhaps an ivory. Ties, cuff-links . . . and shoes?'

Mr Benedict smiled a lot. He walked around in circles. Harper felt dizzy watching him.

'Miss Cathy?'

'You are the master, Mr Benedict. English suits perhaps deserve English shoes?'

Mr Benedict smiled. 'A girl after my own heart, yes. English shoes . . . Church's, and I think we have some from Lob. Two pairs of Oxfords, a pair of brogues, a burgundy derby. And your watch, sir?'

Harper looked at Benedict.

'Your watch?'

Harper shook his head. 'I have one somewhere, tend not to wear it.'

Mr Benedict nodded understandingly, an expression perhaps suited to someone recovering from a serious illness.

'Something understated I think. Breitling and Rolex . . . no, too showy. Cartier?' Mr Benedict shook his head. 'Omega,' he said. 'I think a simple black-face Seamaster.'

He stood back. 'What do you say, Miss Cathy?'

'I say you're a genius, Mr Benedict, no-one like you in the world. I think when you're done he's going to look like—'

'Yes,' Benedict interjected. 'He's going to look just like him.'

'Sonny Bernstein,' Walt Freiberg said. He stood at the desk in the office behind Benedict's fitting room. He held the telephone receiver tight, cigarette in his hand which had burned down to nothing at all. 'You're gonna make some calls. Call everyone you know down there. Start something going, whatever the hell you like. Make him a player.'

Freiberg paused, raised the cigarette to his lips. Saw it had burned down to the filter, dropped it in the ashtray and reached into his jacket pocket for the pack.

'Yes . . . Lenny Bernstein's son. Marcus's people—'

Freiberg paused.

'Not a fucking hope. This is where it stops. Anyone calls, anyone says a thing, you either know nothing or you heard something and it wasn't good. Tell them Sonny Bernstein is a name, that's all. He's a name, has people, his own crew, okay?'

Takes a cigarette from the pack.

'No-one's gonna come down there, believe me. This is what I need. This is a thing I need you to do for me. You got to pay some people then I'll take care of it. Need enough people to be onto this to make it hold up for a week or so, that's all.'

A moment's silence.

'Good enough. Call me if there's anything you need.'

Freiberg hung up, stood motionless, and then reached for his lighter and lit the cigarette.

SEVENTEEN

'An overdose?'

Evelyn Sawyer leaned back and smiled; it was the smile of someone viewing something with the measured slant of hindsight. 'You believe Marilyn committed suicide? That she took all those Nembutal and chloral hydrate tablets herself?'

Duchaunak shook his head. 'No, I don't believe she did Mrs Sawyer.'

'Right,' Evelyn said drily, matter-of-factly. 'I think you could possibly consider Anne Harper's suicide in a similar light.'

'She was murdered?'

Evelyn leaned forward, took another cigarette from the packet. 'I wouldn't say she was murdered, Detective.'

'Then what? What *would* you say?'

There was silence for a moment. The tension between them was hair-trigger sensitive.

'I would say that there was perhaps something that could have been done to prevent such an outcome, and that the *something* wasn't done.'

'There was someone there when she took—'

'Seconal I believe,' Evelyn Sawyer said. 'Something like that.'

'But why?' Duchaunak asked. 'How old was she?'

'When she died she was all of thirty-two,' Evelyn said. 'Twelfth October 1975, a Sunday.'

Duchaunak shook his head, somewhat disbelieving. 'I don't get why she would want to end her life. I don't get—'

'Get what, Detective? How there can be two suicides in the same family so close together?'

Duchaunak didn't reply. He was struggling to focus his thoughts.

'Garrett, my husband . . . he died nearly five years later in August of 1980. He died upstairs, right above where you're

124

sitting now. There was no great similarity between their deaths, Detective, my sister and my husband, but nevertheless there was one specific common denominator—'

'Edward Bernstein,' Duchaunak said.

Evelyn didn't reply.

Duchaunak leaned forward, an expression of concern on his face. 'Does John know how his mother died?'

Evelyn looked back at Duchaunak with a distant and unemotional expression.

'Mrs Sawyer?'

Evelyn Sawyer closed her eyes. Duchaunak believed for a moment she was suppressing tears, but when she opened her eyes once more there was nothing to indicate any real reaction to his question.

'You ever do something, and only years later realize that what you thought you'd done for the best is now going to cause all manner of difficulty?'

Duchaunak nodded. 'Sure I have.'

Evelyn lowered her head, then turned and looked towards the hallway. 'That was one of those, Detective . . . that was definitely one of those.'

'What does he think?' Duchaunak asked.

'I don't know what he thinks now, we haven't spoken of it for years. He was seven years old, and I don't know that he has any real memory of what she was like. He doesn't ask about her, and I haven't offered any information.'

'But originally, when it happened, what did you tell him?'

'I told him she had died, simply that. When he was a little older, when he understood enough to realize that people died in different ways, he asked *how* she'd died. I told him it was pneumonia. There was an outbreak in New York at the time and a half dozen cases were fatal. That's what I told him, and as far as I know that's what he's believed to this day.'

Duchaunak leaned back in the chair. 'He may find out now,' he said quietly.

Evelyn nodded. 'He may.'

'And then you become the person who didn't tell him about his father, and then lied to him about the death of his mother.'

Evelyn looked at Duchaunak. Her expression was both challenging and defiant.

Duchaunak raised his hand. 'You don't get an opinion out of me, Mrs Sawyer,' he said. 'I've lost count the number of times I've decided something and then realized in hindsight that there could have been a better way. This isn't a matter of me coming here to make an issue out of this or even to judge the situation . . . I'm here because I'm concerned about who John Harper is associating with.'

'Does it upset you?'

'What?'

'The fact that Edward Bernstein might die . . . that he might in fact be dead even as we sit here?'

'Does it upset me? Why would you think it would upset me?'

'That his death appears to be the result of a random shooting in a liquor store?'

'As opposed to?'

Evelyn smiled. 'We're not children, Detective. I know why you're here, and I can tell from the way you ask these questions that there is an awful lot more going on than you're saying.' She paused. She looked right through Duchaunak. He felt hollow and insincere. 'How long have you been after him?' she asked.

'Is it that obvious?'

Evelyn Sawyer nodded.

Duchaunak shrugged. 'Seven years, a little more perhaps.'

Evelyn looked away, thoughtful for a moment. 'End of '97,' she said.

'November.'

'A specific incident?'

Duchaunak didn't reply.

'Did someone die? Is that what happened?'

Duchaunak smiled and shook his head. 'No, Mrs Sawyer, no-one died.'

'That you know about?'

'That I know about, yes.'

'You have some persistence, eh?'

'I do.'

'And you have the full backing and support of your department?'

Duchaunak paused. 'I have as much backing and support as I need.'

126

'Which means that this is more than official duty, perhaps something of a personal crusade, Detective?'

'Edward Bernstein is—'

Evelyn Sawyer smiled. 'My turn to interrupt you,' she said. 'We both know all too well who Edward Bernstein is. I don't need an explanation of either the man or his past. Disassociating myself from him and his business colleagues was not the easiest thing in the world—'

'I can imagine,' Duchaunak interjected.

'But I did it, and I got John away from them too. And now, after all this time, because Edward, damned fool that he is, gets himself shot I find myself in a situation where I'm having to walk around the edges of this thing once more.'

'So why did you telephone, John? Why didn't you tell Walt Freiberg to leave John alone—'

'Because Walt Freiberg is not the sort of man you defy, and because there was a shred of truth in what he was saying—'

Duchaunak tilted his head to the right and frowned.

'—Anne might have wanted John to know who his father was.'

'You really believe that?'

'In retrospect no, but in that moment . . . you know how it is . . . emotions enter the picture, you become confused . . . ' Her voice trailed away. 'And then I called John in Miami, couldn't reach him. Called the number of a girl he used to go out with . . . God knows why, but I remembered where she worked, and then when I spoke to him he was unwilling to come.' Evelyn smiled. She looked fatigued. 'John and me, we have a history, you know? We spent the better part of twelve years together, living out of each others' pockets, and when he challenges me it becomes a matter of who can win, rather than a matter of whether or not we're even discussing something important. It went a little like that.'

'I understand.'

'You have children, Detective?'

Duchaunak shook his head. 'No, no children.'

'Wife?'

'No.'

'Reason?'

'Career aspirations, and once they faded the viewpoint that

127

the nature of what I did, the fact that someone would have to be involved in that twenty-four seven . . . well, it didn't seem like the sort of thing someone would want to do.'

'You ever give anyone the choice?'

Duchaunak laughed. 'Not really, no.'

'Fool you, then.'

'Eh?'

'How old are you?'

'Forty-two.'

Evelyn looked him up and down. 'You're serviceably good-looking, reasonably educated . . . seems to me you've denied a decent woman a husband.'

'Perhaps.'

'But then again, you have a raison d'être, do you not?'

'And that would be?'

'Edward Bernstein and his people.'

'I wouldn't say that it was my raison d'être, Mrs Sawyer.'

'But in the absence of anything better it will do.'

'In the absence of anything better, yes.'

'So, enough questions.'

'Just one more if that's okay?' Duchaunak asked.

'Shoot.'

'The things that Edward Bernstein has done, the things you know about . . .'

'And what things would that be, Detective?'

Duchaunak said nothing.

She shook her head and smiled ruefully. 'It doesn't work that way here,' she said. 'I do not choose for Edward Bernstein to be part of my life, whereas you do. I'm in a situation where I'm on the edge of this thing because of John, and when it's over I will do whatever I have to do to keep John out of this. Frankly, in my heart, I don't know that there is a great deal I can do. He will do whatever he feels he should do, and if he chooses a path that I disagree with then I can guarantee that I'll be the very last person in the world he will listen to. You want to find something on Edward Bernstein then you go look yourself. I know these people . . . Walt Freiberg, Sol Neumann, Victor Klein. I have even heard of Ben Marcus, and when it comes to a man like that it is better that his name isn't even mentioned. These things have been going on for a great deal more years than you've been

128

around. Hell, my husband Garrett and a man called Raymond Dietz used to be drinking buddies some thirty-odd years ago, and that was long before Edward Bernstein and Ben Marcus figured it was a good idea to contradict one another. The fact that Garrett and Raymond Dietz ultimately possessed different loyalties is beside the point. These are dangerous people, Detective, I know that and so do you.' She paused for a moment, and then she frowned. 'You don't see what's happening here? You don't see why John Harper has been brought back to New York?'

Duchaunak didn't say anything; merely looked back at Evelyn.

'Walt Freiberg is involved in whatever he's involved in. Maybe he had something to do with Edward being shot, maybe he didn't. Frankly, it doesn't matter. The fact that Edward Bernstein has finally seen some sort of justice pleases me no end. But Walt Freiberg is not a stupid man . . . he is fully aware that you are here, he may even have one of his people watching this house as we speak. He is telling me that he's aware of how much I know. He brought John back just to remind me that he's my only living relative, my sister's son, and if I so much as suggest something incriminating then John will disappear quietly, and it won't be back to Miami. You understand what I'm saying?'

Duchaunak nodded. 'He's blackmailing you into silence.'

'Blackmailing me? Well, if you want to call it that, then yes, he's blackmailing me. John and I may have had our differences, but still he *is* my only living blood relative, and I will not carry a conscience for something that happens to him. That, Detective, is why you are going to get very little out of me.'

'And if something happened to John Harper?' Duchaunak asked.

Evelyn shook her head slowly and looked away towards the window. 'If something happened to him?' She turned back to Duchaunak and smiled. 'I do not believe in violence Detective, but I am of the view that many things in this world are relegated to the level of an eye for an eye in the end – if you know what I mean.'

'Something happens to John Harper, and you will fight back,' Duchaunak said matter-of-factly.

'Me? I look like I'm going to fight anyone? No, Detective, *I* won't be fighting anyone.'

'You have someone who will exact some vengeance for you—'

'I am saying nothing further. I am not willing to put myself in a situation where such things become part of my life. I don't know anything that will help you.'

'But—'

'Hear me on this, Detective. I don't know *anything* that will help you. Are we clear on that point?'

Duchaunak looked down at the floor, and then up at the woman facing him. 'We're clear on that,' he said.

'So, we're done. You go do whatever you have to do and I will carry on with my life.'

Duchaunak nodded. 'Thank you for your time Mrs Sawyer.'

'My time you're welcome to, Detective . . . at my age time is pretty much all you have left.'

Duchaunak rose from the chair and straightened his jacket. 'Up on Fifty-first there's a street sign kind of thing, like a cross. Church building or something. Words read, 'Sin will find you out'. You believe that Mrs Sawyer?'

Evelyn smiled. 'I believe a lot of things, Detective; doesn't mean they're true.'

'Good point,' Duchaunak said.

She walked with him to the front door, opened it, waited until he'd gone down the steps and reached the sidewalk.

'Maybe I'll see you again sometime, Mrs Sawyer,' he said.

'I kind of hope not, Detective . . . but don't take that personally.'

'I never do, Mrs Sawyer, I never do.' He turned right and started walking.

Evelyn Sawyer paused there on the stoop and watched him until he disappeared across the junction at the end of the street. She stepped back into the hallway. When she closed the door behind her the action was decisive, almost as if she believed she could close out the world beyond.

She could not; she knew it. Nevertheless – as with so many times before – she made-believe it would do some good.

EIGHTEEN

'He didn't say where?'

'No, Miss Cathy,' Benedict said. 'Mr Walt said to tell you that the car was outside, that you should have some lunch, that he would call you later.'

Cathy turned to Harper. 'He does this . . . he does this all the time.'

Harper stood in the inner room beyond the store frontage, looking at himself in a full-length mirror. The man who looked back was someone he barely recognized.

'I think we are done,' Mr Benedict said. 'I've had the rest of your things taken to the car.'

'You look like a different person,' Cathy Hollander said. She smiled, walked to the side of the room and stood there for a moment looking at Harper.

'Don't,' he said.

She frowned. 'Don't what?'

'Stand there looking at me.'

'But you look good John . . . you wear good clothes well. You have the build to carry them off.'

Harper turned and looked at Benedict, a stranger who had decided what he should wear. He didn't know how to feel; didn't question it. At some point he'd decided to go with it, just go with it until it took him somewhere he didn't wish to be, and then he would stop. Believed he was in control. Tried to believe there was nothing else here but the generosity of a man who knew his father, and many years before that had known him as a child. Uncle Walt. That was all he was, just Uncle Walt, and if Walt wanted to buy clothes and pay for dinner then so be it. Closer to the truth was that he wanted to stay with Cathy Hollander, and this performance, this small charade, seemed to please her. Now he was doing things to please a woman, and such a route could never bode well.

'We'll go get some lunch,' Cathy said. 'You hungry?'

Harper nodded. 'Hungry, yes.'

'Mr Benedict—' she started.

Benedict raised his hands. 'Not a word. Go to lunch. Enjoy the clothes Mr Harper, enjoy New York . . . it has been a pleasure.'

Harper smiled. 'Thank you, Mr Benedict.'

Benedict lowered his head, a small bow, modest and understated, and then he backed up and turned, passed out through the doorway, closed it gently behind him.

'And who was he?' Harper asked.

Cathy frowned. 'Mr Benedict.'

'I got his name,' Harper said, 'but how does he figure in all of this?'

Cathy shook her head. 'What d'you mean? He's Mr Benedict, your father's tailor.'

'He's a tailor.'

'Yes, a tailor . . . you know what a tailor is, right?'

'I know what a tailor is.'

'Well, that's what he is. He sells suits and shirts and shoes. Your father and Walt come here, a whole load of other people as well, and he sells them their clothes. That's what tailors do.'

Harper nodded. 'We go eat,' he said. 'I'm all out of questions.'

'Good,' Cathy Hollander said. 'Because I'm all out of answers.'

'And after we eat we go to St Vincent's.'

'That a statement or a question?'

Harper shrugged. 'A request maybe?'

'If that's what you want to do then that's what we'll do.'

'I figure I should—'

She shook her head. 'You don't have to explain anything to me, John. You're here for a few days, however long I don't know . . . Walt said to take care of you, to make sure you got whatever you wanted, so if you want to go to St Vincent's then that's where we'll go.'

Harper was tempted to ask how the far the definition of *taking care* went, but he restrained himself.

'So what d'you want to eat?'

'Can we go somewhere regular? Like a normal place that has

132

... like, waitresses ... that come with coffee before you've ordered anything?'

'Sure we can, John, anywhere you like.' Cathy walked across the room and opened the door.

Harper followed her, glanced back at the room as he stepped into the dusty nondescript storefront. He frowned, figured he should ask something else.

The car was out front against the sidewalk. He walked around the back and came up on the passenger side.

'You want to drive?' Cathy asked.

'Sure, if you like.'

'I like,' she said and smiled warmly. 'Always figured I was the kind of girl born to be chauffeured.'

'Is that so?'

'Sure it's so,' she replied. She tossed the keys over the roof. Harper caught them, walked around front, and for a moment it seemed like a kid's game, a game where everyone knew the rules except himself. He stood there for a second, hand on the door, and then he looked to his left and down the street.

'What?' she asked.

He shook his head. 'Nothing,' he replied.

'You don't have that kind of expression when there's nothing.'

He turned back towards her, smiled. 'Kind of expression is that?'

'Ah hell, I don't know ... like you were just considering something real significant.'

Harper glanced down. He pulled the handle. The car door opened. 'Get in,' he said. 'We're going to lunch.'

The call had come as Walt Freiberg was leaving Benedict's shop. A call from Sol Neumann.

'Mr Marcus wants a sit down,' Neumann said.

'Tell me where.'

'You know the place on West and Bloomfield?'

'Somewhere neutral,' Freiberg said. 'Somewhere public.'

'You don't trust us to keep our word on this thing?' Neumann asked.

'Let's not fuck each other around eh, Sol?' Freiberg said. 'Give me a place we can meet and we'll start talking.'

'West Twenty-second near the Flatiron Building . . . restaurant there called The Metropolitan Cafe.'

'An hour from now?'

'Suits us,' Neumann said.

'See you there, Sol,' Freiberg said, and ended the call.

'Sawyer,' Duchaunak said. 'Like Tom Sawyer . . . S-A-W-Y-E-R, first name Garrett.'

Faulkner wrote down the name, turned to the computer ahead of him and started typing. 'Any idea when he died?'

'August of 1980, that's what Evelyn said.'

'A suicide.'

Duchaunak nodded. 'Self-administered cranial ventilation.'

'You what?'

'He blew the back of his own head off.'

'Like eating Mexican fast food.'

Duchaunak frowned.

'It's all over in moments and by then it's too late to regret it.'

Duchaunak smiled. 'Just type the name, do your computer shit.'

Faulkner typed. Duchaunak waited silently, thought about Harper's book, thought about Evelyn Sawyer's comparison between the death of her sister and that of Marilyn Monroe.

'Lock 'n' load, motherfuckers,' Faulkner said.

Duchaunak looked up. 'You got something?'

'Two assaults. June eleventh 1956, and October twenty-second 1974. A DUI in April '68. Possession of an unlicensed weapon—'

'He was part of it, wasn't he?' Duchaunak said, suddenly interested, leaning forward and looking across at the computer screen. 'She said he was buddies with Ray Dietz for a while. She mentioned Victor Klein, Sol Neumann. She sure as hell doesn't forget a great deal.'

'Maybe Garrett Sawyer was with them,' Faulkner said, 'at least until August of 1980.'

'He ever do time?'

Faulkner shook his head. 'No. Arrested a total of eleven times, charged five times, bound over, a couple of arraignments, but nothing ever came of them.'

'And then something happens and he kills himself.'

'Right.'

'Harper found him you know?'

Faulkner turned away from the screen and faced Duchaunak. 'Twelve-year-old kid, and he finds his uncle dead in the house.'

'He tell you that?'

Duchaunak shook his head. 'No, but I figure that's what happened.'

'And the sister, Harper's mother, was a suicide as well?'

Duchaunak shrugged. 'Seems that way but I don't know, Don, I really don't know.' He turned and looked towards the window. 'Lenny Bernstein gets shot, a random thing by all accounts, and then his son shows up, a son no-one knew he had. Everything changes all of a sudden. There's a dead mother, a dead uncle, an aunt who raised the son . . . I don't know what to make of it.'

'Maybe nothing,' Faulkner replied. 'Maybe there isn't any-thing *to* make.'

Duchaunak smiled. He reached up and started massaging his temples. 'With these people . . . with these people there's *always* something to make.'

'So what d'you want me to do?'

'Pull Garrett Sawyer's file. Pull the reports on his suicide, Anne Harper's as well. I want to take a look at them in a little more detail.' Duchaunak rose from his chair.

'And you?'

'Going to go back to St Vincent's, see if Lenny's going to make it.'

'You understand what happens if he dies, right?'

Duchaunak raised his eyebrows.

'You're going to have Ben Marcus to contend with.'

Duchaunak reached for his overcoat. 'One thing at a time. I'm going to see Lenny. I'll tell him how much we all miss him, and when he comes out we're going to throw a little party. We'll have finger food, those little pastry things with shrimp and mayonnaise inside them, shit like that.'

'No pâté,' Faulkner said. 'I fucking hate pâté.' He lifted the receiver on his desk, waved Duchaunak out of the office as he dialled Archives.

Duchaunak went quietly, disappeared from the building. He

took the car and drove towards St Vincent's, thought once more about Marilyn Monroe and how it was all such a stupid, tragic waste.

NINETEEN

'Still here,' Harper said. 'Thought I should at least call and let you know that I was here and that I was staying a little while.'

'Very fucking decent of you,' Harry Ivens replied.

'Everything's okay there?'

'No John . . . we're all behaving like we're seven or eight years old, and while you're away we've been running around the place eating donuts and drawing on the walls with red crayolas. Someone even wrote a bad word on the paintwork near the elevator.'

Harper smiled. 'Business as usual then.'

'So what's the deal?'

'My father got shot.'

'You what?'

'My father . . . he got shot in a liquor store robbery. He's in the hospital, St Vincent's, and there's a very good possibility he isn't going to make it.'

'Jesus Mary, mother of God, John Harper! What the fu—'

'It's okay Harry, it's okay.'

'What the hell is going on? I didn't think your father was still alive—'

'Neither did I, Harry, neither did I.'

'Christ, John, how the hell do you even begin to cope with something like that?'

Harper smiled to himself. He felt awkward, and yet at the same time singularly detached from whatever he was supposed to feel. There was no context, no anchor, no point of reference. This was a once-in-a-lifetime, once-in-a-million kind of deal. 'I don't think you do cope with it, Harry,' he said. 'I think you do what I'm doing now.'

'Which is?'

'Waiting to see if he dies.'

'Goddamnit, John, I don't know what to say.'

'You don't have to say anything. I just figured I should call you and let you know why my aunt was upset—'

'I should think she was.'

'And to let you know that I'll be back in the next few days. I have to see what happens, you know.'

'Sure as shit you do. Jesus, I can't keep my fucking head on. You do whatever you have to do, take what time you need. Things'll be fine here . . . hell, with what you've got to deal with, what happens here isn't exactly fucking relevant is it?'

'I'll be in touch, Harry. Say "Hi" to everyone for me.'

'I will,' Harry Ivens said. 'I will . . . take care, John, okay? And my sympathies to your father. Jesus, I can't believe this, I just can't believe this.'

'I'll call you soon, Harry,' Harper said, and hung up. He backed out of the phone booth in the hospital foyer and turned to see Cathy Hollander standing near the front entrance, talking on her cellphone.

As he reached her she finished the call.

'Everything okay?' she asked.

Harper nodded. 'You?'

'I have to go, I have to do something for Walt. Can you get a cab or something?'

Harper nodded. 'Sure I can.'

She stepped forward, reached out her hand and touched the side of his face. 'You're going to be okay?'

Harper felt a rush of electricity. He wanted to close his eyes, close them just for a moment and be aware of nothing but the touch of her hand on his face. He smiled. 'Sure I'm going to be okay. You go, do whatever. I'll be fine. You know where I am.'

'You'll go back to the hotel after?'

'I should think so,' Harper replied.

She lowered her hand. 'I'll call you . . . maybe we could have some dinner later.'

'Yes, I'd like that. I'd really like to do that.'

She turned, started walking.

'Cathy?'

She turned back.

'I . . .' He paused, cleared his throat. He took a step towards her, reached out and took her hand. She didn't resist him, didn't

138

even look awkward. 'Hell, I don't know if there's something we—'

She shook her head. 'Don't say anything,' she said. 'I've got to go. I'll call you later and we'll go have some dinner, okay?'

Harper nodded, released her hand. She smiled once more and then turned to walk away. Harper watched her go. There was a warmth and humanity that was not at first evident in her manner, something that stretched his patience, made him feel that if he waited for something to happen it never would. Here was an opportunity; he had to seize it or watch it slip through his fingers. He wondered if there was any chance of something with this woman, and if something happened would Walt let him take her away, back to Miami. He could not shake the memory of the first moment he'd really seen her, there in the back of the car as he'd left St Vincent's the first night. The thought that she was the one. Cathy Hollander.

He breathed deeply, slowly; felt the tension within him. He watched Cathy until she disappeared, and then walked to the reception desk, gave his name, said he was there to see Edward Bernstein.

'And your relationship to the patient, sir?' the girl asked. Her name was Clare Whitman. Nancy Cooper was nowhere to be seen.

'I am his son,' John Harper said, and even as he said it he felt it.

'His son?' Clare Whitman asked, aware that their surnames were different.

'My parents weren't married,' Harper explained.

Clare looked awkward, momentarily embarrassed. 'I'm sorry, sir, you understand we have to be somewhat—'

Harper smiled. It was a good smile, a winning smile. 'It's okay,' he said. 'It's not a problem. He really is my father.'

She smiled back. 'Go on up sir.'

Harper turned left, took the stairs, walking with a sense of purpose in his English shoes and tailored suit. He glanced at the two thousand-dollar watch on his wrist. Figured he was owed it, that much at least, for all the years he'd been left to deal with Evelyn, with Garrett's death, with the Carmine Street house and the demons within. Hadn't such things been the very reason he'd left New York? Of course they had. There was the question of why Walt was doing these things, why he was spending money, buying clothes. What had Walt said? A sense of nostalgia, a recompense for failing to look after Harper? Bullshit. Walt Freiberg had a vested interest, an ulterior motive. Walt Freiberg was never nostalgic, or guilty – or stupid.

As he turned onto the second floor risers he asked himself if he hadn't been destined to stay all along. Perhaps Evelyn had been right: *Born in New York John Harper . . . once you're born in New York there's nowhere else that can be called home. You might have run away but everything you ever were is here.*

But she'd been the first one to tell him to leave. First Evelyn, then Duchaunak, then his own father. Why did they want him out of New York? Was Duchaunak planning to gain something from Edward Bernstein's shooting? Was he in some way involved with Freiberg? Harper wondered if Freiberg's insistence that he come to New York somehow prevented Duchaunak from accomplishing his own ends. Was Duchaunak responsible for the shooting of Edward Bernstein?

A feeling of apprehension invaded Harper as he reached the third floor. He wished Cathy Hollander had been with him. He opened the door at the top of the well and walked through.

TWENTY

As was customary at such meetings, neither Ben Marcus nor Walt Freiberg entered the Metropolitan Cafe first. Both Marcus and Freiberg, driven by Sol Neumann and Joe Koenig respectively, came to a halt more than a block away. Words were shared by cellphone, and then Marcus and Freiberg exited their vehicles and walked down together.

Marcus was the first to speak, and only once they were seated in the cafe, once coffee had been ordered.

'My respects to Lenny,' Marcus said. 'This is a bad thing that has happened.'

Freiberg shook his head. 'Lenny Bernstein is tough. He'll come through this.'

'But for now he is out of the picture.'

'He is, but the picture is the same from where I stand.'

Marcus nodded, sipped his coffee. 'We had a meeting, me and my people, hence the call. I wanted to discuss our options Walt.'

'It's very simple. We carry through with the thing that Lenny proposed, or we call it quits and walk away.'

'And if Lenny dies?'

Freiberg smiled, glanced towards the window. 'How long have we known each other Ben?'

Marcus shrugged.

'You ever known me to be on the back step?'

'You have contingency plans.'

Freiberg turned his mouth down at the corners. 'Whatever,' he said nonchalantly.

'So what's the deal with the guy from Miami?'

Freiberg looked puzzled. 'What guy would that be, Ben?'

Marcus smiled. 'Ah, come on, don't piss down my back and tell me it's raining. I hear word that you got Lenny's son up here. Tell me I'm wrong.'

'Seems to me telling Ben Marcus he was wrong wouldn't be a smart idea.'

'So it *is* Lenny's son?'

'You see what you see, Ben—'

Marcus was silent for a moment. He leaned forward then, more intent. 'So he has come up here to clean the slate for what happened to his father?'

'He has come because he wants to be near his father at such a time,' Freiberg replied.

'And he's brought his own people?'

'Sonny?' Freiberg shook his head. 'I'm not one to go asking questions about such things, if you know what I mean.'

'He has a crew, right? This son of Lenny's, he's come up here to make things right after his father's shooting—'

Freiberg raised his hand. 'Enough already . . . enough questions. This is real simple here, real simple. There aren't any fingers being pointed, nothing like that. We don't know if someone put a hit on Lenny, or if it was merely a bad case of wrong place at the wrong time. Sonny Bernstein came up here to be with him, to see his interests were taken care of. Maybe he'll ask some questions, maybe he'll want to dig around and see what he can find. I don't know. I'm not asking. Comes down to it, Lenny's going to be away for a little while. He's doing okay, and it seems there's a chance he'll make it, but before this thing happened you and him were talking business, looking at the idea of doing some work together before Lenny went into retirement.'

'And you want to keep such an option open?'

Freiberg smiled. 'I'm not a man to turn down an opportunity . . . a mutually beneficial opportunity.'

Marcus leaned back in his chair. 'I said earlier that I had a meeting with my people. We took a vote.'

'A vote? That's very democratic of you, Ben.'

'We took a vote on this . . . whether we should go ahead with this proposal of Lenny's, or if we should pack up camp and move out.'

'And?'

'My people want the proposal.'

Freiberg nodded, smiled. 'So we go ahead Ben. That's what you're saying, right?'

'That's what you want to do?'

'Sure, whatever's best for business, Ben, whatever's best for business.'

'And you have Lenny's authority on this, right?' Marcus asked. 'Say he comes through this . . . he isn't going to take this as some kind of bad blood because I made a deal with you?'

'You'll deal with Sonny Bernstein,' Walt Freiberg said. 'That's what he's here for, Ben . . . to make sure that his father's position isn't taken advantage of while he's unwell. He wants what his father wanted, and he has whatever authority is needed to finalize a deal with you.'

'And if something goes wrong, like something happens to Lenny's son, then you call his people in Miami and then we have a fucking war on our hands, right?'

Freiberg closed his hand over Marcus's. 'No-one wants a war Ben, least of all you and me.'

'So that's where we stand.'

'That's where we stand, Ben. At the necessary time, if Lenny is well enough to speak, then you will have his word on this agreement regarding the territories. If Lenny dies, or he is still too unwell to meet with you, then you will have the word of his son.'

'Good enough,' Marcus said.

'And you can let the word out, tell whoever you like, if something *does* happen with Lenny's son then it isn't going to be me they're dealing with—'

'I got the message, Walt, I got the message. Last thing in the world I want is a bunch of crazy Miami cokeheads and psychos running all over New York.' He laughed. 'So we have a thing?'

'We have a thing,' Freiberg replied.

'Next meeting we bring our sites and layouts. I have some people working on some ideas.'

'How many people do I need?' Freiberg asked.

'Including yourself, I'd say you need a crew of eight.'

'And you, Ben? You going to be joining the party on this one?'

Marcus laughed. 'Me? Hell, no. I'm like Lenny . . . find the money, pay everyone, sort out the details, the logistics. I'm too old to be running around with a semi-automatic.'

'You got who you need?'

Marcus nodded. 'I got some good people, people you know. Ray Dietz, Albert Reiff, Victor Klein . . . the usual crew.'

'So, I'll call you . . . we set up a meeting. Choose some place outside the immediate territories. We'll go down there and start working out the details.'

'Good enough, Walt, good enough.'

'You got a date in mind?'

Marcus shrugged. 'Seems to me we might as well go with Lenny's idea.'

'Christmas Eve?'

'You have a problem with that?'

Freiberg shook his head. 'I don't have a problem with that, Ben.'

'Then Christmas Eve it is.'

Freiberg rose, extended his hand. They shook – he and Ben Marcus.

'So, until next time,' Marcus said. 'You take care, Walter.'

'I will, Ben, I will.'

Freiberg gathered up his coat and made his way out of the Metropolitan Cafe.

Ben Marcus watched him go, and then reached into his pocket for his cellphone. 'Make some calls . . . I need you to speak to whoever. Get some details about this Miami character. Get whatever information you can on him. Find out what kind of business he's in down there, what kind of weight he carries, okay?'

Marcus paused. 'You do whatever you have to . . . and call Ray Dietz, find out where he's at on McCaffrey. This boy *has* to be found. Use whatever contacts you have. Don't care how big New York is, he can't hide for ever. Get him found, okay?'

Marcus nodded. 'For sure. Speak later.' The conversation ended, he called Neumann, told him to drive the car down to the Metropolitan and pick him up. He returned the cellphone to his jacket pocket and rose from his chair.

He pulled his overcoat around his shoulders and left the café.

TWENTY-ONE

Four and a half milligrams percent barbiturates, eight milligrams percent chloral hydrate. It took something in the region of thirty-five Nembutal to reach a blood level of four and a half milligrams. To get eight milligrams chloral hydrate someone would have to swallow eighteen or nineteen tablets. Such percentages indicated that she must have taken approximately fifty-five tablets. That didn't include the thirteen milligrams percent pentobarbital found in the liver. That would have taken maybe seventeen more pills. That totalled something in the region of seventy-two tablets. There was no glass, no cup, nothing such as that in the room. Door was locked from inside. Surely no-one could take seventy-two tablets of anything without a drink to wash it down? And not one case – not one out of the many, many thousands of acute fatal barbiturate poisonings on file – had ever revealed a complete absence of residue in the digestive tract. In this case there had been no trace, no capsule residue, no refractile crystals, nothing. And another thing: the amount of pills taken was sufficient to kill between nine and twenty people.

Brentwood, Los Angeles; 12305 Fifth Helena Drive off Carmelina Avenue; warm breeze from the Mojave Desert into the L.A. basin; antique wind-chimes, a gift from Carl Sandburg the poet, whispering their song in the early morning light.

Frank Duchaunak opened his eyes. He rubbed them, felt the gritty reminder of insufficient sleep.

Blonde, beautiful, a glamorous icon, a Hollywood princess, Marilyn Monroe died tragically on Sunday, August fifth, 1962. The troubled, depressive star of more than twenty-five movies was found naked in her bed, a telephone in her hand. A bottle of sleeping tablets lay nearby . . .

Duchaunak had not slept well since the shooting of Edward

145

Bernstein. He looked to his right, over the junction towards the facade of St Vincent's, and he willed himself to go over there, to go see Bernstein lying there in the ICU. The man had been a giant, a legend in his own lifetime, and a single shooting, a single random shooting, the wrong moment, the wrong store . . .

Reminded Duchaunak of the fragility of humanity. Reminded him of Marilyn, and such thoughts became thoughts of Anne Harper, and how everything seemed to turn within its own self-generating circle. Six degrees of separation. He'd been born on the night Marilyn Monroe had died, and such a seemingly disconnected fact had fascinated him for most of his adult life. He knew he was just a little crazy, not the *Jesus told me to stay home and clean my guns*-crazy, but crazy nevertheless.

Frank Duchaunak glanced in the rearview. He smiled at himself; the smile of a tired and slightly desperate man. He lifted the door lever, stepped out onto the sidewalk, locked the car behind him and started over towards the hospital.

'Two visitors in one day,' Clare Whitman said.

'Two?'

'Mr Bernstein's son . . . he's up there now.'

Duchaunak raised his eyebrows.

Clare Whitman leaned forward. 'Is it true?'

'Is what true?'

'Him up there . . . he's really *the* Edward Bernstein?'

Duchaunak smiled. 'I only know one Edward Bernstein. Which one are you talking about?'

She looked awkward for a second, like she'd overstepped the mark. 'You hear things,' she said, as if that was some sort of explanation.

'Things?'

She looked down at the phone, perhaps willed it to ring so she could extricate herself from the conversation she'd started.

'What things?' Duchaunak asked. He was interested in what had been said at the hospital, interested to know if word had gone out.

She shook her head. 'Nothing,' she said. 'Nothing specific.'

Duchaunak leaned forward to read her name-tag. 'Clare Whitman . . . so do me a favor Clare Whitman.'

She looked up.

'My name is Detective Frank Duchaunak. I'm going to be coming down here every once in a while to check on Mr Bernstein. You hear anything, any rumors, any word about Mr Bernstein, anybody coming around here showing more than a passing interest, then I'd like you to tell me about it. You can do that?'

Clare Whitman seemed relieved. 'Yes, Detective, I can do that.'

'That's good,' Duchaunak said. 'That's going to be a great deal of help to me.'

'Right, of course.'

'So I'm going to go up there now.'

'Yes sir.'

Duchaunak turned and started walking, paused as he reached the bottom of the stairs. 'How long's he been here?'

'Mr Bernstein?'

'His son.'

Clare Whitman glanced at her register. 'Half an hour, a little more than half an hour.'

Duchaunak nodded, started up the stairwell.

Vander's Market; delicatessen on the corner of Greenwich and Gansevoort, maybe half a dozen blocks north-west of St Vincent's. Narrow building, tall, and up above the deli are three or four apartments where people lead their lives unaware of the business that is transacted beneath them.

Table in the back right-hand corner. Walt Freiberg, Cathy Hollander, another man with a smallpox-scarred face. Smallpox-face is talking rapidly, his voice hushed, his eyes furtive, and it seems every second sentence he's turning and looking nervously over his shoulder towards the front of the store.

Freiberg is shaking his head, looking down at his hands, glancing at Cathy Hollander to his left. She nods, says something that's all of five or six words, and then Smallpox-face reaches out with his right hand, grips Freiberg's hand and holds it for a moment. Then he's up, sliding out from behind the table and buttoning his coat.

He stands there for a few seconds. He glances towards the street. Cold outside, bitter wind travelling east from the Hudson. Out in the street you can hear sounds from the Fire Boat Station and Pier 53. He doesn't relish the prospect of leaving the deli,

147

but realizes that the conversation is done, the coffee's finished, and Walt Freiberg isn't a man to stay and share lunch with if you're not invited.

'So he's going to do what it takes?' Smallpox-face says.

'He'll do what it takes,' Walt Freiberg says. 'And whenever he's mentioned you call him Sonny Bernstein, not John Harper or John Bernstein, but Sonny Bernstein, you understand? Anyone calls you, anyone from here in New York or any other place, then that's who he is. He's a player of some kind, maybe a big player . . . you're not so sure. He's Lenny Bernstein's son, he's come up from Florida, and he's pissed about his father getting shot. That simple enough for you?'

Smallpox-face nods, would've smiled perhaps but is too preoccupied with whatever runs through his mind. He almost forgets to say goodbye, takes a step, starts to turn, and then turns back and wishes farewell to both Walt Freiberg and Cathy Hollander.

Walt raises his hand. The man walks, black and white checkerboard tiles beneath his feet, and then he's out through the front door and into the street.

'This is going to go?' Cathy asks.

Walt shrugs. 'That a question or a statement?'

'Question.'

'It's going to go, *has* to go – or we're all in the can this time.'

Cathy Hollander nods. A flash of anxiety disturbs her usual imperturbable expression. 'You think Harper will hold up when we need him to? Hell, Walt, he's gonna be dealing with Ben Marcus directly.'

'I think what I think,' Walt Freiberg says drily. 'Let's go . . . I have to speak to someone about something.'

They stand, put coats on, make their way to the front door. Walt Freiberg raises his hand and waves goodbye to an ancient-looking man in a white apron behind the counter. The ancient man doesn't notice.

They step out into the street. Cathy Hollander looks up at the sky – flat like still water, wedding dress-white; figures it's going to snow.

TWENTY-TWO

'Good,' Duchaunak said. 'Good enough to have me start it and finish it in one sitting.'

Harper smiled and looked away, looked around the interior of the hospital cafeteria where they were seated. Pale grey walls, too-high ceiling, acres of silver pipework, endless ducts and vents and a subliminal hum above and beneath everything

'You bring it here I'll sign it for you,' Harper said.

'Can't do that . . . came from the library.'

'You couldn't afford a few dollars to buy one?'

'Couldn't find one.'

Harper frowned. 'Didn't look so hard, eh?'

'Hard enough.'

'So it's such a good book they've stopped selling it.'

'I wouldn't be so cynical. Want to build a reputation and keep your stuff in print, I figure you have to write more than one book.'

'You would know this because?'

Duchaunak shook his head. 'Because of nothing. I don't know squat Mr Harper. Sometimes I think like a detective. Sometimes I figure in a little bit of common sense and come up with something that's close to the truth.'

Harper nodded. 'Fair enough.'

'Like being a detective. You don't build a reputation for solving one case. You get a reputation for solving many cases. You have to keep doing things over and over otherwise you're just a one-hit wonder.'

'Is that so?'

'I reckon it is.' Duchaunak leaned back. 'So what's with the clothes?'

Harper smiled wryly. 'It was my birthday. Uncle Walt took me out and bought me some things.'

149

'Just like old times, eh?'

Harper smiled again. 'Sure, just like old times.'

'That's one helluva suit he got you . . . that English?'

'I believe so, Detective.'

'How much a suit like that cost?'

Harper shrugged. 'God knows. I didn't pay for it.'

'Figure maybe Walt Freiberg didn't pay for it either.'

Harper looked at Duchaunak. 'I have a question for you.'

'Shoot.'

'Heard you paid five thousand dollars for a baseball signed by Joe DiMaggio 'cause you figured Marilyn might have held it one time. That true?'

'You know anything about Marilyn Monroe?'

'You didn't answer the question.'

'No, Mr Harper, I did not pay five thousand dollars for a baseball signed by Joe DiMaggio.'

'Okay,' Harper replied. 'And no, I don't know a great deal about Marilyn Monroe. I do know a little about Arthur Miller.'

'Is that so?'

'Pulitzer Prize 1949. Willy Loman, *Death of a Salesman. The Crucible*.'

'Yes, I know.'

'But you just know about her marriage to him I guess,' Harper said.

'June twenty-ninth, 1956,' Duchaunak replied. He looked up from stirring sugar into his coffee. 'You know she went down to a place called Juarez in Mexico to divorce him on the same day Jack Kennedy was inaugurated just so the press would leave her alone?'

'Why would I know something like that?'

Duchaunak shrugged. ''Cause it's interesting. 'Cause it's got something to do with Arthur Miller and he was a writer like you.'

'He was a playwright not a novelist.'

Duchaunak didn't reply.

'So what's the point of all this?'

'All what?'

Harper looked directly at Duchaunak. 'All this talking back and forth. Coming down here and harassing me—'

'I'm harassing you?'

Harper smiled. 'Well no, not harassing—'

'You just said I was harassing you. If you feel I'm harassing you Mr Harper then I'll leave right now. I wouldn't want—'

'Enough. Enough already. Cut the crap.'

Tense silence between them for a few moments. Duchaunak glanced to his left, towards the door. A doctor walked in, looked around for someone, and then left. The door slammed shut behind him.

'Crap?' Duchaunak asked.

'You know what's going on here,' Harper said. 'You're playing some kind of game with me. You have something on my father, something on Walt Freiberg. I don't know what the hell you've got on them but it has absolutely nothing to do with me—'

'Nothing to do with you?'

'Fuck no. What the hell does whatever's happening here have to do with me?'

'You're involved in this—'

'Involved? Involved in what? What exactly am I involved in Detective?'

'I don't know,' Duchaunak said. He looked down at the fingernails of his right hand. They needed trimming.

'You don't know?' Harper asked.

'Not exactly.'

'Well, maybe vaguely?'

'Vaguely, yes. I can do vaguely.'

'So tell me what the fuck is *vaguely* going on?'

'You don't know?' Duchaunak asked.

'Don't know what? Jesus fucking Christ, what the hell *is* it with you people? Is everyone in New York so fucking obscure?'

Duchaunak leaned back in the chair. 'So who paid for the suit, Mr Harper? Who paid for the watch you're wearing? What is that? That's an Omega, right?'

Harper knew the answer but looked anyway. 'Yes, an Omega.'

'What is that? Fifteen hundred, maybe two thousand bucks?'

'I don't know.'

'Sure you do.'

'Okay, say it is . . . say it's two thousand dollars.'

'So who paid for that?'

'Walt Freiberg.'

'And how the hell did Walt Freiberg get that kind of money?

151

The kind of money that buys English suits and two thousand-dollar watches for someone who isn't so far from a stranger?'

'We're not strangers.'

'Have been for what? Twenty-five, thirty years?'

'He says he kept an eye on me.'

'What the hell would he want to keep an eye on you for?'

'Maybe 'cause my father asked him to?'

'And what kind of people have people who keep an eye on other people? What kind of people do that shit?'

'Rich people.'

'On the fucking money, Mr Harper, on the fucking money. Rich people. Too fucking right rich people. And how do people get rich?'

Harper looked up at Duchaunak. 'Get to the fucking point will you? Say what you're going to say and then go wherever you were headed to when you stopped off here.'

'I wasn't going anywhere but here, Mr Harper. I came here specifically to see your father.'

'Don't tell me, because you're really sorry that someone shot him and you want to make sure he gets better fast?'

'I do, yes.'

'You do? Why would you be so interested in seeing that he gets better?'

'Because it wouldn't be right for him to die like this,' Duchaunak said.

'Right for him? How can a man die right?'

Duchaunak smiled. 'You have a point there, Mr Harper.'

'And your point, Detective? What the hell is *your* point?'

'I think you should leave New York.'

'I know. You told me already.'

'I think you've stayed long enough . . . and I think you know why you should leave.'

'Enlighten me, Detective. Tell me why you think I have any fucking idea what you're talking about?'

'Cathy Hollander.'

'What about her?'

'You know who she is?'

'Sure I do,' Harper said. 'She's Cathy Hollander.'

Duchaunak smiled. 'That's a sharp sense of humor you got

152

there. That's a little dark though, right? Kind of dark humor that threads its way through your book.'

'If you say so.'

'So you know who she is for real?'

Harper shook his head. 'What do you think? I met the woman on Monday, today is Wednesday . . . I don't think that qualifies me as a character referee.'

'You ever hear of Neumann and Marcus?'

'Neiman, like the department store?'

'Neumann,' Duchaunak repeated. 'Like the actor but spelled different?'

'Neumann and Marcus . . . no,' Harper lied. 'I never heard of them. They like a vaudeville duo or something?'

'You should go down the Comedy Store on a Friday evening. You could get like a half-hour slot and work all this out of your system.'

'That where you go?'

Duchaunak didn't rise to the bait. 'So you never heard of these people?'

'Neumann and Marcus? No, I never heard of them.'

'Benjamin Marcus is a bigshot here in New York.'

'That so?'

'Sure it is . . . he's a bigshot, carries a lot of weight—'

'He's like a real fat guy then?'

'No, he's not a real fat guy. You can stop winding, Mr Harper. I got a spring like a car and it won't ever give. You know what I mean, right?'

Harper nodded. 'I know what you mean.'

'Cathy Hollander used to be in with Ben Marcus—'

'In with?'

Duchaunak nodded. 'Sure, used to be.'

'How d'you mean, *in with*?'

'Like she was the girl in the picture, Mr Harper. She was there to hear everything and say nothing, to do what she was asked, to take care of any special guests Mr Marcus might have down to New York—'

'She's a hooker?'

'No, she's not a hooker, Mr Harper. She's a friend of the family, the Marcus family.'

'So why is she with Walt Freiberg?'

Duchaunak smiled. 'There was a wager about something or other and Mr Marcus lost to your father, and Mr Marcus had said that if he lost he would give Cathy Hollander to your father.'

'You're so full of shit,' Harper said. He couldn't help himself; started laughing.

'Whatever,' Duchaunak said. 'These people have a different set of values, a different set of importances than people like you and I.'

'*These* people? Who would they be then, Detective?'

'The people you've been spending time with since you came to New York.'

'And that would include my aunt?'

'Sure it would.'

'You know her?' Harper asked. He was beginning to feel unsettled. Not once had he wished to face the truth of what Duchaunak was implying. Defences were up but starting to wear thin.

'I don't *know* her. I went and spoke to her today.'

'What the hell for?'

'To see if she was the one who asked you to come to New York, or to see if Walt Freiberg told her to bring you here.'

'And?'

'What do you think?'

'I think she wanted me to come,' Harper said. 'I think she believed it was what my mother would have wanted . . . for me to find out that I had a father before he died.'

Duchaunak sighed, glanced towards the door as an orderly came in and walked to the counter. 'Okay,' he said. 'You think what you want to think, Mr Harper, but I have to tell you something, and whether you want to go with me on this or not I still have to give you some kind of an idea of what's going here or I'm going to feel bad about myself. I got enough things to feel bad about without adding myself to the list, okay?'

Harper felt cold and loose within, like something was unravelling inside him.

'Ben Marcus and Sol Neumann are dangerous people. Very, very dangerous people. Your father and Walt Freiberg were, maybe still are, involved with these people. These are not the sort of people you want to have in your life, Mr Harper. You've come here to New York, you've found out something that I'm sure has been very difficult to deal with ... you've got a new suit, a great looking watch there—' Duchaunak stopped mid-sentence, leaned forward, and then he spoke again with a hushed and urgent voice. 'You have to leave, Mr Harper. I'm telling you for your own welfare ... you've *got* to leave New York. Go home, go back to Miami. I'll keep you posted on what happens with your father.'

Harper didn't reply.

'You hear me, Mr Harper?'

Harper nodded. 'I hear what you've said, but you sure as shit haven't told me a great deal.'

'I can't,' Duchaunak said. 'I have to make a judgement call on this, and right now my instinct tells me that the less you know the better. I tell you some of the things that are going down here and you're going to act strange with these people. You act strange with them they'll know it in a heartbeat, and then—'

'What?' Harper asked. 'Then what?'

Duchaunak shook his head. 'Go home, Mr Harper. Please. Would you just go home?'

'I'll think it over.'

'Okay, you think it over.' Duchaunak started to rise from his chair.

'You can lead a horse to water, right, Detective?'

Duchaunak smiled. 'Right, Mr Harper.' He buttoned his overcoat and reached out his hand.

Harper took it without rising.

'Good luck.'

'Thank you, Detective.'

Duchaunak started towards the door.

'Hey!' Harper called after him.

Duchaunak turned.

'So what was the deal with baseball? You didn't pay five thousand dollars for a baseball?'

Duchaunak shook his head. He reached for the door and pushed it open. 'No, Mr Harper, I did not pay five thousand dollars for a baseball ... I paid six.'

Duchaunak pushed the door wide and walked out into the corridor. He was gone before Harper had a chance to reply.

TWENTY-THREE

Harper stayed a while and drank his coffee. Didn't think about the conversation with Duchaunak. Didn't believe his mind flexible enough to take such inferences and innuendoes on board. Looked at the watch Walt had bought him, at the suit he was wearing. Felt like he was pretending to be something he wasn't. At least here there were emotions. At least here he felt a little excitement, a little nervousness. What the hell was the point of such emotions if you didn't experience them once in a while?

Took a cab from the front of the hospital back to the Regent. Driver talked all the way, interspersed with the radio, DJ hammering on about Dizzee Rascal and Social Distortion challenging Franz Ferdinand for the number one spot in the chart.

Harper seated in the back, scanning the streets for anything he recalled of his childhood. New York had changed, it had grown up and become an adult.

'You from New York?' the driver asked.

'Originally, yes.'

'Where you from now?'

'Miami.'

'Miami? Hell, I been to Miami. Miami's a helluva place.'

Harper didn't respond.

'You here on holiday?'

'No, some business I have to see to.'

'You going to be here Christmas Eve, buddy?'

'I don't know,' Harper said. He wondered how far they were from the hotel.

'If you're here, if you stay until Christmas Eve, then you have to take a taxi ride somewhere, okay?'

'A taxi ride?'

'Sure.'

'For what reason?'

''Cause we're collecting money.'

Harper frowned. 'I don't understand.'

'Christmas Eve you take a yellow cab anywhere in the city, anyplace to anyplace else you like, and the money you pay is going to charity. The mayor's even looking at taking all the private cars off the road for three hours in the afternoon so we can raise as much money as possible. You figure you can do that?'

'I can do that,' Harper said.

'If you're here . . . ain't going to be no good you takin' a cab in Miami, right?'

'Right. If I'm here on Christmas Eve I'll take a cab. You have my word.'

'Good man. Good man indeed.'

And then they were drawing to a stop outside the Regent, and from the money that Walt had given him Harper paid the driver, and then he stood on the sidewalk for some minutes after the cab had pulled away and asked himself what he would do now.

He didn't know. He didn't have a clue. He turned and walked up the steps.

Ben Marcus, seated in his warehouse office, takes a call at his desk.

'Ben?' Freiberg says at the other end of the line.

'Walter,' Marcus replies.

'Got a meeting place for tomorrow,' Freiberg says. 'Restaurant with a basement, place called Trattoria St Angelo. Other side of Gramercy Park, corner of East Twenty-fourth and Third. Noon is good for you and your people?'

'Noon is fine Walt . . . we'll see you then.'

'Sure thing Ben.'

The call ended.

Worn-out looking duplex on Vandam Street.

Day is closing down; streetlights contribute their sodium-yellow glow to the proceedings and give the early evening a bruised and exhausted feeling.

House was easy enough to break into, nothing more than two deadbolts and a chain, and Albert Reiff and Ray Dietz sat in the back kitchen waiting. They waited for more than an hour – smoking, saying little or nothing, patience of this kind never in short supply. A great deal of their lives required such a type of patience, and after a while time took on a different aspect for these people. This kind of waiting was easy.

Dietz heard footsteps on the sidewalk out front of the building and rose from the table. He nodded to Reiff, and when Reiff heard the key in the front door, when he knew that it was indeed this house that was being entered, he rose too. They stood each side of the kitchen door, listened as the owner came into the front hallway, as he set something down on the floor, switched on a light, took off his coat perhaps. It was no more than thirty or forty seconds from the point Darryl McCaffrey put his key in the lock to the moment he entered the darkened kitchen, but as he reached out his hand to flick the switch he sensed something was wrong.

Perhaps it was the smell of cigarettes. Darryl McCaffrey didn't smoke. Whatever raised the alarm didn't matter, for even had he identified the specific source of his disquiet he would not have had any time to act upon it. Dietz had a hold on his right arm, gripped it like a vice, and as Dietz pulled him through the doorway Albert Reiff grabbed the back of his neck and pushed him across the room and into the table.

Darryl McCaffrey, thirty-five years old, a social worker for the New York Metropolitan Borough, caught the side of his head on the edge of the kitchen table and went down.

He did not come round for a good eight or nine minutes, and when he did he was not only gagged, he was also duct-taped to a chair, his ankles bound with something, and facing him were two of the ugliest men he'd ever had the misfortune to see up close.

'Mr McCaffrey,' the man on the right said. 'My name is Raymond. This is my friend Albert. Nod if you understand me.'

McCaffrey nodded furiously, his eyes wide, already his bladder ready to release onto the linoleum or explode upwards into the base of his gut.

'Good, so now we're introduced we can get down to the matter at hand. We need to find your brother.'

McCaffrey frowned, eyes wide, started shaking his head.

'Thomas, right? We need to find Thomas . . . and if you

158

co-operate everything will be fine. You don't . . . well . . . if you don't, we're going to kill you.'

Darryl McCaffrey's eyes widened even further. For a second he wondered if it wasn't some sick practical joke.

Then Ray Dietz drove a fist into his chest and he knew no-one was kidding.

TWENTY-FOUR

No-one called. Not Walt, not Cathy, not Frank Duchaunak. Left Harper alone at the American Regent for the entirety of Wednesday evening. He'd eaten alone, right there in the hotel restaurant, and then he'd sat in his room watching TV until he fell asleep. Early hours of Thursday morning he'd woken, still fully dressed but for his jacket and shoes. Shed his clothes, left them where they fell, and crawled beneath the bed-covers. He remembered the sound of rain against the window, little else, and only for a handful of moments before exhaustion folded his thoughts quietly, neatly, and stowed them somewhere beneath consciousness. One day closed, another opened, and he slept through the space in between.

Perhaps the most disturbing moment occurred when he stood in the bathroom a little before nine. For seconds, perhaps as many as ten or fifteen, he had no awareness of his own name. Had he attempted to describe the sensation to someone it would have seemed utterly impossible. But it took place, and took place with such clarity and definition it left him unnerved and disturbed for much of the morning. He wondered if his real identity was being submerged.

He called room service. They told him a number of items had been left at the desk for him; they would bring them up. He ordered some eggs and toast, a jug of coffee. A bellhop came with the trolley, carried the travel-cases and boxes within which his other clothes had been stored. Cathy must have driven them over. Why hadn't she called? Why hadn't she sent a message up, even brought them up herself? Of everyone in New York she was the only one he *wanted* to see. Couldn't get the girl out of his mind. She'd invaded his head and established camp. Harper asked what time they'd been delivered, the bellhop was unsure. Harper thanked him, gave him ten bucks.

He ate in the chair by the window. Looking down from ten floors up, New York seemed like something from a movie. He was detached from it, separate and distinct. He was not part of the city, at least not all of him, and very little of the city was part of him. To let go of that belief was to consider the possibility that Miami was not his home. To consider such a thing meant that he had nowhere to return to. Such a thought worried him. He felt in limbo.

He sorted through the clothes; three suits, a half dozen shirts, two pairs of shoes, four ties, two pairs of silver cufflinks, some silk handkerchiefs, a cashmere double-breasted overcoat and an arran scarf. Tucked at the bottom of one of the boxes was a pair of calfskin gloves, as soft as cotton.

Harper dressed in a navy suit, white shirt, didn't wear a tie. Ties were for business people and gangsters. He felt a little out of character, but the feeling was not unpleasant. He wished he could have called Cathy, was acutely aware that he had no means by which to contact either her or Walt.

It was gone eleven by the time he left. He took his overcoat, the scarf and gloves, and as he left the Regent the commission-aire raised his hand and touched the peak of his cap. Harper acknowledged the man's gesture, remembered that there had been no such greeting when he'd left the previous day. Now he looked like a man with a reason for being, a man with sufficient wherewithal to walk into New York dressed in a couple of thousand bucks' worth of clothes. Judgements were made on how things appeared, not how they were. Harper was reminded that he had, until now, chosen to see exactly what he wanted to see and nothing more. He did not feel equipped, either mentally or emotionally, to go digging beneath the surface. Not today. Not until he acquired some bearings. He turned right onto Hudson, looked up at the Western Union building, and then kept on walking. He possessed no clear purpose or direction, and for the time being that seemed the safest option. The sound of his footsteps seemed to match his heartbeat.

'So what the fuck we got?'

'What we got is a whole load of nothing dressed up as something.'

Duchaunak rubbed his eyes with his clenched fists. He hadn't slept. The conversation with Harper had travelled around and around in his mind like a yellow cab on an open meter. The kid – thirty-six years old but a kid nevertheless – seemed to have no idea who these people were. Five minutes caught up in the lives of people such as Edward Bernstein, Walt Freiberg, Sol Neumann and Ben Marcus, and Harper would willingly have run back to Miami barefoot. And Evelyn Sawyer? Woman seemed to have more secrets than a pyramid.

'So tell me.'

'Well,' Faulkner said. 'There was nothing in the autopsy of either Anne Harper or Garrett Sawyer that indicated they were anything other than suicides. Garrett had a sheet behind him, nothing to get a hard-on about, and aside from the fact that he married Evelyn Harper, sister of Anne, mother to our Junior Bernstein, and was therefore the boy's uncle, there is no other apparent connection to Edward Bernstein.'

'Except we know there must have been.'

Faulkner nodded. 'Saying prayers to intuition and hunch, yes, there must have been.'

'You have no question about that?'

Faulkner shrugged. 'Who doesn't have questions? Course I got questions. Hell, most of this stuff runs on what you think, what you feel, right? What do I reckon? I reckon Garrett was a cog in the machine someplace, maybe even hooked up with Evelyn and was the indirect connection between Lenny and Anne Harper. Makes sense that Bernstein didn't marry the woman, and seems from what Evelyn said that there was no love lost between them.'

'She said that Bernstein pretty much packed his gear when he found out Anne was pregnant.'

'No wonder she wished him dead.'

Duchaunak frowned. 'She never said she wished him dead.'

'You tell some kid their father is dead for thirty years then you have to wish it was true, right?'

Duchaunak nodded. 'Yeah, I suppose so.'

'So we got this kid playing footloose and fancy-free in the middle of all of this,' Faulkner said matter-of-factly. 'He plays by their rules or they're going to do one of two things.'

'Send him on the first plane back to Miami—'

'Or shoot the dumb asshole in the head.'

'He isn't dumb.'

'I know,' Faulkner said. 'I read his book.'

'And?'

'Not my kind of thing.'

'But evidence that he isn't dumb.'

Faulkner laughed. 'He sees what he sees Frank. What's the deal with the clothes, eh? You tell me he's gotten himself all kitted out like his father. Where did they take him? Benedict's place?'

Duchaunak shook his head. 'I guess so.'

'He's selectively dumb. He sees what he wants to see, hears what he wants to hear. When things get uncomfortable he's going to go with them or he's going to run. Freiberg starts dealing with Marcus, Marcus gets the idea that Bernstein's son is nothing more than a newspaper hack from Miami, and I guarantee we'll find him and Walt Freiberg in half a dozen pieces floating in the river.'

'I don't get that he's on their side,' Duchaunak said. He leaned forward and picked up a can of Dr Pepper from the desk.

'There's no sides any more,' Faulkner said. 'The line that separated the good guys from the bad guys got blurred a long time back . . . blurred by the number of people that walk back and forth across it every day of their lives. There is no distinction any more. You show me a guy, any guy anywhere in this city, who didn't take some stolen gear off of his neighbor, didn't buy a carton of smokes at work and pay no mind to the absent duty sticker, eh? You show me one guy who's clean and clear and I'll pay my taxes in full this year.'

Duchaunak smiled. 'The Diogenes routine.'

Faulkner frowned.

'Diogenes. Walked around in daylight with a lantern looking for one honest man.'

'So we can pretty much guarantee that whatever they're planning is going to happen before Christmas. It has to. Bernstein is in the hospital, but Bernstein was never the action hero, not for the last twenty years. Bernstein was always the money man, the arranger for contacts and backhanders. Freiberg is going to run this show, I guarantee you, and I think it's going to be big, and there's going to be a lot of noise, and some people are going to get hurt.'

'And if Harper gets in the way?' Duchaunak asked.

163

Faulkner shook his head, turned his mouth down at the edges. 'He gets in the way that's his own fucking problem. He should've been wise enough to see what was in front of him and not persuaded himself it was something else.'

'Agreed,' Duchaunak said. 'The tail goes on Freiberg. I have to know, Don, I have to know what the fuck these people are doing. This shit fucking eats me alive.'

Don Faulkner smiled, the smile of a weatherworn and veteran cynic. 'Whatever puts wind in your sails Frank. I'll see what I can do about a tail.'

Duchaunak rose to his feet. 'This time, Don, this time I'm going to get 'em so help me God.'

Faulkner nodded understandingly. 'They got a make on Lenny's bullet by the way . . . not that it makes a great deal of difference to anything.'

'What they got?'

'A very old case . . . armed robbery, 7–11 back in January '74. Gun was fired, no-one was hit. Bullet lodged in the wall. The bullet recovered from Lenny Bernstein's chest had the same land and groove marks as the 7–11 bullet.'

Duchaunak frowned. 'Thirty years ago . . . that's fucking bullshit. They've made a mistake, Don . . . they've fucked up for sure.'

'They checked it twice just to make sure,' Faulkner said. 'They came back to me and confirmed that Lenny's bullet was the same gun that was used back in '74. I mean, that in itself counts for nothing. Black market and untraceable guns are constantly circulating; apparently you can still buy G.I. Issue .45s that soldiers never handed back at the end of the war.'

Duchaunak nodded but said nothing. He walked to the small window of his office and looked down into the street. He was silent for some moments, and then – without turning to face Faulkner – he started talking. The way he spoke he could have been alone, and Faulkner sat listening, stayed silent so he didn't interrupt him.

'Thing about New York is it never gets dark,' Duchaunak said. 'It's got to do something to you . . . can't be natural, right? I mean, it gets dark, of course it gets dark, but not the same kind of dark you remember as a kid. Now you got streetlights and all-night stores, bars and strip-joints with neon displays . . . and all of them together add up to it never really being dark enough to sleep properly. Like Vegas . . . you ever been to Vegas?' Duchaunak didn't wait for a reply. 'Seems like daylight all the time, and there's no clocks . . . not in the hotel lobbies, not in diners . . . no clocks. People just lose track of time, they forget to sleep, they just keep on pushing quarters into slot machines until they pass out.'

Duchaunak turned and looked at Faulkner. He smiled, one of those strange and quiet smiles that suggested nostalgic recollection. 'Sometimes I don't sleep until three, four in the morning.' He shook his head and looked down the floor. 'I get so goddamned tired, Don, so utterly and completely exhausted I find it hard to think straight.' He laughed, a short dry sound. 'You won't believe this – you really won't believe this – but I woke up this morning after about two or three hours' sleep and for the life of me I couldn't remember my own name. It was really like that, like I had no awareness of who I was. It didn't last more than maybe five or ten seconds, but I swear to God that I couldn't remember my own name.'

Duchaunak put his hands in his pockets and turned to the window once more. He lowered his head and sighed so deeply it seemed he might empty out and disappear.

'Maybe,' Faulkner said quietly. 'Maybe you should take a couple of days off Frank . . . get some rest, you know? Get your thoughts back on track—'

Duchaunak turned back towards him suddenly. 'My thoughts are on track, Don, my thoughts are completely on track. A little one-lane highway granted, but they're on the fucking money, okay?'

Faulkner raised his hand; a placatory gesture. Duchaunak seemed tied up tight, wound like a Swiss watch.

'This has been going on for seven years, Don, seven years since that whole thing went down. You saw what these people did, you know what they're capable of, and if this John Harper doesn't have the sense to see what's going on and get the fuck out of here then it's his own goddamned fault.'

'You think Freiberg had Bernstein hit?' Faulkner asked.

Duchaunak shook his head. 'I don't know, Don, I don't know. I hope to fuck he didn't.'

Faulkner frowned. 'Why? Why would it matter if it was Freiberg or Marcus or whoever?'

'Because if it's Freiberg then Lenny Bernstein has been betrayed by a man who is in some way a great deal more dangerous. Bernstein kept the reins on Walt Freiberg, kept him in check. If Freiberg has a mind to run the business then it's going to be a great deal louder and messier than it ever was before.'

'Fact is we don't know,' Faulkner said.

'And until we do know there's not a great deal to say about it.'

'I'll see if I can get this tail organized.'

'I'm going to go over to St Vincent's and check on Lenny.'

Faulkner nodded. 'If you see the son you going to say anything?'

Duchaunak shrugged. 'Don't know that it'll make a deal of difference.'

Faulkner sighed audibly. 'Christ, if he only knew. If he had the slightest idea about his father, about people like Sol Neumann and Ben Marcus . . .' His voice trailed away into silence.

Duchaunak didn't reply. He put on his overcoat and opened the office door. 'Later,' he said.

'Later Frank.'

Duchaunak closed the door silently behind him and made his way down towards the street.

Moments later the door opened and Sergeant Oates looked into the room. 'You seen Sampson?' he asked.

Faulkner shook his head. 'No, why?'

'I got a bad one for him . . . some guy got himself beaten to death. Duplex down on Vandam Street.'

'Anyone we know?'

Oates shook his head. 'McCaffrey, Darryl McCaffrey, social worker I think. Neighbors called it in.'

Faulkner frowned. 'Don't know him. If I see Sampson I'll tell him you're after him.'

'Fuck no, don't say a thing. He hears I'm looking for him he'll leave the fucking building.'

Faulkner smiled.

Sergeant Oates closed the door.

TWENTY-FIVE

'No question about it.'

Sol Neumann looked directly at the man facing him, a man with a bad case of smallpox-scarred skin. 'I'm taking what you're telling me directly to Mr Marcus. You understand what that means, right?'

Smallpox-face, a dark-haired man in his mid-forties called Micky Levin, looked right back at Sol Neumann, his gaze unerring, unflinching. Sol Neumann didn't scare him. Sol Neumann was only so tough because of Marcus. Take Marcus away and Sol Neumann was nothing more than five and a half feet of stiff shit in a two thousand-dollar suit.

'You know me, Sol, eh? You know me for how many years? I tell you something you take it to the bank, right? When did I ever give you something that wasn't kosher, eh? Tell me one time Sol, one time when I gave you something that wasn't straight like a railtrack?'

Sol Neumann raised his hand and silenced Levin. 'Sonny Bernstein, right?'

'That's right, that's what they called him. On my mother's fucking life—'

'Your mother's dead, Micky.'

'On my mother's fucking grave then, what the fuck does it matter, eh? I stood there and listened to that motherfucker Freiberg, so help me God he's a fucking Jew . . . you believe it? I have to celebrate Passover knowing that that two-bit shoeshine motherfucker—'

'Okay, okay, okay. Enough with getting a hard-on for this guy, okay? So you tell me again . . . you were there, Walt Freiberg, the girl, right?'

Micky Levin was nodding furiously. 'Yeah, yeah, me and Walt Freiberg and the girl.'

'And Freiberg said that Sonny Bernstein would take care of this thing?'

'Right, right, you got it . . . Sonny Bernstein would take care of this thing.'

'He make any reference to a crew in Miami, anything like that?'

Micky shook his head. 'He didn't say nothing about a crew, no. He didn't say nothing directly.'

Neumann shook his head. 'And what the fuck is that supposed to mean? Did he say something or didn't he fucking say something?'

Micky Levin shrugged. 'Freiberg . . . he said that Sonny Bernstein was pissed about his father getting shot, that was all. Said he was pissed, that it wasn't good that this had happened because Sonny Bernstein had a reputation for causing trouble.'

'He said that?'

Micky Levin nodded.

'You're sure?'

'I'm sure Sol, I'm sure. He didn't say nothing specific about a crew, but I got the feeling that this guy was some kind of player.'

Sol Neumann leaned back in the chair. He looked around the narrow, windowless office at the back of the West Ninth Street Diner, an office where many such meetings had taken place over the previous years. What these walls had heard; what words the floor, the furniture, the redundant wooden colonial-style ceiling fan had absorbed – and never understood their meaning. Summer of '94, heady and intoxicating, heat so bad there was no way anyone could have stood to be in the room more than ten or fifteen minutes, and Sol Neumann and a weasel-faced man called Haywood Roebling had tied a guy called Kent Bayard to the chair where Micky Levin now sat. Tied him tight with duct tape, his wrists, his ankles, even around his neck, and then they beat the crap out of him in the hope that he'd tell them the drop-times on a bookie's pick-up schedule. Kent Bayard was not a bad man, nor a stupid man, but he was a man with a heart defect, and he seized up and stayed dead after twenty-five minutes of Sol Neumann's hospitality. Haywood Roebling didn't make it beyond Christmas; he got hit with an assault and battery charge from way back when, something to do with a bottle-bleach blonde and a jealous husband from Brooklyn Heights; a week in pre-arraignment lock-up and someone shivved him in the kidney. Haywood didn't have his Blue Cross up to date and he died in triage at Pace University Beekman Hospital.

'You done good, Micky,' Sol Neumann said, and from the drawer ahead of him he took a flat brown envelope. He tossed it over to Levin; Levin snatched it from the air and had it inside his jacket within a heartbeat.

'So go do your worst, eh?' Neumann said.

'Consider it done,' Levin replied, and rose from the chair. He backed up two steps, turned, opened the door, and disappeared into the diner.

Neumann leaned forward and lifted the telephone receiver. He dialled a cellphone number. It rang three, four, five times, and then someone answered.

'Micky comes to see me,' Neumann said. 'He gives me the impression that the minor *is* going to stand for the major . . . I need whatever information you can get on what he's got in Miami.'

Neumann listened, nodded, half smiled.

'Good enough,' he said. 'What goes around goes around, right?'

Another pause.

'Well, let the orchestra tune up, eh? The show goes on. We need cars like I said, four of them. Get hold of the garage guy who does the spray-jobs. I'm gonna need all the guns you can buy for the money I gave you. Speak to the people you usually deal with. Come back to me with specifics when you've got them. Mr Marcus is going to want a daily progress report, okay?'

Neumann paused, listened again.

'Whatever you got. Call me later.'

Neumann set the receiver back in the cradle. He stood up, buttoned his jacket, then walked around the desk and took his overcoat from the stand behind the door. He was out of the building and heading down the street within moments.

On West Ninth he turned right towards Fifth. Head down, walking a straight line, crossed the junction onto East Ninth and kept on going. Took a right onto Broadway and made his way to the Eighth Street Station. Boarded a train up to Union Square, bought a newspaper at a stand. Up the steps into daylight, and then he cut north-east across the park and was lost somewhere in Gramercy.

Only when he reached St George's off of Rutherford did he stop and make a call from a kiosk on the street.

'Get Mr Marcus on the phone.'

He waited as the message was passed. He heard the familiar sound of Marcus clearing his throat.

'We're on,' Neumann said quietly.

'Sure?'

'Yes Ben, I'm sure.'

'You got confirmation?'

'Yes . . . from Levin. He saw Freiberg himself, Freiberg and the girl, and he said again that the thing is going to go forward, that the kid will stand for Lenny if it comes to that.'

'You on the way back?'

'I am.'

'You got someone working on the Miami end? I need to know everything there is to know about this boy and the strength of his Miami crew.'

'Yeah, someone is going to make some calls and find out what he can.'

'Okay. Make it as fast as you can . . . we have the meeting at noon.'

'On my way.' Neumann replaced the receiver and stepped out of the kiosk. He tugged his collar up around his throat and began walking back the way he'd come.

Up above the sky was clear, the breeze from the East River bitterly cold. He wanted a cigarette bad but he was trying to quit. Why, he didn't know. Not a question of health. One of his girls had pulled a face and said it was like kissing an ashtray. He exhaled a lungful of white mist and made believe. Smiled to himself. Head down again, walking fast, like he was trying to lose a tail.

In a narrow-fronted bookshop on the corner of Desbrosses and Hudson, a place that he could have missed had he turned his head for just a second, John Harper found a dog-eared and battered copy of *Depth of Fingerprints*. He took it to the counter, paid three dollars, made sure that he passed it face up so the counter clerk did not see the picture on the back. In all likelihood, even had she seen it, she would not have connected the two. Harper believed he had not so much changed as become an entirely different person. The intervening fifteen years of emptiness and frustration had modified and altered his features. He was not the same man, neither inwardly nor outwardly.

He left the store and walked across Watts and Canal Street, running a parallel to West and Washington, and then he was bearing east almost automatically, something pulling him that way, something preternatural and instinctive. Within minutes he had turned right onto West Houston, and it was then that he realized he was only a block from Carmine. He had walked back to his childhood, the stop at the bookstore representative of the one occurrence of worth between his leaving New York and his return. Seventeen years, and all he had to show for it was a battered paperback in a brown paper bag buried in his overcoat pocket. Harper stood for a moment, stood and imagined looking back at himself. He had on a tailored suit and white shirt, a pair of hand-tooled leather shoes, a seven hundred-dollar cashmere overcoat. The man he now appeared to be was perhaps the man he had intended to become. He'd believed such an identity would be found by leaving. He had found it, ironically, only upon his return.

For some time he vacillated, uncertain about whether he should go and speak with Evelyn. He knew little of the truth of his father. He believed Evelyn knew everything. He stood on the corner of Clarkson and Seventh, hands buried deep in his pockets. He was summoning sufficient courage to confront the past, and in considering this he realized that what he was really confronting was an unknown future. What Evelyn would tell him could only serve to influence how he felt about himself, his roots, the place from which he'd come. That, regardless of anything else, would inevitably alter tomorrow, next week, the months and years ahead of him. Past became present became future. That simple.

Harper, in no doubt as to his *need* to know, took a last deep breath, gritted his teeth and started walking.

TWENTY-SIX

For a long while Duchaunak stood with his face a few inches from the glass.

Every so often he reached up and rubbed a hole in the condensation created by his breath. He made-believe he was looking at someone he knew nothing about. He quietly watched as they fought against the damage that had been done to the body.

Frank Duchaunak believed that Edward Bernstein was dying. Bernstein was not a quitter, never had been, but what he was battling with had ripped right through him and out the other side. The bullet had come like an invading force – swift, merciless, without the faintest sense of remorse or compunction. *Fuck you*, it said. *Fuck you for getting in the way. Fuck you for being there you . . . you human being!* It had punctured his right lung, broken some ribs, grazed his heart, God only knew what. The doctor had explained each element of the injuries sustained: Duchaunak had stood listening patiently, and though he had understood very little of what he was being told he did understand the final comment the doctor made.

'Not a normal person.'

'What?'

The doctor shrugged, glanced towards the window through which they could both see the still form of Edward Bernstein. 'Not a normal person,' he repeated.

Duchaunak frowned. 'What d'you mean, not a normal person?'

'Normal people don't come away from something like that, especially someone of his age. The caliber, the close range, the internal hemorrhaging . . .' The doctor shook his head. 'Takes a particular kind of individual to come away from that. Remarkable enough that he's still alive after this many days. Tonight it will be five days since he was shot – quite something, believe me – what we have here is quite out of the ordinary.'

Duchaunak had heard that, clear as a bell, and then the doctor had left him alone in the ante-room, his face almost touching the glass, his mind turning over every connection he had made with Edward Bernstein during the previous seven years.

Watching Edward Bernstein die was like witnessing the slow-motion departure of a member of his own family.

Duchaunak smiled. There could only be a handful of years between himself and Harper. Evelyn Sawyer had maintained a lie all these years, telling her own nephew that his father was dead. Harper had never spoken to Bernstein, whereas Duchaunak had talked with the man many times. Ironic, but Duchaunak was perhaps closer to family than Harper himself.

In some small and quiet way he almost resented Harper's appearance so late in the game. He resented whoever had pulled the liquor store robbery. He resented the fact that Bernstein had possessed sufficient nerve to challenge the guy, to scare him into reacting the way he had. More than everything else he resented the fact that the man who had arranged and orchestrated whatever was to occur before Christmas now possessed the perfect alibi. And if the job went down, and if it was successful, and if Edward Bernstein recovered from his injuries and walked away . . . well, wouldn't that have been the perfect crime? The D.A. wouldn't even give Duchaunak the time of day. *You want me to build a case against a man who was in hospital . . . not only in hospital but in Intensive Care suffering a serious and life-threatening gunshot wound as a result of attempting to prevent a liquor store robbery . . . you want me to put a man like that in court and ask a jury to take me seriously . . . Jesus Christ, who do you think we are? In fact, who the hell do you think* you *are? Get the hell outta here and go do something useful with your life!*

Duchaunak shook his head resignedly and glanced at his watch. He figured he would kill for a cigarette.

The Marcus crew was already at the restaurant by the time Freiberg and Cathy Hollander arrived. Freiberg's people came in twos, separate cars, a few minutes apart. Neverthless, had anyone been watching the front of the building it would have seemed strange. Between eleven-forty a.m. and a few minutes past noon, a total of seventeen people arrived. It was too early for the lunchtime traffic and, besides, the Trattoria St Angelo was never that busy, even on a Friday night. But no-one was watching, and thus the event went unnoticed by anyone but those directly involved. Such a meeting was in some small way an historic event. A collaboration between Ben Marcus and Lenny Bernstein – men who'd been neither friends nor enemies for thirty or more years. The last time Marcus and Bernstein had spoken it had been about Cathy Hollander, a wager that had seen the woman traded between them, nothing more than a commodity. Thus there was a degree of tension present when she first saw Ben Marcus and Sol Neumann seated at a table at the far end of the basement room.

Beside Neumann sat Victor Klein, Henry Kossoff, Albert Reiff and Karl Merrett. Beside Marcus were Ray Dietz, Maurice Rydell and Lester McKee. Eight in all, eight familiar faces from such country clubs as Queensboro, Five Points, Green Haven and Attica.

The Bernstein crew were also graduate members of such select establishments: Joe Koenig, Edgecombe and Fulton; Charlie Beck, Altona, and back of them came Larry Benedict, who'd done time at Five Points, Leo Petri – also Altona and Fulton – and finally Ricky Wheland and Ron Dearing. With Walt Freiberg and Cathy Hollander they made up the Bernstein eight. Sixteen crew members, Ben Marcus himself as the prime co-ordinator, a position that should have been held jointly with Lenny Bernstein.

Marcus rose and came forward to greet Walt Freiberg. They shook hands. Marcus nodded politely at Cathy Hollander but didn't speak. There was nothing but business here.

Neumann came behind Marcus and assisted in showing Freiberg and the others to their seats. Glasses and ashtrays were set ahead of each chair, alongside them notepads, pencils, a detailed map of Manhattan's west side, south from Tribeca and all the way north to Chelsea.

The atmosphere in the room was awkward, but Freiberg and Ben Marcus sat at the head of their respective tables, and when Marcus rose to speak he seemed at ease. The Bernstein crew took this as a sanction from Freiberg that Marcus would lead the discussion.

'On the one hand,' Marcus started, 'this is a difficult time, but I have always been a man to look towards the optimistic angle of any situation I am faced with.' He glanced at Freiberg. 'Despite whatever differences I may have had with Lenny Bernstein, there has never been a shortage of respect. We have had our common enemies, and we have had our common aspirations. It has been said that in order to have a challenge one must choose a worthy opponent, and let me be the first to say that Lenny Bernstein, if nothing else, has always been a worthy opponent. His absence here is evident, and if he should fail to recover from this recent and terrible situation that has befallen him, then I shall be the first one to grieve for him. Lenny Bernstein is a fighter, and I trust that he will come through this.'

Marcus paused. He reached for a glass of water and took a sip.

'As you are all now aware, before this terrible accident Lenny and I had a meeting. We discussed the possibility of both our crews working together as a precursor to Lenny moving out of New York, retiring if you like, and the assumption of territorial control by myself. New York is not the place we remember. The city has lost its culture and its heritage. You look anyplace in New York you'll find the blacks and the Spanish. They deal crack and such things. They whore their sisters out. Then we have the Eastern Europeans, speaking languages none of us can under-stand. Ed Koch was bad enough, Guiliani was a nightmare, and this guy Bloomberg? The truth is that I don't know where the hell they got this guy from. Lenny felt his time to retire had come. That was the truth. I believed this was a good opportunity for all of us. Lenny came to me with his proposal, and though there were no specific details forwarded, we nevertheless both felt that such an agreement would work.'

Marcus turned towards his own crew. 'We took a vote, and we decided unanimously that we would respect Lenny Bernstein's proposal . . . and in discussion with Walt Freiberg here it has in fact been concluded that we will carry forward with this idea. That is the reason behind our meeting today.'

Marcus looked at Walt Freiberg. 'Walt, is there anything you would like to say?'

Freiberg smiled, rose to his feet. 'Ben here has given you the reason we're here. He's also had one of his own people, Victor

Klein—' Freiberg looked at Klein and nodded in acknowledgement. 'Ben has had Victor work on some preliminary ideas for something that we are looking to initiate on Christmas Eve—'

'Christmas Eve?' Karl Merrett asked. 'Jesus, Walt, that's a week from now.'

'A week, yes,' Freiberg replied. 'We're not talking safecracking or bearer bonds, nothing complex . . . we're talking a straightforward armed robbery . . . or, rather, *robberies*. We're looking at four teams of four men, three mechanics and a driver, in and out, very limited internal co-operation required. It will be a number of armed offensives against selected targets, and from start to finish each one should take no more than thirty minutes.'

'You say robberies,' Charlie Beck asked. 'How many are we talking here?'

Freiberg glanced at Marcus. Marcus nodded. 'There will be four, each offensive co-ordinated to begin at the same time precisely. Four different locations, four different crews, a total haul expected to clear twelve or thirteen million dollars.'

'With no internal co-operation, right?' Henry Kossoff asked.

Marcus cleared his throat. 'The internal co-operation, Henry, as is usually the case in such matters, will be the unwillingness of your average citizen to risk his life for someone else's money. We have names of people within each site, and these people have whatever access codes we need. Like I said, it's not going to be a complicated business.'

'And the teams are going to stay within their own crews?' Joe Koenig asked.

Marcus shook his head. 'Two from each crew in each team. This is going to be a joint operation . . . split teams, split proceeds above and beyond the required amount for the purchase of Lenny's territory and connections.'

'We're buying Lenny Bernstein's territory out of the proceeds?' Karl Merrett asked.

'We are indeed. Seven and a half million dollars,' Marcus replied.

'Seems to me there's some issues here,' Lester McKee said. 'Not to throw anyone a curve, but is it entirely necessary for us to pull four actions simultaneously to raise this money?'

Freiberg laughed. 'If you have seven and a half million dollars

Lester, then I think we'd all be interested to know what line of work you're in.'

The gathered crews laughed. It seemed to ease the tension slightly.

Freiberg glanced at Marcus. Marcus nodded.

'The reason we're doing it this way is because of Lenny Bernstein,' Freiberg said. 'We looked at the possibility of doing some work with Mr Marcus . . . we discussed this idea and we were all taken with it. Yes, of course, there could be some other way to raise seven and a half million dollars, but why the hell write a check when you can use someone else's credit?'

Once again there was a smattering of laughter.

'It is what it is,' Freiberg said. 'We make this thing work then seven and a half million goes to Lenny, the rest is divided between you guys. Everyone wins on this thing. We get enough to go our own ways and do whatever the hell we want to do, and you people end up with most of Manhattan to play with.'

'We're here,' Marcus said, 'to look at the ideas Victor has put together. Anyone has a problem with this they can speak with their own people once this meeting is done and replacements can be worked out. I'm going to have some words with Walter here, and Victor is going to bring up some pictures and maps and tell you what he's been working on.'

Victor Klein rose and moved to the front of the room. He had Sol Neumann help him drag an A-board to the edge of the table, upon which was an enlarged version of the map that sat ahead of every chair.

'Some of you Bernstein guys know me,' Klein said. 'I did some time at Attica and Green Haven . . . know Walt from Attica, Charlie Beck here from the Haven . . . and Cathy I know too. Some of you others may have heard of me. Anyways, what we have here is an outline for four sites I've been working over. East Coast Mercantile and Savings on West Twelfth,' – he pointed to a spot on the map – 'American Investment and Loan on Bethune and Greenwich. Next we have New York Providence on West Ninth and Washington. Finally, Associated Union Finance on West Broadway . . .'

Marcus took Walt Freiberg by the arm and steered him away from the table. They walked to the back of the room together.

'There's going to be some things I need to do Walter,' Ben Marcus started.

'Things?'

'I need to address a couple of issues . . . kind of delicate to speak about before the whole crew. People know people. People have a drink and say things out of turn, not because they mean to, but because it comes into their minds and they don't have a hold on their tongues, right?'

Freiberg nodded.

'So, like I say, there's a couple of details I'm going to want to iron out in the process of putting this thing together.'

'How many exactly?' Freiberg asked.

'Two right now, perhaps three.'

'People I know?'

Marcus smiled. 'Who *don't* we know Walt . . . tell me who *don't* we know?'

'You going to give me some names?'

'I'm going to give you Levin and Hoy.'

Freiberg shook his head. 'And maybe I'm going to want to do a little housecleaning myself before we move out, so if we're going to clean up our details then there has to be a little give and take, right?'

Marcus nodded. 'Right, sure there does. Do me the courtesy of letting me know if it's someone on my payroll directly, would you?'

'Of course Ben, of course.'

Marcus reached out a hand and they shook.

'Good,' Marcus said. 'That's good.'

'So we go back and see what your man Klein has put together?'

'Of course,' Ben Marcus said.

And the two men made their way back to the table.

TWENTY-SEVEN

It was ten after two.

Harper stood at the end of Carmine Street. He felt transparent, insubstantial. He felt like the child he'd once been, but with something missing. His innocence? His fundamental belief in the goodness of people? His intuition, his trust in humanity, his vision for the future, his dreams? He closed his eyes for a moment. So many things were missing. And where had they gone? He'd been unaware of their absence until now. Why was it always at the point where nothing could be done that one realized some action was needed?

He started walking, mouthing the house numbers to himself, his lips moving silently like a child learning to read.

Someone sees me they're going to call the cops, he thought to himself, and then he imagined what he would do if he were witness to his passage. Hometown boy made good, back to visit the folks, back to show them how leaving had been the reason for his success.

Without realizing it, he had reached Evelyn's house, the place of his introduction to the world. He stood there for some time. He tried to remember what his mother had looked like but, as with so many times before, he struggled to find even a vague resemblance. He could recall vividly how Evelyn had looked thirty years before, even Garrett with his ruddy face, his penetrative eyes, but his own mother . . . ?

Harper looked to his left down the street. He looked up at the house. He wondered if Evelyn was inside watching him.

He went up the steps, raised his hand to the knocker. His heart thumped in his chest.

Five, six minutes later he resigned himself to the fact that she was not home. He had knocked a dozen times, stood patiently waiting for the slightest sound from within, even leaned down and looked through the keyhole. There was nothing.

From his pocket he took the brown paper bag, unwrapped it, withdrew the book. He opened the front cover and turned to the title page. From his inside jacket pocket he took a pen.

For Evelyn, he wrote, his hand unsteady as he did so. *Thank you for everything. Much love, John.*

He closed the book. He leaned once more and pushed it through the letter flap. He heard it land on the hallway floor within.

He stood there for a few moments more, then turned and went down the steps to the sidewalk. He walked to the junction of Bedford, crossed over onto Seventh and headed north-east towards St Vincent's. He became aware after a little while that everything looked different. At first he believed New York had changed, but it had not. His absence had been not only temporary, but irrelevant. Evelyn was right: once you were born here it was inside you. No matter how far you walked, no matter the direction, you took the city with you, and being part of itself it would always draw you back. Like mercury.

By the time he reached Sheridan Square it had begun snowing. It was the eighteenth of December, a week until Christmas.

Later, much later.

Cathy Hollander stood at the window of her apartment on East Fourth. Through the front window she could see the side of the Russian Orthodox Cathedral. She found it ironic that she was surrounded by religious buildings – six churches within as many blocks. Ironic, not because she was without any personal religious beliefs, but because her life had taken such a seemingly contradictory direction. But then wasn't religion merely a set of ideas or beliefs? If that was the case then she was perhaps the most religious person she knew. She had some very definite ideas, and back of those some very specific beliefs. She believed that Edward Bernstein would die, and for this she felt some sense of loss. Regardless of his life, regardless of all that he had done, she understood an aspect of his character that appeared unknown to the world. In the months since she'd met him he'd spoken of his son – a son unaware of his existence – on many, many occasions. The depth of regret had been evident in

Bernstein's expression each time he'd spoken of John Michael Harper. Such bitter irony. In the past few days John Harper had discovered that he did indeed have a father, and the father – the one who had longed to speak with his son – was unaware of Harper's presence. Was that not the cruellest trick to be played by God?

And Harper himself? Cathy believed that he would die as well. Why? Because he was there. No other reason. John Harper had walked himself right into the middle of something he could never hope to understand. He would be used, played, maneuvered, and then – perhaps in the very moment he truly understood what was happening – he would probably be murdered. Such was the way of the world it seemed. Certainly the world that she herself was part of; a world off its axis and spinning ever faster into darkness.

She sighed. She shook her head. She turned away from the window, away from the impressive facade of the Russian Orthodox Cathedral, and from a bottle on the mantel she refilled her glass. She walked through to the small kitchen and sat at the table. She looked around the walls, at the few pictures tacked to the front of the refrigerator, a dying plant in a wickerwork pot near the sink, a trash bin that contained nothing more than several weeks' worth of empty cigarette packets. This was her life. For now at least. Nothing more nor less than this. She wondered what her own mother and father would say if they were still alive. She closed her eyes, imagined them standing in the doorway looking at her, felt the tension within; the threat of tears behind her eyelids. She opened her eyes. She raised the glass to her lips, swallowed the inch and a half of whisky, set the glass on the table and rose.

From the bedroom she took her coat, stood for a moment looking down at the unmade bed, and tried to remember the last time she'd slept in it. She could not. Seemed that each day folded seamlessly into the next, and there were no divisions in between. She stepped back, turned, crossed the front room and opened the apartment door. Once outside she locked it securely, not because there was any great necessity for security, but merely out of habit. Had someone broken in they would have believed no-one lived there, or that someone had left several months before and didn't plan to return. The refrigerator was empty, as were the drawers, the cupboards; nothing more than a single cardboard box beneath the window, containing a handful of tee-shirts, some underwear, a clean blouse, an unworn pair of shoes. Such articles, such characterless and insignificant articles, were representative of Cathy Hollander's life. She took the stairs down, and as she walked away from the few things that represented herself she understood that this was the person she had become, and having become this person she could never be herself again.

Cathy Hollander.

'. . . is not her real name.'

'Did you follow me here or what? Did you follow me here to tell me whatever you're telling me?'

Duchaunak smiled. 'I didn't follow you, no.'

'I came yesterday. You were here. I come today—'

'And here I am again.' Duchaunak raised his right hand and massaged the back of his neck.

Harper frowned. He stood for a moment looking down the corridor over the detective's shoulder. Ten minutes was all he could take; ten minutes standing and watching the old man through the glass. Then he'd turned away and left, intending to go get something to eat, and found Duchaunak in the corridor. Like the man had followed him, perhaps waited outside for him to arrive, and then come right on in to piss him off.

'You waited outside and then followed me in here?'

Duchaunak shook his head. 'I came to see Lenny—'

'Why the fuck are you calling him that? Lenny? What the fuck is that? His name is Edward Bernstein, right? Edward fucking Bernstein, not Lenny—'

'It's his nickname—'

'I don't give a fuck what it is. It's not his *name* okay? Not his proper fucking name. If you're going to talk about him then at least use his proper fucking name eh?'

'You're upset, Mr Harper—'

'Oh fuck off, I'm upset. What the fuck would you know? I don't even know why you're here—'

'Because I've spent much of the past seven years following that man, and I want to know what happens to him.'

Harper stood motionless. He felt anger welling inside him. He clenched his fists and stared at Duchaunak.

Duchaunak raised his hands. 'This isn't a confrontation, Mr Harper.'

'Get the fuck out of here.'

Duchaunak lowered his hands and smiled. 'I can see that you're having difficulty with this.'

'I said get the fuck out of here, Detective . . . you have no right coming here and saying these things to me.'

'And your father has no right stealing money from people and killing—'

Harper started towards him, raised his fist, looked like he was going to let fly at Duchaunak.

Duchaunak backed up, tried to turn, seemed to lose his balance and leaned against the wall.

Harper reached Duchaunak before he had a chance to gather himself, raised his hand and gripped his coat lapel. 'Just get the fuck away from me!' he snapped, the anger and frustration evident in his voice. 'Go away! Leave me the fuck alone!'

Duchaunak twisted away from Harper, and then suddenly twisted back. Harper's grip was lost, and Duchaunak ducked sideways and tried to push Harper away.

Harper, incensed beyond anything he'd felt before, raised his fist again and took a swing at Duchaunak.

Duchaunak ducked but Harper's fist caught his shoulder and sent him sprawling to the ground with some force.

Harper stepped back, stopped dead, looked down at Duchaunak and realized what he'd done.

Duchaunak didn't speak. He looked embarrassed.

Harper turned and started to walk away.

'I'm not here to harass you, Mr Harper,' Duchaunak said as he started to get up.

Harper slowed and turned. 'Leave me alone.'

'I will,' Duchaunak said. 'I will leave you alone, but you have to understand that I'm here to help you with this . . . I'm not trying to make this thing any worse than it already is.' Duchaunak was on his feet, brushing down his clothes.

'What the fuck do you want with me?' Harper asked. 'Really?'

Duchaunak shook his head, straightened his tie. 'I came here to see what I could do.'

Harper didn't reply.

'And I came here to see whether you took my advice.'

Harper shook his head. 'I didn't go back to Miami, Detective.'

'I can see that Mr Harper.'

'And this thing with Cathy Hollander? What the fuck is that?'

'Cathy Hollander isn't her real name.'

Harper nodded. 'Is that so?'

'It is.'

'And what *is* her real name?'

Duchaunak looked directly at Harper. His gaze was unflinching. 'I don't know.'

'Maybe it's Cathy Hollander.'

'It's not.'

'How can you be so sure?'

'Because there is no-one called Cathy Hollander anywhere in New York who looks like her.'

Harper laughed awkwardly. 'Maybe she came from somewhere outside New York.'

'She has no Social Security number, Mr Harper. She has no job, no car, nothing registered in her name except the hotel room you happen to be staying in—'

'You're checking up on me—'

'No, I'm checking up on Walt Freiberg and Cathy Hollander, and you just happen to be on the edges of this thing because of your association with them.'

'And now it's a felony to use another name?'

'No, Mr Harper, it's not a felony to use another name. I'm not interested in her because she uses an alias.'

'You're interested in her because?'

'Because she's spent the better part of the last six months living with your father, and now she spends all her time with Walt Freiberg as far as I can tell, and before she met your father she used to hang around with Ben Marcus, and anyone who has anything at all to do with Ben Marcus becomes a subject of intense curiosity for me almost immediately.'

Harper was silent for a few moments. He turned away, unable to hold Duchaunak's gaze. When he looked back at the man he realized how utterly exhausted Duchaunak looked.

'You look like you have ghosts following you, Detective . . . like a man on the verge of a nervous breakdown.'

Duchaunak smiled, his expression almost sardonic. 'My captain, he says that.'

'Maybe you should take some leave,' Harper said. 'Did he suggest that?'

'No, he didn't . . . he told me to leave Len—to leave Edward Bernstein alone.'

'But you don't pay any mind to what people tell you?'

Duchaunak shook his head. 'Not when it comes to Edward Bernstein, Walt Freiberg and the Marcus crew.'

'The Marcus crew?'

'Ben Marcus, Sol Neumann, the other people who work for them.'

'And these people are what, Detective?'

'Some of the worst people New York has to offer.'

'Is that so?'

Duchaunak frowned, tilted his head to one side. 'You ask me that question . . . why d'you ask me that question like that?'

'What question?'

'When you say that . . . is that so? You say "Is that so?" like you're challenging me, like you don't believe a word I'm saying.'

'I wouldn't say that I didn't believe a word you're saying,' Harper replied. 'I believe some words, I don't believe others.'

'What don't you believe, Mr Harper?'

Harper smiled. He shrugged his shoulders. 'I don't know what I believe, Detective. And with just as much certainty I don't know what I *don't* believe—'

'Now you're beginning to sound like a true New Yorker . . . obscure, Mr Harper, very obscure.'

'So what are you here to tell me? You've come to tell me to go back to Miami again?'

Duchaunak put his hands in his pockets. He looked down at his shoes, seemed to notice something, and then proceeded to clean the upper part of his right shoe against the back of his left leg. He inspected his shoe once more and then looked up at Harper once more.

'Let's go get some coffee, Mr Harper. Let's get out of here and just go get a cup of coffee someplace, eh?'

'And you will tell me what the fuck is going on here?'

Duchaunak nodded. 'Yes, Mr Harper, I'll tell you what's going on here.'

185

'For real this time . . . not this back and forth bullshit okay? I go someplace with you, we sit down and you give me some straight answers about all these things.'

'Okay, Mr Harper.'

'Okay.'

Duchaunak turned and started walking.

Harper, glancing once more over his shoulder in the direction of his father, followed him.

TWENTY-EIGHT

Jessica McCaffrey had made it out of the lower east side of New York and into college with nothing but sheer determination and a big heart. Just as her brother Darryl believed he could help the community with his social work, so Jessica possessed a vocation to nurse. Strictly speaking she should have wound up a hooker, maybe a crack mule, but she kept it together despite losing parents, despite her brother Thomas edging ever closer to the kind of people she'd sworn she would never associate with. There was a point, a few years before, where she believed she could have saved Thomas from his own irresponsibility and greed, but Thomas didn't walk with the Lord, Thomas didn't see eye to eye with Jesus, and though she had pleaded with him to let God into his heart she had not succeeded.

So she studied, she worked two jobs, she sat exams, she graduated, and in November of the previous year she'd been selected to serve her internship at St Clare's in the theater district, right there on West Fifty-first, half a dozen blocks away from Carnegie Hall.

When the two men appeared at the front door of Jessica McCaffrey's house, a house she shared with a fellow nurse called Cassandra Wilson, she at first believed they might be police. A couple of times detectives had arrived to speak with her about Thomas's whereabouts, and when they greeted her, smiled politely, told her they wanted to ask some questions about him, she wondered what trouble he had gotten himself into this time.

She did not yet know, and would not know until Raymond Dietz told her, that her older brother, Darryl, was already dead.

The men came into the house – not because she allowed them, but because they were a great deal stronger than she. One of them, a heavy-set man with penetrating eyes; a man who later said his name was Albert, held a gun in his hand. She'd seen such a gun before. It was a .38 caliber revolver.

Once inside Albert searched the house and confirmed that no-one else was there.

Raymond Dietz sat Jessica McCaffrey down in the kitchen, sat right across from her at the plain deal table, and told her that they needed to speak with Thomas.

Jessica McCaffrey – unafraid to cry, believing that Jesus was truly on her side and thus all that happened was His will, that God moved in mysterious ways, that there was a sense of balance and divine justice in all things – told Raymond and Albert that she had not seen Thomas for more than a year.

She told them the truth; it did not, however, appear to satisfy them.

Even when Raymond held her right hand flat on the surface, even when Albert used the handle of the .38 to break two, perhaps three of her fingers, she continued to assert that she knew nothing of Thomas's whereabouts.

After another series of unresolved questions, Albert took her right arm by the wrist, and raising her hand above shoulder level he brought her elbow down swiftly onto the surface of the table. The elbow and much of her radius shattered in several places.

Jessica McCaffrey remained conscious only long enough to tell them that once more she did not know where her brother was.

Finally, seemingly satisfied that she was telling the truth, Ray Dietz and Albert Reiff left the house through the back door.

They left nothing – no fingerprints, no hairs, no physical indication of their visit.

They left nothing with Jessica McCaffrey, nothing but a vacant stare and a .38 caliber rose centering her forehead.

Three blocks north-east. Man standing on the junction of West Fifteenth and Seventh. Cursing the snow which now falls with some sense of purpose. Pulls his overcoat collar up around his neck. Curses the latecomer who was supposed to meet him there fifteen minutes before. Bag he carries is heavy despite its minimal size. Brown paper bag, like a grocery kind of thing, but inside there are three .38s, a box of Glaser Safety shells, two cartons of double-aught shot. Kind of bag you don't want someone to look inside unless they're the buyer.

Looks at his watch. Curses again. And then he sees his mark, standing there on the facing corner. Relieved. Can't wait to hurry back inside and get some coffee, smoke a cigarette.

Waits patiently until the traffic clears. Buyer hurries across towards him, hands in his pockets, and only when the buyer is within ten or twelve feet does he recognize him: Micky Levin.

'Micky?' the seller asks.

Micky frowns, shakes his head. *You don't know me, don't know my name*, that gesture says.

The seller is having second thoughts. If Micky Levin is buying then Micky Levin isn't *really* buying. Micky Levin never bought anything for himself in his life. He's a carrier, a gopher, a hired hand, a runner, a small-timer with high hopes and flexible loyalties. He'll never be anything but someone's boy.

'Everything?' Micky asks.

The seller nods. 'Everything,' he says.

'Do I need to check it?'

The seller's eyes widen. 'When did you ever need to check anything from me?'

Micky smiles. 'I didn't.'

'So we're good then?'

Micky shrugs. 'I have to check . . . you understand this isn't my gear, right? I'm just fetchin' an' carryin', you know what I mean?'

The seller nods. 'I know what you mean.'

'And this is a taster, right? This stuff is good then we're gonna need one helluva lot more. You make good on this and there's a lot of money gonna change hands.'

The seller nods, his mouth turned down at the edges thoughfully. 'So you're in on something—'

'Hey, you know better than that,' Levin says.

The seller is irritated. Micky Levin is a two-bit piece of shit. He doesn't have the right to share the same sidewalk, let alone speak like he's hit the big time.

Levin shakes his head. 'I ain't got nothing. I ain't into anything, you get me?'

Seller wants to slap Micky down the street and west three blocks, but he minds his fists and his mouth. Needs the trade.

'Back there,' Micky says, and indicates an alleyway fifteen or twenty feet down the sidewalk.

'I'm walking,' the seller says, and turns, starts in that direction, and Micky's following on behind him, glancing back towards the other side of the street.

The seller pauses at the entrance to the alley, glances back at Micky who is three or four steps behind him, and then turns and walks right on down there.

Micky slows up. He turns and heads back the way he's come. He waits on the sidewalk, blocks the alleyway from view with his body, and when two or three minutes have passed he backs into the darkness, turns, and hurries down there to the fence at the end.

The seller – a wiseass, no-good, two-faced motherfucker called Johnnie Hoy – sits against the fence, hands in his lap, snow turning him pale grey, face kind of pushed in to one side, switchblade jutting awkwardly from his right eye, left eye open and staring, expression kind of surprised but at the same time resigned to the fact that if he was going to go then it would be in such a way as this. People like Johnnie Hoy didn't die of coronaries or strokes or diabetes or cancer; people like Johnnie Hoy were shot in the forehead or garrotted, stuck in the neck with a shiv down in Fulton Pen., or they took a long drop with a short rope off a fire escape someplace in Brooklyn Heights. It was part of the life, part of the world within which he had lived, the same world which now had killed him.

'Cocksucker,' Micky Levin says. It's almost a whisper, nothing more than that. And then he takes one step forward and lets fly with an almighty kick to Johnnie Hoy's head. The sound of the vertebrae shattering in his neck is like a firecracker. Blood jettisons across the toe of Levin's shoe.

Micky leans down and picks up the paper bag. Looks inside. Three .38s, a box of Glaser Safety shells, two cartons of double-aught shot. Bundles the top of the bag tight, tucks it under his arm.

'Sol?' Levin asks.

Sol Neumann steps from the back right-hand corner of the alleyway.

'So we're good?'

Neumann nods, clears his throat. 'Good enough.'

Levin buries his hands in his overcoat pockets. 'Cold as fuck,' he says.

190

'Get outta here, go home,' Neumann says, and nods his head towards the street-end of the alley.

'I'm gone,' Levin says, and starts walking.

'Hey.'

Levin turns back towards Neumann.

'You keep your ears and eyes open for any sign of this McCaffrey guy, right?'

Levin shakes his head. 'It's all I hear about Sol. McCaffrey, McCaffrey . . . Jesus, who the fuck *is* this loser?'

'He ain't no-one,' Sol Neumann replies.

Levin smiles. 'For someone who's no-one he sure seems to have pissed off a lot of people.'

Neumann raises his hand. 'Enough already. Do what you're asked. Keep your eyes and ears open, okay?'

'Right, right. McCaffrey.'

'Thomas McCaffrey. Black guy. You hear anything you let me know.'

'Sure thing Sol, sure thing.' Levin turns and starts to walk away. Tiny drops of blood remain at the toe of each footstep, stark red against the snow.

Sol Neumann stands for a moment and watches until Levin has vanished out into the street. He lifts his left foot and places it against Johnnie Hoy's chest. With his right hand he tugs the knife free, wipes it on Johnnie's coat, and then folds it up. 'Fucked you up, eh?' Neumann says. 'Dumbass piece of shit you are, so help me God.' He pauses a second more, looks down at the collapsed form of the man against the fence, the blood covering his cheek, running down his neck, the way the snowflakes touch it and dissolve instantly. By the time someone finds him they'll have to defrost the asshole.

Neumann puts the switchblade in his pocket. He backs up one, two, three steps, and then he turns and hurries out onto West Fifteenth. The snow comes down faster as he walks. The mess of footprints in the alleyway will be gone within seconds. The lights from the storefronts reflect back at him. The feeling of Christmas is in the air, and Sol Neumann believes this Christmas will be one he remembers.

He is right. Johnnie Hoy will not be found until late the following morning. By the time they get to identifying him word will already be out that Johnnie was out of the show for keeps, wouldn't be clearing his tabs or making good at the track. Easy come, easy go.

Sol Neumann heads back towards the Fourteenth Street subway station. He takes a train, stays on all the way down through West Village to Canal Street, walks back up Sixth to a small Cantonese restaurant. Inside it is warm, a welcome respite from the snow and bitter wind. He removes his overcoat, nods at the waiter, and then goes to the rear of the restaurant. He takes a chair facing Ben Marcus.

Ben Marcus looks up, raises an eyebrow. 'Mr Hoy won't be joining us?'

Neumann shakes his head. 'He couldn't make it.'

'A shame . . . the char sui bun is very good indeed.'

Neumann smiles. 'Another time perhaps.'

'And McCaffrey?'

Neumann shakes his head. 'Marie fucking Celeste.'

Marcus is quiet for a moment, and then leans forward, his voice hushed. 'I said I wanted him found, Sol. I meant just that. I need him found within hours, not days. Tell your guys that the man who finds him is in for a twenty-five bonus.'

'Ben—'

Marcus shakes his head. 'I don't want a discussion. I want McCaffrey. Twenty-five grand to the man who finds him.'

Neumann doesn't reply.

Marcus reaches for a bottle of sake and then leans back in his chair. 'So we eat,' he says, and then fills glasses for them both.

Sol Neumann smiles, unfolds a napkin. Killing people makes him hungry.

TWENTY-NINE

Southside Johnny and the Asbury Dukes singing 'Love On The Wrong Side Of Town'.

Jukebox back and to the left, like an old Wurlitzer. Coffee shop, quaint but hip, last man standing against the Seattle conglomerates. Tables with red and white-checkered cloths, waitress dressed like some old-time '50s kind of theme. Button-badge said 'Angela'.

'Just straight,' Duchaunak said. 'None of this foam or steamed milk or walnut shavings or anything else . . . just straight coffee with cream and sugar.'

Angela smiled beautifully, like she didn't even have to try and look good, just rolled out of bed like Veronica Lake. She turned to Harper. 'And you, sir?'

'Same again but no sugar.'

'Anything to eat? Cinnamon Danish, Banoffee pie?'

Harper shook his head.

Angela looked at Duchaunak. Duchaunak asked if they did a plain ring donut. They did; he said he'd have one.

She drifted away with a degree of elegance and grace that belonged to a George Petty pin-up, not a coffee shop.

'Pretty girl,' Duchaunak said.

'She is.'

'You're not married?'

Harper shook his head. 'You?'

'No, not married.'

'Ever been?'

'I look like the marrying kind to you?'

Harper smiled. 'I know some girls that don't give a rat's ass what a man looks like.'

'The kind of girl you pay for, right?'

'No, not the kind of girl you pay for. What do you take me for?

I don't mean that kind of girl . . . I mean the kind that's looking for a husband because the idea of having a husband and raising a family is more important than what the guy might look like.'

'I don't know any girls like that, and besides I'm not the marrying kind.'

'How come?'

Duchaunak smiled wryly. 'Cops are like nuns. They marry the lifestyle, the job. If they're fortunate enough to find a girl who'll put up with being second best all the time then good luck to them. I sure as hell haven't seen a great number of my colleagues make a success of that kind of life.'

Angela returned. She set the cups on the table. A jug of cream, a bowl filled with sachets of sugar, some brown, some white.

Harper looked up at her. She was a very attractive woman; made him think of Cathy Hollander, wondered where she was, what she was doing.

Southside Johnny faded. Tom Waits started up with 'The Ghosts Of Saturday Night'.

Duchaunak was sorting through the bowl of sugar sachets. He took out one of each, brown and white, and laid them side by side near his coffee cup. He went through a little ritual, picking up a sachet, holding it by the upper edge, flicking it so the sugar settled to the bottom. He tore the top, emptied half the sachet into his cup, and then folded it over neatly and put it on the table. Took a spoon and stirred his coffee – clockwise twice, anti-clockwise three times. He did the same with the second sachet – flick, tear, pour, fold, stir – and then he took the first sachet, unfolded the top and emptied the remainder in his cup.

'What the fuck is that?' Harper asked.

Duchaunak looked up. 'What?' He glanced around the room as if there was something to see.

'That shit with the sugar sachets.'

Duchaunak frowned.

'The thing with opening them and putting half in your cup, and then this stirring routine . . . what the fuck are you doing?'

'Er . . . it's nothing . . . just a thing I do . . . like for good luck, you know?'

Harper shook his head, his eyes squinted. 'You what?'

'It's nothing. It's just a thing I do. Half and half, brown and white sugar.'

194

'What's the fucking matter with you? You got OCD or something?'

'OC what?'

'OCD. Obsessive-Compulsive Disorder. You know, like people who have to turn the lights on and off five times before they can go to sleep. That kind of shit.'

'No, I haven't got OCD.'

'Then what the hell're you doing all that for?'

Duchaunak looked up at him. 'Don't make something out of nothing—'

'You're the one who's making something out of nothing . . . all that opening sugar sachets and closing them up again for good luck. What normal person does that kind of thing?'

'The company you're keeping I don't think you have any right to be making judgements on who's normal and who's not.'

'Meaning?'

'Meaning that you got yourself into something deeper than—' Duchaunak shook his head. 'Christ, I don't know, I can't even think of a suitable metaphor for the depth of shit you're in.'

'So give me a clue.'

Duchaunak leaned back and sighed. 'You ever seen *The Godfather*?'

'Which one? It's a trilogy.'

'Ah fuck, I don't know. I only ever saw one of them.'

Harper smiled. 'Then you're missing a great deal. You should go rent out all three of them and watch them back-to-back. Lot of people have an opinion about the third one—'

Duchaunak raised his hand. 'I didn't come here to talk about Godfather movies.'

'You asked me if I'd seen the movie, right? You started this thing about *The Godfather*.'

'I know I did. Hey, I'm sorry. Let's back up a minute and start over.'

'Sure, whatever you say.'

'Right. Okay. So you seen some gangster movies.'

Harper nodded. 'I've seen some gangster movies.'

'So you know that people like that . . . well, people like that, they steal and kill one another and all that kind of thing.'

'Sure they do. That's what being a gangster is all about. That's their job, isn't it?'

195

'So that's who you're dealing with right now.'

Harper didn't reply.

'You understand what I'm telling you, Mr Harper? The people you are associating with . . . Walt Freiberg, Cathy Hollander, yes?'

'They're gangsters . . . like in *The Godfather*. Gangsters like in the movies, right?'

Duchaunak smiled, then turned his mouth down at the edges. 'Gangsters, hell I don't know. *The Godfather*? It was just what came to mind. I was simply trying to give you a point of reference.'

'A point of reference? Marlon Brando or Al Pacino? Or maybe Andy Garcia, eh? And Cathy Hollander? Is she more like Talia Shire or Diane Keaton?'

'You're missing the point, Mr Harper—'

'The point? What point would that be, Detective? You come down here and run this same crap on me? What the hell is it with you?'

'I'm doing my job—'

'I don't understand how this can be part of your job.'

Duchaunak leaned forward. He placed his hands flat on the table. 'My job, Mr Harper, is to stop people breaking the law—'

'And you're here right now, right here in this coffee shop with me, on *official* business, yes?'

Duchaunak paused, looked awkward.

Harper slid his coffee cup out of the way and leaned forward. 'On official business, Detective, working on a case, an active case supported by your department, authorized by your precinct captain, and I am in some way directly or indirectly involved in an ongoing police investigation—'

Duchaunak gestured stop.

Harper fell silent.

The detective reached for his coffee cup. He drank some, set it down, pulled his jacket together and buttoned it in the middle. He started to rise from his chair.

'What the fuck are you doing now?' Harper asked. 'You going to go to the bathroom three times before you can drink any more coffee?'

'I'm sorry to have wasted your time, Mr Harper—'

'You're not leaving.'

Duchaunak frowned. 'That a question or a statement?'

'A statement,' Harper replied. 'Sit the fuck down for Christ's sake. Sit down, drink your goddamned coffee, tell me what the fuck is going on here.'

Duchaunak looked uncertain.

'Sit down,' Harper repeated.

Duchaunak sat down. 'You want to hear what I have to say?'

'No, I don't *want* to hear what you have to say, but I feel like I've got to at least give you the time of day. I've been here . . . what? Four days, give or take? You've been wandering around the edges of whatever the fuck is going on here the whole time. Every visit I make to the hospital you seem to be there. You went to see Evelyn, right? You've either got some weird compulsion playing out here, or there is something going on.'

Duchaunak leaned forward, almost a mirror-image of Harper. 'I don't believe there is something going on,' he said quietly. 'I *know* something is going on.' His tone of voice and body language had taken on the air of something conspiratorial.

'And what is it that you *know* is going on, Detective?'

Duchaunak shook his head. 'Your father . . . your father is a man with a reputation.'

'So I understand.'

'What do you understand?'

Harper shrugged. 'Hell, anyone who has a tailor has to either be loaded or royalty or something, right?'

'His tailor,' Duchaunak stated drily.

'Sure, his tailor. Where the hell d'you think I got the clothes from?'

Duchaunak smiled. 'His tailor . . . right. You mean Lawrence Benedict.'

'Benedict. Mr Benedict. That's him.'

'And Walt Freiberg told you he was your father's tailor?'

'Sure. Didn't only tell me. Took me over there and bought me a load of—'

'Stolen designer suits, right? And before you say anything further, nobody *bought* anybody anything when you went to see Lawrence Benedict. Lawrence Benedict, or Larry as he's known, doesn't sell suits to your father or Walt Freiberg. Larry Benedict

197

runs a business trading stolen designer wear through a store-front, back of which you will find an office where an entirely different business is taking place.'

Harper didn't say a word. He sat looking at Duchaunak with his unwillingness to face the truth struggling to remain intact.

'He runs a chain of illegal bookmakers right from the Lower East Side through Bowery, Little Italy, Tribeca, Soho, and as far north as the Manhattan end of Eighth Avenue. And Larry Benedict works for Lenny Bernstein, the conductor, the composer, whatever the hell he wants to call himself.'

Harper shook his head. 'You're full of crap. I went to see that guy and he was a fucking tailor, okay? He used all this tailor's language and he talked about English shoes and the way European people have their clothes different from us . . . Christ, it was a foreign language.'

'So he knows something about clothes.'

'Sure, he knows a great deal about clothes, he's a tailor—'

'Who's done two stretches in two different penitentiaries for armed robbery, and has been directly or indirectly involved in at least seven additional heists that we know of.'

'Heists? What heists?' Harper shifted uncomfortably in his chair.

'Heists. You know what a heist is, Mr Harper?'

'Sure, it's like a robbery—'

Duchaunak nodded. 'Sure it is, but it has to involve firearms or violence. That's the difference between a straightforward robbery and a heist. A heist is an armed robbery, a robbery where people usually lose their lives as well as their money. That's what a heist is, Mr Harper.'

'And you're telling me that the tailor, Mr Benedict, has been involved in these things?'

'I am.'

Harper was silent for a moment. He looked down at his coffee. It was cooling rapidly, a thin film of skin forming on the top. He felt tight in his lower gut, almost nauseous. He believed his coffee would remain right where it was.

'And Uncle Walt?'

Duchaunak did the knowing smile thing again.

Harper wanted to smack him.

'Uncle Walt?' Duchaunak said. 'Like Uncle Walt Disney,

198

right?' He laughed. 'Your Uncle Walt is possibly the most dangerous of them all.'

'Them all?' Harper asked.

'Yes, of them all. Walt Freiberg, Ben Marcus, Sol Neumann, Micky Levin, Ray Dietz, Johnnie Hoy, Larry Benedict, a few others who you probably haven't heard of yet.'

'And Cathy Hollander?' Harper asked, almost not wanting to ask the question but somehow compelled to.

'Cathy Hollander?' Duchaunak asked. 'Or Diane Sheridan, perhaps Margaret Miller . . . any one of the dozen or more names she's used over the years.'

Harper was wide-eyed and disbelieving.

'Oh yes, indeed,' Duchaunak went on. 'Your Cathy Hollander, sweetheart though she may seem, has been a busy girl over the years. Solicitation, check fraud, false identities; skipped a bail bondsman in Brooklyn Heights on a two-count felony eighteen months ago. Used to spend all her time with Ben Marcus's people, but then she got involved with a scam alongside Larry Benedict, and that's how she met your father.'

Harper frowned.

'She was the runner on a whole mountain of illegal books on a game at the tail end of last season. The Cardinals slaughtered the Mets, both ends of a Sunday doubleheader, and Cathy Hollander, though she wasn't using that name then, was instrumental in ensuring that Larry Benedict kept his show on the road. Rumor has it they turned more than a quarter million dollars on that game alone. That's how she knew your father, and then something happened and she stopped working for Ben Marcus and started working for Edward Bernstein.'

'A quarter million dollars,' Harper said, and even as the words came out of his mouth he was uncertain why he'd said them, didn't even make sense as words, but he was trying to find something as a point of reference.

'You ever seen quarter of a million dollars, Mr Harper?' Duchaunak asked.

Harper shook his head.

'Pocket change.'

'You what?'

Duchaunak smiled the knowing smile. 'To these people a quarter of a million dollars is pocket change. Maybe seven or eight years salary for me. They made it on one lousy Sunday game. You believe that?'

Harper shook his head. He had no idea what he believed.

'So that, Mr Harper, is the kind of thing you've got yourself caught in the middle of—'

'Caught?' Harper exclaimed. His voice sounded awkward, almost as if he was standing over to the right and listening to himself. 'I'm not *caught* in the middle of anything, Detective.'

'You're not?'

Harper shook his head. 'No, I'm here because I wanted to be here.'

'Is that so?'

Harper hesitated.

'Evelyn Sawyer called you, remember? And who was back of Evelyn Sawyer? Walt Freiberg, right? *Uncle* Walt. He was the one who wanted you here. He wanted you here so much that I figure he might have threatened your Aunt Evelyn.'

'Bullshit,' Harper said.

'Maybe not directly, Mr Harper, but Evelyn was the one who said it.'

Harper frowned, shifted in his chair, leaned forward again.

'She said that Walt Freiberg was not the sort of man you defy.'

Harper shook his head. His throat was dry, his mouth like he'd been touching his tongue to the terminals of a battery. He wanted a glass of water.

'You're having a little difficulty with all of this, I understand that,' Duchaunak said. 'It isn't a matter of trust or belief or anything else. I'm not asking you to believe what I say. All I'm asking you to do is open your eyes and look at what's going on around you . . . ask yourself if all of this doesn't seem awful strange. You get a call from Evelyn. She insists you come to New York. When you get here she tells you your father, a father you never knew you had, is not only alive but up in St Vincent's with a potentially fatal gunshot wound. You go over there. You want to see him. You want to find out if the man you thought was dead for the past thirty-something years is in fact alive, is in fact your father, and who do you run into? You find yourself in the company of Walt Freiberg, a man you haven't seen since you were a kid. With him is a girl, this Cathy Hollander, and she's all sweetness and light, friendly as hell, and they look after you, put

200

you in a hotel—' Duchaunak stopped mid-flight. 'Who's paying for the hotel?' he asked suddenly.

Harper looked away towards the window. Felt like his head was a balloon full of smoke.

'Mr Harper?'

Harper looked back at the Detective.

'The hotel? You know who's picking up the tab?'

Harper sighed. 'Walt is . . . well actually, I figure he is. The room was booked under Cathy Hollander's name.'

Duchaunak smiled. 'Walt Freiberg will be paying it then.'

'What makes you so sure?'

'Cathy Hollander never paid for anything in her life.'

Harper closed his eyes. He gritted his teeth. He was silent for a few moments, and then he opened his eyes and looked directly at Duchaunak. 'How do I know what you're telling me is the truth?'

Duchaunak nodded. 'You don't.'

'So what on earth is the fucking point of me sitting here listening to what you have to say?'

'The point?'

'Yes, what is the point of me sitting here listening to something that you cannot substantiate or prove?'

'Because I want you to do just that,' Duchaunak said.

'What?'

'Substantiate and prove everything I'm telling you.'

Harper laughed, more an expulsion of nervousness than a laugh.

'I need your help bringing all of this together,' Duchaunak went on. He leaned back, and as he leaned back Harper realized that the man was perfectly serious.

'You're serious, aren't you?'

Duchaunak nodded. 'I am.'

'You want me to help you . . . help you do what exactly?'

'Something is going to happen, something big I reckon, and from everything I can tell it's going to happen before Christmas. I need your help finding out what it is.'

Harper frowned. 'I don't get it.'

'It isn't rocket science, Mr Harper. These people – Walt Freiberg, Cathy Hollander, whoever else might be involved – they're going to pull some kind of job before Christmas. We don't know what it is, we don't know who else might be involved ... all we know is that it's going to happen, and realistically, facing the fucking music if you like, the only real hope we have of finding out ahead of time is you.'

Harper said nothing in response.

Duchaunak sat motionless, staring right back at him.

'Me,' Harper said eventually. 'The only hope you have is me.'

'Right.'

'Then you have no hope at all.'

'Is that so?'

'That *is* fucking so,' Harper said. 'I didn't come here to work undercover bullshit for the New York police department for Christ's sake. I came here to see my father in St Vincent's after somebody fucking shot him. Don't you figure I've got enough to deal with here considering he's supposed to have been dead for thirty years already.'

'I think—'

'Frankly, Detective, I don't give a rat's ass what you do or do not think. I'm here for as long as I need to be, as long as it takes for him to die, or to come out of ICU and say something to me, and then I'm going all the way back to Miami to pick up where I left off, to come to terms with the fact that my father—'

'Is one of the most highly regarded and successful bankrollers in New York's criminal hierarchy. He funds these things Mr Harper, he puts up the money for these actions, and Christ only knows what he's managed to rake off of the top in payback. Your father is—'

'Dying in St Vincent's, Detective . . . and that's as far as I want to take it.'

'Mr Harper . . . if lying and cheating and robbery and murder are an art then your father is Velazquez.'

Harper frowned. 'You what?'

'Velazquez,' Duchaunak repeated.

'Who the living fuck is that?'

Duchaunak smiled. 'Don't play the fool, Mr Harper.'

'I'm not playing anything, Detective, I don't have a fucking clue what you're talking about. Who is this Velazquez? He's another of these people, another of these criminals my father and Walt Freiberg are supposed to be involved with?'

202

'Velazquez was a painter, a seventeenth-century Spanish painter,' Duchaunak replied.

'Velazquez the painter? Jesus, why the hell didn't you say you were talking about the painter?' Harper's tone was sarcastic and sharp. 'Now . . . hell . . . now it all makes complete sense.'

'I was drawing an analogy, Mr Harper. I think you know exactly what I was saying.'

'You were saying that if murder and robbery and whatever the hell else were an art, then my father was Velazquez, right?'

'Right.'

'And without any ability to prove this, is that slander or libel or both?'

Duchaunak leaned back in his chair. 'What do you think of Cathy Hollander?'

'What do I think of her? I don't think a great deal, Detective.'

'I think she still works for Ben Marcus.'

'And you're telling me this because?'

'Because if Cathy Hollander is still working for Ben Marcus then there is every possibility that some further harm may be done.'

'Further harm? You're saying that this Ben Marcus might have had something to do with the shooting?'

'I don't know.'

'Fuck me, Detective, what the hell is this? For Christ's sake, is there anything that you *do* know?'

'I think there is a power struggle going on.'

'Between?'

'Your father and Ben Marcus . . . and now your father is in St Vincent's I believe there will be a power struggle between Ben Marcus and Walt Freiberg. I think there will be a war over the New York territories. Where two sides want the same thing and in order to get it they go out and start killing one another.'

'I know what a war is, Detective.'

'Well, if you want my opinion, that's what I think is going to happen.' Duchaunak shook his head slowly and leaned back in the chair. 'There's a history here, a long history. The way business has been done in New York for the last twenty or thirty years is changing, and changing fast. This isn't the same city, on the surface or underneath. Used to be that we had to deal with murders and robberies, the usual criminal trade. There were

203

drugs, but not drugs in the quantity we have now. Now there are black gangs, drive-by shootings, Hispanics and Puerto Ricans, even organized crime from Europe, places like the Czech Republic and . . . Christ, only last week we dragged someone in for a killing and he could not speak a word of English. He was Polish. Had to have a translator from the Polish Embassy. You get that? He was here, right here in New York, came into the city on a forged passport and visa just to kill someone who was interfering with a cocaine trade that was being controlled in Warsaw. That's the city we now have. Your father, Walt Freiberg, Ben Marcus . . . these guys are dinosaurs, they're old school. Their time has long since gone. It wouldn't surprise me if they were involved in a war amongst themselves to hang onto the last remnants of their original territories. And I think you're going to find yourself right in the middle of it if you don't leave New York. But then I've told you that a few times already, and you seemed determined not to listen to me.'

Neither of them spoke for a few seconds.

'Your mother,' Duchaunak said.

'What about her?'

'She was Evelyn's sister.'

'Yes, you know that . . . you went and talked to Evelyn, remember?'

'How'd she die?'

Harper felt uncomfortable again, almost as if he was fighting everything that Duchaunak was telling him. His viewpoint would be challenged by something Duchaunak said, he would counter it, undermine it, and before he had time to reassemble his mental defences there was another barrage on its way. Three days before he'd been on his way out to Blackwater Sound. Now he was fencing with a New York police detective.

'She died of pneumonia,' Harper said.

Duchaunak nodded, smiled with his mouth but not his eyes.

'What?'

'Nothing, Mr Harper, nothing at all.'

'Something about my mother? You're implying by your expression that there was something else about my mother's death.'

'I am?'

Harper raised his hand. 'Enough of this,' he said quietly, and then he started to rise from his chair.

Duchaunak reached out, touched his forearm and indicated the chair. 'Sit down, Mr Harper. Sit down and listen to what I have to say.'

'Fuck you,' Harper said. His tone was direct, unwavering.

'Just a minute or two longer . . . a minute or two longer for me to tell you a story, Mr Harper . . . just a little story, okay?'

Harper paused for a moment.

Duchaunak nodded, smiled with some degree of sincerity.

Harper sat down.

'Tell you something about child abductions.' Duchaunak placed his hands palm to palm on the table, and when he spoke he moved his hands as if to emphasize each phrase. 'Child abductions,' he repeated. 'Children being taken from public places. Fairgrounds are good, open-air shows, aquariums, zoos, places like that, right? People go there, usually a man and a woman together, man and a woman who could pass as a couple, in some cases *are* actually a couple. They take clothes, wigs, make-up, all sorts of stuff; things to change the way a kid looks so they can get the kid out of there to a waiting car. One thing never changes, though.' Duchaunak looked up at Harper. His expression was designed to solicit a response.

'What thing?' Harper asked.

'The kid's shoes.'

'The kid's shoes don't change?' Harper asked.

'Right. Place like that these people wouldn't necessarily have a specific child in mind. They'd scope out a likely target, follow them, wait for the parents to be elsewhere, and then the child would be gone in the blink of an eye. They bring clothes, wigs, all sorts of things like I said, but for some reason they don't bring shoes. Could never predict the size of the child's feet, and so they never brought shoes.'

'And?'

'And therefore a kid would go missing, the parents would freak, alert security. Security would close the gates, call the police, parents would be taken to the exits, and everyone would be asked to leave slowly. Parents would stand at the gates and identify the kid by their shoes.'

205

'Okay,' Harper said. 'Okay. Fair enough. Good advice for when I have kids and someone abducts them.'

Duchaunak laughed. 'That was not the point of telling you that.'

'Oh? No? You're sure? I thought you were handing out pearls of wisdom—'

'I told you that for a reason.'

'Okay, good . . . you had me worried for a moment. And what was the reason for telling me this?'

Duchaunak smiled knowingly. '*Vincit omnia veritas.*'

Harper tilted his head to one side. 'And what the fuck does that mean?'

'It's Latin.'

'That's what it means?'

'No, that's the language.'

'So what the fuck does it mean?'

'It means that truth conquers all things. There is always one thing that you cannot hide.'

'Right . . . yes, okay. Thin, a little weak with the connection there, but I get the point.'

'Okay, so you get what I'm saying?'

Harper shrugged. He wondered how close Duchaunak was to the edge. 'And that relates to me . . . how exactly?'

'These people – Walt Freiberg, Cathy Hollander, Larry Benedict, Marcus, Neumann, all of them—'

'My father?'

'Your father too, Mr Harper, very definitely your father. There is a single, simple fact that cannot be hidden despite all the gestures, the suits, the fancy restaurants. There is something here that cannot be avoided.'

'Which is?'

'The truth of who they are. The fact that they've been stealing whatever they've set their hearts on, Mr Harper, stealing like there was no tomorrow.'

Harper and Duchaunak looked at one another in silence.

'And then there's Garrett Sawyer,' Duchaunak eventually said.

Harper shook his head.

'Assaults, two of them. One in June '56, another in October of '74. Possession of an unlicensed weapon in December of 1966. Things like that.'

'Garrett Sawyer shot himself in the head Detective.'

'Did he?'

'What the fuck is this now? Of course he did. I found him for fuck's sake!'

'I figured you did. I'm not questioning the fact that you found him. I'm just questioning whether or not he actually shot himself in the head.'

'You ever see someone who's shot themselves in the head, Detective?'

'As a matter of fact yes, several times, Mr Harper.'

'So you know better than I. It's not exactly something you can mistake for a bad case of the flu, right?'

Duchaunak smiled. 'No, Mr Harper, it's not, but I believe that murder is something that can be relatively easily mistaken for suicide.'

'You're telling me that Garrett Sawyer was murdered?' Harper shifted uncomfortably in his chair.

Duchaunak didn't reply, merely sat there looking back at Harper.

Harper felt his heart beating in his chest a little faster, felt agitation and emotional disturbance. 'Now I figure you've said enough,' he said quietly, and as the words left his lips he rose once more, stood with determination. 'I am gone.' He took the cashmere overcoat from the back of his chair and put it on. 'Even now I am walking away from here, leaving this coffee shop, calling a cab and going back to my hotel.'

'Cathy Hollander,' Duchaunak said. 'Or Diane Sheridan, or Margaret Miller?'

Harper closed his eyes, breathed deeply. 'You . . . you are a sad and difficult person, Detective. You need some help. Some kind of professional help. Is there no service that's provided with your line of work, someone you could talk to, someone that could help you make sense of this madness?'

'No, Mr Harper, there isn't.'

'No kind of health plan you subscribe to?'

'Humor ever the last line of defence, eh?'

'I'm not smiling, Detective.'

'Go speak to Evelyn.'

'Evelyn? What the hell would I want to go speak with Evelyn for?'

'The truth. The one thing that they cannot hide. Ask her about your mother. Ask her how your mother died, Mr Harper . . . ask her to tell you the truth about what really happened twelfth of October 1975. Tell her you spoke with Frank Duchaunak and he told you to ask her how Anne Harper was just like Marilyn Monroe. You go ask her about that and see what she says.'

Harper raised his hands. 'I'm leaving.'

'That's what I want you to do. If you're not going to help me get these people, then I want you to go back to Miami as fast as you can.'

'So, I'm leaving right now. Something we can agree upon, okay?'

'You know what I mean. Leave New York, Mr Harper . . . just for a little while, just 'til after the New Year. I'll keep you posted, I'll let you know what happens with your father, but for God's sake leave New York—'

Harper turned and started walking. Ten, twelve feet from the table he heard the feet of Duchaunak's chair scraping on the floor as he rose.

'Leave the city, Mr Harper!' Duchaunak called after him. 'Trust me, you need to leave the city!'

Harper shoved the door open and walked out onto the street. The gust of wind and snow that caught him sent him back against the wall to his left. He snatched at the front of his coat and pulled it tight around his throat. He hurried to the junction and crossed the street, kept walking until he reached a convenience store with an overhead canopy. He buried his hands in his pockets, looked along the street for a cab.

Fifteen minutes later, hurrying up the steps to the entrance of the American Regent, the commissionaire held open the door and acknowledged Harper as he passed through into the foyer.

'Mr Bernstein,' he said, and nodded.

Harper paused, turned, frowned. 'Harper,' he said. 'My name is Harper.'

The commissionaire smiled knowingly. 'Of course, Mr *Harper*.'

And by the time Harper realized that the man believed him to be someone other than himself, he was near the desk, asking for his key, making his way towards the elevator.

Once inside his room he went to the window, watched as the

snow came down thick and fast. The wind caught great swathes of flakes and hurled them this way and that, and Harper found himself transfixed by their random motion, the unpredictability of their patterns. And through the snow he could see the lights of New York, and it reminded him of the way the lights looked from the sea as he'd cut out so many times before. The water turquoise and cerulean, the sky clear, a view all the way west to Joe Bay, the smell of salt clearing the nostrils, Key Largo and the Swash drifting away behind him . . .

Such things were his life, not here; here amongst the madness of obsessed police detectives, women with multiple names, people from his childhood bringing disturbance and disruption . . .

Harper thought to leave; to take the remainder of Walt Freiberg's money and fly out that night. Go home, just like Duchaunak said; back to Miami, back to a world that appeared altogether safer.

But John Harper did not go. Knew he wouldn't before he even considered it. Blood-ties perhaps. Perhaps not. The reason did not appear to matter. He found that he couldn't leave; however hard he tried to believe Frank Duchaunak was right, he found he could not leave.

He needed to speak with Evelyn. He needed to know the truth about his own mother.

That, if nothing else, was reason enough to stay.

Dark grey Buick on the corner, no more than a block from the Regent. Don Faulkner reaches into his pocket and takes out a cellphone. Calls Duchaunak. Phone rings twice and Duchaunak answers.

'Harper's back in the hotel,' Faulkner says.

Listens for a moment, shakes his head.

'Frank . . . Frank, listen to me for Christ's sake. Go home, eh? Just go home for a couple of hours will you? Get some sleep. I'll keep—'

Faulkner falls silent, looks agitated, and then 'I know, I know . . . all I'm saying is that I can stay here and keep an eye on him. You've been up for God knows how long. Just go and get a few hours' sleep, okay?'

Faulkner nods. 'Yes, okay. Yes, I will. If I say I will, then I will, okay?' Closes his eyes for a moment, exasperated perhaps. 'Yes, alright . . . okay. You go home, I'll call you there if he appears.'

Listens for a few seconds more and then says, 'Right, okay . . . tomorrow. I will see you tomorrow.'

Faulkner pockets his cellphone, reaches for a cigarette and lights it. He exhales smoke, shakes his head. 'Crazy motherfucker,' he says to himself. 'Crazy, crazy motherfucker.'

Outside, beyond the windows of his car, the snow comes down in waves.

THIRTY

Kid, no more than eight, maybe nine. Bright red slicker, kind of pull-down woollen hat to keep his ears warm, knee-high rubber boots, heavy treads leaving unmistakable footprints in the snow. Running alongside him is a dog, kind of rat-mongrel thing with eyes too big, yapping excitedly. Dad a good ten yards up the street, all three of them on the way home from nowhere important.

Kid went by the name of Tyler Russell, rat-mongrel dog was called Bucket, which meant nothing of any great significance, but kind of cute, kind of name an eight-year-old gave a rat-mongrel and it made folks smile.

Bucket heads down the alleyway off of West Fifteenth and Seventh. Tyler goes after him, shouting his name. Dad turns at the junction, realizes he's lost his kid and the dog, sighs exasperatedly and heads back the way he's come. Cold. Too damned cold to be out with a kid and a dog. Turns right down the alleyway. Can see the footprints of both of them. Shouts his son's name.

'Tyler?'

No answer.

Pinprick twinge of awkward nerves somewhere in the lower gut.

'Tyler!' he shouts, and it comes out sounding strange, perhaps the acoustics of the alleyway, the thick snow, the frozen air. Perhaps nothing more than the irregularity with which he raises his voice.

'Tyler!' he shouts again, and this time he gets kind of anxious. Starts to walk more rapidly. Wondering what the fuck has happened.

And then he sees them. Tyler standing stock-still, Bucket sitting up on his haunches right beside him. Kind of Christmas-card picturesque. Little boy, little dog, thick virgin snow with no footprints but their own. Relief. Like a wave of something that comes up from the vagus nerve. Like something tight had a hold of him and then suddenly let him go.

'Tyler . . . What are you doing?' Dad asks. 'We have to get home, sweetheart.'

Comes up back of them – taller, can see over his son's head – and figures there's something not right when Tyler doesn't turn or speak or respond in any way.

Bucket whines like the rat-mongrel kind of thing that he is, and his head is tilted to one side, like even he – a handful of dog no bigger than a cat – realizes that something isn't right down here.

That's when Dad sees the guy on the floor. Right there on the ground like he's telling a story, waiting for someone perhaps, taking a rest and smoking a cigarette.

Except he isn't waiting or resting or telling a story. He's dead. Deader than Elvis. Side of his head all broken up and covered in blood, and the blood has run down his neck and throat, down across the lapel of his coat, and it's frozen solid and looks like nothing natural.

Dad says, 'Oh my fucking Christ almighty.'

Tyler turns, looks down at Bucket, whispers, 'You hear that, Bucket . . . Daddy said the F word.'

All night he was cold. Heating was up, way up high, and Harper realized before too long that the cold he felt had grown from within. He'd slurred back and forth between wakefulness and unsettled rest until the early hours, and then – even as the snow got bored with Manhattan and figured it would head south-west to whitewash New Jersey – he'd drifted into something vaguely resembling sleep and stayed there until six.

First message came from the desk at ten after seven.

'Hollander,' the guy had said, and then spelled it unnecessarily. 'H-O-L-L-A-N-D-E-R,' and Harper had patiently waited for him to finish, and then told the clerk that if Miss Hollander called again he should pass on the message that he wouldn't be around until after lunch.

Harper wanted a little time, a little breathing space. Things were coming at him from over the edge of reality, things that he was struggling to hold on to, struggling to see where they connected to whoever he thought he was before he'd returned to New York.

Remembered something from Hemingway, something about quitting things. If you quit things, whether good or bad, it left an emptiness. If it was a bad thing the emptiness filled up by itself; if it was a good thing you had to find something better or the emptiness would remain for ever. Made sense to Harper when he set the receiver in its cradle. In Miami he'd possessed something resembling a life. Here, well here he really possessed nothing. Nevertheless, in speaking with Duchaunak, with Cathy Hollander, even with Evelyn, it was becoming more and more evident that he knew little if anything regarding his own past and heritage. He was uncertain if he *wanted* to know – really know – but simultaneously he knew he *had* to know. There was an emptiness and it could not be left alone.

Hence he felt compelled to see Evelyn; compelled enough to order breakfast, to eat it, to shower and shave and dress, to stand at the window a little before eight and ask himself if it was too early to take a cab to Carmine and see what she had to say.

He walked down to the street, stepped into a coffee shop, and used up half an hour looking at a newspaper without paying any mind to what he was reading, and then he called the cab, drove over there, and felt the tension in his gut.

Whatever it was it was going to come, and there was nothing he could now do to stop it.

'When?'
'A little after seven.'
'And he said what?'
'I didn't speak to him directly.'
'Who did you speak to?'
'The clerk at the desk . . . he called Harper's room for me.'
'And?'
'Message came back that he wouldn't be around until after lunch.' Cathy Hollander sat on the edge of her bed. Seemed she was tense all the time now. Because of what was happening, everything inexorably rolling forward against all odds. Days now, just days away, and she would be through and out the

other side. Or dead. There was always that possibility. Known that from the start. But had it stopped her? Hell it had.

'After lunch?'

'That's what he said, Walt . . . that he'd be around after lunch.'

'And what the fuck does that mean, for Christ's sake?'

Cathy shook her head. She looked towards the window to her right. Snow had stopped altogether. Sky was pale grey, flat, nothing out there. 'I don't know Walt . . . I don't know what that means.'

'He sick or something?'

'I don't think so, seemed fine the last time I saw him.'

'Which was?'

'Wednesday . . . you remember . . . when you called me on the cellphone? I was at St Vincent's then, had just dropped him off. That was the last time I saw him.'

'And he seemed okay?'

'Sure, he seemed okay.'

'You didn't call him yesterday?'

Cathy sighed, shook her head. 'Walt—'

'You were busy, right . . . sorry, yes of course. We were all a bit fucking busy yesterday, weren't we?'

'To say the least.'

'Okay, it is what it is. Give it an hour or so and call the hotel again. See if he's in. If he's in go up and see him, make sure he's okay. Last thing we need is the kid flaking out on us, right?'

'And if he's not there when I call?' Cathy asked.

'Come on over to the house. Just come on over to the house and we'll figure out what to do with Harper after lunch.'

'See ya later, Walt.'

'Sure thing sweetheart, see ya later.'

Cathy Hollander hung up the phone.

She stood for a moment, dressed in nothing but her underwear and a robe, and then walked through to the bathroom.

She turned on the shower. She asked herself what the hell she was doing with her life. She didn't have an answer. Truth be known, she figured she didn't want one.

'Four, perhaps four-thirty a.m.'

'And Harper was still in the hotel?'

'Christ Frank, I guess so. I waited outside until I couldn't keep my eyes open any more, and then I drove home. He didn't come out the front, that much I do know. If he climbed out the window and scaled down the back wall and disappeared into the night, well that's another fucking story entirely.'

Duchaunak was silent for a few seconds. He looked out of the window of his too-small kitchen. He wondered if he had what could actually be called a life.

'Okay, Don, okay. You called the hotel yet?'

'I called just five minutes ago.'

'And?'

'Like I said Frank, he went out.'

'Right, right,' Duchaunak replied distractedly. 'He went out . . . wonder where the hell he's gone.'

Don Faulkner didn't reply. There was nothing he could have said that would have helped.

'The desk guy have any idea?'

'No,' Faulkner said. 'Harper didn't say anything to them.'

'But he did get the call, right?'

'Right, just the one call. Cathy Hollander. That was early, a few minutes after seven. Harper got the message and told the clerk what I just told you.'

'What the hell is he doing?' Duchaunak asked, but he was asking himself.

Faulkner stayed silent.

'Freiberg maybe . . . but then what would Freiberg be doing operating independently of the girl? Maybe he's gone to see Marcus.'

'Or the aunt?' Faulkner suggested.

'Could be, could be.'

'Truth is that we don't know Frank, and there isn't a helluva lot of point trying to second-guess the guy. I can go over to the aunt's, but without knocking on the door and seeing who's inside I wouldn't know if he was there or not. And Marcus, well he could be any number of places.'

'Yes, I know, Don, I know,' Duchaunak said. 'You get someone onto Freiberg?'

'Not yet. I spoke to a couple of guys on leave and they weren't interested. I'm still trying to figure something out.'

'Right, right . . .'

Faulkner knew Duchaunak's attention wasn't on what he was

saying, nor what he was hearing. He could almost sense the wheels turning inside the man's head.

'Let it be what it is,' Duchaunak said eventually. 'We're not going to spend all morning running around the city looking for the guy. I'm going into the office; see you there in an hour or so.'

'Sure thing, Frank, sure thing.' Faulkner hesitated for a moment.

'What is it?' Duchaunak asked.

'I did some checking up—'

'On what?'

'Remember the bullet match . . . the one they dug out of Lenny and the 7–11 robbery in 1974?'

'Sure, yes, what about it?'

'They took someone in for the 7–11 . . . took someone in and questioned them.'

Duchaunak said nothing.

'Frank?'

'Yeah, I'm here. Who'd they take in, Don?'

'Guy in the 7–11 said it was two people. They only ever questioned one person about it—'

'The name, Don, the name . . . what the fuck is this?'

'Garrett Sawyer.'

'You're bullshitting me!'

'As God is my fucking witness, they took Garrett Sawyer in on the 7–11 job, but there was no evidence, no ID. He wasn't charged with anything and they let him go.'

'And the gun that was used turns up thirty years later and someone shoots Lenny Bernstein with it . . . what the fuck kind of coincidence is that?'

'Exactly that,' Faulkner replied. 'A *fuck* of a coincidence.'

'Okay, okay, I have to go,' Duchaunak said. 'I'll call you later . . . we'll catch up on this thing, okay?'

'Sure, Frank . . . speak later.'

Duchaunak hung up.

Faulkner stood there with the receiver in his hand. He looked at it for a little while as if he was uncertain of what he should do with it. Fact of the matter was that he was concerned for Frank Duchaunak. Seemed to him the man needed some kind of professional help. Therapeutic kind of help.

Faulkner sighed, shook his head, set the phone in its cradle.

He walked to the front hall and put on his overcoat. He tried to ignore the sense of disorientation that came with so little sleep. He opened the door and stepped out into the cold. He figured he'd walk to a diner, get some breakfast before he drove over to the precinct house. At least if he ate enough he'd have sufficient energy to keep it all together.

THIRTY-ONE

'Why? I told you why already.'

'Tell me again, Ev . . . give me something I can use.'

'Use?' Evelyn smiled wryly. She turned and looked towards the kitchen window. Her face was half in and out of shadow. Harper had not been aware of how she had aged.

'I got your book . . . the one you put through the letter box.'

Harper nodded.

'I did buy it you know? Originally, back when it was published.'

'You told me.'

'I bought it, I read it, and I was pissed off with you for a very long time.'

'I know. I didn't mean—'

Evelyn raised her hand. 'It doesn't matter, John . . . dirty water beneath burned bridges.'

Harper took a pack of cigarettes from his pocket, offered her one.

Evelyn smiled. 'Thought you were trying to quit.'

Harper shrugged.

She stepped forward and took a cigarette from him. 'Didn't try so hard, huh?'

'Seems that way,' he replied.

Evelyn was on-edge, goading him. All these years behind them, everything that had happened, and even now he didn't understand why it had to be a battle of wills. He decided not to rise to it; he was no longer an awkward teenager; he no longer considered her the enemy.

Harper offered Evelyn a light, but she had a box of matches in her housecoat pocket. She moved from where she stood by the sink, came and sat facing him at the plain deal kitchen table.

'Something you can use,' she echoed. 'And what would you classify as something you could use, John Harper?'

'Tell me something about Anne.'

Evelyn's eyes widened. 'Your mother? What do you want me to tell you about your mother?'

'What she was like—'

'She was like you,' Evelyn interjected. 'She was a lot like you.'

'How so?'

'Wilful, determined, arrogant sometimes.'

'Arrogant?' Harper shook his head; had never considered himself arrogant.

'No, maybe not arrogant, more like headstrong, stubborn sometimes. She could be like that. Tell her she couldn't have her own way and she'd tear the house down until you gave in.'

'Did she love Edward?'

Evelyn laughed, but the sound she made gave away something of her awkwardness. She was neither comfortable nor familiar with being asked such questions. 'I don't think she was old enough to know what love was when she met Edward Bernstein.'

'She grew to love him?'

'Grew to love him, no, I don't think so. I think your mother was in love with what she *thought* was Edward Bernstein. Who she thought he was and who he actually was were not the same person.'

Harper frowned. 'How d'you mean?'

Evelyn flicked ash into the ashtray. She took another drag of her cigarette and looked intently at Harper. 'Why are you asking me these questions John?'

'Because you're the only family I've got, Ev, and you're the only person who really knows anything about my mother and father.'

'Anne is dead, has been for nearly thirty years. The past is the past. It belongs right where it is, and I'm not of a mind to go dragging it back where it doesn't belong.'

'I need to know, Ev.'

'Need? That's a little strong, isn't it?'

'I don't think so . . . and besides, I figure you owe me some truth.'

'Owe you? I don't reckon I owe you anything.'

'For lying, Ev. I believe that you owe me for lying about my father.'

'Ha!' Evelyn snapped. 'You're talking about people owing things. What about your mother and my husband? How the hell do you think I feel, eh? How in God's name do you think I feel? Tell me that, John Harper—'

Harper leaned forward. The cigarette he held had burned down to the filter. He dropped it in the ashtray. 'What do you mean, Ev? Their deaths were five years apart . . . they weren't connected.'

Her expression changed. It was nothing, and yet it was something. Enough to cause Harper to lean his head to one side and look at his aunt more closely. The shift was like the shadow of a cloud across a field. Harper was beneath it as it passed, and he felt that second of transient coolness.

'What?' she asked, noticing the way he looked at her. She sounded defensive.

'You tell me.'

'There isn't anything *to* tell.'

'They were connected,' Harper said matter-of-factly. 'Tell me how their deaths were connected, Ev.'

'They were *not* connected,' she said. She scowled. Her features were cold, her eyes flinty. 'Your mother died of pneumonia. Five years later Garrett took his own life.'

'Did he do that? Did he really take his own life?'

'What the hell is this?' she said. 'What the hell is going on here? You've been talking to that crazy cop, what was his name? Frank something-or-other . . .'

'Duchaunak.'

'That's the one. He's been speaking to you—'

'And to you it seems. He came here, didn't he? He asked you about my mother and Garrett, didn't he? He asked what happened to them and you told him something that you haven't told me. I'm right, aren't I?' Harper leaned forward, his tone of voice insistent. 'Aren't I?'

Evelyn leaned back. She shook her head slowly. 'I think you should leave now, John. I really think I've had enough of this kind of talk.'

Harper leaned back; he smiled coldly. 'I'm not leaving, Ev. I'm not leaving until you tell me what happened. Tell me the truth

220

about them . . . tell me the truth about your sister and your husband. What happened to them, Ev? Tell me what really happened to them all those years ago—'

'Enough!' she snapped. Her voice was loud, sudden, harsh, abrupt. 'Enough for God's sake!' She looked away. She was incensed, furious. She turned back to Harper after a moment, and the directness of her gaze unnerved him. It had been many, many years since Evelyn Sawyer had pinned him with such a stare. 'I don't give a damn what you think . . . you have no right, no right whatsoever, coming here and telling me what I should and shouldn't tell you. You want to come back here and get involved with these people then that's your own responsibility, and you cannot hold me accountable for what might happen—'

'I hold you accountable for the truth,' Harper said. He was angry. His fists were clenched. 'I spoke to Duchaunak and he told me—'

'Aah, what the hell does he know?'

'More than I do, but not as much as you, right? How come it's my parents we're talking about, and yet I'm the one who knows the least about them?'

'Because there are some things it is best *not* to know.'

Harper shook his head. 'I'm not thirteen, Ev. I'm not a kid any more. I went away and grew up. I did a whole load of things in the years I was away—'

'But evidently failed to learn a very simple lesson.'

Harper frowned.

'To leave the past where it is, and to stay out of things that can do no good. You come back here—'

'You *insisted* I come back here, Ev . . . you remember the phone calls you made to Nancy Young, and calling the newspaper? You remember doing that?'

Evelyn didn't respond.

'You *insisted* I come down here, Evelyn, you made it almost impossible for me to refuse.'

'I know, I know—'

'And now I'm here, here at your request, you're doing everything you can to send me back to Miami. You and the cop. So tell me, tell me why you are so goddamned frightened about what I might find out? Is it about Anne? Eh? Is it about my mother?' Harper leaned forward. He felt tension in his stomach, anger rising in his chest. 'Or is it about the mysterious, dying Edward Bernstein? Is that who this is really all about?'

'You don't know what you're talking about—'

'Well, of course I don't know what the hell I'm talking about, Evelyn! No-one in this goddamned city seems to have a straight answer for anything!' Harper banged his fist on the table and Evelyn jumped. For a split-second she looked afraid. *Really* afraid. Harper held his fist there for a moment, right there ahead of him, like if there had been something to hit there would have been nothing to prevent him.

Evelyn looked back at Harper with a cold, hard glare.

'Speak Evelyn . . . speak before I break something, for Christ's sake.'

'You don't want to hear what I have to say—'

'What you have to say is *exactly* what I want to hear! Goddamnit, what is it going to take to get someone to say something direct around here?'

'You know how long that cop has been after your father?'

'Duchaunak? No, I don't know, Evelyn. Pray tell me. How long has Frank Duchaunak been after my father?'

'Seven years, a little more. November of 1997 he started gunning for Edward Bernstein, and in all that time, regardless of an apparent complete lack of support from his department, he has not quit. Evidently he had reason enough, don't you think?'

Harper watched Evelyn. She was animated, her words sharp and quick, directed right at him.

Harper closed his eyes and shook his head. He could feel the tension and pressure, could see how his knuckles had whitened. He experienced a moment of clear and instinctive foreboding, an unmistakable, intuitive gut-reaction that told him to back up and walk away.

'Reason enough?' he asked, and even as he asked it he wondered whether he wanted to hear the answer.

'Edward Bernstein has been Duchaunak's raison d'être for the last seven years; that's how it seems to me.'

'Is that what he said?'

Evelyn laughed. 'No, of course he didn't say that. Frank Duchaunak was appropriately obscure in everything that he said. He even lied to me.'

'What did he lie about?'

'About his motivation for following your father for all this time.'

'What did he say?'

Evelyn shook her head. 'It was not what he said, it was what he didn't say.'

Harper waited for her to speak. She lit another cigarette.

'And?' he prompted.

'I asked him how long he'd been after your father. He told me seven years. Told me he'd started back in November of '97. I asked him if someone had died, and he told me no.'

Evelyn fell silent. For a moment she looked as if she wasn't done, but Harper sat there for some seconds before he realized that nothing further was coming.

'He told you no,' Harper stated matter-of-factly.

Evelyn nodded. 'Right, he told me no.'

'That no-one had died.'

Evelyn nodded once again.

Harper shook his head. 'I've lost the thread here, Evelyn . . . I'm not sure what you're saying.'

She smiled, but the smile said something of bitterness and regret. 'It's not difficult, John. You're a bright boy, always have been. Duchaunak started pursuing your father because of something that happened in 1997, November of 1997. I asked him if he started after your father because someone had died, and he lied. He told me no.'

'So someone did die?' Harper asked.

'Oh yes,' Evelyn replied. 'Someone died alright . . . someone most definitely went and died.'

Cathy Hollander stands in the front room of her apartment, receiver in her hand. Waiting.

'Hi . . . yes, hi there. I was on hold . . . I think I got cut off. I called a minute or so ago. I was after—'

Interrupted. Pauses. Listens.

'Yes, that's right, John Harper.'

Waits another moment.

'Right, okay. Yes . . . er no, no problem. Thanks for your help.'

Shakes her head. Frowns. Hangs up. Lifts the receiver again and dials another number.

'It's me.'

Glances left towards the window.

'Gone out somewhere. Left a couple of hours ago.'

Listens. Looks down at her shoeless feet.

'No, I didn't leave a message. I'll come over to the house like you said. I'll check after lunch.'

Nods understandingly.

'Sure thing Walt, sure thing. Okay, see you in a little while.'

Nods once more. 'Okay, goodbye.' Hangs up. Sets the phone down on the counter. Pauses in the doorway for a moment. Expression pensive, uncharacteristically deep, and then Cathy Hollander leaves the kitchen and walks across the front room to her bedroom.

Faulkner stands as Duchaunak bursts through the door of the office.

'Where?' Duchaunak asks.

'Alleyway off of West Fifteenth and Seventh.'

'Sure it was there? He wasn't killed someplace else and moved?'

Faulkner shakes his head. 'Hell Frank, we don't know . . . guy was so frozen they have to defrost him before they can do the autopsy.'

Duchaunak frowns, angles his head to one side, starts laughing – kind of an awkward laugh precipitated by facts that seem wilder than fiction.

'At a guess he was killed last night, we don't know when, won't know for sure until the coroner's done his thing, but whenever it was, they left him in the alleyway all night and he froze solid . . . froze like a fucking popsicle.'

'Aah, Jesus Christ, what the fuck is going on here?'

Faulkner frowns.

'This thing, this goddamned thing. We got Lenny laid up in Vincent's, his son has disappeared, and now Johnnie Hoy, one of the only people who ever gave us anything that we could use on Bernstein gets knifed in the fucking eye and left out in the cold for some poor kid to find.'

'You think that's why he was killed?'

'I don't think, Don, I *know* that's why he was done. Freiberg and Marcus are doing something, maybe separate, maybe

224

together, but whatever the fuck it is there's gonna be some housework.'

Faulkner shakes his head. He sighs exhaustedly and sits down. 'It's going to be bad, isn't it?'

Duchaunak nods slowly. 'As bad as it gets and then some, I reckon.'

'I can take my annual vacation now?'

Duchaunak laughs. 'Sure, Don, sure . . . have a good time. Send me a freakin' postcard okay?'

'So now?'

Duchaunak opens his mouth to speak.

The phone rings.

He leans forward, lifts the receiver. 'Yep.'

Eyes widen, starts to frown.

'Where?'

Nods, snaps his fingers at Faulkner. *Pen*, he mouths.

Faulkner leans across with a pen. Duchaunak takes it, writes something on the jotter ahead of him.

'Pier 49,' he says. 'Good enough, Mike . . . many thanks.'

Duchaunak sets down the receiver. Looks across at Faulkner.

'Mike Donnelly at Despatch . . . just took a call for a black and white out near Pier 49.'

'For what?'

Duchaunak shakes his head. 'Get your coat, we're going out there.'

Faulkner starts to rise. 'But it isn't ours, Frank. How can we just go out on some random call when we haven't been given it?'

'It isn't a random call, Don.' Duchaunak is by the door, turning the handle, opening

'What, Frank? What the fuck is it?'

Duchaunak is out and down the corridor. Faulkner goes after him, tugging his coat on as he goes. Nearly loses his balance at the end, one hand against the wall, picking up speed as Duchaunak starts to run.

THIRTY-TWO

Harper was shaking his head.

'You don't want to hear about this, do you?' Evelyn asked. 'You want to hear about your father, what happened with him and your mother, right?'

Closed his eyes. Tension was visible in everything about him. Wound up tight; watch-spring tight.

'You going to say something?'

Harper slowly shook his head again, eyes were open but he was looking at the floor. He found it hard to breathe, a tightness in his chest that was suffocating.

'You want a drink or something?'

'No Evelyn . . . just give me a minute will you . . . just need a minute or two.'

Evelyn leaned back. There was something relaxed in her manner, almost as if telling the truth had taken the weight and tension from her shoulders and passed them to Harper. She did not seemed pleased that he was suffering, evidently suffering, but she did seem relieved that whatever she'd told him was no longer held tight inside her like a clenched fist.

'What d'you want me to say, John? I kept all of this away from you. All those years I knew what was going on. I knew what he was like, the people he associated with. That's why things were so difficult here. He sent Walt Freiberg over here; time and again the man came with things for you. Money, clothes, toys, things for your birthday, for Christmas. Keeping those people out of your life was a full-time job in itself. You don't even know the half of it—'

'So tell me,' Harper said. 'Tell me the half of it that you never told me before . . . for Christ's sake Evelyn, tell me *anything*.'

Evelyn looked fatigued, not just tired but fatigued; the bone-deep exhaustion that comes from carrying something that

226

drains every ounce of strength from within, not only physically, but mentally and emotionally.

'The late-night phone calls, the threats. Times I would go to collect you from school and Walt Freiberg would be there in the street, right there in the street standing beside a car, and in the car was your father watching every move you made. One time . . . one time I went to get you and they were there. I couldn't see you anywhere, not in the street, not in the yard behind the school, and I was convinced they'd taken you, convinced that finally he'd persuaded you to get in the back of that car and they were just taunting me, letting me know that they had the money and the power to make anything happen the way they wanted. They scared the hell out of me. Those people really, really scared the hell out of me.'

'I never knew any of this—'

Evelyn laughed, suddenly, abruptly. 'What could I have told you? Your mother died when you were seven years old. Your father left when you were two . . . I say *left* when you were two, but hell John, Edward Bernstein was leaving from the moment he found out Anne was pregnant. I knew who these people were long before your mother ever confronted the truth. She fell in love with whatever she believed Edward Bernstein was . . . she even convinced herself that he wanted you, that he would have stayed and raised a family.'

Evelyn looked away. She was silent for some time. When she turned back there were tears in her eyes, heavy and swollen. She blinked, and those tears rolled down her cheeks. She took a tissue from the pocket of her housecoat and touched it to her eyes.

'How did she die, Evelyn?' Harper asked.

Evelyn smiled, a sense of nostalgia and pain evident in her expression. 'She died lonely and afraid, John, lonely and afraid.'

'But how? *How* did she die?'

Evelyn looked away once more, away towards the window. The mid-morning light was flat and clean, the sky clear. It gave the room a still and monochromatic atmosphere. She looked like a ghost of herself, a woman caught in the middle of something that could not have been worse had she tried.

'Whatever the truth is—' Harper began.

Evelyn waved his words aside. 'The truth is the truth,' she said quietly. 'It is not the truth that scares us, John, it's the way we believe others will take it.'

'So tell me,' Harper said. 'Tell me how she died.'

'It was a Sunday . . . twelfth of October 1975. I don't even remember where you were, maybe out with Garrett or something. You were seven years old, you had your own way of dealing with Anne's episodes—'

Harper frowned. 'Episodes?'

'That's what me and Garrett called them, Anne's episodes.'

'Like crazy stuff?'

Evelyn shook her head. 'She was in a bad situation, John, a real bad situation. She knew about your father, she knew what he was doing. Walt was around as well. Walt was friends with Garrett . . . not serious friends, more like acquaintances. They had the time of day for one another, you know what I mean?'

Harper nodded. He shifted in his chair. He felt nauseous from smoking.

'But that's beside the point,' Evelyn said. 'We're talking about Anne, right?'

'Right, Ev, talking about Anne.'

'So I was out somewhere, maybe went to the market or something. Anne was upstairs, had come to stay with us for a few weeks but ended up staying the better part of a year. She had her own room, you had a smaller room down the hall, and she used to sleep in in the morning. She always had a helluva time getting up, your mother.' Evelyn smiled. 'Anyway, I came back. The place was quiet, real quiet. I figured she'd maybe got out of bed, got dressed perhaps, gone out somewhere . . .' Evelyn hesitated, sat motionless, silent, looking back at Harper for some seconds. 'She was in her room.' She glanced upwards, up towards the ceiling. 'She was up there in her room . . .'

Harper felt his breath catch in his chest.

'I knew something was wrong when I reached the landing.'

Harper wanted to move, felt he had to, but at the same time such a thing seemed utterly impossible.

'I went along there like I was walking towards—' She shook her head. 'I don't know what I felt, John . . . something like fear, something like a premonition. Whatever it was I knew there was something behind her door that I didn't want to see, and then

228

when I got there, when I tried the handle and it was locked . . . it was then that I knew.'

'Knew what?'

'I knew . . . hell, John, I knew she'd killed herself.'

Harper didn't move. Didn't blink. Held his breath for seconds, minutes perhaps. Tears filled his lower eyelids, rolled lazily down his cheeks. He did nothing to stop them.

'I don't know what she took; I could see that she'd taken something.' She paused. 'I remember,' she said, and looked at Harper. 'You were out, out somewhere with Garrett, and when you came back I stayed downstairs with you while Garrett went up and covered her over. I had opened the door to her room with another key, and then I waited downstairs until you came home. I told you she was sleeping . . .'

'Why, Ev . . . why?'

'Why did she kill herself?'

Harper shook his head. 'Yes . . . no . . . hell, I don't know, Ev. Christ almighty.' He closed his eyes and leaned his head backwards. 'Why didn't you tell me?'

'Tell you? I don't know, John. I meant to tell you. I meant to tell you about your father, especially after your mother died, but I could never bring myself to it.' Evelyn smiled. She wiped her eyes with the tissue. 'I held onto the idea of telling you for so long. Garrett used to fight with me about it, said that it wasn't right for a child to grow up not knowing the truth about his own parents. And you know what I used to tell him?'

Harper shook his head. It was an involuntary response to a question; he really had no idea what he was thinking, no real understanding of what he was hearing.

'I used to tell him to give me a little longer, give me a few more months, a handful more weeks. I used to tell him that I just needed a little more time to make you feel as if you had a family with us.'

Harper opened his eyes. He looked at Evelyn; she looked away abruptly, uncomfortably.

'I used to convince him that before too long you would start to think of me and him as your parents. That's what I used to tell him. He told me I was crazy, that you would never see us that way, and I s'pose he was right, wasn't he, John?'

Harper opened his mouth to speak.

Evelyn raised her hand. She shook her head and smiled. 'That's not fair. I shouldn't have said that.'

Harper was speechless. He wasn't expected to answer the question, but it didn't change the fact that it had been asked. It seemed to hang in the room like a ghost.

'Anyway, that's what I used to tell him, and I managed to keep him from telling you himself, and then—'

'He died too.'

Evelyn nodded, bowed her head. Her hands were twisting together, the tissue rapidly disintegrating under the assault. 'And then none of it mattered. Anne was dead. Edward was gone. Garrett killed himself.' Evelyn looked up. 'And it was just you and me, John, you and me against the world.'

'Why did she die, Ev? Why did she kill herself?'

Evelyn's eyes widened. She looked momentarily surprised. 'It isn't obvious now?'

Harper shook his head.

'To get away, John, to get away from Edward Bernstein and everything he represented. That's why she killed herself, John. Finally, after everything that happened, it was the only way she could escape.'

THIRTY-THREE

Something about the smell of the water. A couple of weeks before, Duchaunak had been up at the Fire Boat Station and it had been exactly the same. Rank, fetid, corrupt almost. Something about the odor that stayed in his nostrils, hung on his clothes for some considerable time afterward. Combined now with the coppery taint of blood it tightened his throat, made his stomach turn.

Not the kind of job for a normal person, he thought, and watched as Don Faulkner stepped around the lake of blood and leaned closer to the battered form of a man.

A handful of seconds, really no more, and then Faulkner stood up straight, turned and nodded at Duchaunak. 'It's him alright, Frank.'

'Sure?'

'No question. Come see for yourself.'

Duchaunak stepped around the blood, reached out, and took Faulkner's hand so as not to lose his balance, and then he too was squatting beside Micky Levin, a man he'd known almost as long as he'd known Edward Bernstein. There was no doubt really. No doubt of who it was. It had been more wishful thinking on Duchaunak's part. These people – violent, brutal, utterly beyond redemption – were nevertheless the people that consumed the vast majority of his time. In essence they were his extended family. To lose one was to lose yet another person who somehow existed on the same wavelength, and whichever way Duchaunak looked at it it seemed an injustice. Ultimately, if all of them died or were incarcerated, then he would be alone. Duchaunak smiled to himself.

'What?' Faulkner asked.

Duchaunak shook his head.

'You smiled at something.'

231

'Nothing, Don . . . just a thought.' Duchaunak stood up. 'So what do we have here?'

'Apart from blunt trauma, massive blood loss, and a dead Jewish gangster?'

'Apart from that.'

'I think we have the beginning of your war.'

Duchaunak opened his mouth to speak, but was cut short by the shrilling of his cellphone. He took it from his pocket.

The conversation was brief, terse almost, and the expression on Duchaunak's face darkened like some incipient storm. Less than a minute and he closed the phone and returned it to his pocket.

'We got a meeting with the man,' he said quietly.

'Aah hell,' Faulkner said. 'What the fuck now?'

Duchaunak stepped back and started to walk away from Micky Levin. 'I don't know, Don, I don't know.'

'Well, what are we going to do about Micky?'

'Let the uniforms handle him. They'll have someone down here shortly, someone from Homicide.'

Even as the words left Duchaunak's lips a dark sedan came hurtling down towards the pier.

'What'd I tell ya?' he called out, and Faulkner hurried after him, unwilling now to share any words with the assigned Homicide Unit.

They made it away from the scene before any such challenge took place, and turning, looking back over his shoulder as the car pulled away, Don Faulkner wondered if it really could get as bad as he thought.

'You've seen this before, right?' he asked Duchaunak.

Duchaunak shook his head. 'Not here, no. Chicago, maybe ten years ago, something like that. Early nineties, hadn't long been in the Department. Was a war, territorial thing primarily.'

'Bad?'

Duchaunak nodded. 'Bad enough.'

'You think we're going to get such a thing here?'

Frank Duchaunak looked towards his left, out of the window into the Lower West Side. 'Think it's going to be worse, Don,' he said, his voice almost a whisper. 'Honestly, I think it's going to be worse.'

*

Callbox near The Regent. Sol Neumann stands shivering while some fat guy gesticulates and shouts at someone on the phone. Eventually the fat guys maneuvers himself out of the box and rolls away down the sidewalk. Neumann leaves the door open. Fat guy left his body odor inside. Neumann dials a number, waits patiently.

'News?' he asks.

He frowns, starts to shake his head. 'Look,' he says, his voice firm, assertive. 'There isn't any fucking time for such things. You find him now. You go out there and find this black mother-fucker right fucking now, you understand? It ain't difficult. There's people who know him. He lives in New York. He has family here—'

Neumann falls silent as he's interrupted.

'No, no fucking way. You listen to what I'm saying. I just saw Mr Marcus and we have hours. You understand what I'm telling you . . . we have *hours*. You get whoever the fuck you need and get out there and walk the fucking streets until you find this McCaffrey. That's all there is to it. I'm calling back in two hours and there better be some fucking word on this asshole, okay?'

Neumann doesn't wait for a reply. He slams the receiver back on its hook and barges out of the callbox. Seems to him that threats – implied or direct – work better than bonuses.

Cathy Hollander stands on the steps of the house. A quiet shadow of madness haunts her, follows her wherever she walks, waits for her around corners and reminds her that it is still there when she reaches it. It is a shadow that has been accompanying her for some considerable time. She wonders when this will end, and then reminds herself that she must not think such thoughts. Such thoughts lead only one way, and it is not a way she can afford to take.

She takes the last two steps, reaches up and presses the buzzer. She can hear it echo within. The sound of footsteps, a woman's footsteps, and then the door opens and Walt Freiberg's wife stands there smiling. She looks so much older than Cathy remembered her.

'Hello dear,' she says. 'Come on in, Walt said you were coming over.'

Cathy takes a deep breath and crosses the threshhold.

'You'll be staying for lunch?'

Cathy says nothing.

'Of course you will dear,' Eleanor Freiberg says gently. 'Let me take your coat.'

THIRTY-FOUR

After that word – *escape* – had left Evelyn's lips there was silence in the kitchen on Carmine Street.

Perhaps, beyond the window, the world had ceased its revolutions. Perhaps not.

The world, whatever it was, whatever it might have represented, seemed to change in Harper's mind. Its metamorphosis was swift and irreversible. Where he'd once held a memory of his mother he now possessed an awkward and distorted nightmare. Where there had been no father, no visible memory, no recollection at all, he now faced a brutal and unforgiving reality that he could not step away from no matter how hard he tried. What was once there was now absent; what was once absent now crowded against him like a vast and unrelenting wall of emotional pressure.

'You want a drink?' Evelyn asked. Her tone was gentle, almost sympathetic.

Harper looked up. He tried to smile. The muscles in his face did not respond well. He felt that his expression conveyed only pain and confusion.

Evelyn leaned forward and placed her hand over his. Her skin was warm and soft, the skin of someone old. 'I'll get you a drink,' she said, and rose quietly from her chair.

Evelyn busied herself with glasses, a bottle of brandy, and when she returned to the table Harper found the thought he wished to express. The words did not follow and he experienced little more than abject hollowness.

Evelyn shook her head slowly as she sat down. 'Don't even try to think about it,' she said. She poured brandy into both of the glasses, slid one across the table to Harper.

He lifted the glass and as the brandy touched his lips he inhaled sharply. The aroma of the spirit cleared his nostrils, produced a burning sensation behind his eyes. He drank it down in one go, waited for the warmth to fill his chest.

He set the glass on the table and Evelyn refilled it.

'Everyone survives,' she said.

Harper smiled weakly, shook his head. 'No they don't.'

'You know what I mean.'

'I know what you mean, Evelyn, yes. But sometimes you reach a point where you wonder if surviving could ever be enough.'

'Or if just surviving is all you will ever do?' she said.

'Is that really why she died . . . because she couldn't escape?'

Evelyn looked down at her hands. She held her own glass carefully, as if afraid to break it. 'She used to speak to me of how difficult it all was. Used to tell me things that she never would have told Edward, never would have told Garrett. I was her sister, we were closer than anything . . .' Evelyn looked up. 'Your mother never did anything by halves John. If she did something then she really did it. When she fell in love with Edward she *really* fell in love. It was never an insubstantial thing with Anne, never half-minded. Finally, after she realized that he wasn't going to be your father, wasn't ever going to be her husband, she felt there was no reason for her to go on. And then she took the most certain way out. Like I said, she never did anything by halves.'

'And he knew that she committed suicide?'

'Edward? Of course he knew. He came here afterwards, the day of your mother's funeral, and he tried to take you away from me. Garrett stood up to him. Garrett knew what Edward Bernstein was capable of, but nevertheless he stood up to him.' Evelyn smiled. 'Don't know that I was ever more proud of Garrett than I was that day.'

'Where was I?'

'I sent you away with a friend of mine . . . you remember a woman called Francine? Had a daughter, a year or so younger than you called Grace?'

Harper shook his head. 'I don't know . . . vaguely, I think.'

'I sent you to her house for a few days. She took care of you until everything was over.'

'What happened?'

Evelyn closed her eyes for a second. 'You really want to know?'

'Of course, Ev.'

'He came and told me that he was your father, that he had a right to you now. He said that Anne would have wanted it that way, that she would have wanted you to be with him.'

'And you didn't agree?'

Evelyn laughed suddenly. 'Agree with him? God no, not a prayer. I didn't even have to think about it, and neither did Garrett. I don't think Garrett knew what he was taking on, but he stood right there in the doorway—' Evelyn raised her hand and pointed at the exit to the front hallway – 'Right there. Garrett stood right there and prevented Edward from coming in here. I can see them now, Edward looking over Garrett's shoulder and shouting at me, demanding that I tell him where you were. Garrett didn't back down.' Evelyn paused, smiled to herself.

'What?'

'He was scared. Garrett was scared alright. He had his hand behind his back and I could see him clenching his fist, his knuckles all white. He would never have raised his hand to Edward, never in a million years, but that day I believe he was ready to do whatever it took.'

'And you thought it best I stay unaware of all of this . . . all these years?'

Evelyn said nothing for a moment, and then she smiled ruefully. 'I asked something of that detective,' she said. 'Asked him if he'd ever made a decision, ever said something untrue because he thought it was best, and then couldn't go backwards and undo the damage. That was how it was, John. I did what I thought was right at the time, and then the more time went on the more I felt it wasn't necessary.'

'Until now.'

Evelyn shrugged her shoulders. 'I don't know, maybe . . . Christ, John, how can you ever judge what you would have done had circumstances been different? If Walt hadn't called, if he hadn't insisted I call you I don't know what I would have done. Maybe I would've let Edward die—'

'Maybe he won't die, maybe he'll recover.'

'When did you go over there last?'

Harper thought for a moment. 'Yesterday. They have him in a room by himself, like an intensive care room.'

'If there's any justice in the world he will die,' Evelyn said coldly.

'I don't think Detective Duchaunak wants him to die.'

'I think you're right,' Evelyn replied. 'I think for some considerable time our detective has been obsessed with Edward Bernstein.'

'You were going to tell me about that. There was someone who died back then? When was it, 1997?'

Evelyn nodded. She didn't speak.

'And he told me some things about a girl that hangs around with Walt Freiberg, a girl who was apparently involved with Edward for some months, and then before that with someone called Marcus.'

'Ben Marcus?' Evelyn asked.

Harper looked up.

Evelyn's eyes were wide, her expression anxious, and Harper said 'Yes, Ben Marcus. Why? You know him?'

'Of him . . . I know *of* him,' she said. 'Walt Freiberg is involved with Ben Marcus now?'

'I don't know Evelyn. I don't seem to know a great deal of anything going on here, remember?'

Evelyn leaned forward. 'You shouldn't see him again John,' she said. Her voice was quiet but direct. 'I know you won't go back to Miami, not until you know what happens with your father, but—'

'Duchaunak said the same thing,' Harper interjected. 'That I should leave New York.'

'He said it for a reason,' Evelyn said.

'What is it with him? Why is he so obsessed with my father?'

Evelyn shook her head and sighed. 'Because he believes that Edward is responsible for all of his unhappiness.'

Harper frowned. 'You what?'

'Detective Duchaunak believes that Edward Bernstein destroyed his life.'

'Destroyed his life? Isn't that a little melodramatic?'

'No, John, not melodramatic. Not when you understand what happened to him.'

Harper leaned forward. 'So what happened?'

Evelyn smiled, almost sardonically. 'He believes that Edward was responsible for the death of Marilyn Monroe.'

238

Harper started laughing. 'What the hell—'

'I'll tell you,' Evelyn interjected. 'I'll tell you what happened back in November of '97.'

THIRTY-FIVE

Captain Michael McLuhan. Third generation Irish-American; face like a wrestling match. Sharp words, often abrupt, a naturally awkward and aggressive nature. Seven kids though, eldest nineteen, youngest eleven; almost one a year once he got started, and when he spoke of them his entire demeanor and manner changed. When he talked of his children he could have been some compassionate gentle soul. Cops who worked for him knew him well. When he called – when he wanted some facetime – well, if you were smart you opened your mouth first, opened it as soon as you entered his office. Smart cops in trouble said 'Captain McLuhan, how are the kids doing?' as the very first thing, and the stripes he gave them for whatever they'd done were always less in number and scarred infrequently. Mention his family before he got a chance to tear you a new asshole, and the odds were on coming out of that office still walking straight.

Now it was Duchaunak and Faulkner, both of them seated on the other side of his desk.

'So?' Captain McLuhan asked Duchaunak.

'Micky Levin,' Duchaunak replied.

'No question?'

'No question.'

'And we had a dead Johnnie Hoy a little while ago.'

Duchaunak nodded. 'We did indeed.'

'And your take on this?'

'They're starting a war.'

'A war?' McLuhan leaned back in his chair. He put his hands behind his head.

'A war.'

'Between . . . ?'

'Walt Freiberg and Ben Marcus.'

McLuhan nodded. He glanced at Faulkner. Faulkner said

nothing; carried the slightly distant expression of a man who was on the edge of a fight and wasn't looking to get hurt.

'And why would there be a war starting between Walt Freiberg and Ben Marcus?'

Duchaunak frowned. 'The territories?' he said, a rhetorical question, his tone a little disbelieving. 'That, and the fact that I believe Ben Marcus did the hit on Lenny Bernstein. You know about the bullet—'

'Bullet?' McLuhan asked. 'Oh, let me think now . . . do you mean the bullet that they dug out of Lenny Bernstein which matched some gun used in a robbery thirty years ago?'

'Yes,' Duchaunak said. 'Garrett Sawyer was questioned on that robbery. Garrett was married to Evelyn Sawyer, and she was the sister of Anne Harper who had a child with Bernstein—'

McLuhan rolled his eyes, then looked at Faulkner with an expression that spoke of patience stretched to its limit. 'You're still hobby-horsing this whole thing, aren't you? The number of conversations you and I have had about Edward Bernstein and Walt Freiberg, about Marcus and Neumann and the whole lot of them—'

'For very good reason—' Duchaunak started.

'Don't interrupt me, Frank,' McLuhan said sharply. He withdrew his hands from the back of his head and gripped the arms of the chair. 'I am not in a good mood today. Not only do I have to deal with you pair, I have to deal with some whacko who's killed a brother and a sister, beat the pair of them to death on different days in different places. The girl was a nurse for Christ's sake, Jessica McCaffrey, and Sampson has to go tell her relatives that both her and her brother have been killed. I am already a man on the edge, and the last thing I need is to be interrupted while I'm talking. There are very few things that upset me more than being interrupted Detective Duchaunak.'

Duchaunak nodded apologetically.

'Right then. You never saw the Department Counsellor, am I right?'

'I saw her.'

McLuhan nodded slowly. 'Right, you saw her . . . and how many *times* did you see her Frank?'

Duchaunak hesitated.

'Frank?'

241

'Once,' Duchaunak said.

'Right . . . you saw her once. And she scheduled weekly meetings for you that were supposed to continue until further notice.'

'I saw her, Captain, I saw the woman.'

'You saw her once, Frank. *Once.*'

'You ever seen her?' Duchaunak asked. 'The woman is about as useful as a solar-powered torch.'

Faulkner withheld himself from laughing. He turned away, raised his hand to his face and cleared his throat.

McLuhan glared at him.

'I did go and see her, Captain. I went and told her and she asked me all manner of bullshit questions about whether or not my father hugged me enough when I was a kid. Christ, the thing was like a made-for-TV fucking movie—'

'It was a requirement Frank, a fucking *requirement* of your evaluation. It wasn't a nice fucking idea. It wasn't a go-and-have-chat-with-the-nice-shrink-lady-when-you-feel-like-it-and-every-thing's-going-to-be-fine. It was a condition . . . let me say that again. It was a *condition* of you staying on the job. The fact that you didn't do it and you are not already suspended is by the sheer fucking grace of God. That, and the fact that you pair of smashers actually manage to get some halfway-decent results on something useful every once in a while. Now we're back in here trawling through the same old routine again. Frank Duchaunak and his obsession—'

Duchaunak opened his mouth to speak.

McLuhan raised his hand, extended a finger and wagged it back and forth like a stern teacher. 'Listen to what I'm saying, Frank. We are back in here talking to you about the same fucking obsession you have with these people. It's Bernstein and Marcus, Neumann, Freiberg, Charlie Beck . . . and then you have all of their goddamned families back of them. Where's Raymond Dietz and Albert Reiff? And who's that other asshole you keep going on about?'

'Joe Koenig,' Duchaunak said.

'Right, Koenig . . . Joe Koenig . . . so where the fuck are these guys this time?'

Duchaunak looked sideways at Faulkner, and then he turned

back to McLuhan. 'They're around, Captain. They're always around.'

'Is that so?'

Duchaunak looked back without expression.

'And they're around now? I mean . . . I mean they're right here in this room now Frank? Are they with you all the time? Do you hear their voices when you go to fucking sleep at night?'

Duchaunak closed his eyes and shook his head. He looked overwhelmed, at the end of some internal road and now uncertain of where he'd believed it would take him.

'For God's sake, Frank, Edward Bernstein is in the hospital dying of a gunshot wound. Who knows that his own people didn't set the thing up to have him out the way—'

'We know it wasn't a set-up, Captain. We know that it wasn't a planned shooting.'

McLuhan nodded. 'I've seen the security footage yes, but it doesn't change the fact that once again we are walking down the same beaten-to-shit path and there isn't anything at the end but your fertile and overactive imagination.'

'But there's something else now, Captain—'

'I know there's something else, Frank . . . there's two dead something-elses, but that does not, I repeat *does not* change the fact that you have no standard assignment authority, no back-up, no departmental protocol behind you. You are, and not for the first time I might add, flying by the seat of your fucking pants. Jesus, you guys are like Wing and a Prayer Incorporated. I have nightmares about what you pair are doing. I wake up in the early hours of the morning in a cold sweat worrying about what thunderstorm of shit you're going to bring down on me tomorrow. Can you not let Homicide just do its job with Levin and Hoy? Can you not let Edward Bernstein, who may or may not be the Devil Incarnate and all his unholy tribes in human form, die in fucking peace in St Vincent's Hospital? And now this thing about Bernstein's son? Where the fuck in left field of all left fields did that motherfucker come from?'

'Miami.'

'Hey! It's not a fucking joke, Frank! You think I'm joking? I *look* like I'm joking here?' McLuhan's face reddened, his eyes like hot dark stones. 'Pretty easy to tell when I'm joking, Frank . . .

243

I'm the first one to fucking laugh. You see me laughing? You see me laughing, Frank? No? I didn't fucking think so—'

'Captain McLuhan—'

'No Frank! That's it! That's *fucking* it! Enough is enough! You're on suspension.' He turned and looked at Faulkner. 'You're reassigned to—' He stopped mid-sentence. 'What the fuck am I thinking? Fuck you too! You're on suspension as well. Frank Duchaunak and Don Faulkner are suspended.'

'You have to be—' Duchaunak started.

'I have to be *what* Frank? I have to be insane not to have done this a month ago. Out of my office. Let me deal with my two homicides. Let me assign some real homicide detectives to this thing, and you pair can go off and sit in a diner somewhere for a fortnight and feel repentant about all the stress and high blood pressure you have caused, and work out how the fuck Edward Bernstein arranged the assassination of JFK and started the Iraq fucking war from his hospital bed. Christ, you pair are probably responsible for decreasing my lifespan by about five fucking years!'

Duchaunak rose from his chair. His fists were clenched.

Faulkner started up as well. 'Frank—'

Duchaunak turned, glared at Faulkner. Faulkner didn't say another word. He kind of hung somewhere between seated and standing and didn't know where to look.

'Captain McLuhan, you can't do this . . . you really cannot do this.'

'I can do anything the fuck I like. What does it say on my door? It says *Captain*, right? *Captain* Michael McLuhan. That means that as far as you guys are concerned I really can do anything the fuck I like. I am suspending you. I am suspending you for *real*. For a fortnight, perhaps longer. Maybe if I don't see either of you for two weeks my blood pressure will come down and I will start to believe that you are not off your fucking heads. Then I might reconsider. Taking into account the way this has gone before I will assign you to something else, give you a week, and then begin to wonder what the hell made me think anything would be different.'

Duchaunak's face was red with anger. A sweat had broken out across his forehead. Don Faulkner had decided to sit down, and he sat there like a man who knew he'd been defeated.

'Now, do you understand what I have said here? Do we actually *understand* one another, Frank?'

'There's going to be a war,' Duchaunak said, his voice tense, the words making their way out through gritted teeth. 'There's going to be a war . . . going to be a whole lot more dead people lying around the streets of your precinct, and—'

'Enough, Frank! That is enough! Out of here . . . right now!' McLuhan rose and started around his desk. His shoulders were hunched forward, his fists clenched; looked like a Chicago bareknuckle fighter who'd taken fifty on the side to break bones.

Faulkner was up and at the door before McLuhan had reached Duchaunak. Duchaunak hesitated, and then he too took three or four steps backward and stopped in front of Faulkner.

'Go now, Frank, before I really lose my temper. Two weeks, both of you. Come back after the New Year. Come back and see whether I haven't died from a coronary, and then we will talk about your careers in the New York police department, okay?'

Duchaunak opened his mouth to speak.

'Think, Frank. Think about what you're going to say before you say it.'

Duchaunak looked over his shoulder at Faulkner. Faulkner shook his head, reached back and opened the door.

'Nothing is a good thing to say right now,' McLuhan said. 'Go do something else until after Christmas . . . just go do something else, Frank, anything but chasing Edward Bernstein. The guy is a ghost, a fucking spectre . . . he doesn't even exist any more.'

Duchaunak closed his eyes for a second, lowered his head, and then he turned as Faulkner held open the door.

Duchaunak waited until Faulkner had quietly closed the door, and then he started down the corridor.

'Frank?'

Duchaunak didn't reply.

'Frank, wait up for God's sake.'

Duchaunak stopped walking and waited until Faulkner caught him up.

'Frank—'

'Leave me be, Don. Leave me be for a day or two. Go home. Go and see whoever you go and see when you're not working. Leave me alone for a little while. I'll call you, okay? I'll call you and we'll figure out what we're going to do.'

'We're not going to *do* anything, Frank.'

Duchaunak raised his hand and Faulkner fell silent. Duchaunak smiled as best he could, an expression of philosophic resignation and bone-deep fatigue. 'Tomorrow,' he said quietly. 'Maybe the next day . . . I'll call you.'

Faulkner knew better than to argue. He raised his hand and gripped Duchaunak's shoulder for a moment, and then he started to walk away.

Duchaunak watched him go. He hesitated for a moment, turned and looked back towards McLuhan's door, wondered for a moment if he should attempt to handle the man by himself. He inhaled deeply, exhaled, and then seemed to accept the fact that nothing further would be achieved today.

He buried his hands in his pockets. He walked slowly, head down, and made his way to the end of the corridor. He took the stairs. Never took the elevator. Frank Duchaunak didn't do elevators; never had and never would.

THIRTY-SIX

'Cleaning things up, yes . . . it's always necessary when things are changing. Like the shift between seasons. Things have to die to make room for things that need to grow.'

Freiberg rose from where he was seated at the dining table and walked to the window. He paused in silence, his back to the room, and when he turned the smoke from his cigarette and the backlight seemed to make his face disappear into nothing. Cathy Hollander looked down at the remnants of her lunch. Her appetite had not been good. She'd made her excuses so as not to offend Eleanor Freiberg, that she'd been a little off-color all morning, and Eleanor had smiled and accepted her apology gracefully. Eleanor always smiled, always saw the very best in everything. Eleanor Freiberg was married to one of the most vicious and uncompromising gangsters in New York, and yet the face she wore for the world you would have believed her married to a priest. Cathy believed Eleanor was quietly drowning beneath a tidal wave of valium and gin. How else could she have survived?

'So what we do is what we do, and such things are not pleasant,' Freiberg went on. 'They are a necessity my dear, always a necessity. If Marcus and his people want to prune their own trees then that is their business, right?'

Cathy smiled. She took a cigarette from her purse and lit it.

'And your plans?' Freiberg asked.

'I'm a New Yorker, Walt, always have been, always will be. I go where the money goes, know what I mean?'

Freiberg stepped towards her and sat down. 'Tell me something,' he said quietly. He stubbed out his cigarette, leaned back and crossed his legs. 'I have known Ben Marcus for many, many years. Despite the countless conversations I have had with the man, good and bad, I could not say that I truly understand him. You were with him for quite some time—'

'Hardly,' Cathy said. 'A few months, perhaps three or four.'

'Even so, a few months being around him, involved in things that weren't official business, you must have come to some sort of conclusion about him.'

'I wouldn't say I was *around* him, Walt . . . I spent most of my time in hotels. You know the life people like me live as well as anyone.'

Freiberg smiled understandingly. 'He hurt you, didn't he?'

'Hurt me? I think he hurts everyone who has anything to do with him eventually.'

'You tried to leave?'

Cathy looked away towards the window, caught in a wave of oppressive claustrophobia. She gripped the arms of the chair, felt her knuckles whiten. 'A hundred times, Walt, a hundred fucking times.'

'How did you end up with him?'

Cathy laughed nervously. 'Same way everyone else ends up with him.'

'You owed him money.'

She nodded. 'Right.'

'A lot?'

'Enough.'

'More than ten?'

'Twenty-eight grand, Walt. I owed him twenty-eight grand and change.'

'Gambling?'

'Yes.'

Freiberg sighed and shook his head. 'And he had you work off the debt?'

'Yeah . . . he had me work off the debt.'

'Until this thing with Edward.'

Cathy was silent for a time. She looked down at her hands, now wrestling with each other in her lap, and then she looked directly at Freiberg. Her eyes were cold, hard, unflinching. 'When the thing happened with Edward, when Edward took me away from Ben Marcus it saved my life.'

Freiberg raised his eyebrows. 'Marcus was going to kill you?'

'No Walt, he wasn't going to kill me, but I was a day or two away from killing him, and we all know how that would have ended.' She shook her head slowly. 'I didn't plan anything Walt. I can't say that I ever planned anything in my life. I was way out there though, out wherever the edge of your sanity is, and I had already given myself a choice. I was going to make a run for it, and if he came after me, because it would have been Ben Marcus who came after me personally, I vowed I would kill him. I might have done it, but Sol Neumann, Victor Klein, Ray Dietz – any of those guys who were close to him – would have hunted me to the ends of the earth and killed me right back. It was do or die for me Walt, do or fucking die.'

Freiberg shook his head and exhaled deeply. 'Just in the nick of time, eh?'

'Too right.'

'And things were okay with Edward?'

Cathy smiled. 'Edward is a gentleman, Walt, you know that better than anyone. The guy's a saint compared to Ben Marcus. Edward never laid a hand on me. Edward treated me like a human being—' Cathy Hollander felt her words catch in her chest. 'Jesus, Walt, why the hell does this shit have to happen to the people who don't deserve it?'

'Way of the world sweetheart, way of the world.'

'He's going to be alright, isn't he?'

Freiberg looked at her hard. 'Honestly?'

'Honestly.'

'I don't think so. You want my gut feeling on this, I think his time is done.'

Cathy felt tears welling in her eyes. She reached for her purse, withdrew a tissue and held it to her face.

Freiberg leaned forward, closed his hand over hers. 'You have to let this go,' he said quietly. 'He and I . . . Edward and I . . . have been family for as many years as I can recall, and I have to let him go too. This is the way these things work out, and if you knew Edward as well as I do, you would understand that going out like this is what he'd want. Wasting away in some godawful nursing home, sucking his lunch through a straw and pissing in a plastic bag is the last thing in the world he'd want. You have to look out for yourself, and you have to look forward, right? That's what Edward would want.'

Cathy nodded.

'You should get to know his son. John Harper seems like a good man.'

Cathy laughed. 'Harper? Jesus, Walt, the guy's right off the farm.'

'You listen to me, Cathy Hollander, you've got to look out for yourself. You have to make a decision now because things are going to get tough and bloody for a while. It's going to end at some point. The control of the city is going to change, and then you're going to have to make a choice between staying with me or making something of your own. You don't owe Marcus any more, and you sure as hell don't owe me anything. You're not going to come out of this empty-handed. Edward would have taken care of you, and it's my responsibility to do what he would have wanted. And this guy, John Harper, he's a smart guy. He wrote a fucking book for Christ's sake. You write a book then you can't be a retard, right?' Freiberg laughed, squeezed Cathy's hand reassuringly. 'Maybe you should make a little time to get to know him. He's got nothing here once Edward's gone. His aunt, she's a cold one. John never saw eye-to-eye with her. He isn't going to stay in New York because of her. He's going to go right back to Miami, right back to Florida where the sun shines every fucking day, where no-one has anything on him or you. It's worth considering, Cathy, it's worth looking at the possibility of going somewhere where no-one knows your name or your face. Stay here in New York and you'll always be remembered as Ben Marcus's girl, even Edward's. You're known as the girl who paid a debt for Ben Marcus, and that, believe me, is not the way you want to be known no matter who's running the show after we're gone.'

'You're really going to pack up the circus and go, aren't you?'

Freiberg smiled. 'I'm hitting the late years. This used to be a city where you could get something done, make some serious money. Everything has changed. The seventies, they were our heyday, that's when we were kids. The eighties there was all the money that came in with the business people and the cocaine. You should've seen the parties these people had, the money they threw away.' Freiberg smiled and shook his head. 'If we'd been regular people with regular jobs we'd be looking at Florida retirement brochures. Truth is, if Edward dies there isn't going to be anything here. I'm not a king Cathy, never have been and never will be. That's something that Edward could do, but me? I don't think so. I'll be on my way once everything's settled with Marcus. But you? You're on your own. That means there's room for someone else. I know that no two people are alike, and just because you're close to Edward doesn't mean that his son would be anything similar, but he seems like a good man, and he could take you away from this and help you make something better. This is not a life you want to die for, Cathy. This is the sort of life you live for as long as it isn't dangerous, and the moment it gets truly dangerous you take the best ticket out.'

There was silence for a little while. Cathy could hear the sound of her breathing, feel the beating of her heart.

'You hear me?'

'I hear you, Walt.'

'I make any fucking sense to you, or am I just another piece of furniture?'

'You aren't furniture Walt. You aren't ever going to be close to furniture. I hear what you say.'

'And?'

Cathy looked up, smiled and frowned simultaneously. 'What d'you want me to say?' She laughed. 'You want me to call him and ask him to marry me? I heard what you said, Walt. I listened. I paid attention. Lot of shit is going to go down before I have to think about what I'm going to do.'

'Sure as hell it is, but when it starts it's going to be fast. It'll be over before you know it, and then you're going to be high and dry. You have to make a plan, Cathy. You have to think about what you're going to do, and have your options worked out.'

'You going to be my career counsellor?'

'Smartmouth all you like sweetheart . . . this is a brutal fucking thing that's going to happen, and once it's done Edward is not going to be around to protect you from the backlash.'

Cathy raised her hand. 'I got it, Walt, I really do. I have my ideas, okay? I got into this trouble by being impulsive. I got some things worked out—'

'And John Harper . . . he figures somewhere in the things you've worked out?'

Cathy smiled. 'I'm going to tell you? You're a gambling man. Walt. You get a hand you keep it tight until it's ready to show, yes?'

251

Freiberg smiled. 'We're done with this,' he said. 'I get the feeling my little lecture was unnecessary.'

'I'm going to do what I have to do, Walt. Don't worry about me.'

Freiberg raised both his hands. 'Conversation is over,' he said. 'You call the hotel, find out where he's at . . . if he's there go see him and we'll arrange a meet. I want to know what the deal is with this cop . . . I want to know whether he's chasing John the way he chased Edward.'

'You're a good man, Walt Freiberg,' Cathy said. She leaned forward, held his face between her hands. She kissed him once – gently, as a daughter would kiss a father – and then she let him go.

'Go make the call,' Freiberg said. 'Go make the call and we'll see what damage has been done.'

THIRTY-SEVEN

For some reason Harper mentioned Garrett. Why, he didn't know. Perhaps it was the house, the fact that all his memories of Carmine were encapsulated within the events of that day. When Harper said his name he could see how swift and merciless the reaction was. Evelyn stopped dead in her tracks, had started to speak of Duchaunak, of Edward Bernstein, of why these men had become adversaries, and later Harper wished that the thought of Garrett had never come to mind.

'They're crazy people,' she said quietly. 'All of them. Edward Bernstein, Ben Marcus, Albert Reiff . . . all of them . . . as crazy as it gets.'

Harper leaned forward. 'How do you know these things Evelyn? How do you know what happened, about all these people, their names, what they did . . . how do you know about all the people who've died?'

She smiled. It was a smile tainted with sadness and regret. It was the expression of a woman discovering a painful truth she had long expected, and having expected it had somehow reconciled herself to it before its arrival. 'Because of Garrett.'

'Garrett?' Harper asked. 'But Garrett is dead.'

'I know, sweetheart. I know he's dead, but you mentioned his name and there he is, right there in front of me.'

Harper frowned. 'I don't understand, Evelyn. I don't understand what Garrett has to do with this.'

'You ever wonder why Garrett killed himself? You ever ask yourself that?'

'Endlessly,' Harper replied. 'I was twelve years old for God's sake. I can close my eyes even now and see him . . . I can see the room . . . everything. Of course I've asked myself why he did it.'

'You ever wonder if it wasn't a suicide?'

Harper said nothing. He remembered Duchaunak asking the

253

same question, and the thought of Duchaunak reminded him that Evelyn had started telling him about Edward Bernstein, what had happened to start the cat-and-mouse game.

'Well?' Evelyn prompted. 'Did that thought ever cross your mind?'

'Duchaunak asked the same thing,' Harper said.

'Seems to me Frank Duchaunak may have his own agenda. Who knows where his loyalty ends and his obsession begins. You ever consider that? That he might have an awful lot more to do with these people than he's saying?' Evelyn shook her head. 'Regardless, Frank Duchaunak, whatever kind of crazy he might be, is not a stupid man.'

'So Garrett was murdered? Is that what you're saying?'

'I'm not *saying* anything, John . . . I'm suggesting that there might be a different set of events and facts to explain what happened to my husband.'

'You think he was murdered?' Harper asked.

Evelyn smiled. 'The jury's still out.'

'But you consider there is a strong possibility that Garrett did not commit suicide?'

Evelyn sighed. 'I was married to him. I married the man because I loved him. I am not an impulsive or spontaneous woman. I married him because I believed he was a good man, and though there may have been mistakes, though he might have been involved with people he shouldn't have been, even involved in things that were not right, he was still a good man at heart. I also believe I knew him well enough to know he wasn't one to bail out when things got bad. I don't believe that he was the kind of man who would kill himself to avoid facing the truth.'

Harper stubbed out his cigarette. He rose from his chair and walked to the window. 'So what *are* you saying, Evelyn? What are we *actually* saying here?'

She turned towards him. 'I'm saying that nothing is exactly what it appears to be, John. I'm saying that there has been a great deal of loss and hurt and pain connected with my life. Your father is the same. He chose to do something with his life, and though I don't believe he regrets his decision I still believe that where he is now is testament to the hard reality of such a life.'

'He was shot in a liquor store robbery Ev . . . a random thing, a random shooting. Hell, it could have been anyone there—'

'Could have been, John, but wasn't. Edward was there, right there when someone came in to commit a robbery. Seems to me that those who live by the sword—'

Harper stopped her. 'Don't give me the lecture, Evelyn. The last thing I need right now is some cliched religious quotes. You'll be telling me it's karma next—'

'Maybe it is.'

'So what is the deal with these people then? Garrett died . . . how many years ago?'

'Twenty-four.'

Harper threw up his hands. 'Twenty-four years. Jesus . . . quarter of a century, Evelyn. I seem to be missing something here. He died twenty-four years ago, and yet you know all about these people, all these things they've done—'

'I don't know everything, John, not even half of it I'm sure.'

'But you know something, right?'

'I read the newspapers. I watch the TV. I listen to what people say . . . I just pay attention. For God's sake it isn't that hard to find out what happens in this city—'

'Bullshit, Ev, that's just so much bullshit. You know about these things because you *want* to know about them. You read the papers and watch TV? Not a hope. You don't find out things like that without doing something to find out.'

'Okay, okay. Enough, John. You're right. I know about them because I made the effort to find out.'

'But why? Why would you want to know this stuff?'

Evelyn sat stock-still. Her eyes were bright, fierce almost. Her hands were clenched, her whole body rigid with suppressed emotion. 'Because these are the people that took my life away John. These are the people that took away my sister and my husband—'

'You don't know that, Ev. You said that you didn't know whether or not Garrett was killed . . .'

'I know enough, John. I know that Garrett is dead, your mother too. Whether they were murdered or they killed themselves doesn't even matter now. The truth is simple, even simpler in hindsight than it was at the time. If Edward Bernstein had not been part of our lives, if they had never met him, never been involved with him, then they would both be alive . . .'

'You don't know that, Ev. How can you possibly know something like that?'

She smiled, a tense and awkward smile. 'Because I know Edward Bernstein. I know what he's like. I know what he's capable of—'

'What he's capable of? What the hell d'you mean, what he's capable of?'

Evelyn shook her head. 'You don't see it do you? Christ, I couldn't even begin to explain what these people have done. I don't know . . . it's not fair on you. It's not fair to bring you here and open up this can of worms. This is exactly what I prayed would never happen. This is why I never told you about him, why I never mentioned his name, why I told you he was dead for all these years. This is a life that I never wanted to see you become part of—'

'I'm not part of anything, Ev—'

'No, you're not, and because you aren't you're alive and well, you have a job, you aren't dead or in jail or—'

'Or anything,' Harper said. 'I'm not anything, Evelyn . . . I'm no-one. No roots, no family, no history, nothing. I live down there in Miami on my own. I have a dead-end, meaningless job—'

'Meaningless? You wrote a book, John. You wrote a book, a very good book if you want to know my opinion. And now you write for a newspaper. You don't rob banks or carry a gun. You don't spend half your time looking over your shoulder to find out which of your closest friends is going to kill you.' Evelyn stopped talking. She looked at Harper and shook her head. 'You don't get it, John, and I don't know that you ever will. I don't even know that I *want* you to get it. This is a bad business. These are dangerous and unthinking people. This Walt Freiberg . . . Walt Freiberg is a man who possesses no heart, no soul, nothing as far as I'm concerned. Walt Freiberg is a horror . . . an absolute horror of a human being—'

Evelyn paused to catch her breath. Her hands were shaking, her eyes rimmed with tears. She looked crushed, defeated.

She took a deep breath and held it for a moment. Shaking her head slowly, she rose from her chair and held out her hand towards Harper.

Harper stayed exactly where he was.

'I never wanted this life for you, John . . . never wanted you to be part of it, never wanted you to even know of it. I always said I was sorry that you left for Florida, and I was . . .' Evelyn took another step forward, reaching out her hand even further. 'I *was* sorry to see you go, but at the same time it gave me a great feeling of relief. At least in Florida there was a chance you would never become involved in this life.'

Harper stepped back, and back once more until he was stopped by the counter. He moved to the right, began making his way towards the door.

'Don't go, John,' Evelyn said, a note of pleading in her voice.

Harper shook his head. 'I'm going, Evelyn, I have to get out of here—'

'No,' she said, and tears started to well from her eyes. 'Stay here with me, John . . . stay here and we can protect each other from these people—'

But Harper stepped past her and took his jacket from the back of the chair. 'I'm going, Evelyn. I'm going back to the hotel to take some time to think about all of this. I don't know what to believe. Did my mother kill herself? Was Garrett really murdered? Who the hell is Cathy Hollander and Walt Freiberg and what the hell do they have to do with me?' He gritted his teeth, raised his fist as if he was preparing to put it through the door. 'Jesus Christ! You're right, Evelyn. I suppose I did have a life. I may not have had much of a fucking life, but it was something. I was down there in Miami minding my own business . . . Christ, I was on the way to a fishing tournament when the paper called me—'

'John . . . please—'

'No, Evelyn. Enough is enough. I'm leaving now. Don't say anything else. I've heard everything I want to hear.'

He hesitated for a split-second, almost as if he was willing her to challenge him.

She sat down heavily, looked at him with an expression of utter despair. Not a word came from her lips.

Harper nodded his head once, an acknowledgement of her silence, and then he left. He closed the front door silently while behind him, there in the small kitchen on Carmine Street, a room that represented all of his childhood years, Evelyn Sawyer buried her face in her hands and wept.

Harper had reached the junction before he registered any real emotion, and when he did it almost took him off his feet.

THIRTY-EIGHT

Cathy Hollander shook her head and set the receiver back in its cradle.

'Not there?' Freiberg asked.

'No. He went out and hasn't come back.'

Freiberg nodded. 'Okay,' he said quietly. 'Okay, okay, okay . . .'

'What do you want me to do?'

'Leave it for now,' he said. 'Go home. I have some things to see to. Call him again in the morning . . . no, second thoughts, go to the hotel in the morning. Go over there and see him in person. Make sure you actually see him. Find out what this cop has been saying to him. We can't have him falling apart on us right near the end.'

Cathy Hollander nodded.

'You can handle this?'

Cathy smiled. 'I could handle Edward,' she said.

'So be it,' Walt Freiberg said. 'John Harper is your responsibility from this point on.'

Cathy Hollander tried to smile. She found she could not. She wondered where this thing would end; if indeed it would end. She wondered, when all was said and done, if she would be alive to tell the tale.

'It's going to work out,' Walt Freiberg said, and he reached out and took her hand.

'Promise?' she asked.

Freiberg smiled; shook his head. 'Never promise anything Cathy,' he replied. 'Promises—'

'Were made to be broken, right?'

'Right.'

Cathy squeezed Freiberg's hand.

'Now go,' he said, his voice almost a whisper. 'There are things that have to be done.'

Looking like he'd walked from an auto smash, in itself nothing short of a miracle, Frank Duchaunak, cold and bitter, hands buried in his overcoat pockets, stood on the corner of Hudson and West Broadway watching the front entrance of the Regent. The urge to go up there, to stand in the corridor on the tenth floor, was almost overpowering. He wanted to see John Harper, wanted to find out what was happening, what he'd been told to do, what Freiberg had asked of him, because he knew there would be something. Frank Duchaunak *knew* there would be something.

After leaving the precinct house he'd considered making a trip to St Vincent's. Instead he'd called, learned that Lenny Bernstein was neither better nor worse. The man was in a coma, as good as, and nothing had changed since the day before.

And thus he'd walked out here, out to Hudson, out to the hotel where he believed John Harper was hiding from the world.

Three or four times he'd started away from the facing sidewalk, even made it as far as the curb, but then he'd turned back. He was a man torn between two opposites: his duty and his intuition. Duty dictated that Harper was off-limits, not only from the viewpoint that Duchaunak was suspended, but from the viewpoint that Harper himself had in no way violated any law. No matter the crime, there was no law that provided for random investigation of a perpetrator's relatives. Against this was Duchaunak's intuition, of such conviction it pained him. Walt Freiberg was keeping Harper in New York for a reason. A specific and definite reason. Walt Freiberg never did anything without rationale or motive. Not ever.

Finally, unwillingly, Duchaunak started walking away from the Regent. Had he waited a further ten or fifteen minutes he would have seen Harper himself, head down, hands buried in his coat pockets almost in mimicry of Duchaunak, walking the street as if drawn by something. His movements were automatic, unthinking, and he seemed to be fighting with something that pulled him in the opposite direction. Had the detective seen him he would perhaps have been unable to approach him. Perhaps not.

Duchaunak went home. Once inside it started to snow again. He sat and watched from his window, much as Cathy Hollander, much as John Harper, all of them looking out into the same city. Different lives, different perspectives, different reasons.

Three blocks west of Carmine, corner of Washington and Leroy, a man called Charlie Beck flicked a cigarette into the gutter, and then entered a narrow doorway to his right. A faded awning read West Side Boxing Academy. He shrugged off his coat and handed it to a man standing in the foyer. They exchanged acknowledgements without words, and then Beck walked through a second door into the gym. Place smelled rank – old sweat, dried blood, much pain. He raised his hand to Walt Freiberg who was standing against the back wall sharing words with a fighter. Beck waited until the fighter had walked away, back towards a makeshift ring at the far end of the room, and then he sauntered across to Freiberg, smiling as he went.

'We're good?' Freiberg asked.

'Good as Wenceslas,' Beck replied, and then he grinned like a fool and shook Freiberg's hand.

'What have we got?'

'M-16s. Got some .45s, .38s, few other bits and pieces.'

'Vehicles?'

'Spoke to Henry Kossoff and Victor Klein. We're going to use E-250s, four of them. Black.'

'And after?'

'Secondary vehicles will be elsewhere.'

'We're going to use the parade as cover, right?'

Beck nodded.

Freiberg didn't speak for a moment. He and Beck watched as a flyweight black kid caught a roundhouse and staggered against the corner.

'Gut feeling?' Freiberg asked. 'You think it was Marcus who put the hit on Lenny?'

Beck turned. 'I do Walt. I think he had Lenny hit because he didn't want to see the deal through.'

'And now he's cornered . . . now he has to see it through because he doesn't want Sonny Bernstein to bring some dangerous friends up from Miami.'

'Fucking irony, eh?'

'More than a fucking irony . . . thing's a piece of theater.'

'Fuck 'em all, eh?'

Freiberg nodded. 'Good as it gets, Charlie . . . fuck 'em all.'

THIRTY-NINE

It was a quarter after eleven when Cathy Hollander put her hand on his arm. She was saying something, something that Harper later could not easily recall; something about trust, about the way in which people were no longer able to trust one another, and it was then, as she said those things, that she put her hand on his arm.

Later he would remember the smell of her.

Later he would remember the way her hair looked, the way she sort of half-turned her face, and half-smiled, and then there was a sound from his own lips that was like someone laughing. Perhaps half a someone.

It was an awkward moment. A moment of tension. A moment Harper had read about, written about in a book called *Depth Of Fingerprints*, something that was now part of an earlier life.

She had been near the wall, the window behind her, and her hair had been several shades of some indistinct color, a color like gold perhaps, or copper; perhaps sun-bleached mahogany.

He had slept soundly. Slept from dusk 'til dawn really. Slept ten, eleven hours, even longer. He could not remember the moment he lay down and closed his eyes, just as he could not remember the time when they opened again, seemingly without thought or intention, seemingly without any real purpose. His mind – stretched beyond the limits of natural flexibility – was now quiet and numb.

He knew he was awake when she knocked at the door. He'd been dressed – pants, a tee-shirt, even one shoe – and when he opened the door she'd looked down at his feet and smiled. Like she'd known. Or someone had told her.

'You have on one shoe,' she'd said.

'Come in,' Harper had replied.

And then she had. Walked right past him; sort of breezed in as if it was her own suite of rooms, and the smell of her had haunted the space around him like a ghost. Harper believed that when she left he would still be able to smell her on his clothes.

'You don't look well,' she'd said. It was here that Harper's memory failed him. He remembered taking off the one shoe as opposed to putting on the second. He remembered that. He remembered standing there with the shoe in his hand, being suddenly struck by the thought that perhaps he'd slept like that – his suit pants, his tee-shirt, his one shoe.

He'd smiled absent-mindedly, shook his head, nodded then. 'Don't look well?' he echoed. 'No . . . of course not . . . don't feel well either.'

There was a child somewhere. Laughing. Running. Sound of a child laughing and running. Happy child.

Frank Duchaunak lay there for a long time, remembering the sound of the happy child. Child running down the hallway outside his apartment.

He lay there trying to remember his name, but all he could think of was Norma Jean Baker, and how Death had come to visit. August fifth, 1962, and Death had come like the mailman.

After a while, a handful of minutes, maybe an hour, Duchaunak turned on his side. He tugged the pillow from beneath his head, folded it in half and used it to support his neck. From where he lay he could see the beige and ochre monotony of his room. *It is the vista one would be comfortably accustomed to if one were a psychiatric patient*, he thought, and smiled to himself, like such a thought mattered, like there was anything that really mattered.

He stayed there for a while longer, absent of thought, of movement, and then he glanced at the small green-faced, three-dollar digital clock that flashed on the nightstand. Nine minutes past eleven the green digits flashed, and he knew it was morning because the clock evaluated everything with a twenty-four-hour perspective.

Eleven-o-nine, Duchaunak thought. Eleven-o-nine and I'm still in bed.

He unfolded the pillow, lay it flat, allowed his head to sink into it, and closed his eyes. He went back to sleep, not because he was tired, but because there was nothing left to get up for.

*

'There aren't any answers,' Albert Reiff said.

The man facing him opened his mouth to speak. There was a lot of blood around his mouth, beneath his nose also. He had a tooth missing in front, though he could have lost that some while before. One of his eyes was kind of puffed-out, like it was getting ready to swell up, to turn purple, sickly yellow, and black maybe.

'Don't say anything else, okay?' Reiff raised his hand. He had big hands, long fingers, but they weren't the kind of fingers you'd play piano with. Albert Reiff wasn't a piano-playing kind of guy. 'You say anything else you're just going to insult me further. I'm not stupid. I look like a stupid person to you? Eh? Do I? Tell me the fucking truth Mouse . . . do I look like a stupid person to you?'

The bloody-faced guy, Mouse by all accounts, shook his head vigorously. 'No Al—' he started, but Albert Reiff raised his hand and slapped Mouse.

'Did I say to fucking talk, Mouse? Hey, did anyone hear me say you should start talking now?' Albert shook his head. 'No, I didn't fucking think so.'

Mouse blinked furiously, like he was trying to communicate something in morse. He had the wide eyes of a frightened man, a cornered man, and the way he shifted in the chair, shifted without really moving, he looked like maybe he'd pissed himself and it was real uncomfortable.

'So tell me what he said,' Reiff said. 'Tell me *exactly* what he said, Mouse.'

Reiff was silent for a moment, and then: 'It's okay . . . I'm giving you permission to speak now.'

Mouse shook his head.

'Aah fuck, you have to make this all melodramatic and personal. You have to make an issue about this when it really wasn't fucking necessary.' Reiff shook his head, sort of turned and looked over his shoulder. 'Ray?' he called out. 'Ray . . . come here and listen to what Mouse has got to say for himself.'

Mouse made a sound; a sound like he was all full of air and was deflating rapidly. Sounded like everything inside him sort of collapsed.

Raymond Dietz appeared in the doorway behind Albert Reiff. He carried something in his hand.

'What?' he said.

Reiff smiled. 'Mouse doesn't seem to have a great deal to say for himself.'

'Isn't it always the way . . . always the way with these guys. And what the fuck kind of name is Mouse . . . more like fucking Rat!' Dietz laughed coarsely and came up behind Albert Reiff. He was over Reiff's left shoulder, looking down at Mouse who sat shivering, both his hands nailed to the arms of the chair, torn duct tape around the lower half of his face and throat, his ankles tied tight, one shoe removed and much of his right foot hammered to a pulp inside his sock.

'So what's the deal, Mouse?' Reiff asked. 'What *is* the deal with the man's son, eh? What is the deal with this Sonny Bernstein?'

Mouse shook his head. He closed his eyes tight and lowered his chin to his chest.

'Nothing to say then?' Dietz asked.

Mouse was silent, motionless but for the muscular twitches caused by so much pain.

'Fuck you,' Albert Reiff said, and with that he stood up and moved to the right.

Dietz was fast, faster than even Reiff expected. He stepped to the left, snatched Mouse around the throat, and with one swift arc he drove a screwdriver through the man's temple.

Mouse's eyes opened wide and stared back at the pair of them. He blinked once, his hands tugging furiously at the nails that pinned them to the chair, but all of it was involuntary, a simple muscular reaction, for Mouse had been dead the moment the screwdriver punctured his frontal lobe.

'Get someone to fix up this shit would you?' Reiff said. He glanced at his watch. 'I have to drive over the other side of town and pick my kid up for lunch.'

'Sure thing,' Dietz replied. 'I'll get some cleaners down here.'

Reiff nodded. 'See you at the thing tonight.'

'Sure, see ya tonight.'

Reiff made his way out of the room through a narrow doorway at the end of an unlit corridor.

Ray Dietz stood for a moment, hands on his hips, looking down at the dead body in the chair.

'Mouse,' he said quietly. 'You're a fucking prick.'

*

There was silence between them for quite some time. Harper sat on the edge of the bed, his head turned to the window. The curtains were half-drawn, and the light that filtered through cast much of the room in shadow. The impression was one of late afternoon.

Cathy Hollander sat on a chair near the door, beside her a small circular table upon which sat an ashtray. She'd lit a cigarette, set it in the tray, and then seemed to have forgotten it. It burned regardless, arabesques of smoke ghosting upward, each subsequent arc of grey following the next as if playing catch-as-catch-can to the ceiling.

'What happened, John?' she eventually asked.

Harper did not respond, neither moved nor spoke.

'John. Tell me what happened.'

Cathy leaned forward for a moment, and then leaned back once more. She seemed effortlessly assured, confident in everything she did and said.

Harper looked at her for some little while before speaking. A faint smile played around the corners of his mouth. 'I was wondering about something,' he eventually said. Strange, but his voice did not sound the same. Sounded like some part of him had been left behind somewhere. He figured sometime, soon perhaps, he would have to retrace his steps and find it.

'Wondering?' Cathy asked. 'Wondering what?'

'Whether everything that Frank Duchaunak has been telling me is true, or if he's one half-crazy motherfucker.'

'What did he tell you?'

'That my father is involved in New York's criminal under-world. That Walt Freiberg is his right-hand man. That there's a guy called Ben Marcus who seems to control some part of New York's territories, and there's going to be a war between him and Walt.' Harper paused for a moment, turned and looked towards the window, turned slowly back and looked at Cathy. 'And,' he added quietly, 'I have been wondering about you.'

'About me?' Cathy asked, a flicker of curiosity in her eyes. 'I've told you about me.'

'I wouldn't say that you've told me about you at all.'

She laughed briefly. 'Sure I have . . . about what happened with Ben Marcus and your father—'

Harper shook his head. 'You didn't tell me about Diane Sheridan or Margaret Miller—'

'Oh, come on!' Cathy exclaimed. 'Who the fuck told you about that? The cop? Did he tell you about Diane Sheridan and Margaret Miller?'

Harper nodded. 'He did yes. He told me they were aliases you used.'

Cathy smiled, nodded her head. 'He was right.'

Harper frowned. 'He was right? You used those names?'

'Sure I did . . . and I seem to remember using the name Lauren Briley. I think I even used the name Veronica Lane one time, like a play on Veronica Lake.'

Harper shook his head. 'I don't understand. Why would you have reason to use different names?'

Cathy shook her head. 'You really are straight out of the woods aren't you? You really don't have a clue about the kind of life I've led.'

Harper said nothing.

'I've been a hustler of one kind or another my whole life, John. I've danced in sleazy bars, I've escorted Japanese business-man in Vegas. I've served cocktails to society widows, ferried trays of warm beer to slot-machine junkies in Atlantic City. I've seen every corner of life from the bottom up and the top down. People like me live four or five lives simultaneously. You lose a job in some place, you disappear for three months, you go back with different make-up and a different name and no-one asks any questions, you get my drift?'

'And you've been arrested?'

'Sure have sweetheart . . . arrested, charged, arraigned, bound over, spent three or four nights in the holding tank more times than I care to recall. Even been driven to the state line of Texas and politely asked not to come back.'

Harper was smiling. 'You're shitting me.'

Cathy shook her head. 'Do I look like I'm shitting you?'

'No, you don't.'

'Right. What possible reason could I have for telling you anything but the truth. I don't have anything to prove to you, and I sure as hell don't feel there's any need to have you think of me as something other than I am. I've pretty much done everything you can do apart from hook for a living—'

268

'Hook?' Harper asked, even as it dawned on him what Cathy was saying.

'Hook, right . . . like be a hooker. Jesus, you really are a little naïve aren't you?'

Harper raised his hand. 'I've had three or four conversations with Duchaunak, and each time I've come away with a very different viewpoint about everybody I know here in New York, even people I don't know—'

'What has he told you? What has he told you about the people here in New York?'

'Christ, loads of things, all manner of stuff, and I really don't know whether to believe any of it or not.'

'Such as?'

'He's never said anything direct . . . he never does. He makes inferences. He implies something, and then when I try to pin him down to something precise he says he doesn't know.'

'Which doesn't seem a very substantial way of going about things, if you don't mind me saying.'

Harper nodded. 'It's like trying to catch a smoke ring. He said something a while back, something about my mother having committed suicide. I was told she died of pneumonia, have always believed that, and Duchaunak implied that she committed suicide.'

'And did she?'

Harper shrugged. 'I went to see Evelyn and asked her about it.'

'And what did she say?'

'She confirmed it. She told me that my mother committed suicide because it was the only way she could escape from my father.'

Cathy Hollander looked at Harper for quite some time. Thirty seconds, perhaps a minute, and then she rose from the chair and walked towards him. She sat down on the bed beside him.

'What else did he say?' she asked. Her voice was gentle, sympathetic almost.

'He said that my Uncle Garrett, Evelyn's husband, the one I found dead, the one who shot himself in the head—' Harper turned and looked at Cathy. He was very aware of her closeness. 'Duchaunak said that such a suicide could very easily have been murder.'

Cathy was nodding slowly. She placed her hand on Harper's arm; he was intensely aware of the pressure it created.

'What else?' she asked.

Harper shook his head. 'I don't remember. So many things . . . so many different things. Some of them he said like they were facts, other things like they were possibilities. I got confused . . . so confused.'

Harper felt Cathy pulling at his arm. He felt himself losing his balance as he sat there on the edge of the bed. He went sideways, just a few inches, but he came to rest with his head against her shoulder. He could smell her perfume, feel the sensation of her hair against his cheek, and for a moment he believed that he'd not been so close to a woman for as long as he could recall. He opened his mouth to speak again, to say something, anything, as if he felt he should continue talking to justify her gesture of empathy and consolation.

'Ssshhh,' she whispered.

Harper fell silent. He could hear her breathing, feel the beat of her heart. He felt her hand in his hair then, her fingertips grazing his cheek, and for a moment he closed his eyes.

'You need to come and see Walt,' she said. 'You need to come and speak to Walt . . . Walt will tell you the truth about all of this, John. Walt knows everything that happened, and what Frank Duchaunak and Evelyn have told you is only the half of it.'

Harper turned slightly, once again felt her very real warmth and closeness.

Cathy moved her shoulder slightly and Harper eased back. Their faces were almost touching.

'I don't want—' Harper started.

Cathy reached up her right hand and pressed her finger to his lips. She shook her head slowly. 'Don't think,' she said. 'Don't talk . . . no more questions, okay? You're going to get dressed and we're going to go see Walt, and then things will start to make sense.'

Harper nodded, closed his eyes for a moment.

Cathy Hollander kissed his forehead. 'It's going to be alright,' she said. 'Trust me, John, it's going to be alright.'

Harper looked up at her. He felt her nose graze his cheek. He moved his head slightly. He felt her tense up, just a fraction,

270

something almost imperceptible, but she did not withdraw. John Harper swallowed. His throat was tight. It was difficult to breathe. He raised his hand, felt it travel in slow-motion, and then he held his palm against her face. He moved forwards, felt her lips against his, and for a heartbeat they were connected. Then, suddenly, unexpectedly, he sensed her inhale and flinch. Just like that. She pulled back and his hand was no longer touching her face.

'No,' she said. 'John . . . no . . .'

'Yes,' he whispered, and leaned forward once again. Their lips met, this time with greater pressure, and when he opened his mouth slightly he felt her yield in return. He reached behind her, held her against him, and then she started to struggle, raised her hand and pushed against his shoulder.

'No, John!' she snapped, and moved backwards. She stood up suddenly, and it seemed she would lose her balance.

Harper reached out to steady her but she brushed his hand aside and stepped back even further.

'We can't do this,' she said, and in her eyes was such an expression of loss and hurt that Harper believed he had truly offended her.

He opened his mouth to speak, to say something that would make sense.

'Don't say anything,' Cathy said. She walked towards the window and sat down in the chair.

Harper rose and took a step towards her. 'I'm sorry—'

'Don't be . . . please don't be sorry . . .'

Harper shook his head. 'It's my fault. I'm sorry. I didn't mean to upset you. Just let it go, okay? I really don't want you to think that—'

She laughed. 'I've let it go,' she said. 'Okay? We're okay on that? It never happened, alright?'

Harper nodded, felt he had to agree. Didn't want to. Agreeing with her was the last thing in the world he wanted to do.

'It's gone,' she said. She brushed her hair away from her face. 'We're going to go see Walt,' she added. 'Right now. We go see Walt, okay?'

'Okay,' Harper said.

'Everything's just as it was,' Cathy said.

Harper smiled, reached for his jacket, and knew that everything was not just as it was; knew that it would never be the same again.

Not a word passed between them as they left the room.

FORTY

Four minutes after noon.

Duchaunak opened his eyes. He could not remember if he had slept during the previous hour, but he vaguely recalled a sense of dreaming.

He lay there for a little while, and then he sat up, his legs over the edge of the mattress, the pillow in his lap.

He looked around the room: the TV and VCR in the corner, the shelving unit holding a stack of tapes, the titles of which he could read from where he sat: *The Misfits, Monkey Business, Niagara, Some Like it Hot, Bus Stop, How to Marry a Millionaire, The Prince and the Showgirl*. He had every one of them, and how many times he'd watched them he could never hope to recall.

Not a life really, is it? he thought. *Not really, officially, what one would call 'a life'.*

Frank Duchaunak lay back again. He looked at the ceiling. He wondered, just for a moment, what would become of him.

'I need to go back,' Harper said as they reached the end of the corridor.

Cathy frowned.

'I need to get a tie.'

'You what?'

Harper raised his hand, sort of pulled his unbuttoned shirt collar tight around his throat. 'A tie,' he said. 'I want to get a tie.'

'Okay,' Cathy said. 'I'll wait here.'

Harper returned the way they'd come, unlocked and entered the room, walked to the chair near the window and from the back of it took a dark blue silk tie. He paused a moment to knot it, watching his hands do their work in the mirror beside the wardrobe.

He looked at himself. White shirt, cuff-links, a tailored suit, a tie, a watch, clean shoes. He nodded. He tried to smile. He didn't know what to think, and thus he tried to think nothing at all.

He left the room, walked back to where Cathy Hollander stood by the elevators.

'You look good,' she said. 'You scrub up well.'

Harper shook his head, hesitated as if in thought, and then turned and looked at Cathy. The expression on his face was almost vacant. 'Let's go,' he said quietly.

'Right,' she said, and took his arm.

'He said nothing? Nothing at all?'

'Right.'

'Nothing at all is no fucking use to me, Sol.'

Neumann nodded. He sat facing Marcus. How many years he's worked for the man, the number of times they've been faced with such situations, never once the faintest suggestion Marcus would direct his anger at him, but still Neumann was unnerved. Ben Marcus was unquestionably the most intense man he had ever known.

'Who spoke to Mouse?'

'Dietz and Reiff,' Neumann replied.

'You didn't go down there?'

Neumann shook his head. 'I couldn't Ben, I had that other thing to handle.'

'What thing?'

'The thing with the cars . . . I had to make sure everything was ready with the cars.'

'I should've sent Dietz to handle that and you should've seen Mouse.' Marcus rose from the chair behind his desk and started pacing back and forth between the window and the door. He was silent for a minute or two, his brow furrowed, and then he paused and turned towards Neumann. 'They killed him, right?'

Neumann nodded.

'And you trust them for this . . . they wouldn't get riled and kill the guy because he upset them?'

'Hell Ben, they're as good as they come. Remember that thing with the cop's brother a while back? Ray and Albert handled that better than I could've done. They would've given Mouse every opportunity to tell them whatever he knew.'

274

'So are we of the opinion that Mouse knew something and evaded them, or that Mouse knew nothing?'

Neumann shook his head. 'I can't guarantee anything, but I'd say the latter.'

Marcus walked back to his chair and sat down.

'But hey, Mouse Jackson isn't exactly at the top of the fucking totem pole in Lenny Bernstein's crew, know what I mean?'

Marcus nodded. 'I know, Sol, I know . . . but it seems strange that something as big as this wouldn't have already filtered its way right through the ranks.'

'Bigger it is the less people know, right? Something like this you have to keep under wraps right until the very moment it goes loose . . . otherwise, hell, who the fuck knows who's got who on whose payroll?'

Ben Marcus sighed and leaned back against the chair. 'So, we're none the wiser; we really don't have a clue who this guy is, this Sonny Bernstein. We get words that mean nothing. He's this, he's that, he's the other, but nothing specific. If this guy's the player that Freiberg says he is then he's done one hell of a job of disappearing.'

Neumann shrugged his shoulders. 'Heard of a guy one time . . . Cuban guy I think, worked for the Mafia for some fifty odd years. Name was Pereira . . . no, Perez, Ernesto Perez. Fifty years working for the Mafia, and when they finally got him there was no fucking record anywhere . . . no passport, no driving license, no Social Security number, nothing.'

'What you saying, Sol, that this Sonny Bernstein works for the Mafia?'

'I'm not saying anything, Ben, 'cept that people can exist without being on any official record.'

'Official records I'm not concerned about. I just want to know if there's some reliable word on this guy in Florida, anything that will tell me whether I'm up against an army or a fucking ghost.'

Neumann shook his head. 'These things seem good, Ben. Victor's done some good work. We got weapons, we got the vehicles being arranged. He's got names of managers in each branch, the people with access codes. He's done his usual straight-up job. The practice runs have gone well. People from our crew and Bernstein's lot seem to be working together. Hey,

Sonny Bernstein is here, whoever the fuck he might be . . . seems to me everything's going to roll forward just like you agreed with Lenny. Fact that we never intended to go through with the agreement is beside the fucking point now . . . way it seems, we could come out the other end of this thing with a great deal more than when we went in.'

'I can't deal with what *seems* to be, Sol. I need to know the facts; I need to know exactly what these people are going to do now Lenny's in St Vincent's.'

'I think you've hit the problem right there, Ben,' Neumann said. 'I get the idea even *they* don't know what they're going to do.'

Marcus said nothing.

Neumann sat motionless.

'And McCaffrey?' Marcus finally asked.

Neumann hesitated, and then he shook his head.

Marcus closed his eyes. He inhaled slowly, exhaled again. 'Nothing?'

'We found the sister, the brother as well. We got nothing from either of them. Rumor has it McCaffrey's dead.'

Marcus opened his eyes and looked at Neumann. 'Rumor?'

'Well—'

'I want his head, Sol. I want McCaffrey's head in a bag by the end of the day. I don't know how many times this has to be ordered. Get me it now. I am *ordering* that McCaffrey be found.'

Neumann did not respond.

'Go,' Marcus said.

Neumann didn't move.

'*Now*, Sol . . . go now, and bring me this nigger's head.'

FORTY-ONE

'Frank Duchaunak,' Walt Freiberg said, 'is basically a good man. Fact of the matter is that his heart is in the right place . . . difficulty is that his mind isn't.'

Cathy smiled, glanced across the table at Harper, and seeing that he too had smiled she seemed to relax. They'd shared no more than a dozen words in the cab. Cathy had called Freiberg on his cellphone, arranged to meet him in a restaurant on West Third near the Judson Memorial Church. It was no longer snowing, but the drifts from an earlier fall had banked against the storefronts and curbs. 'Feels like Christmas,' Harper had said, and then turned and looked at her, his tiredness evident, his emotions frayed, his mind stretched at the seams, and she had reached out and touched his hand, and they seemed, perhaps, to be conspiratorial, to be on some similar wavelength, communicating with no words. She had nodded, half-smiled, glanced away and out through the window, and Harper had looked down, closed his eyes, and then silently exhaled. They were pretending. He knew that. Was aware that she knew it too. They had almost coincided for a moment in the hotel room, and then the moment had gone. Everything from this point forward would be varnished with a gloss of pretense.

Cathy paid the cab, and once through the doorway of the restaurant they had waited no more than five or six minutes before Freiberg arrived.

He seemed in good spirits, shedding his overcoat, laughing with the maître d' joining them at the table towards the rear of the room.

It was Cathy who mentioned Duchaunak's name, commented on the fact that Harper had encountered the man on more than one occasion, that the detective had been telling Harper all manner of things, that Walt should perhaps clarify the facts, take away the uncertainties, put everything right.

It was then that he'd said the thing about Duchaunak, that the man's heart was in the right place, that his mind wasn't.

'Addiction,' he went on. 'The power of an addiction is always greater than the addict's loyalties. So it is with Frank Duchaunak.'

Harper frowned. 'He's on drugs?'

Freiberg laughed. 'No, John, he's not on drugs. I was about to give you an analogy.'

Harper leaned back in his chair just as the waiter arrived.

Freiberg ordered – hot chicken salads, fresh granary rolls with Normandy butter, other things – and once the waiter had stepped away he edged his chair backwards, crossed his legs and lit a cigarette.

'Frank Duchaunak carries an obsession—'

'I spoke to Duchaunak,' Harper interjected. 'He told me a great deal of things. He told me that I should go and see Evelyn and clarify things about my mother . . . and at the same time he told me to leave New York.'

'For any particular reason?'

'Because there was going to be a war.'

'A war?'

'Between my father, or at least you . . . a war between you and a man called Ben Marcus.'

Freiberg smiled, looked like he was going to laugh but didn't. 'And when did he tell you this?'

Harper thought for a moment. 'Thursday.'

'And he came to see you at your hotel?'

'No, I met him at the hospital, and then we went to a coffee shop.'

'Right, right,' Freiberg said quietly. 'And what else did Frank Duchaunak tell you?'

'He told me about Mr Benedict, said he traded in stolen clothing, and that he runs a chain of illegal bookmakers from the Lower East Side to Eighth Avenue. He said that he worked for my father.'

'He did, did he? And what did Evelyn say?'

Harper shook his head. 'This hasn't been easy Walt . . . this has been one helluva couple of days.'

278

'I know, Sonny, I know . . . tell me what Evelyn said.'

'She told me about my mother . . . that she didn't die of pneumonia, that she took an overdose. Duchaunak knew about it, he knew the truth about her.'

'What makes you think that?' Freiberg asked.

'Because he was the one who told me to go over and see her. He told me to go and ask Evelyn how my mother was like Marilyn Monroe.'

'Jesus Christ, this guy has a nerve. I can't see how he can say this shit and get away with it.' Walt looked angry. His fists clenched and unclenched. He suddenly stopped and took his cellphone from his jacket pocket.

'What're you doing?' Cathy asked.

'I'm going to call Charlie.'

Cathy shook her head. She put her hand on the phone even as Walt was punching in the number. 'No,' she said. 'There's nothing that Charlie's going to do that isn't going to cause more grievance.'

Walt Freiberg looked at her. Cathy looked right back at him, didn't look away.

Harper watched Freiberg's profile, could see the knot of muscle beneath his ear that swelled and relaxed as he gritted his teeth.

'Okay,' Freiberg said, almost a whisper, and then he turned back to Harper.

'Seems everyone has had a go at telling you a story,' he said. 'Don't know about you, but seems to me one of the oldest rules in the game applies here.'

Harper shook his head. 'Oldest rules? What oldest rule?'

'Thirty minutes,' Freiberg said. He sort of smiled knowingly. 'Thirty minutes into the play, if you haven't figured out who the fall guy is then maybe it's you.'

Duchaunak glanced at his watch. 'Just before one,' he said.

The telephone receiver was tucked beneath his chin and against his shoulder. He was seated on the edge of the bed trying to tie his shoelace while he spoke.

'Don't go over there,' Faulkner said. 'Leave it be.'

'I don't want to leave it, Don, I want to go see the guy now.'

Duchaunak took the receiver in his hand and stood up. With his free hand he pressed his temples between thumb and middle finger. Everything about his body language spoke of exhaustion, frustration, irritability. He paced back and forth as he listened.

'What're you going to tell him? That you're there officially?'

'Of course I'm not going to go over there officially,' he said, interrupting Faulkner. Silence for a moment.

'I can't have you fuck this up any more than it's already fucked up, Frank—'

'For Christ's sake, Don, give me some credit. I can go and speak to the guy. Jesus, he's on his own in the hotel . . . as far as I know he's on his own. I can go over and speak to him, one human being to another. I'm perfectly capable of going over there and holding a civil conversation with him.'

'McLuhan called me in and put me on something else you know.'

'You what? He took you off suspension?'

'No, he didn't take me off suspension . . . he pulled me in to help Sampson on this double murder thing. He put me on a desk, taking calls you know? Following up the cranks, the usual kind of crap that goes along with such a thing.'

'What double murder?' Duchaunak asked.

'You remember, the one with this brother and sister . . . Darryl and Jessica McCaffrey?'

'He didn't call me, Don . . . McLuhan didn't call me.'

'I know Frank, I know . . . and he told me to dissuade you from any attempt to harass Bernstein or Harper, anyone at all.'

'I am going to go over there, Don. I'm going to go to the Regent and see Harper.'

'I know you are Frank . . . be careful for fuck's sake, will you?'

'Okay . . . okay, Don. Tonight. I'm going to go over there tonight.'

'Call me . . . okay? Let me know what the hell you're doing.'

'I will, Don, I'll call you tomorrow.'

'Okay, Frank. You take care now.'

'I will.' Duchaunak stepped back, set the receiver in its cradle, sat down on the edge of the bed and put his head in his hands.

'Never figured it would be this hard,' he said to himself. 'Never figured it would be this fucking hard.'

*

280

'Tell you something about your father,' Walt Freiberg said. He took a warm roll from a basket in the center of the table and broke it in half. He spoke as he buttered it thickly.

'Couple of years back, when exactly doesn't matter, Frank Duchaunak came and found Edward in a restaurant not far from here. I was there with him. Me, Edward, another couple of guys just having some dinner, minding our own business.'

Freiberg tore a section from the roll, put it in his mouth, raised his serviette and wiped his lips.

'So Frank comes over, right to the edge of the table, and he says hello to us, he shakes Edward's hand. He knows the guys around the table. There's no strangers there, right?'

Harper nodded, aware of little else but Cathy Hollander beside him.

'So Frank is standing there. Edward asks him if he'd like to sit down, perhaps have something to eat. Frank smiles, he shakes his head. "I'm not hungry," he says. "Shame," Edward replies. "Food here is really good." It kind of goes back and forth like this for a minute or so, and I look at Edward and I can see that he doesn't really get why Frank is standing there. So eventually Edward asks him. He says, "What d'you want, Detective? Why are you here? You come over and speak with us, you don't want to eat. What's the deal here?"'

Freiberg smiled, reached for his glass and took a sip of wine.

'So we're all waiting for what Frank has to say. He hesitates for a moment, like for some kind of dramatic effect, and then he says, "You know a man was killed today?" "A man was killed today?" Edward asks him. "Yeah, a man was killed. Don't worry Edward, he wasn't an important man. He was just a guy in a jewelry store on West Houston. Hell, I don't think he would've lasted much longer anyway. He was pretty old, getting on in years, you know?" "No, as a matter of fact I don't know," Edward says to him, and Frank says, "Sure you do, Edward . . . little jewelry hit your people pulled on West Houston. Security guy there, got himself hit in the head real fucking hard . . . Well . . . I figured it wouldn't have been polite not to let you know what happened to him."'

Freiberg reached for his glass again, took another drink.

'So Edward says, "And why would this concern me Frank? What does this have to do with me?", and Frank says, "I don't

281

know Edward. I just figured you might want to know. I just spent four and half hours by the old guy's bedside in the hospital, waiting for him to come round so he could tell us something about what happened. Only problem is he never did come round. He gave up less than an hour ago, and I thought it was only common decency to come over here and tell you." "Common decency," Edward said. "What the hell are you talking about?" "Talking about one of your people," Frank said . . . stood right there at the end of the table and said that to your father. "Talking about one of your people . . . some no-good two-bit asshole who works for you . . . works for you on one of your robberies. He gets a little unruly, a little freaked, and he whacks some poor old guy in the head and the guy dies. Not a word. Not a single fucking word and he's dead. That's what I'm talking about Lenny," he says. Calls him Lenny right there in front of his friends. "That's what I'm talking about Lenny." And Edward sits there and doesn't reply. Doesn't say a goddamned word.

'I was with him the whole time. We'd been living out of each other's pockets for, like, two, three weeks, and if there was a robbery on West Houston then it was news to me. But Edward doesn't challenge Duchaunak. He knows that if he challenges him, riles him, then Duchaunak will just go off into left field and never make it home. He lets Frank Duchaunak stand there for a little while longer, and then when Frank starts to feel awkward, when he starts to look like he's made an asshole of himself, Edward stands slowly, walks around the edge of the table and takes Duchaunak's arm. He walks him to the door, smiling all the way, and if you'd seen them they would have looked like long-lost catching up on stories from home. Edward walks him out into the street, right out into the street, and then he calls a cab. The cab comes, he puts Frank inside it, and just as he's about to close the door Duchaunak leans towards the open window.'

Freiberg leaned forward, almost in echo of what he was describing.

'Edward sees Duchaunak leaning towards him, and he bends down to hear what the guy has to say. "Given the time again," Frank says. "Given the time again . . . with hindsight, with everything behind you, with everything that has happened, would you make a different choice?" And Edward thinks for a moment, almost like he's teasing Duchaunak, and then he says "Choice, Frank? What the hell made you think that this was ever a matter of choice?"'

Freiberg smiled and leaned back in his chair. 'That, John Harper,' he said, 'is the kind of person your father is, and if you want to know the truth about him then you ask me. You don't ask Frank fucking Duchaunak, and you sure as hell don't ask Evelyn Sawyer. You ask me. And you want to know why?'

Harper raised his eyebrows.

'I'll tell you why, Sonny. You ask me because I was there . . . all the way along the line, regardless of what happened . . . good, bad or indifferent, I was there. That's the facts, my boy . . . those *are* the facts. I was there. No fucker else was. You want to know something about Edward Bernstein then you've come to the right place, okay?'

Harper nodded. 'Okay.'

'So you want to know some stuff?' Freiberg asked.

'Sure, Walt, sure.'

'Shoot,' Freiberg said. 'You ask me whatever the fuck you like and you're going to get an answer. May not like it, but hell, you find me anyone on God's green earth who likes everything that goes on, eh?'

'Anything?' Harper asked.

'Sure as hell, Sonny, anything. Ask away.'

FORTY-TWO

Ben Marcus, Sol Neumann. Both of them standing back of the desk. Neumann standing to the right, Marcus leaning forward, hands on the back of his chair, a chair he would ordinarily be seated in.

Ahead of them sat Raymond Dietz and Albert Reiff, other regulars – Maurice Rydell, Henry Kossoff and Karl Merrett. Seated, chairs gathered together in a sort of half-circle, and already the room was filled with smoke as they sat and listened to Marcus, listened and never questioned.

'Easy is not in this vocabulary,' Marcus said. 'Easy is for other people – kids, schoolteachers, people who work in libraries. What we have in front of us is an asshole of a thing. No bones about it. No questions. Maybe the toughest thing you ever done. All of you.'

Marcus pulled out his chair and sat down. He rested his forearms on the desk, hands together, and he took a moment to survey the faces in front of him.

'Johnnie Hoy. Micky Levin. May they rest in peace. Just because they messed up doesn't mean they don't deserve a moment of respect now they're gone.'

A murmur of consent.

'This is a tough business. We all know that. People walk between the lines. Lines are very easy to see. Step over the lines and you have to set things right again. You don't get things right, then you have to be put someplace where you aren't going to interfere with business. Johnnie, Micky, they knew where the lines were. Maybe they believed that there was room for a little sidelining. Maybe not. Doesn't matter now.'

Marcus turned and looked up at Sol Neumann, standing there at the side of the desk, arms folded, face implacable.

Marcus turned back to the small audience.

'Mouse Jackson. We had some words with him.' Marcus looked at Dietz and Reiff in turn. 'He wasn't able to give us anything. From all appearances, Lenny Bernstein got himself shot up in a liquor store robbery. Wasn't anything. Some wild kid with a .38 as far as we can tell. They have Lenny in St Vincent's, but his son is here, and as far as we know, simply because we've heard no word to the contrary, everything is going to roll forward on the twenty-fourth. Seems everything is going to make time, just like we figured with Lenny. And then when the thing is done we'll have what we always wanted, and Lenny . . . well, Lenny would have done whatever the hell he wanted, but now?' Marcus shook his head. 'Maybe he'll make it, maybe he won't. Doesn't matter a great deal to me. I respect the man. *Have* to respect the man after everything he's done, but just 'cause I respect him doesn't mean I'm going to be sorry he's dead.' Marcus waved his hand in a dismissive fashion. 'Whatever,' he added. 'These things always have a way of working themselves out.'

Once again, a murmur of consent from the five seated men.

'So everything goes . . . everything goes as if nothing has changed. This guy, this Sonny Bernstein, seems he will stand for his father, and whatever he says is going to be the same as if Lenny himself had said it. That's the way we're treating this business, and if it comes out the way we figured then everyone's going to go home happy.'

Marcus eased back his chair and stood up.

'But there is still this one thing, and I am not happy. You have all done what you were supposed to do. We have vehicles, we have weapons, we have the people we need. Victor has provided the floor plans and names we need. We know what we're after and we have a way to get it.'

Marcus paused and surveyed the gathered faces. 'However, despite this, I am not happy. I am not fucking happy at all.' His fists clenched, and the tension in the room tangibly increased. 'This Thomas McCaffrey is still somewhere. He may already be dead. The point is that we don't know. This is something that we cannot forget about. This is something that has to be fixed, and fast. You understand?'

The gathering nodded, looked at one another, looked back at Marcus.

'Whatever it takes we find him. Get word out to whoever you know. Speak to the people you trust, even to the people you don't. You need buy-money then you speak to Sol. When it's done the man who found him gets twenty-five bonus. That's all there is to it. I want this Thomas McCaffrey found before this thing goes off on the twenty-fourth.'

Once again the men nodded in affirmation.

'So, until the night before, we don't meet again. Not any of us. Not in the same place. No phone calls from landlines. Use payphones. Don't use cellphones. Everyone knows the drill. Anyone wants me they go through Sol, understood?'

The men nodded, grunted their acknowledgements.

'So let's get out there.'

They all rose, all five of them, and as they left they each shook hands in turn with both Ben Marcus and Sol Neumann.

Once the office was vacated Marcus turned to Neumann. 'I see Lester McKee was not present.'

Neumann nodded.

'Trouble?'

'Enough.'

'Someone's going to take care of it?'

Neumann nodded. 'Someone's going to take care of it.'

'Did he do the thing with the trailer . . . the one with the cigarettes out of the McCarren Park warehouse?'

Neumann shrugged. 'Fuck knows.'

'He did something else?'

'He did something else.'

'We're going to lose him?' Marcus asked.

'Yep.'

'And on the day? Who's going to take his place?'

'Albert has a boy we can use.'

'Not his own kid for Christ's sake . . . that kid has to be the dumbest motherfucker ever to walk the face of the earth.'

Neumann smiled. 'No, not his own kid. Some other kid he knows.'

Marcus raised his hand. 'Whatever, whatever. Just take care of things right, okay?'

'Ben,' Sol Neumann said, in his voice a tone of disappointment and surprise. 'When did I ever—'

Marcus reached out and gripped Neumann's shoulder. 'Never

is the answer to your question Sol,' he said. 'I'm not talking about you ... I'm talking about these other assholes. Hell, they're good people, but this is the big one, right? This is the thing. This is the one that makes everything come together, and I cannot afford any fuck-ups, know what I mean? I made an agreement with Lenny, an agreement I never intended to keep. Now, events unforeseen, I have to keep this agreement. I got Lenny's kid up from Miami, and as far as I know the guy's a fucking ghost. I got this McCaffrey guy on the loose. I got his dead brother and his dead fucking sister ... a fucking social worker and a nurse for Christ's sake! You imagine how that's going to look on my résumé? I got too many variables Sol, too many variables. I don't sleep so well when there's variables.'

'Take it easy Ben, take it easy,' Neumann said. 'This thing has been worked out professionally. Victor knows what he's doing, and this McCaffrey guy has gone somewhere and I figure he isn't going to come back. If I were him I'd pick a direction and just keep fucking running. Believe me, nothing is going to go wrong, Ben, nothing is going to go wrong.'

'I know, I know, I know. I just cannot have anyone out of step on this. There's going to be a meeting with Freiberg. I have any loose ends, anything looks out of place, then I'm going to have to kill him. That's just the way it's got to be. I get the idea Freiberg has created a mirage around this guy. I don't care who he is, how many people he knows down in Miami ... fact that we're not getting any substantial word on him tells me that it's a scam. Way it feels right now I'm going to have to kill Walt Freiberg, maybe this Sonny Bernstein as well. People around them will fall into line fast enough. Freiberg has made himself the head of Lenny's crew. He disappears, then that crew will become ours and we can still pull this thing on the twenty-fourth. I don't want to do that, but if that's what needs to happen then that's what will happen.'

'Ben, it's okay. Go to the club will you? Go see one of those girls and get a fucking massage or something. You're making something out of nothing. It's going to go fine ... believe me ... it's going to go fine.'

Ben Marcus smiled and reached for the door handle. 'Ever the optimist, Sol, ever the optimist. How'd you get to be so fucking optimistic?'

Neumann smiled back. 'Dropped me on my head when I was born . . . been as cheerful as fucking springtime ever since.'

FORTY-THREE

'You *know* she killed herself,' Harper said matter-of-factly.

'You heard me,' Freiberg replied.

Harper turned to look at Cathy Hollander.

Evelyn had stated the facts the way she saw them, the way she believed them to be. Confirmation was everything. One person is opinion, two people . . . well, two people say the same thing and you can pretty much take it to the bank.

'And why do you think she killed herself?'

'Why?' Freiberg echoed. He pushed his dinner plate to the side and leaned forward. Harper thought the man looked like something from a '40s classic – Edward G., Jimmy C., Humphrey B.; Sidney Greenstreet and Peter Lorre somewhere out back in the kitchen sharpening things and looking scary, all hooded eyes and high-key lighting. 'Why does *anyone* do such a thing?'

'Two of them did, my mother and Garrett Sawyer, both in the same house and five years apart.' Harper shook his head. 'What the fuck was that all about?'

Freiberg leaned forward. 'People kill themselves for two reasons. There's something they want they can't have. There's something they've got they don't want. That's pretty much it. Doesn't get an awful lot more complicated than that.'

Harper was silent for a moment. Once more he looked at Cathy. She smiled understandingly. Harper looked at her lips, the way the muscles tensed when she changed her expression. He wanted to know why she had pulled away. He wanted to kiss her again, make her yield.

He turned back to Freiberg. 'She had something she didn't want,' Harper said matter-of-factly.

'Something she didn't want? What d'you mean?'

'Evelyn told me . . . that Anne was aware of the life my father was leading and felt she couldn't escape from it. That's why she killed herself.'

Freiberg smiled. It was a dry and humorless smile. 'Is that what she told you?'

Harper nodded. 'Yes. Why?'

'Because, my dear friend, it was exactly the opposite.'

'The opposite? I don't understand.'

'Anne Harper didn't kill herself to get away from something. She killed herself because the people who loved her, at least the people who *said* they loved her, were hell-bent on making her leave your father. That's why your mother died, because her sister, your Aunt Evelyn and her husband, other people who knew her at the time . . . all of them were doing everything they could to make her leave your father. That was what happened Sonny, that was *exactly* what happened.'

Harper was frowning, looking sideways at Cathy Hollander, then back to Walt Freiberg.

'It isn't difficult,' Freiberg said. 'Your father and your mother, like Romeo and Juliet, the Montagues and the Capulets, and all manner of bullshit thrown in there by people who had no goddamned business getting themselves involved. Evelyn and I never saw eye-to-eye as you know. There was always something with that woman, something undercover, something unspoken. Never said what she meant, never meant what she said. I mean, for Christ's sake, look at the bullshit lines she fed you. Your father is dead. Goddamnit, you're how old? Thirty-whatever fucking years of age before you find out that your father isn't dead; all these years, he's alive and well and living in New York. And then this thing with your mother . . . dying from pneumonia, that's what she told you, right?'

Harper looked back at Freiberg, didn't move, didn't say a word.

'That's right, isn't it?' Freiberg asked again. 'She told you that your mother died of pneumonia?'

Harper nodded.

'So what the hell is that? The truth about your parents is right there in front of you all this time. She tells you just what she wants you to know and nothing more. That was always her way. That's just the person she is, Sonny. She didn't want your father around Anne, believed that what she thought was right for your mother was more important than whatever the hell anyone else might think, even Anne herself. Anne lived under a cloud. Jeez, she was one of the prettiest, brightest girls I ever knew. She was a real sweetheart, and smart too, very smart indeed. And yet you could see something else there, like there was something that haunted her. You could just feel the way she lived under this oppressive cloud all the time, and that came from Evelyn.'

Freiberg shook his head, ground his cigarette into the ashtray and lit another.

'And Garrett? Garrett was a good man. I knew Garrett long before he ever met Evelyn. Garrett Sawyer was a tough bastard, didn't take no crap, but he got himself in with Evelyn and that was the end of that. Guy was never the same again. We used to go out, me and Edward and Garrett, used to go out and see people, used to play cards over in Atlantic City with Ray Dietz and Victor Klein, a couple of guys who now work for Ben Marcus. We caused some trouble, we upset some folks, but we never did any real harm. We were young, and things never seemed to be as serious as other people made them.' Freiberg smiled. 'One time . . . I tell you about this one time with me and Garrett—'

Freiberg stopped mid-flight. He shook his head. The smile vanished. 'Hell, I'm sorry, kid. You don't want to be hearing good ol' boy stories about me and Garrett Sawyer. Where was I?'

'Garrett and Evelyn,' Cathy said.

'Right, right . . . Garrett and Evelyn. Yeah, so I knew him before he ever met her. I knew Garrett when he was a hired hand for this freight company downtown. Hard-working guy, real hard-working. Never complained, never a bad word out of his mouth about anyone. And then he met Evelyn, and Evelyn was something else. She was like whatsername in that Brando movie, the one where the sister comes to visit.'

'*Streetcar Named Desire*,' Cathy said.

'Right, the sister . . . the one who was in *Gone With The Wind*.'

'Vivien Leigh . . . she played Blanche DuBois.'

'Right, right, Blanche DuBois. She was like that, all airs and graces and ideas above herself, that's just how she was. From the moment Garrett met her he was walking on eggshells with everything he did. He was a regular guy, a real straight-up Joe, and then she came sailing in like the Queen Mary and kicks the wind out of his sails—'

'Why did he shoot himself?' Harper asked.

Freiberg shrugged his shoulders. 'You asking me whether I think he wanted out of the thing with Evelyn?'

'I'm asking why he shot himself, that's all. You knew him. You knew what he was like—'

'You knew him too kid, you were almost a man when that thing went down.'

'I was twelve.'

'Okay, fine, you were twelve. You weren't a baby, though. You lived in the same house as Garrett for more than ten years. Why d'*you* think he killed himself?'

Harper smiled, like he was embarrassed, like he'd been asked something intensely personal in front of the whole class.

'So?' Freiberg said. 'What's your view on this?'

'I don't think I'm qualified—'

'Qualified?' Freiberg asked. He laughed coarsely. 'This isn't Harvard. We don't need qualifications. I'm asking for your opinion Sonny . . . just your opinion about a man who lived under the same roof as you for a decade or more. That's all. Don't make something out of it that isn't there.'

Harper turned once more and looked at Cathy. His right hand was on the table, and even as his eyes met hers he felt her hand close over his own. *Port in a storm*, he thought. *None of this matters. None of this is important. Everything here in New York will someday be of no significance.*

Cathy nodded. 'Speak,' she whispered. 'It's okay.'

'I think . . . I think he was hiding a secret,' Harper said.

'Hell, everyone has secrets kid. Show me someone who doesn't have secrets and I'll show you a dead guy.'

Harper was shaking his head. He smiled. The expression was of someone exhausted but resilient. 'Not just *a secret*,' he said. 'I'm talking a big fucking secret.'

'Whatever the hell went down in that house . . . Christ, it's all years back, it doesn't matter anymore, right? The past is the past. All that matters is today, tomorrow. Christmas is coming. You have to be happy about that. Everyone's happy about Christmas.'

'I don't know that happy is something I can use right now,' Harper said.

'Sure it is,' Freiberg replied. 'You have to work yourself out of this serious attitude thing you got going on—'

'What the hell's the matter with my attitude?' Harper asked. 'I've been here, what . . . six days? I'm starting to unravel a little now. I'm starting to wonder whether I can really hang all this together and stay upright for more than ten minutes at a time. I go see Evelyn. I ask her some questions. She breaks up like a storm cloud and the tears come. She tells me the truth. She tells me my mom committed suicide, that she died lonely and afraid. That's what she said, Walt. She said that Anne Harper died lonely and afraid. You have any idea how that makes me feel?'

Freiberg raised his hand, opened his mouth to speak.

'It was a rhetorical question,' Harper said. 'I don't want you to even try and answer it.'

Freiberg nodded, closed his mouth.

'So I get that. I get that small detail right between the eyes.' Harper paused. He could feel Cathy Hollander beside him, their knees touching, her hand still closed over his. He wanted to move it but the pressure of her skin against his own seemed to give him some small measure of comfort. She was the only person who had managed to retain some aspect of humanity amidst everything that was happening.

'And then Evelyn suggests, she *implies* that maybe everything that happened with my mom and her husband wasn't precisely as it appeared to be.'

Freiberg's eyes seemed to tighten. He angled his head to one side and looked closely at Harper.

'She kind of rolls out this theory on a maybe, just a maybe, nothing definite, okay? She gives me a few words of suggestion that *maybe* Anne didn't kill herself, that *maybe* Garrett didn't kill himself either—'

'What the fuck is she—' Freiberg started.

'Exactly,' Harper interjected. 'This is six days of my life, Walt, six days and everything has changed. Everything that I've been told is once again being turned on its head. Evelyn says that Anne killed herself to get away from my father. You're saying that she killed herself to get away from Evelyn and be *with* my father. Who the hell am I supposed to believe?'

293

Freiberg smiled. It was nothing more than a cool, matter-of-fact change in expression. 'You believe whoever has lied less,' he said.

'Which means you?'

'If I have lied less to you then, yes, it means me.'

'This is bullshit,' Harper said. 'I don't want to do this. I don't want to play this game. This is a nightmare. That's how it feels, like a fucking nightmare, and as I'm walking through it I don't even have the idea I'm asleep, that it really doesn't matter what the hell happens because at some point in the not-too-distant future I'm going to wake up.'

'What d'you want me to do?' Freiberg asked.

Harper shook his head. 'I don't know, Walt, I just don't know . . .'

'You want me to answer any more questions?'

'I don't think I dare ask any more questions. I'm getting to the point where I'm scared to find out something else that's going to kick me while I'm already down.'

'You're a tough guy. You walked through all of this and came out the other side. You even wound up smart enough to write a book.' Freiberg turned and looked at Cathy. 'She read your book,' he said. 'She read your book and said you were a fucking genius. Hell, you even made her cry.'

'Did you read it?' Harper asked Freiberg.

Freiberg looked bemused for a moment. 'Me? I look like the kind of person who reads books?'

Harper sensed an element of irony in Freiberg's voice. He wanted to turn and smile at Cathy, wanted to ask her what had made her cry, but he couldn't. If anything he felt a little embarrassed.

'So what d'you want to know?' Freiberg repeated.

'The cop,' Harper said. 'What *is* the deal with this guy?'

Freiberg shook his head. 'Who the hell knows. Guy's out on a limb. Been a cop for God knows how many years. Who knows what he's involved in, what his vested interests might be.'

'But with my father . . . why does he have this thing about my father?'

'Anyone mention the name Lauren Sachs to you?'

Harper frowned, shook his head.

'Not Evelyn . . . she didn't tell you about Duchaunak and a girl called Lauren Sachs?'

'No,' Harper said. 'Who the hell is Lauren Sachs?'

'Okay, okay, okay.' Freiberg sighed and leaned back in his chair. He reached up and loosened his tie. 'You want to know about Lauren Sachs then you're going to need to know about someone else.'

'Someone else?'

'Sure,' Freiberg said. 'You're going to need to know about Ben Marcus.'

'Evelyn mentioned him . . . I heard that name before when I spoke to Evelyn. Who is this Ben Marcus?'

Freiberg glanced at Cathy.

Harper was aware that she had withdrawn her hand. He turned and looked at her but her face was directed towards Freiberg.

'Ben Marcus,' Freiberg said quietly. 'Ben Marcus is the man responsible for the attempted murder of your father.'

FORTY-FOUR

Eight minutes after two p.m.

Ray Dietz, Albert Reiff, Maurice Rydell, Henry Kossoff, Karl Merrett. The noise of the bar filters through from the front, and beyond that the street, the sound of cars passing like a tired man sighing. North of the cross-over between Bowery and Little Italy, there on the junction of East Fourth and Lafayette, another oasis, another watering hole, another microcosm of this shadow of New York, the sour and darkened underbelly; the real world.

'Four cars,' Rydell says.

'Four cars,' echoes Merrett.

Dietz looks up from a clipboard, upon which are notes, detailed, all of them with margins and headings and times and locations. 'Drivers are Charlie Beck and Joe Koenig from Lenny's crew, Henry Kossoff, and Maurice from ours.'

Kossoff and Maurice Rydell each nod in turn.

'Walt Freiberg will be running the show from their end. As you know we've got Larry Benedict, Leo Petri, Ricky Wheland and Ron Dearing—'

'Jesus, I hate that motherfucker,' Karl Merrett interjects.

'Whatever,' Dietz says. 'Personal feelings are irrelevant now. We do this thing and then we're done. It's the end of an era. Nothing's gonna be the same after this one.'

Henry Kossoff nods towards Albert Reiff. 'Hey, what's the name of this boy we're using instead of Lester?'

'Lewis Parselle.'

'He's good?'

'Good as we need.'

Kossoff frowns. 'Doesn't sound like much of an assurance to me.'

'*My* assurance is good enough for you,' Reiff says. His voice is brusque and sharp.

'And what the hell is that supposed to mean?'

Dietz raises his right hand. 'Ladies, ladies, ladies, enough. We got business to see to. Take your sandpit squabbles home and put them in a fucking box until after Christmas, okay?' He looks at Kossoff and Reiff in turn. His expression is tough and uncompromising. 'Okay?'

Reiff nods in the affirmative, as does Kossoff. The tension dispels.

Karl Merrett laughs and everyone relaxes.

'I know feelings are high,' Dietz says. 'We got Lenny Bernstein in St Vincent's and we don't know anything about his son, nothing except he's s'posed to stand for him and give the word. This is what we have, and this is the best it's going to get. We deal with it, just like we dealt with everything before, right?'

There is a murmur of considered affirmations from around the table.

'So we go through it again, and we do the same tomorrow, however many times we got to to make sure we have everything straight. We all agreed on this?'

They are. There is no room, no time, no place for disagreement.

'Okay then,' Ray Dietz says. 'Karl, we start with you.'

Duty Sergeant, man by the name of Warren Oates, stands in the doorway. Wears his face like it doesn't fit, like it's someone else's and he's seeing how it works. It doesn't. Resigned himself to the fact that it's too late to take it back, that he'll always look this way; carries that shadow of resignation around his eyes, in the stoop of his shoulders, in the quiet tension of his jawline.

'Who is it?' McLuhan asks.

'Jackson,' Oates replies.

'Mouse Jackson?'

'The very same.'

'What'd they do to him?'

'Nailed him to something through his hands.' Oates holds out his right hand like it will help to understand the concept. He closes his fingers slowly, almost like he's imagining the pain. He can't. Never could. Get your head around that kind of pain and you faint right where you stand.

'And?'

'Taped around his mouth and throat, around his ankles too, but they took off his right shoe and beat his foot to pieces.'

'Fuck me, that's got to hurt,' McLuhan says, and he scrunches his toes inside his shoe.

'And then there was the screwdriver,' Oates says matter-of-factly.

'The screwdriver?'

'Right.'

'What fucking screwdriver?'

'The one sticking out the side of his head. That was the thing that killed him.'

McLuhan nodded, leaned back in his chair and crossed his legs. 'You figure that might have been a good thing to tell me first?'

Oates shrugs. 'It was all good to tell you . . . don't seem to make a difference in what order.'

'Where was he found?'

'Under a bench in Washington Square Park.'

'Aah, Jesus Christ, you'd think they'd have the decency to keep this thing out of public view goddamn it!'

McLuhan rises suddenly and thumps his fist on the desk. 'Fuck these people!' he barks.

Oates doesn't bat an eyelid, doesn't move a muscle. He's either seen this so many times he isn't fazed, or he's beyond the point of caring. His expression doesn't shift.

'You thinking something?' McLuhan asks.

Oates shrugs again. 'Thinkin' that maybe there's going to be a war.'

'No!' McLuhan snaps. 'No, no, no! That is *not* what I want to hear! There is *not* going to be a war, for fuck's sake!'

Oates smiles wryly. 'Not on your watch, right?' he says.

McLuhan glares at him. 'Fuck you!'

'It is what it is, Captain . . . we got Micky Levin and Johnnie Hoy, now Mouse Jackson, all of them directly or indirectly connected to Ben Marcus. We got Lenny in St Vincent's, bleeding out like there's no tomorrow. You tell me you don't see a war coming, eh?'

McLuhan raises his hands. 'Leave me alone for a while,' he says. He turns and sits down again. He looks like a beaten man.

'You want me to do anything on this thing with Mouse?'

'Where is he?'

'City morgue I reckon,' Oates says.

'Make sure Forensics pulls him apart, the bench also . . . see if there's anything that tells us where they killed him. Hell, Oates, you know this shit as well as anyone. Get whatever you can, and whatever you get let me know as soon as possible, okay?'

'Okay, Captain.' Oates smiles. 'Have a nice day.'

'Hey!'

Oates pauses, turns.

'Is there anything, *anything* at all on these McCaffrey people, the social worker guy and his sister?'

Oates shakes his head. 'There's nothing yet. Got a lead on another brother . . . Thomas McCaffrey, though no-one seems to have heard word of him for some time.'

'And what the fuck is he, a brain surgeon?'

'No, he's a crook, he was the black sheep of the family. Did a stretch in Attica. Coincidentally, he was in Attica at the same time as Johnnie Hoy and Ray Dietz.'

McLuhan shakes his head and looks down. Feels like someone ran over his life with a twelve-wheeler.

'Make this shit go away will you, Sergeant . . . do whatever you have to to make this shit go away.'

FORTY-FIVE

Freiberg cleared his throat. 'By the time everyone walked away . . . everyone that could still walk, six people were dead. Apparently, and I don't know if this was someone's effort to sensationalize it, the health and sanitation people had to come down and hose the blood from the sidewalks. She was amongst the dead, killed by a single bullet that went through the back of her neck from behind and exited through the lower part of her face. Couldn't have been worse for her family. They were Catholics, good Catholic people, and she had to have a closed coffin at the funeral.'

Freiberg shook his head slowly. 'That was November of '97, all of seven years ago, and, understandably, Frank Duchaunak has not been able to let go of it. That's the kind of thing you wind up carrying for life.'

'Where was it?' Harper asked.

'South-Western Mercantile Bank on Canal Street.'

'And he'd only been in New York a short while?'

Freiberg nodded. 'Weeks I think, maybe a month or two. Came from Chicago, transferred here because this was where she was from.'

'And she looked like Marilyn Monroe.'

'Dead ringer . . . almost scary. Her name was Lauren, Lauren Sachs. Hell of a nice girl from all accounts. Native New Yorker, family in Stuyvesant I think, still there as far as I know.'

'How did he meet her?'

'I don't know, Sonny. How does anyone meet anyone else these days? Friends of friends, work connections, who the hell knows? Duchaunak was out in Chicago, he got transferred here, all set to get married I reckon, and then this thing happens.'

'Tell me.'

Freiberg smiled, shrugged his shoulders. 'What's to tell, John?

It was a bank robbery, an armed bank robbery. You've seen the movies, you know how these things supposedly go.'

'And Edward . . . my father . . . he was there?'

'Christ no. Your father? Not a prayer. He was probably out of the state, more than likely someplace like Jersey City. He was never in the vicinity of these things. There was never any direct connection between your father and the work he did.'

'So what *did* he do?'

'He paid for it.'

'He paid for it? I don't understand—'

'He was the banker. He put the money up. He financed the whole operation. That's what he did, and that's what he was doing right until the moment he was shot. That's what your father has spent his whole adult life doing, John: working with people like this, paying their way, financing these operations and then taking whatever percentage was his. And Ben Marcus, he's the same. Years ago there were no divisions . . . everyone worked alongside each other. Then it seemed to be divided, your father on one side, Ben Marcus on the other.'

Harper took one of Cathy's cigarettes and lit it. His mind was struggling to contain itself. He was silent for a good minute. He sat there without moving, the cigarette burning; didn't say a word.

Freiberg eventually broke the quiet tension. 'And that's why Frank Duchaunak has pursued your father all these years.'

Harper looked down at the table. All of a sudden whatever appetite he might have had, had vanished.

'I am—' he started, and he looked up at Freiberg.

Freiberg smiled, angled his head to one side. 'Whatever you were going to say, first and foremost, you are your father's son.'

Harper shook his head. 'I don't know how to deal with this,' he said quietly, almost to himself.

'Sure you don't,' Freiberg replied. 'Tell me someone who *would* know how to deal with this. You've been walking around the edges of this thing since you got here.' He leaned forward, rested the backs of his forearms on the table. He held a matchbook in his fingers which he turned over, back and forth, back and forth, and Harper watched him do it, almost mesmerized. 'This is a big thing,' Freiberg went on. 'This is a fucking giant, and not only do you have to deal with the reality of who your father is you

301

also have to deal with all the attachments and extras. This thing with Evelyn . . . Christ's sake, Sonny, I find it tough to get my head around that and I've known the woman for as many years as you've been alive. And, aside from everything else, you have Frank obsessive-fucking-compulsive Duchaunak treading on your toes every time you take a step left or right.' Freiberg smiled broadly, and there was something in his eyes, something sincere and earnest, that made Harper feel as though the man had some inkling of what he was going through. 'It all comes back to family, you know? Whatever the fuck else might be going on it all comes back to family. You had a mother, you *have* a father, and right now he's laid up in St Vincent's with a bullet hole in him, and what little life he has left they're trying their damnedest to keep from leaking right out of that fucking hole, and the person that did that to him, the asshole who figured it might be a good idea to see the last of your father, well I can guarantee he's somewhere right now eating his two hundred-dollar lunch, talking with his people and figuring out what he's going to do with your father's territory when he dies.'

Harper looked up suddenly, his eyes wide.

'Sure as shit and shinola,' Freiberg said. 'His name is Ben Marcus, and he's been snapping at your father's heels for as long as I can remember. This guy is the source of all this trouble. If Ben Marcus hadn't been such a greedy motherfucker, if he hadn't gotten it into his head that his own territory and business wasn't big enough, then your father would not have been shot. He wouldn't be up there in St Vincent's on a life support machine, Evelyn wouldn't have had to confront the truth and pull your life to pieces, and you'd be somewhere down in Florida minding your own business and getting on with your life. That's what Ben Marcus has done, and that's what he needs to pay for.'

Freiberg sat back and nodded his head. He relaxed his shoulders and crossed his legs. He was silent, like he was waiting for Harper to say something.

Harper looked at Cathy Hollander. Cathy looked at Freiberg.

'Ask her,' Freiberg said. 'Ask *her* about Ben Marcus. Christ, she was around the guy for God knows how long . . . if anyone can tell you what a complete asshole Ben Marcus is then there's your girl. The man is dangerous, truly fucking dangerous.'

Cathy turned back to Harper.

Harper raised his eyebrows and Cathy averted her eyes for a moment.

'Well?' Harper asked.

'He's right,' Cathy said. 'Everything that Walt told you is right.'

'That this Ben Marcus is responsible for the shooting of my father?'

Cathy did not respond.

'Cathy? Is he? Is this guy the one who had my father shot?'

She nodded her head.

'Is that a yes?'

She turned to look at him, dead-center, up close. 'Yes,' she said emphatically. 'I believe Ben Marcus ordered the shooting of your father.'

The Gordian knot of emotions, tied tighter than Sunday shoes, started to weaken at the center.

Harper held it together. *Not here*, he thought. *I cannot deal with this here.*

'And this Duchaunak character?' he asked Freiberg. 'This thing with Duchaunak's fiancee? Is it true that she was killed in a bank robbery?'

Freiberg nodded.

Harper shook his head. He breathed deeply a couple of times. 'And my father was responsible for this?'

Freiberg laughed. 'Was he fuck! That was Ben Marcus's gig. That was a Ben Marcus job through and through. Half a dozen gorillas with semis and M-16s thundering their way around the place. No class Sonny, the guy has no fucking class. Granted, your father fronted the money but it was Marcus's people that did it.' Freiberg smiled. 'Wake up and smell the java kid . . . you know *exactly* what I'm talking about. This isn't TV, this is the real deal, the real fucking deal. This is what people like us do. This is the life your father led until Ben Marcus—'

'Until Ben Marcus got someone to shoot him, right?'

'Right.'

'Jesus.' Harper seemed like a man on the edge as he looked at Freiberg. 'Evelyn was going to tell me about this. She said that Duchaunak believed my father was responsible for all his unhappiness . . . this is what she was talking about, wasn't she?'

Freiberg shrugged. 'As far as I know Duchaunak figures your

303

father for everything from the Wall Street Crash to the Hearst kidnapping. What we got here is a cop who is supposed to be under some kind of psychological care, s'posed to be getting his thinking patterns ironed straight by some headpeeper. This is the kind of guy we're dealing with here; the kind of person who's devoted his time and energies to making your father guilty of everything that's happened in New York for the last seven or eight years, probably much longer.'

Harper frowned. 'But why?'

'Why is he after your father?'

'Right. Why does he think something like that if it isn't true?'

'Because your father has managed to sidestep the guy a good few times, and every time he does that Duchaunak loses the thread just that little bit further. He's gotten himself a little fixated on the subject—'

'Why this? Why does it have to be this way? Why couldn't he be a schoolteacher? Why couldn't he be an engineer or a computer guy, something like that?'

Freiberg smiled. 'Same reason you'll never really be a newspaper journalist.'

Harper frowned.

'You're a writer. There's a whole lot of difference between a guy who can write a book, and some guy who puts together column inches for the daily rag. Hell, I'm not going to knock someone who works for the press, man's got to earn a living right? But there's a difference, one helluva big difference, between that and writing a whole fucking book.'

Harper nodded. There was a difference, no doubt about it.

'So why'd you do it?' Freiberg asked.

'Write the book?' Harper asked. 'Hell, I don't know, Walt . . . it was just there. I felt like I had to.'

'You didn't have a choice, right?'

'I s'pose not, no.'

'Well, that's why your father does what he does . . . hell, that's why we all do this. 'Cause we don't have a choice. That's the truth right there. We don't have a choice.'

'Don't have a choice?' Harper said, in his voice the strain of incredulity. 'What d'you mean, no choice? How can you even begin to compare something like writing a book with robbing banks and killing people?'

Freiberg shook his head. 'I'm not doing any comparing here,' he said. 'All I'm saying is that when it comes down to it, when you take everything away and confront the reason why someone does something – good, bad or indifferent – it all comes down to purpose. The guy has a purpose to do something, that's the thing that drives him, makes him determined, and whether you're talking about Frank Duchaunak or Edward Bernstein or Albert Einstein it doesn't matter. The thing is the drive. What the guy feels is the drive. That drive is going to carry him forward, and where it carries him? Well, frankly, there's as many different destinations as there are people, right?'

'I don't know what to say,' Harper said.

Freiberg nodded, in his expression something that spoke of empathy, almost compassion for Harper's predicament. 'Then don't say anything,' he replied. 'You do whatever you have to do with what I've told you. I've got to do what I have to do. I have to make this thing right—'

'What thing?'

'This thing with Lenny . . . with your father. Ben Marcus had someone shoot him and I can't let that lie. Me and your father, well, me and your father have been as close as anything for a good many years, and regardless of the rightnesses or wrong-nesses of what's happened there is a certain justice that has to come about.'

'You're going to kill Ben Marcus?'

Freiberg laughed. 'Hell no, kid, I'm not a murderer. I'm not going to kill Ben Marcus, but I *am* going to do something that's going to make his life very difficult for a very long time.'

'What're you going to do?'

Freiberg shook his head. 'As far as you're concerned I'm not going to do anything. You don't want to get involved. You don't want to be any part of this thing, believe me. You have your own life. You should stay however long you feel is right, and if your father passes away then you have to make a decision about whether you want to stay for his funeral and whatever. You decide to go, then no-one's going to stop you. You can go right back to Miami and pick up where you left off, make believe this was all some bad dream you managed to survive. You can forget about me, about Cathy, forget all about Evelyn, crazy mother-fuckin' bitch that she is—'

'Walt!' Cathy interjected.

Freiberg sort of half smiled, looked embarrassed. 'Sorry, no offence,' he said. 'Anyway, like I said, you have to make whatever sense of this you can. You have to decide for yourself, basically because no-one else is going to make any decisions for you; and if you need anything from me, if you need money, a plane ticket, whatever, then you only have to let me know and it will be taken care of.'

'And Duchaunak?' Harper asked.

Freiberg looked puzzled. 'Duchaunak? What about him?'

'I should tell him I'm going?'

'Fuck him. You want to go you just go, that's all there is to it.'

Harper looked at Cathy. She tried to smile but it seemed from the awkwardness of her expression that she was unwilling to venture any suggestions. Harper turned back to Walt. 'You think I should go?'

'I don't think anything. Guiding principle of my life is to think as little as possible as often as I can.'

'Seriously, Walt . . . you think I should go back to Miami and try to forget all of this?'

'You can't ask me something like that. How could someone else ever answer a question like that? If I make the decision then I'm the fall guy whichever way it goes. Anything bad happens then it's going to be because I influenced your decision, right?'

'I have a little more responsibility for myself than that.'

Freiberg smiled knowingly, almost sardonically. 'Everyone has as much responsibility as they need until something comes along that they don't want to be responsible for, know what I mean? You can say whatever you like, it isn't going to change my view on this. There's a thing I have to do. It's a personal thing. That's all there is to it. You're no more involved in that than you are in . . . hell, I don't know . . . whatever the hell else you aren't involved in. This is a business matter, that's all, and whether you stay or go isn't going to make any difference in what I do. Do I think you should stay? Do I think you should go back to Florida? Those are questions I will not answer for you, because whichever way it goes I'm going to wind up wrong, you understand?'

Harper nodded slowly. He understood perfectly well. There was little else to say.

'So what are you going to do?' Freiberg asked.

Harper smiled wryly. 'I don't know.'

'There isn't any hurry. You can take whatever time you like coming to a decision. There isn't a deadline here.'

'I want to go back to the hotel,' Harper said.

'Now? You want to go now? We haven't even finished lunch.'

Harper shook his head. 'I don't have a great deal of appetite Walt. I want to go back to the hotel and sleep for a while. This is too much for me to deal with. There are too many things I'm trying to work out, and I really don't feel so good, you know?'

Walt Freiberg leaned forward and closed his hand over Harper's. 'I understand kid, I really do. This has all been a bit fucking much, right? Cathy here will get you back to the hotel, right, Cathy?'

'Sure thi—'

'No,' Harper said. He glanced at Cathy. He felt awkward, perhaps couldn't deal with being alone with her just at that point. 'It's okay. I want to go by myself. I'll take a cab. I'll just go out and take a cab and see myself over to the hotel. I need to have a rest. I need to get some space away from all of this and figure out what I'm going to do.'

'Sure you do,' Freiberg said. 'You do whatever you want. Let us know if there's anything you need and we'll get it taken care of.'

Harper tried to rise from his chair. He was unsteady on his feet and Cathy Hollander reached out her hand to assist him.

Harper hesitated for a moment, and then he took it. He steadied himself, maneuvered his jacket from the back of his chair and around his shoulders, and edged out from behind the table.

He stood there for a moment, his face all but empty of expression, his eyes kind of flat and blank.

'You're going to be okay,' Freiberg said without rising from his chair. 'Things are going to work out, Sonny . . . they always do.'

Harper nodded without really absorbing what Freiberg had said, and then he turned and started walking towards the front door of the restaurant.

Cathy Hollander made as if to follow him.

'Let him go,' Freiberg said. 'Let the kid go . . . he needs some time to himself.'

Cathy hesitated, turned and looked at Freiberg.

307

Freiberg smiled. 'He got to you, didn't he? Eh? Tell me the truth now, sweetheart . . . that boy did whatever he did and found his way under your skin. Tell me I'm wrong.'

Cathy Hollander said nothing, didn't even crack her face with a smile. She merely turned at the sound of the restaurant door opening and the sight of Harper almost stumbling out into the street.

Freiberg smiled – all high, wide and handsome. 'You know what they say sweetheart?' he joked. 'You want to find out if they love you, well you let 'em go and see if they come back.'

FORTY-SIX

Neumann smiled. He had a gold tooth three back on the right. It caught the light at an angle.

Ben Marcus leaned forward and steepled his fingers together. 'Why?' he asked. 'I need a reason?'

Neumann smiled again. 'No Ben, you don't need a reason. No-one needs a reason for anything. I'm just curious, that's all.'

'Because she made a fool out of me,' Marcus replied. 'She was here and then she went with Bernstein, and she made a fool out of me.'

Sol Neumann shook his head and frowned. 'I don't get it. Best as I recall it was a straight deal. He wound up with the girl, fair and square, right?'

Marcus shook his head. 'You're missing the point Sol. It wasn't that I lost. It wasn't that she was the deal and she went with Lenny Bernstein. It was that she didn't say a word, not one word of complaint. The fact that she said nothing made it clear that she wanted to go more than she wanted to stay with me. That's why, Sol . . . as simple as that.'

'So when? Before or after?'

'After. The whole thing goes down and then you get her.'

'You want me to do it personally?'

'Whatever you like, Sol. You do it yourself or you have someone do it. All I want to know at the end of the day is that Cathy Hollander is dead, okay?'

'Okay,' Sol Neumann said, a little taken aback by the force of Marcus's dislike for the girl. 'Whatever you want, Ben, consider it done.'

Marcus nodded. 'Good enough,' he said quietly, and went back to reading his newspaper.

*

Sometimes he takes out photographs. There are a few, perhaps four or five, and though she smiles, though she is laughing, none of them capture the spirit that was Lauren Sachs. Unbeknownst to Duchaunak she bears an uncanny resemblance to Anne Sawyer. Had he known this he perhaps would have believed that God was no crueller than when inflicting irony.

And when he holds the photographs he can see his hands shaking, and it is not the tremens of a drunk, nor the anxieties of a neurotic; it is the suppressed emotional reaction of a man afraid, a man both lonely and afraid.

This is a life, kind of. This is an existence, to apply the broadest sense of understanding to the term. This is what he is, and what he is seems altogether driven by something external. A planet in orbit that remains merely because of a star's magnetic influence. Were the star to implode, or burn, or even shift its axis, the planet would spiral away into darkness and vanish. As if it had never been. As if it had been a figment of the imagination.

As far as Captain McLuhan was concerned there was no life. It ceased from the moment Duchaunak was suspended, and would resume when he was reinstated. *If* he was.

Duchaunak sets the pictures down on the kitchen counter. He touches each in turn. Five of them. In only one is he present, and at the moment of the taking, as the finger of the photographer was depressed to capture that split second, Lauren had turned her eyes fractionally to the right and smiled. As if at someone else.

There had been no-one else there but Duchaunak. He alone knew that. But now, now and forever, it seems that she is almost ignorant of his presence.

It breaks his heart.

It breaks his fucking heart.

Later, a vague collection of random and empty minutes, he gathers up the pictures and returns them to a worn and tired envelope.

He folds the envelope along all-too-familiar creases, creases that will soon come apart, but he will not throw the envelope away, for there in the right-hand corner as he turns it over, inscribed in her nonchalant hand, it says 'Me and Frank, Summer '96'.

Me and Frank.

Me *and* Frank.

His eyes swell with tears.

Fuck it, he whispers to himself, and those words, almost inaudible, come back at him in echo.

Fuck it.

The Gordian knot unravelled.

Tie undone, hanging loose from his collar, his eyes bloodshot. Like the ghost of some Atlantic City poker player still haunting the tables, a player found dead in his chair, his heart collapsed from the pressure, his liver like a small, polished stone.

Feels like someone has gathered up every part of his life and then set them on fire, and he – in his desperation to extinguish the flames – has stamped everything to pieces.

The damage is broad, indiscriminate, irreversible. The damage, whichever way he looks at it, is done.

John Harper shed his jacket, let it drop to the floor. Walked like an automaton to the chair under the window and collapsed into it. He felt the chill breeze from the inched-open window beside him but lacked the motivation or will to lean out and close it.

Stayed there for a good thirty minutes, and then moved slightly to ease the pressure in the small of his back. Leaned his head to one side, closed his eyes, tried to imagine himself aboard the *Mary McGregor*, the breeze cutting out of Joe Bay or Blackwater Sound, tried to recall the Dry Tortugas, the footprints of turtles, the reefs, the clear water, the citrus, the coconut . . .

Remembered nothing but the tense claustrophobia of Evelyn's kitchen on Carmine Street; how the sound of her breathing had changed as she spoke of her sister, Harper's mother, the mother who never died of pneumonia, the mother who styled herself after Marilyn and took the shortest road away from the longest disappointment . . .

Harper made a sound. It was nothing more than a breathless sense of anguish rising from his chest, but in the solitude of that room on the tenth floor of the American Regent it was not a human sound. It scared him.

He opened his eyes. A sudden surge of energy filled his body and he rose awkwardly from the chair. He paced back and forth for a handful of seconds, then made his way urgently to the bathroom. No sooner had he flung open the door than the rush of nausea almost doubled him over. He made it to the sink before he heaved with such force that he felt something tear in his trachea. Nothing came but intense pain; the pain of emptiness, of nervous hysteria, of a man teetering on the brink of something altogether deeper than his own capacity to understand.

He believed, as he kneeled there on the floor – head down, hands gripping the edge of the sink above him – that every emotion and feeling, every fear and doubt, every hope and broken promise that he'd heard and experienced in the previous days, had finally located him.

John Harper, he of the wasted life, he of the futile gestures towards nothing of significance, had finally been discovered. This was a judgement for his life. This was the penalty for his laxity and procrastination. There was a lesson to be learned here: that life moved whether you moved with it or not. This other life, a life he'd been unaware of, had grown without him, become something that owned him, despite his absence. He was paying the price for his own shallow ignorance.

For thirty-something years the truth had been here. He had never asked. He had not wished to know. Had he been so blind as to think that it would never find him? If nothing else, Garrett's suicide should have raised sufficient questions for him to . . .

To what? To interrogate Evelyn further? To insist the police re-open the inquest into his death?

Harper let go of the sink and sat down on his haunches. He did not know what to think. He did not *want* to think.

He closed his eyes tight, and for a time there was just silence and darkness. He prayed it would stay that way, at least for a while.

Dry heaving now. Duchaunak leans back and opens his mouth as if to scream, but nothing comes out. Not a sound.

Heart like a trip-hammer. *Ka-chunk, ka-chunk, ka-chunk*. Head hurts. Hard to focus. Needs a drink but doesn't dare. Long, lonely, interminable road; nothing at the end; nothing but further longing and loneliness.

He grips the cool edge of the bathroom sink. Grips it hard.

Leans his full weight back and feels the thing straining at the wall. Stays like that for some time, a minute, perhaps more, and then he stands straight, looks at his reflection, wonders what it would be like to put a gun in his mouth and blow the back of his head off.

Like someone did to Garrett Sawyer at 66 Carmine.

Duchaunak turns on the cold faucet, cups his hands beneath and sluices water onto his face. His eyes sting. He keeps them closed until the sensation subsides.

He wonders what will happen. Wonders if McLuhan will call. Wonders if they'll leave him out here on his own, forget his name, and someday he'll be part of that great history of New York deaths: three weeks and the neighbors call someone because the smell is so bad.

Duchaunak smiles at his own wet reflection; believes that somewhere he lost it, and then – as a second thought, close behind, heel-to-toe – he wonders if whatever he lost was never really his in the first place.

'It is what it is,' he whispers, and then he tugs on the light cord and closes the door as he leaves.

Harper gone, Cathy Hollander and Walt Freiberg finished their lunch. As the waiter walked away, the bill paid, Freiberg leaned forward. 'I never trusted her,' he said.

'Not trusting her and killing her are two very different things,' Cathy Hollander replied.

'That's as may be, but if I'm leaving when this thing is done . . . if I'm leaving New York, never to come back, then I don't want to spend the rest of my life knowing that Evelyn Sawyer is still breathing.'

'So what are you going to do?' Cathy asked.

'Do?' Walt Freiberg asked. 'What am I going to do? I'm going to wait until the dust has settled on this thing, wait until things quieten down, and then I'm going to go over to Carmine Street and shoot the bitch in the fucking head.'

'Simple as that,' Cathy Hollander replied.

Walt Freiberg rose from his chair and buttoned his jacket. 'Sure it is,' he said quietly, his voice almost a whisper. 'It really is as simple as that.'

FORTY-SEVEN

Evelyn Sawyer had slept little since her last discussion with John Harper.

She was not a woman to introspect, to turn inward and view her motives or reasons for the decisions she'd made. What was done was done; there was little that could be changed about it now, and John Harper had in some small way chosen to walk back into this life. He could have left. He could have turned around and taken the next flight back to Miami. But no, Walt Freiberg and Edward's hooker girlfriend had been there to seduce him with their money, their lies, the faces they wore for the world.

The truth? That truth, pure and simple, was that no-one knew the whole truth. No-one but Evelyn. And she could never have told Harper. Such a thing would have broken him.

That Sunday morning she turned from where she stood at the window near the kitchen sink. Time had moved so fast. There had been no time for anything, not for herself, not for consideration of her position, nor for any kind of resolution regarding what Anne would have wished.

What *Anne* would have wished. Not what Evelyn would have wished, but what Anne would have wished.

Anne was dead. Anne had killed herself, October twelfth, 1975; maybe someone had been there . . . hell, Evelyn thought, someone *had* been there, but Anne had brought it on herself. Everyone brings their own destiny to pass.

Even she: Evelyn Sawyer, widow of Garrett Sawyer, a widow of the war.

And now another war would come, and people would die, and the old would make way for the new, and she would more than likely be left to survey the walking wounded, the dead, the damaged. Perhaps John Harper would make it through the other side. Somehow Evelyn doubted it. John Harper had left this life. You could not leave it, and then later return and expect yourself to be prepared. You had to grow inside it, grow as part of it, and its nature had to grow within you.

This was a different world: fast, brutal, unrelenting.

This was the world Edward Bernstein had created, and though Harper was his son, would never be anything other, he was no more a part of this than his mother had been.

And look – Evelyn thought to herself – just look what happened to her. Had it not been for Anne Harper, had it not been for her weakness, then Garrett would still be alive.

'Burn in hell,' Evelyn Sawyer said, and her voice, there in the silence of 66 Carmine, was like the hiss of a branding iron.

She lowered her head, felt the muscles tighten in her throat, and started to cry.

'His precise words, sir . . . no calls, no visitors.'

'But I'm—'

'I'm sorry sir. I cannot ignore the wishes of a guest in the hotel. The privacy of our guests becomes our responsibility from the moment they check in. I cannot put a call through to Mr Harper's room. I hope you understand sir, but such a thing becomes a matter of the hotel's credibility and reputation—'

'It really is nothing more than a few words—'

'Once again, I'm sorry sir. I don't wish to be unhelpful, but unless there is some specific aspect of the law that has been violated I cannot override a guest's request for privacy. Mr Harper called down this morning and stated emphatically his wish not to be disturbed. Now, if you wish to leave a message?'

'Yes, a message . . . I'll leave a message.'

'Very good sir. First of all your name?'

'Er . . . my name . . . '

'Yes sir, your name.'

A moment's hesitation, and then: 'Actually, it doesn't matter.'

'Sir?'

'It doesn't matter . . . I'm sorry to trouble you.'

'You're not going to leave a message?'

'No, I've decided against it. Thank you anyway . . . thanks for your help.'

'Very good sir. You have a nice day now.'

'Yes, okay . . . yes . . . have a nice day yourself.'

The line went dead.

Duchaunak set the receiver back in the cradle. He stood motionless. Didn't even appear to be breathing.

He thought to go there, go right over to the American Regent and demand to see John Harper. What could he say? Couldn't say a goddamned thing. Security would throw him out. McLuhan would find out what he'd done and have him charged with harassment; either that or fire him. Could McLuhan fire him for something like that? Duchaunak believed not, but then McLuhan wouldn't be firing him for that alone.

Duchaunak took three steps to the right and sat down in his armchair. Hadn't slept, nothing to speak of. Had wrestled with the sheets for an hour or so and then got up, padded back and forth across the room for a while and then sat in the kitchen eating Cheerios from the box. If he'd had any sleeping tablets he would have taken some. Maybe too many.

Duchaunak smiled; wry smile, almost accepting of his own paranoia and perverse sense of irony.

Everything was fucked. That was the truth. That was as good a place as any to start.

He closed his eyes, leaned back his head, and starting to half-sing, half-speak something in a slow and mournful voice:

'I want to be loved by you . . . just you . . . nobody else but you . . .'

After a while the light through his eyelids seemed to fade. Sleep took him silently, and he went without protest.

'What'd they say?'

'No visitors, no calls.'

'No question he's there?'

'No, he's there alright. Got back soon after he left us and hasn't come out since.'

'You're certain?'

'Walt—'

'Okay, Cathy, okay. Just tell whoever you've got over there to let you know if he makes a move anyplace, alright?'

'Walt, I've got it covered. Charlie Beck's keeping an eye on the place. Trust me, okay?'

'Good enough. Leave him be. Least we know where he is,

right? Come on back here and we'll go over this stuff once more.'

'Half an hour.'

'No problem, see you then.'

'Right.' Cathy Hollander hung up the phone and stepped out of the callbox. She tugged her coat tight around her throat and started walking.

Twenty yards down the sidewalk and it started to snow. Christmas was everywhere – peoples' faces, the bright eyes of children, storefronts, grubby-faced Santas ringing bells and collecting nickels and dimes at street corners and junctions, the vari-colored lights strung from doorways and fire escapes – but Cathy Hollander saw none of it.

Christmas, right now, was the least of her concerns.

Harper did not surface again until gone three p.m.

He could not remember when he had called the desk, when he'd requested no calls or visitors. Perhaps seven, maybe eight that morning. He lay there for a further fifteen or twenty minutes before he gathered sufficient will to rise and use the john. He dared not look at his own reflection in the mirror. He felt he'd confronted a little too much reality for one week.

He returned to the bed, sat on the edge of the mattress, thought to call down for cigarettes but didn't.

Already far beyond the point of trying to determine the truth, he felt that perhaps there was no real or specific truth. There was merely the truth of individuals. Freiberg, Duchaunak, Evelyn Sawyer, and then the truth of his father, Edward 'Lenny' Bernstein: the conductor, the orchestrator, the criminal.

Harper smiled to himself. It was all so much crazy bullshit. Who were these people? What the hell had happened during this past week?

Suddenly he thought of Harry Ivens, the fact that he hadn't called the man for . . . for how many days? Yesterday, the day before? He couldn't remember. Harper reached for the telephone and dialled the number. He sat there patiently, the phone ringing four or five times before the answer service kicked in.

'*Miami Herald* . . . how can I help you?'

'Hi there . . . er, yes . . . I wanted to speak to Harry Ivens.'

'I'm sorry sir, Mr Ivens cannot be reached today.'

Harper frowned. 'Cannot be reached? But I need to speak with him . . . can you not get a message through to the service desk and let him know that John Harper is on the phone?'

'I'm sorry sir, I can't do that.'

'Can't? What d'you mean you can't? I don't understand . . . is there a problem with him? Is something wrong?'

'No sir, there's nothing wrong.' The voice at the other end smiled sympathetically. 'It's Sunday sir. Mr Ivens does not come in on a Sunday. I can take a message and he'll pick it up first thing tomorrow.'

'It's Sunday . . .'

A pause at the other end. 'Yes sir. Sunday. All day. Right to the very end.'

'Yes . . . right . . . of course.' Harper laughed nervously. 'Okay . . . thank you.' He withdrew the receiver from his ear, looked at it quizzically. He frowned once again, shook his head, and then set the phone down.

'Sunday,' he said to himself. 'Jesus. I've been here a week.'

FORTY-EIGHT

Eleven minutes after nine, darkness shrouding the city.

An hour earlier Frank Duchaunak had been asked to leave by the lobby staff. He'd argued with them for a good fifteen minutes, argued with them to the point of losing his temper. He hadn't lost it, hadn't really created a scene. The threads that held everything together were fragile enough as it was. He knew he was close to the edge, knew also that no-one was really certain of the precise location of that edge until they went over it. Everything was catch-as-catch-can until someone was caught. No way was it going to be him.

John Harper called down for coffee, a ham and mustard sandwich, a pack of Luckies.

Hotel staff wondered who he was; why the mystery; why the cop had come late in the evening and demanded to see Harper, and yet when challenged, when asked for a warrant, some authority to go right on up to the tenth floor and disturb a hotel guest, he had backed down, been almost *too* polite, and then refused to say which precinct he was from.

This was New York; this was the American Regent, a hotel that retained a box of possessions left by guests that bore no description or comprehension of their use. A microcosm of all that was good and bad with the world. Such things came as no surprise, and yet still raised eyebrows, begged questions; questions that would remain unanswered because no-one really wished to know. The man on the tenth floor was Edward Bernstein's son: enough said.

And Harper – his life broken up in pieces and scattered across New York – sat at the window and ate his sandwich. He watched the snow come down and thought of Christmas. Christmas, he figured, belonged to some other world, a world he'd once been part of, a world that continued to revolve somewhere like a carousel. He'd stepped off. How, he didn't know, but he had, and now he could not even find where he'd alighted, let alone reverse his footsteps. What was done was done. He knew that.

Later, lying on the bed and staring at the ceiling, he wondered if he would ever see Miami again. He considered it for quite some time; came to the conclusion that he didn't care.

A week had passed, seven days; everything had changed; nothing could ever be the same. Harper wondered if he, perhaps out of desperation, out of loneliness, had not brought all of this into being. He smiled to himself. *Perhaps if I sleep*, he thought . . . *perhaps if I sleep and dream, and wake tomorrow, I will find it has all been a nightmare.*

The man he'd become was not the man who'd left Florida.

The thing that unsettled him was that such a thought brought nothing but relief.

John Harper closed his eyes, and he knew, with as much certainty as was possible, that tomorrow he would have to make a decision.

Sol Neumann stepped back from the edge of the table and glanced to his left.

'He's dead?' Ray Dietz asked.

'Deader than Elvis,' Neumann said.

'What was his name?'

Neumann frowned and shook his head. 'How the fuck would I know his name? What d'you think we got here? You think me an' this schmucko were dating or something?'

Dietz laughed. 'Fuck, Sol, I only asked if you knew his name.'

'He was some guy,' Neumann said. 'He was some guy that sprayed cars for a fucking living. He was given a job, he did the job, and then he came to get his money. That's all I fuckin' know, okay?'

'Hey, take it easy, would you? What the fuck you doin' bustin' my balls here? So it's just some fucking guy, okay. Just some fucking guy who's got a biro sticking out the front of his face. Fuck man, couldn't you have shot him, maybe strangled him or something . . . you have to stick a biro through his eye? Jesus, we aren't animals, Sol.'

'Now who's bustin' whose balls, eh? Shut the fuck up,

Raymond. Just shut the fuck up and help me get him in a gunny sack.'

'Where's he goin'?'

'Maurice is going with the Parselle kid. Down to Pier 46 and put him in the Hudson River.' Neumann indicated the slumped form of the dead paintsprayer with a nod of his head.

Dietz took a step closer to the table. He looked down at the guy, the way his head was lolled to one side, the way that nothing more than an inch of biro now protruded from his right eye. His left eye stared vacantly back at Dietz. Dietz shuddered involuntarily. 'It's fucking brutal, Sol. Seriously . . . I mean this is just fucking brutal what you did to the poor bastard. There's got to have been a more humane way to do this.'

'Humane? What in fuck's name are you talking about, humane? The guy was going to blab. The guy was all ready to be a fucking radio station. It is what it is, Raymond. He knows the deal. He knows how things work. He's all grown up now, Raymond. He pulls a fucked-up stunt like that . . . hell, he was up for the big time, he was up for a good bundle of money. He knew what might happen when he started in on this thing.'

Dietz backed up, raised both his hands. 'Enough already. The guy's fucking dead, okay? We get him in the bag and take him outside, end of fucking story okay?'

'Okay. Good. Don't know what the fuck that was all about. Jesus, anyone'd think we were on a Girl fucking Guide outing.'

Dietz shook his head. He figured it would have been best to take the biro out of the guy's eye before they folded him into the gunny sack, but he couldn't do it. Just the thought made him nauseous.

Eight minutes later the guy in the sack was edging out of an alleyway in the trunk of a beat-up Plymouth Valiant. Name was Jimmy Nestor. Used to spray cars for a living, sometimes went out on a boost, sometimes smoked too much weed and got high and mighty ideas about stinging some dumbass motherfucker for a ten grand bonus and disappearing to California.

Jimmy Nestor, hophead that he was, didn't know where the edge was. Not exactly. Went over it, as was always the case with those who were unrealistic about their own limitations.

Next place he would see would be the cool depths of the Hudson River – black, almost without end, and real fucking lonely. Much the same as the rest of his life, loser that he was.

FORTY-NINE

'But that's not possible, Mr Harper.'

Harper shook his head. He glanced towards the window. The snow had come down thick and fast during the night. New York looked clean, perhaps for the first time in a year.

He turned back and looked at Frank Duchaunak. Duchaunak carried the shadows and ghosts of a man who had not slept for a very long time. He'd arrived early, called from down in the lobby, and Harper – without thinking – had lifted the receiver.

Seven minutes it had taken Duchaunak to persuade him; seven minutes and finally Harper had conceded defeat.

'Okay,' he'd said. 'Come on up.'

And here they were – the lost one from Miami, the crazy one from Chicago.

'I don't see how you can be certain about any of this,' Harper said.

'Why d'you say that?'

'The stuff I've heard.' Harper once again turned towards the window. He closed his eyes for a moment and shook his head. 'I hear one thing I think is true. An hour later I hear something else which sounds just as plausible.' Harper directed his gaze towards Duchaunak and said nothing for some seconds.

Duchaunak was neither unsettled nor awkward in that silence. It seemed for a small while that neither of them breathed.

'I don't know what is true, Detective, and I am quite sure that no-one else does.'

Duchaunak smiled. 'Are you saying that you'd take the word of someone like Walter Freiberg over a New York police detective?'

Harper tilted his head to one side and raised his eyebrows questioningly. '*What* you are is irrelevant, Detective, it's *who* you are that matters.'

323

'Who I am?'

'Let's be brutally honest with one another,' Harper said. 'From what I have heard and seen so far I don't know who is the more crazy, you or Walt Freiberg.'

'The Marilyn Monroe thing?'

Harper shrugged. 'The Marilyn Monroe thing. The thing with the sugar sachets. The fact that you turn up here looking like a beat-to-shit wino—'

Duchaunak instinctively ran his fingers through his hair in a vague attempt to straighten it. His hand then gravitated towards his chin where he ran it across the rough stubble of his chin. 'I didn't have a great deal of time—'

'It doesn't matter, Detective . . . this is not a personal issue. You seem to me to be a very driven—'

'I am Mr—'

Harper raised his hand. 'Let me finish, Detective.'

Duchaunak nodded awkwardly. 'Yes, sorry . . . please go on.'

'As I was saying, you seem to be a very driven man. You seem very focused about what you're trying to achieve here. I'm still trying to come to terms with the fact that I have a father, a father I have been unaware of for more than thirty years.' Harper paused, inhaled deeply. 'A father that is a criminal, possibly a murderer . . . and the truth, Detective, the truth is that I have reached a point where I am having great difficulty finding a reason to stay.'

'I need you to stay, Mr Harper.'

'You *need* me to stay? You've spent most of your time trying to convince me to leave.'

'Yes, I know. But now I need you to stay.'

'For what purpose?'

'To help me end this thing, to help me find sufficient reason to put these people away.'

'Walt Freiberg?'

'Walt Freiberg, your father, Neumann, Ben Marcus, all of them.'

'But especially my father, right?'

Duchaunak nodded.

'And why the change of heart?'

'Because right now you seem to be the only link I have with these people.'

Harper frowned. He shook his head. 'I don't understand . . . this is your job, right?'

Duchaunak glanced to the left, a split-second reaction, perhaps involuntary.

'You got canned,' Harper said matter-of-factly. 'You got fucking canned, didn't you?'

'I didn't get canned, Mr Harper, as you so elegantly put it.'

'So what's the deal here? You're not on this officially, are you? You've come here without a warrant, without any official sanction, haven't you?'

'I've come here to ask for your assistance . . . to appeal to your sense of civic duty.'

Harper sneered. 'You're telling me I should do what you want out of civic duty?'

Duchaunak nodded.

'And why the hell should I do anything you want me to do?'

'Because helping me would be the right thing.'

Harper laughed coarsely. 'The right thing? According to whom? According to you? Walt Freiberg? Or maybe Evelyn Sawyer?'

'According to the law, Mr Harper.'

'Oh, come on! You're going to have to do an awful lot better than that to get my vote, Detective. You want me to do anything you're going to have to give me one helluva good reason.'

'Because these are bad people—'

Harper cut in. 'And I'm supposed to have a conscience about what other people have done?'

Duchaunak shook his head. 'I'm wasting my time, Mr Harper. I came here because I thought you might have some degree of common sense, some vague semblance of responsibility—'

'What d'you mean, responsibility? I haven't done anything.'

'But your father has. People in your family have. That carries with it some sense of responsibility.'

'That's your viewpoint,' Harper said. 'That is your viewpoint and your viewpoint alone. What these people have done is their business, not mine.'

'It's your business when you can do something to help stop it and you choose not to.'

'And what makes you such an expert on this thing? Why are you so driven when it comes to my father and Walt Freiberg?'

325

Duchaunak shook his head. 'I have my reasons.'

'Because of Lauren Sachs?'

Duchaunak inhaled suddenly. His eyes widened and he looked at Harper as if Harper had shot him.

'Walt Freiberg told me,' Harper said.

Duchaunak did not respond.

'I spoke to Walt and he told me that Lauren Sachs was killed, but that the robbery was organized and perpetrated by Ben Marcus and his people.'

'He would tell you that,' Duchaunak said. 'Of course he would tell you that . . . you think he would admit to having been involved in something like that?'

'You see what I mean, though?' Harper asked. 'What I said about being told one thing, and then being told something else which sounds just as plausible. My father's dead. No, he's not dead. He's alive and well and living in New York. Oh fuck, no he's not. Someone just shot him in a liquor store robbery. My mother died of pneumonia. Did she, fuck . . . she committed suicide in the Carmine Street house and my Aunt Evelyn found her and never told me. Then I'm told about this girl, the one you were going to marry. Evelyn implied that someone had died, and that was the reason you were so obsessive about my father. She said that you attributed all your unhappiness to something my father had done. Then I find out from Walt that it was your fiancée Evelyn was talking about, but he said that Ben Marcus was responsible for her death.' Harper smiled. His expression was bitter and filled with resentment.

'I understand, Mr Harper—'

Harper laughed. 'No you don't. You haven't got a clue what I'm talking about.'

Duchaunak didn't reply.

'Go on, Detective, tell me one more time how you understand.' Harper leaned forward in the chair. His movement was meant as nothing but a challenge.

Duchaunak shook his head and looked down. 'I don't understand. You're right. I don't understand.'

Harper leaned back, reached for the cigarettes he'd ordered from room service and lit one. 'I quit smoking,' he said. 'I'd quit for the best part of three months before I came here, and now I'm smoking again. I am so fucking pissed off with you people.'

'You people?'

'Yes, Detective, *you people*. You and Evelyn Sawyer, Walt Freiberg, this Cathy Hollander or whatever her name is. I'm even pissed off with people I don't know and people who are already dead . . . that's how mightily fucking pissed off I am.'

Duchaunak rested his elbows on his knees and placed the palms of his hands together. He moved his hands as he spoke to emphasize what he was saying. 'I'm not going to tell you that I understand how you feel, Mr Harper. I don't, and I'm not going to pretend to. I have been working on these people for seven years. What they have done, the things that have happened around them . . . this is the stuff of nightmares. These are crazy, evil, destructive people. I am sorry to speak to you like this, sorry that this is your father we're talking about, but the truth is the truth Mr Harper. Edward Bernstein, Lenny as they call him, has been one of the most prominent New York criminal underworld figures for the past thirty or forty years—'

'I don't want to *know*, Detective.' Harper started to rise from his chair. 'I want you to leave now—'

'Sit down, Mr Harper!' Duchaunak snapped.

Harper dropped back into the chair as if he'd been forcibly pushed.

'You sit back down and hear me out,' Duchaunak said, his tone just as direct. 'You listen to what I have to say, and then you make a decision. This isn't something you can run away from. This is the truth, goddammit. This is the truth and you're going to listen to it whether you like it or not. I could have you arrested—'

'Arrested?' Harper said. 'Have me arrested? What in God's name are you talking about?'

'Aiding and abetting a known felon. Withholding information directly related to an ongoing criminal investigation. Obstructing justice. You want me to go on?'

Once again Duchaunak and Harper stared at one another in silence.

'Right then,' Duchaunak said. 'You listen to what I have to say, and then you make a decision about what you want to do, okay?'

Harper did not reply.

Duchaunak nodded. 'So, like I said, this *is* what it is, Mr Harper.

These are the facts. Your father, Edward Bernstein, has been involved, directly and indirectly, with many of the most lucrative armed robberies in New York during the last thirty or forty years. It has been estimated, and there's no way in the world this could ever be accurately determined because he's probably been involved in a great deal more than even we know about . . . but conservative estimates put the total financial damage somewhere in the region of a hundred to a hundred and twenty-five million dollars. Like I said, that's just the stuff we know about. The body count is somewhere in the region of forty-five people. Once again, those are just the ones we know about. No doubt there are a number of good citizens and assorted criminals weighted down and sunk in both the East and Hudson Rivers. We don't know for sure, and in all honesty we probably will never know. Your father has also spent a considerable number of years in the care of the state at two different times in his life. Walt Freiberg has also done two terms of imprisonment, one for aggravated assault, another for possession of a concealed weapon with intent. Third time we get him he gets the deep six.' Duchaunak looked up at Harper. 'That's the expression we use for—'

'I know what it means,' Harper said. 'Third strike he gets life without parole.'

Duchaunak nodded. 'Your father is a clever man, exceptionally so, and his cleverness is matched only by his ruthless nature and his seemingly limitless greed. Walter Freiberg is his right-hand man, his consigliere, the one who organizes things when someone needs to disappear.' Duchaunak leaned back in the chair. He seemed to relax a little, perhaps because he believed Harper was listening, perhaps because there was something reassuring in the sound of his own voice as he reiterated the reasons for his own tenacity. 'When your father and Walt Freiberg have set their minds on something there has been nothing sufficient to stop them. The law is irrelevant, a mere inconvenience they pay lip service to every once in a while. They want something, they go and take it. As far as they're concerned it's as simple as that.'

Harper slid back in the chair. He felt smaller, like he'd been crushed.

'There have been killings, Mr Harper, killings that really

328

warrant the term "executions". People have died because they disagreed with your father, because they said some word that upset Walt Freiberg. Lives have been used up as if they had no value at all. This is what we're dealing with here . . . these are the kind of people we are involved with.'

Harper sat up a little; he edged forward and rested his elbows on his knees. The smoke from the cigarette curled up around his face and made his eyes water. He did nothing to stop it.

'There have been gangland shoot-outs over streets, blocks, parts of New York that your father believed he controlled, and those who challenged that ownership.'

'Marcus,' Harper said, his voice strained. 'You're talking about Ben Marcus, right?'

'Ben Marcus, yes,' Duchaunak replied. 'You know about Ben Marcus?'

Harper looked up at Duchaunak and shook his head. 'No, not really. Like I said before, Walt told me that the robbery where your fiancée was killed was carried out by Ben Marcus, and that Marcus was the one who had my father shot.'

Duchaunak opened his mouth to say something, and then closed it. He shook his head, seemed puzzled.

'What?' Harper asked.

'Ben Marcus . . . Walt Freiberg told you that Ben Marcus arranged to have your father shot?'

'Yeah, that's right,' Harper replied. 'Hell, let's be blunt eh? Walt told me that Marcus put a tap on my father.'

Duchaunak smiled knowingly and shook his head slowly.

'What?' Harper asked.

'Cannot be, Mr Harper. I'm afraid that Walt Freiberg did not tell you the truth.'

'You what?'

'There is no way Ben Marcus ordered the shooting of your father.'

'What're you talking about? Of course he did. That's what all this is about isn't it? A battle over the territories. Ben Marcus wants my father's territory . . .' Harper stopped suddenly, sort of half laughed, but it was a strange and humorless sound. 'Jesus, listen to me. I cannot believe I'm sitting here saying these things.'

'Go on, Mr Harper.'

'Right, yes . . . a battle over the territories. Ben Marcus ordered the shooting of my father because he wants to take his territory.'

'Not possible,' Duchaunak said. 'Like I said, that's just not possible.'

'How so?' Harper said. 'How is that not possible?'

'I'll tell you exactly how it's not possible, Mr Harper . . . and then maybe, just maybe you'll listen to what I have to say.'

FIFTY

Nine-sixteen a.m. Longshoreman called Danny Fricker stands on
the edge of the steps near one of the Pier 42 loading platforms
and lights a cigarette. Leans on the railing, rusted and wet,
smells the all-too-familiar odor of garbage and hopelessness that
comes up from the river. Back and to his left is the Christopher
Street Station, ahead of him and across the water he can see
Castle Point, Elysian Park and Hoboken. Once went with a girl
from Hoboken, name of Sally Tomczak; Polish girl with a voice
like an angel, used to sing in a club called The Rosa Maria until
her parents found out the kind of men who went there. That was
ten years before, and as far as Danny Fricker knew she married
some dumb Polack and now the only singing she did was
lullabies for her babies. Helluva shame. Helluva waste. Life
seemed to have such things down cold, the way it could give you
something grand and then snatch it right away.

Danny Fricker smokes, he thinks, he smiles nostalgically, and
then he glances down to the edge of the water and sees a gunny
sack come to rest against the stonework.

Takes him twenty-five minutes and the assistance of two other
guys to drag that thing out of the water. They use long wooden
poles with metal hooks on the end, the things they employ to
catch hold of netted cargo coming down on a crane. Slits open
the sack with a boxcutter, and the sight and smell from within is
enough to turn everyone's breakfast to mystery meat and spray-
paint the dockyard. Ironic in some small way, though they
wouldn't have known that at the time.

Danny Fricker calls the deputy chargehand, brute of a man
called Bill Rissick. Rissick radios the dockmaster, dockmaster
comes down and immediately calls the police. Despatch sends a
black and white, an ambulance and a deputy coroner. Deputy
Coroner is the only one who can do on-site examinations and

authorize the movement of a body. He's the one who opens up the gunny sack and turns the body onto its back, notes the ballpoint pen protruding from the eye socket of the victim, and once his initial evaluation is complete he instructs the driver and attendant medic to take the body to the central morgue where a forensic pathologist will perform an autopsy.

Police Detective Gary Sampson takes statements from Fricker, his two buddies, the deputy chargehand and the dockmaster. He gives them leave to resume their day, tells them not to worry about it. They will, undoubtedly, because such a thing as this is rare within a lifetime, and once experienced there is little one can do to forget it. The images, the sounds, the smells, the feelings – such things are held in perpetuity within the memory, and they can backflash unexpectedly. And it's Christmas for God's sake. Kind of a world is it when shit like this happens so close to Christmas?

'Fucked-up world if you want my opinion,' Fricker tells Sampson.

Sampson nods, thinking not only of a man in a gunny sack with a biro in his eye, but also of Darryl and Jessica McCaffrey, a brother and sister murdered, related by blood but seemingly unconnected, a case that appears to be going nowhere, more than likely never will.

'You're right there,' he tells Fricker. 'Really very fucked up indeed.'

'Not a question of luck,' Walt Freiberg told Joe Koenig. 'It's never a question of luck. Relying on luck, attributing anything to luck, good or bad, is merely a way of excusing your own lack of preparation.' Walt smiled. 'Edward used to say that . . . he'd say, "Walt, you have to understand that luck is a stupid man's way of telling the world he couldn't figure the odds."'

Koenig laughed, and then his expression became a little more serious. He leaned forward in his chair, leaned closer to Freiberg, almost as if he believed he would be overheard. 'He isn't going to make it, is he?' he asked.

Freiberg shook his head. 'Joe . . . hell Joe, I don't fucking know. He's a tough guy, as tough as they make 'em, but he's old. People at the hospital are surprised he's stayed alive this long.'

'But everything goes forward regardless, right?'

Freiberg nodded, put his cigar in the ashtray. 'There's been a lot of talk,' he said. 'Lot of rumors, lot of hearsay. Some of it I've heard, most of it I haven't wanted to. What we got worked out goes ahead. In my mind there was never any doubt about it.'

'And the kid is going to hold up?'

'Sure, he'll hold up. He doesn't have to do anything directly . . . he just has to be here and keep everyone thinking he's something he ain't. This has been too long coming for us to start all over.'

Koenig shook his head, back in the chair. 'So whaddya reckon? You think it was just bad luck that Lenny was in the liquor store when that thing went down?'

Freiberg smiled. 'Bad luck? Hell no, he just didn't figure the odds.'

'What is on the film says everything. That's the truth of it, Mr Harper. The footage from that night tells us everything we need to know.'

Harper looked at Duchaunak, shook his head, shifted around in his chair. He seemed unable to control either his thoughts or his body. He turned towards the window, inhaled, held his breath for a few seconds, then looked back at Duchaunak, but his focus was off. He was looking right through the detective and into the corner of the room.

'Mr Harper?'

Harper snapped to. 'I'm with you,' he said, seemingly alert, but his voice told of exhaustion and a depth of battered emotions.

'So you understand what I'm saying to you?'

Harper nodded. 'That the robbery started before my father went into the liquor store.'

'Seven minutes before.'

'Seven minutes,' Harper echoed. 'Must've felt like a lot longer than seven minutes to the people in the store.'

Duchaunak nodded. 'In fact, Mr Harper, it appears that the car that your father was in must have been several blocks away, and already the robbery was in progress. Your father was in the wrong place at the wrong time. It was bad luck, just simple bad luck . . . a coincidence of the worst kind. He walked into a liquor store, went right to the back, apparently to buy some wine, and

333

failed to notice that on the other side of the central aisle a man was holding the owner of the store at gunpoint. When your father came around the top of the aisle and started towards the till he obviously saw what was happening, and for whatever reason he decided he was going to do something about it.'

'And he got himself shot?'

Duchaunak nodded. 'He got himself shot.'

'And you're sure the robbery was occurring before my father arrived there?'

'Like I said, it started before your father even stopped the car. According to the CCTV tape the perp walked into the store a good seven minutes before your father arrived. There was a hiatus of about three minutes while the perp waited for another customer to leave, and then he took the gun from his jacket and threatened the store owner and his wife.'

'So Ben Marcus couldn't have ordered the shooting?'

'Seems to make sense, eh?'

'Seems to make sense.'

There was silence for a few moments, and then Harper looked at Duchaunak directly, unflinching, his eyes cold and hard. 'So what do you want?' he asked. 'What is it that you want me to do, Detective?'

FIFTY-ONE

Twelve after eleven a.m. Detective Gary Sampson files a brief summary of the morning's events, attaches a photocopy of his initial interview notes for the case file. Calls the central morgue from his desk, waits on hold for seven minutes, and is then told that the John Doe from Pier 42 is still in a line.

'We had a busy night,' the attendant tells him.

'Didn't we all?' Sampson replies, and leaves his cellphone number so they can call him when the results are out.

Hangs up the phone, thinks to call his wife regarding arrangements for collecting his mother. She's coming over for Christmas, coming over from Atlantic City. Brother's coming too, and it'll be the first time the family's been together for the better part of five years. Last time was his father's funeral, but the less said about that the better.

Sampson tugs his jacket from the back of the chair and starts out of the office. Places to go, people to see, he thinks, in this very, very fucked-up world.

Three-dollar ballpoint pen.

Trace evidence: chips of glass, paint, metal, plastic, particles of dirt and soil; natural fibers, hair – human and otherwise; man-made fabrics – acetate, rayon, nylon, polyester, orlon; everything falling within the comfortable parameters of 'matching', 'consistent with' and 'within the limits of the examination'.

The word 'forensics' meant 'related to debate or argument'.

There was no argument here.

Deputy Chief Forensic Pathologist Anthony Damilano was comfortably familiar with the four types of death – accident, suicide, natural and murder; this was undoubtedly the last. Angle of the three-dollar ballpoint conclusively proved that the victim had not held it against the upper part of his eye and then forced himself against it, perhaps using a wall, even the surface of a table, as a support to stabilize the object. This ballpoint had entered the socket from a point slightly above eye-level and to the victim's left. Someone had stuck the thing into him with sufficient force to break the clip off against the upper rim of the eye socket. The victim had been tied into a gunny sack and thrown into the river. Helluva way to spend Christmas, Damilano thought, and started work on the prints.

Duchaunak cleared his throat. 'As far as we know there are three dead, perhaps four,' he started. 'Two of them from Marcus's camp, one named Micky Levin, another name of Johnnie Hoy. Johnnie Hoy was found in an alleyway off of West Fifteenth and Seventh. Little kid found him, eight years old I think. Johnnie had been left out there all night. Someone stabbed him in the eye, dragged him out there and left him all night. Frozen fucking solid he was, and this little kid goes walking his dog and finds this guy.' Duchaunak smiled resignedly. 'Not the sort of thing you want playing on a kid's mind at Christmas, eh?'

Harper stared blankly at a point somewhere between himself and Duchaunak. It appeared he hadn't blinked for several minutes.

'There's another guy,' Duchaunak went on. 'Kid called Lester McKee. He's a regular character in this business. Anything goes on in the Marcus territories and you'll find Lester.' Duchaunak paused, as if for effect. 'Thing is, Mr Harper, we haven't been able to find him. We've looked, kept our eyes and ears open, but there's been no word about Lester McKee for quite some time. And I'll tell you, he isn't the sort of kid who just takes off to see his ma in Poughkeepsie.'

Harper closed his eyes.

'Micky Levin we found down on Pier 49 with the side of his head staved in. When I got home I had to scrape bits of him out of the welts of my shoes.'

Duchaunak paused to see if Harper would react. He did not. Duchaunak went on talking.

'And then, on your father's side, we have a guy who goes by the name of Mouse Jackson. Friend of mine called me and told me that he was found dead beneath a bench in Washington Square Park. There was trace evidence of adhesive on his wrists and ankles, on the lower half of his face; indications that he'd been gagged and taped to something, that he'd had nails driven through his hands.' Duchaunak shook his head resignedly. 'Fuck knows what that was all about, maybe some kind of seasonal motif, eh?' He shook his head. 'One of his feet had been beaten to a pulp, but the thing that killed him was the screwdriver through his temple—'

'Enough.'

Duchaunak frowned. 'I beg your pardon?'

'Enough,' Harper repeated. 'Enough already.'

'I have plenty more where that came from, Mr Harper.'

Harper shook his head. He rose from his chair and turned his back on Duchaunak. He walked to the window and stood there looking out and over New York. 'This is the war, right? The war you were talking about.'

'This is nothing, Mr Harper. This is a little warm-up before the main act.'

'And the main act? What will the main act be, Detective?' Harper turned slowly and looked at Duchaunak.

'I don't know, Mr Harper . . . and that's precisely why I need you.'

'What time?'

'Early.'

'How early?'

'A few minutes after nine as far as we can tell.'

Walt Freiberg is silent for a few seconds.

Cathy Hollander stands in the callbox, her palms sweating, her heart audible as it beats nervously in her chest.

'And the cop is still in there?'

'Yes.'

'Fuck!'

'What d'you want me to do?'

'Want you to do? Jesus Cathy, I don't *know* what I want you to do! What the fuck do *you* think you should do?'

'Walt—'

'I'm sorry, that was uncalled for,' Freiberg interjects. He falls silent. She can hear him breathing. This is perhaps the first time she's heard him rattled, like everything isn't running smooth and simple how it's supposed to.

337

'There isn't anything we can do,' he finally says. 'No-one's going in there to tell Harper he shouldn't talk to the cop, right? So the cop talks to him. What the fuck, eh? We go talk to Harper when Duchaunak has left and we turn everything back the right way round again.'

'You think we can?' Cathy asks.

'Hey,' Freiberg says, and he starts laughing. 'Who the fuck are we dealing with here? There isn't anything we *can't* do. We have time, not one helluva lot of time, but we have time.'

'So I stay here?'

'Where are you?'

'Callbox about three blocks from my apartment.'

'Christ no, get inside. Hell, Cathy, you're going to freeze your ass off. Get Beck to stay by the Regent and call you when the cop leaves. I'll come get you and we'll go over, see Harper, sort this thing out once and for all, okay?'

'Okay,' Cathy says, doubt evident in her voice.

'Hey, what is this? Once more with feeling . . . we go over there later and sort this thing out, okay?'

'Okay,' Cathy says, and tries to sound as sincere as she can.

'Good enough,' Freiberg says. 'Call me when the cop leaves and we'll go to work.' He hangs up before Cathy has a chance to acknowledge him.

Cathy Hollander sets the receiver back and opens the callbox door. The wind cuts at her face, tightens the skin around her eyes. She stands for a moment, and then starts walking. She is several blocks from home and it is bitterly cold. She thinks to ask herself what kind of life she has created, but does not dare.

'Jimmy Nestor.'

'Who?'

'James Nestor. Jimmy Nestor,' Damilano says. 'That's what flags up on the prints. He has a sheet. Seems he was a booster.'

'Age?'

'You've got access,' Damilano says. 'Pull up the file.' He waits while Detective Gary Sampson accesses the database and retrieves Nestor's file.

'I know this guy!' Sampson says. 'I didn't recognize him. He had that biro sticking out of his eye an' everything. I've pulled this guy in three, four times. He and his cousin run a chop-shop

338

on Mulberry . . . er, no . . . I think it's Mott, one of those streets just over into Little Italy. He does the chassis numbers, paint jobs, the whole thing. His cousin takes 'em, he fixes them up. I think Jimmy's done a turn in Green Haven . . . yep, here we are, did a year and a half for grand theft auto back in '99.'

'So I got the body and you got the name,' Damilano says.

'Good job. We'll take it from here. Thanks for getting back so soon.'

'Not a problem.' Damilano hangs up the phone and turns back to the naked, battered body of James Roosevelt Nestor a.k.a. 'Bird' a.k.a. 'Chester'.

Sampson hangs up as well, then lifts the receiver to call Despatch.

'I got a place over in Little Italy I want to check out. You got another squad you can send with me?'

'Sure we got another squad,' Despatch duty sergeant snarls at him. 'We got four or five . . . in fact I got one comin' outta my ass even as we speak. Hell, let's make it a party, let's send the whole fucking precinct down to Little Italy. We can have pizza—'

'Hey!' Sampson yells. 'Cut that fucking crap out will ya? I just called to see if you guys have another squad.'

'No, we don't have another squad Detective, and if today is anything like yesterday you aren't going to get a back-up squad until after the New Year, so you have a real good Christmas, okay?'

'Asshole,' Sampson says, and hangs up the phone. He calls across the room to his partner. 'Hey Sonnenburg, we got a day trip.'

Yale Sonnenburg looks up from the document he's reading. He nods, reaches around back of the chair for his jacket and rises, still reading the pages.

'What the hell is that?' Sampson asks.

Sonnenburg smiles. 'It's my wedding vows,' he says. 'I have to learn my wedding vows in Hebrew.'

Sampson shrugs. 'Whatever floats your boat man, whatever floats your boat.'

FIFTY-TWO

'And that's all you've got?' Harper asks.

Duchaunak nods his head. 'That's all I've got, Mr Harper.'

Harper shakes his head. 'That there might be a robbery—'

'Oh, you can take it from me, Mr Harper, there *will* be a robbery. I have no doubt about that.'

'Okay, okay ... so you're telling me that this thing will happen. You don't know exactly when, but you think it's going to be Christmas Eve. You think that people who work for my father and people who work for Ben Marcus are going to be involved, that they're going to do this heist together, right?'

Duchaunak nods in the affirmative.

'And that's what you've got,' Harper repeats; a rhetorical question.

'That's what I've got.'

'So, even though they are opposing criminal fraternities they are going to do something together?' Harper pauses. He scratches his head. 'That's ... no, I'm sorry, there's something I just don't get here ...'

'It's been done before,' Duchaunak says. 'It happened in Chicago a few times. You get these guys from opposing families, and then someone comes up with something that's too big for one organization alone, and so they work it out together. It's the strangest goddamned thing. They shoot the hell out of each other, they walk on each others' territories, all this shit for years, and then suddenly they find something they can't do with the resources they each individually have and so they pull a robbery together, they cut up the proceeds, and once the dust has settled they're shooting the hell out of one another all over again.'

'That doesn't make sense—' Harper starts.

Duchaunak smiles knowingly. 'Don't try and apply any logic to this, Mr Harper. One thing you cannot do ... one thing you

340

will never be able to do is apply logic to what these people do. This is another race of human beings who happen to occupy the same planet as us.' Duchaunak shakes his head. 'You try and rationalize this within your own frame of reference and you'll overload. I wouldn't even try.'

'And how do you *know* that they're going to do this thing together?'

'I don't *know* anything, Mr Harper. It's not a question of what I know, it's a question of—'

'Whatever,' Harper interjects. 'The bottom line is you want me to talk to these people. You want me to see Walt Freiberg and Cathy Hollander, whoever else might be around—'

'And find out what they're going to do.' Duchaunak finishes it for him, leans back in his chair and crosses his legs.

Harper looks away towards the window. 'You've lost it, you really have lost it, Detective—'

'Hey, I didn't get personal,' Duchaunak retorts. 'What is this? I'm asking you to do something to help me and you get personal.'

'*You* didn't get personal?' Harper asks, his voice starting to rise. 'What in fuck's name are you talking about, you didn't get personal? You've spent the last week convincing me that these people are one crazy, fucked-up bunch of psychopaths and bank robbers and how I should get out of New York as fast as I can, and then all of a sudden, right at the point where someone's put you on a leash, you're asking me to go amongst them, all nice and polite, and just ask them where they might be having their next armed robbery. Jesus, if that isn't personal then I don't know what is.'

Duchaunak is silent.

'Well?' Harper asks.

'Well what?'

'You have anything to say?'

Duchaunak shakes his head. 'Point taken, Mr Harper. It *is* personal. In fact, looking at it the way you've just put it, it couldn't be more personal. I'm sorry to have troubled you.' Duchaunak starts to rise from his chair, reaches for his overcoat.

'Hey, what the fuck is this?' Harper asks.

Duchaunak frowns, shakes his head. 'I'm leaving,' he says matter-of-factly.

Harper smiles, starts to laugh. There is a tone of sarcasm when he speaks. 'I see,' he says. 'Backwards psychology. You are so predictable.'

'So predictable?' Duchaunak asks. 'It's not a matter of being predictable or anything else Mr Harper. What you say is true. I can't argue with you. This is a complicated situation, and in all honesty it's unfair of me to expect you to get any deeper into it.'

Duchaunak pulls on his overcoat, starts for the door.

Harper seems uncertain. The conflict of thoughts, of emotions, is displayed on his face. 'Wait,' he says.

Duchaunak pauses.

'Back up a minute will you?'

Duchaunak turns and looks at Harper.

'This thing, this robbery you're talking about . . . this thing goes forward and people are going to die. Is that what you're saying?'

Duchaunak shakes his head. 'An armed robbery is an armed robbery, Mr Harper. By definition it involves the use of firearms, the commission of a felony, a very serious felony, and the people carrying out this robbery have every intention of escaping with not only the money but also their lives. If a situation arises where deadly force is exercised in an effort to stop them, well all I can tell you is—'

'Enough with the police shit okay? Just tell me the fucking truth,' Harper interjects. 'They do this thing, some people are going to die . . . that's all I'm asking you right now. Yes or no, tell me if some people are going to die.'

Duchaunak nods. 'Yes, Mr Harper, some people will almost definitely die.'

Harper is silent for quite some time. He looks through the window, ten floors above street level, ten floors above New York, and all he can hear in the room is the frightened beating of his own heart.

He turns and smiles at Duchaunak. 'Why are you such a crazy bastard?'

Duchaunak looks down at the floor. 'Stress of the job?' he asks. 'I don't know, Mr Harper, I really don't know . . . maybe just because someone around here has to be crazy to make life a little more interesting.'

'And you need my help because you've been pulled off this thing?'

Duchaunak nods.

'And if I don't help you, then you're out in the back end of nowhere all on your own?'

'A little melodramatic, Mr Harper.'

'Melodramatic but true, right?'

'Right.'

'So what do you want me to do . . . what do you want *exactly*?'

Duchaunak steps away from the hotel room door. He advances two or three steps further into the room and buries his hands in his overcoat pockets. 'What I want, Mr Harper, is for you to do everything they want you to do. You are here for a reason. You are not here because Evelyn insisted you come. You're here because Walt Freiberg made her insist. He needs you here for some reason. Somehow, and this I cannot figure, you play some part in this thing, and it has something to do with the fact that your father was shot. If Walt Freiberg believes that Ben Marcus had your father killed, then there may very well be some arrangement that they've reached. This is what gives me the idea that they're working together. That's as much as I know, and even that is guesswork. You're here because you are Edward Bernstein's son, and this fact counts for something in whatever Walt Freiberg has planned. I just need you to speak to them, to make them think that you're willing to be as much a part of this thing as they need you to be . . . and whatever they tell you I need you to report back to me.'

'And that's all?' Harper asks.

'I'm asking for as little as I can, Mr Harper, and believe me, if there was any way to have you completely uninvolved in this then that's the way I would prefer it. I am in the proverbial shit . . . in fact I am rafting down a rapid of shit, there are holes in my canoe and I don't have a paddle. That's how *in the shit* I am.'

'So you better leave.'

'You what?'

'You better leave, Detective, and you better make sure as many people see you leave as you can manage. If your theory is correct, if I *am* needed in some way, then this hotel will be being watched by whoever, and as soon as you leave Walt Freiberg will come over, or maybe Cathy Hollander or whatever her name is, and they will want to find out what you have told me, what crazy ideas you have been filling my head with, and then they will tell me how everything you've said is utter insanity and that it's time for me to get the real facts.'

Duchaunak takes a card from his pocket and hands it to Harper. 'On the back is my cellphone number. Don't call me from another cellphone, call me from a kiosk in the street, a public phone in a train station or a shopping mall, somewhere like that. Don't phone me at the precinct or at my home. Call me and tell me where you are and I will come meet you or call you back from another public phone.'

'Because if they figure out I've spoken to you—'

Duchaunak shakes his head. 'Don't even go there, Mr Harper . . . believe me, don't even go there.'

'So leave,' Harper says.

'I've left already,' Duchaunak replies, and opens the door. He steps out into the hallway and closes the door silently behind him.

John Harper, late of Miami, Fla., stands near the window and closes his eyes. Had he been a religious man he might have said a few words, but he is not, and thus says nothing. Tries to think nothing too, but that is harder. He backs up a few feet, sits down, leans back his head and sighs.

'Unbelievable,' he says quietly. 'Un-fucking-believable.'

Three minutes and eleven seconds later the phone rings.

FIFTY-THREE

'Go through them again,' Marcus said.

Sol Neumann cleared his throat. 'For us we have Ray Dietz, Albert Reiff, Maurice Rydell, Henry Kossoff, Karl Merrett and the kid that's come in to replace Lester McKee. His name is Lewis Parselle.'

'And for the prosecution?' Marcus asked, smiling sarcastically.

'Freiberg himself, Ricky Wheland and Ron Dearing as drivers, Joe Koenig, Charlie Beck, Larry Benedict and Leo Petri.'

'And the girl?'

Sol Neumann shook his head. 'Freiberg has her on point down at Bethune and Greenwich.'

Marcus shook his head. 'She's a smart girl, Sol. Don't underestimate her.'

Neumann nodded in agreement. 'Smart she may be, but the whole thing is out of her league.'

Marcus smiled, started laughing. 'Let me tell you something, Sol. You can hear me on this thing or you can choose to know best. Regardless of Lenny Bernstein being out of the picture he is not really out of the picture, you get what I mean? These people, Freiberg especially, have worked with Bernstein for so many years that they think like him. This thing will go down just as if Bernstein was right behind it, just like he was running everything.'

'And the kid? What the hell do we do about him?'

'Give it until tomorrow. We get word he is someone, or we don't. If we get no word, or the kid is something out of someone's imagination, then Freiberg is going to get himself killed. That's the way it is. I can't be dealing with this runaround shit. He's some Miami bigshot ... hell, if he's that fucking big then we would have heard something reliable. Who the fuck does Freiberg think we are? He thinks we're three days off the farm? There's no doubt this thing will run. Too big, too much planning to just let it all fall apart, and there's too much at stake. And it'll go forward regardless of whether Walt Freiberg is dead or alive.'

Neumann didn't speak.

'You get any word on the man himself?'

Neumann shook his head. 'Same as yesterday, the day before. They got him hooked up to everything and then some. Still don't know if he's going to make it.'

Marcus shook his head. 'So the kid will stand for him like Freiberg said. We get word the kid is good then it stays as planned. No word then Freiberg is dead. It is what it is. The thing goes down, we wind up with the major pieces. Freiberg will be gone, the kid will disappear wherever the hell he came from. What the fuck, eh?'

Neumann nodded. 'What the fuck.'

Marcus nodded. 'So call 'em in, all of them. We meet at seven at the Indiana Club and go through everything again.'

'You want me to call Freiberg?'

Marcus shook his head. 'I'll call Freiberg.'

Sol Neumann rose from where he was sitting.

'And Sol?'

Neumann looked down at Marcus.

'I want to lose the cop as well.'

'The crazy one?'

Marcus nodded. 'Yeah, the crazy one. Someone should've put that poor son-of-a-bitch out of his misery a long fucking time ago.'

'Couldn't agree with you more, Ben, couldn't agree with you more.' Neumann turned towards the door, on his face an expression of relief. Ben Marcus had not asked about Thomas McCaffrey.

At one-nineteen p.m., afternoon of Monday, December twenty-second, kneeling in a slick of blood that was making its way west towards Mulberry, feeling that same blood seeping through the knee of his regulation green coveralls, listening to the heart, feeling the pulse as it slipped away beneath his finger, wishing that the guy over his shoulder would stop screaming at the top of his voice for *Somebody to fucking do something . . . Jesus Christ, what the fuck is going on here? Can't somebody DO SOMETHING!*

One-nineteen p.m., afternoon of Monday, December twenty-second, Blue Cross medic Keith Kurtz pronounced Detective Yale Sonnenburg dead.

Simple as that.

Bullets – two of them – one through the side of the guy's neck, one in the lower part of his stomach. Second one punctured his leather belt. Clean hole right through. Bullet was lodged somewhere in the mess of guts behind. Maybe the belt was the only reason his stomach stayed inside his shirt. Big bullet. Close range. A nine milli, maybe a .357. There were guns all over the place, lot of blood, because the guy that shot the cop was dead too. Mexican, Puerto Rican perhaps; olive skin, dark hair, face pretty wrecked from what Kurtz could see as he knelt beside the dead body of Yale Sonnenburg. Looked like the Mexican took two or three shots as well. One seemed to have gone through the bridge of his nose.

Kurtz didn't know that Sonnenburg was due to be married in less than a week. Had he known it wouldn't have made a difference. Shit like that doesn't count for much in the face of a nine milli.

The other cop just carried on hollering like he was a fire siren. Kurtz's partner, a weatherworn, seen-it-all-before twenty-five-year veteran called Alfredo Langa, steered the hollering cop into an alleyway off of Mott Street. Kurtz figured the place was some sort of chop shop, like an auto-parts warehouse or something. Cans of paint everywhere, like big steel drums of the stuff, and all bright yellow. Yellow like sunflowers.

Kurtz radioed his central despatch to have them send out some more cops and the deputy coroner. He also told them to send a doctor, someone who had the authority to sedate the other cop.

Kurtz checked the dead cop's jacket for ID, found it tucked inside his left breast pocket along with a sheet of paper covered in blood and lines of type. Looked like some foreign language, Hebrew or somesuch. The guy's shopping list maybe – lox, bagels, cream cheese, chicken livers, who the fuck knew? Whatever it was, it sure as hell wasn't a great deal of use to him now.

Kurtz smiled to himself. You had to maintain your sense of humor, he thought. However insane this stuff got, you had to keep your sense of humor together.

Later his girlfriend, cute brunette called Patti Hayes, would ask Keith Kurtz how his day had been.

He'd smile, shrug his shoulders, and say, 'Same ol' same old. Another day, another dead guy,' and she would kind of half-laugh and punch his shoulder playfully, and then ask him if he wanted to roll up a Jimmy Durante and get boosted.

That was Keith Kurtz's life.

That was Yale Sonnenburg's death.

Gary Sampson went running down the street, Alfredo Langa chasing him, and though Langa thought the cop had flipped because of the auto-shop guy he'd killed, it wasn't that at all.

Detective Gary Sampson – twice decorated for valor, once commended by the Mayor's Office, three times receiver of a one-eighty-one for excessive force – was really running away from something else.

Something to do with being Yale Sonnenburg's best man maybe; something to do with telling Yale's girlfriend she was a widow before she'd even started.

For a long while Evelyn Sawyer was quiet.

For a long while she said nothing at all. When the sense of frustration and grief became too much she climbed the stairs and stood in the upper landing for some minutes. Her breathing was shallow and indecisive, almost as if she was fighting something within.

After a while she turned and opened the door, stood for some minutes at the foot of the bed.

She could almost see everything as it had been. She could see Anne, the way her hair was spread across the pillow, the way her knees were tucked up towards her chest as if she'd experienced some terrible, constricting pain.

Many years had passed, and yet it was all here, as if it were mere moments ago.

A heartbeat. Less perhaps.

Evelyn backed up and turned around. She opened the facing door and stood looking into the room where her husband had killed himself.

348

Everything was here. 66 Carmine. The house she'd never been able to leave, never been able to walk away from. To leave would have been to betray them both. At least that's what she'd felt. And both Anne and Garrett had been betrayed enough.

'It's coming to an end,' she said.

Eventually she left the upper landing and went downstairs.

She lifted the telephone receiver from its cradle in the hallway and dialled the operator. 'New York Police Department,' she said.

She waited patiently, no more than thirty seconds or so.

'Hello . . . er, yes. I'm not sure . . . I was trying to find a particular police detective.'

A moment's silence.

'Precinct number, no . . . I'm sorry, I don't know that. His name? Yes, of course. His name is Frank Duchaunak.'

The line went silent and Evelyn Sawyer stood without moving. She looked towards the light coming through the frosted glass panel in the front door. The light was blurred through her tears.

After a while there was someone at the end of the line.

She listened, and then said: 'No, no-one else . . . I need to speak with Detective Duchaunak only. Do you know when he'll be available?'

She tilted her head to one side and frowned.

'Oh . . . I see. Right. Yes, of course . . . thank you for your help. No, that's fine thank you . . . goodbye.'

Gently, almost in slow-motion, she replaced the receiver in the cradle and bowed her head.

She could hear footsteps upstairs as they crossed the landing and reached the top of the stairs behind her.

But for that sound – in itself no sound at all – 66 Carmine was silent.

FIFTY-FOUR

The Hollander woman looked even better.

Perhaps she did it on purpose, Harper thought.

Even her voice on the telephone, her seeming concern for his welfare, the sense of empathy he felt as she told him she understood how difficult things must be – all of it seemed so effortlessly simple, and yet so perfectly effective. She had rejected him. That was the truth. And yet the way she spoke it seemed that everything was how it was before.

What was it about Cathy Hollander that made him feel so defenceless?

They arrived within twenty minutes. Where she'd called from Harper didn't know, didn't ask, but it was almost as if he wanted to see no-one but her. Walt came too, smiling, generous of word and action, bearing gifts – a bottle of liquor, a carton of Luckies, his smile high, wide and handsome. All of these things communicating a sense of warmth and fraternity, as if here – here in this small heartbeat of New York – they were all in this together.

'You look good,' Walt told him. 'You got some rest?'

'I got some rest, yes.'

'I'll fetch some glasses,' Cathy said. 'We'll have a drink.'

Walt went to the window, looked out over the city. 'There is little that can compare to New York at this time of year.' His tone was measured and calm; he seemed effortlessly in control of himself – unhurried, at ease. 'And New York is the most beautiful city in the world?' He turned and smiled at Harper. 'It is not far from it. No urban night is like the night out there. Squares after squares of flame, set up and cut into the ether. Here is our poetry, for we have pulled the stars down to our will.'

Harper frowned.

'Ezra Pound,' Walt said, and stepped forward. 'There's a little culture for the evening.'

Cathy handed him a glass, one also to Harper.

'I have been here for as long as I can recall, and yet Christmastime in New York always seems to possess an air of magic that is inimitable.' Walt raised his glass. 'A toast,' he said. 'To Edward, to health, wealth and happiness . . . and to the spirit of Christmas in New York.'

Cathy laughed. 'Such theater,' she said. She turned and smiled at Harper, a warm and effusive expression of affection it seemed. 'I can't take him anywhere,' she quipped.

'It's good to see you Sonny,' Walt said. He looked down at the glass in his hand. It appeared he was trying to find the words to say what he wished. 'I have . . . I have been worried—'

'Worried?' Harper asked.

Walt smiled, shook his head. 'Well . . . no. Worried is perhaps a little too strong. I have been thinking about your position here, how hard it has been for you. You've been here how long?'

'Last Monday,' Harper said. 'I've been here a week.'

'Christ almighty, just a week? Seems you've been here . . . God, I don't know how long.' Walt stepped away from the window, pulled the chair out from under a small table against the wall. Sitting sideways, his left arm on the back, he indicated the sofa to his right. 'Sit down Cathy,' he said. Cathy did so, and then Harper made his way to the bed and sat also.

'Like I said, I've been thinking,' he went on. 'A great deal of things have happened in a very short time. Thing have been said—'

'Walt, you don't need to—' Harper cut in.

Walt raised his hand. 'It's okay. This isn't a lecture. There's just a couple of things that have been playing on my mind and I wanted to get them out, you know?'

Harper didn't respond; Walt Freiberg was going to speak whether Harper wished him to or not.

'Things have been difficult since your father . . . since Edward was shot,' he said. For a moment he looked away, his expression pensive. There was a depth to his eyes, maybe nothing more than shadows, perhaps the way the light fell, that created the impression of a man exhausted. Walt Freiberg seemed somehow

351

burdened despite his calmness; that was the only way Harper could describe it.

'For many years we have worked together.' He waved his hand nonchalantly. 'Now it is not a matter of what we have done, the business we have been involved in . . . that is not the point we are discussing.' He looked directly at Harper. 'This is not a moral issue John. This is an issue of justice and rectitude.'

Harper frowned. 'Justice?'

Walt nodded. 'Justice and rectitude.'

'How so?'

'Ben Marcus.'

'Ben Marcus? I don't understand.'

Walt Freiberg set his glass on the small table beside him. He turned the chair beneath him and leaned forward, his elbows on his knees. For a while he said nothing, looking down at the floor, looking at his own hands as he steepled his fingers together. When he looked up the shadows beneath his eyes seemed even deeper.

'Ben Marcus. Hell, Sonny, Ben Marcus needs to pay for what he's done to Edward.'

'To pay? Pay for what Walt? I'm missing something here.'

'Jesus, isn't it the easiest thing in the world to understand?' For a moment he looked angry, and then his face suddenly calmed. 'I'm sorry, I'm not mad at you, I'm mad at the situation.' He smiled awkwardly, shook his head.

'I still don't get the thing about Ben Marcus—'

'It's really simple. Ben Marcus ordered the shooting of your father, and I, for one, cannot let this lie John . . . I just cannot let this thing lie.'

Harper shook his head. 'I spoke to Frank Duchaunak—'

Freiberg frowned. 'Duchaunak was here?'

'Oh, come on Walt, don't take me for a complete idiot. I know very well that you're aware that Duchaunak was here. Don't insult me by telling me you haven't been watching every move I've made since I arrived.'

Freiberg smiled broadly. He looked at Cathy. 'Smart guy eh? Didn't I tell you that this was a smart fucking guy?'

Cathy nodded, and for a moment it seemed she didn't know where to look.

'And don't patronize me either, Walt. And don't call me

Sonny. And don't think that I've spent a week in New York wandering around with my eyes closed.'

Walt Freiberg raised his hands in a conciliatory gesture. 'Hey John, don't get me wrong—'

'I'm not getting you wrong, Walt. I'm getting you right. I'm here for a reason. God knows why but you insisted that Evelyn get me here. I want to know why. I want you to tell me *exactly* why you brought me here. I want you to tell me the truth, and none of this half-assed bullshit about this, that and the goddamned other. Tell me what you want, tell me now, and at the same time tell me how much I'm going to get out of it.'

'How much—'

Harper turned to Cathy. 'Will you tell him that I'm not stupid? He doesn't seem to be hearing me too well.'

Cathy started to say something but was interrupted by Walt Freiberg.

'You're misunderstanding me, John,' he started.

'No Walt, *you* are misunderstanding *me*. I've been played like some dumb country hick farmhand out of the back-end of nowhere for the past seven days, by you, by Evelyn, and by this crazy fucking cop. I want to know exactly what is going on. I want to know *precisely* what you people are doing, what *precisely* it has to do with me, and if there's something you need my help with then I'm going to want to come away from here with an awful lot more than I arrived with. *Now* do we understand one another?'

Walt Freiberg nodded. 'Okay,' he said quietly. 'First things first . . . tell me what the cop told you.'

Harper smiled, shook his head. 'What the cop told me doesn't matter. The cop is crazy. That guy paid I don't know how many thousands of dollars for a goddamned baseball. He's been suspended. He's off whatever case he thought he was on. He doesn't have a hope of coming anywhere near whatever the hell you're doing because even his own people think he's lost it.'

'Whatever,' Freiberg said. 'He came here to tell you something . . . what did he say?'

'He told me that Ben Marcus could not have put a hit on my father.'

Freiberg nodded. He looked down at the floor once more and

shook his head. 'And why did he think that Ben Marcus could not have done this?'

'Because, according to the CCTV footage from that night, the robbery was already taking place before my father's car even reached the curb. The guy with the gun was in the liquor store seven minutes before my father even showed up.'

'Right,' Freiberg said. He reached into his pocket, took out a packet of cigarettes and lit one. 'Do you know what Cabernet Sauvignon is?'

Harper frowned. 'It's a type of wine.'

'Right, yes. It is a type of wine. There are many different types of Cabernet produced, and your father was partial to a particular variety. It wasn't that expensive, forty, maybe fifty dollars a bottle, but he liked it a great deal.'

'And the point of telling me this?'

'The store where he was shot ordered that wine for your father. They ordered it in especially for him. He asked them to, and they were more than happy to oblige. Sunday nights he would drive over there and collect a case of that wine for the forthcoming week.'

Freiberg paused to light a cigarette.

'It wasn't difficult,' Freiberg went on. 'It was simply a matter of knowing a little of Edward's routine. Edward was not a frightened man. He wouldn't have even given the issue a second thought, wouldn't have changed his routine even if he'd been told that someone was going to hit him there. Your father would merely have gone there with a couple of people, that's all. Your father . . . well, he didn't change what he wanted to do for anyone.'

Harper didn't say a word.

'So it was not difficult to have someone there. It was no remarkable feat on Marcus's part to predict approximately when Edward would be there. He could quite easily have had cellphone contact with some hoodlum outside the store. Marcus has Edward's car followed, and as soon as he starts making his way towards the store the call goes out, the shooter goes in the store, the thing kicks off just in time for Edward to show up. All Marcus's shooter has to do is keep that robbery going until Edward shows up. It was a simple effect . . . an illusion was created, and in that way anyone who believed it was a vendetta between Marcus and your father would have been easily convinced that it was not. Why? Because the shooter was already in the store before Edward arrived.'

Harper looked at Cathy. She nodded her head to confirm what Freiberg had said. 'It's true,' she said. 'Most times I would go down there with him. I know the store, must've been there twenty, thirty times.'

'So that's how complicated it was,' Freiberg said. 'And that little trick certainly fooled your cop.'

'He's not *my* cop,' Harper said.

'He's not?' Freiberg asked.

'What the fuck is this? What are you asking me that for?'

Freiberg shook his head. 'It is not easy to determine where your loyalties lie, John.'

'My loyalties?'

'Yes, your loyalties. A loyalty to family, or a loyalty to the law.'

Harper laughed sharply. 'This is so manipulative, and not even inventive manipulation. Jesus Christ, Walt, give me some fucking credit will you? Who the hell d'you think I am, eh? You want something, you ask me, okay? You need something from me then tell me what you need and I'll tell you whether or not I'm prepared to give it. It isn't complicated, Walt, it really isn't this fucking complicated.'

Cathy leaned forward. 'Tell him, Walt ... tell him what's going on. If he doesn't understand then he can't help.'

Freiberg nodded. He looked at Harper, then at Cathy, then at Harper once more. 'I will tell you what you need to know,' he said quietly. He waited for some word, some reaction from Harper, but there was nothing. 'And I will tell you what we need from you. You will not have time to think about it, John – at least not a great deal of time – and if you decide not to help us then we will have to act regardless.'

'Cut to the chase, Walt. Enough of this,' Harper said.

'Day after tomorrow,' Cathy Hollander interjected.

'The day after tomorrow, Christmas Eve, we take some actions,' Walt said. 'What those actions are you do not need to know. They are things that were arranged by your father, and have been organized for a considerable time. They involve both myself, the people who work for Edward, and also a number of people in the employ of Ben Marcus. We are, in effect, collaborating in a series of actions that will realize a considerable return—'

'You're going to hit some places, right?' Harper said. 'What are they? Banks? Finance houses? Diamond cutters?'

'The first thing,' Freiberg said.

'Banks . . . you're going to hit some banks, and you guys are going to work with Marcus's people. That's what you're telling me?' Harper looked at Cathy. She nodded in the affirmative.

'And I have something to do with this. You want me to be a getaway driver, right?'

Walt Freiberg laughed. 'No, John, we do not wish for you to be a getaway driver.'

'Then what? Tell me what you want.'

'Tomorrow,' Freiberg said, 'there is a meeting. That meeting was supposed to take place between your father and Ben Marcus. Your father cannot be there for obvious reasons, and so I am going to take his place.'

Harper was silent for a few seconds. He looked at Cathy, then looked once more at Freiberg.

'I will be there to stand for your father, to speak for him, to agree to the terms of a sale.'

'A sale? A sale of what?'

'Your father's territory,' Freiberg said matter-of-factly.

Harper frowned. 'How the—'

Freiberg raised his hand. 'Your father made an agreement with Ben Marcus. He wanted to retire, had considered it for some time, but he did not wish to go away with nothing to show for the work he had done and the territory he owned. He spoke with Ben Marcus, and between them they agreed that Edward would sell his interests in his New York territory. They agreed a price—'

'And after the agreement was made Ben Marcus had my father shot so he wouldn't have to pay the money,' Harper interjected.

Freiberg nodded. 'We think so. Edward had already started letting some of his people go. He'd started to settle old debts for his friends, gave money to people and helped them move out of New York. He was closing up the empire if you like. It was something he was ready to do, and I was not averse to the idea. To a degree, the fact that some of his affairs and relationships were being concluded put him in a vulnerable position. Once he'd made his agreement with Marcus we believed everything would roll forward, but there was a suspicion that Marcus might renege on the deal – and I suspected there might be an attempt on your father's life—'

'And yet he continued to do the same things, to follow the same routines?' Harper asked.

Freiberg smiled. 'Like I said before, Edward was not a frightened man. He figured Marcus wasn't ballsy enough to do what he did, but he was wrong, and we were faced with the reality of no deal, no Edward, and Marcus in a very strong position due to the fact that some of our people had already left New York and could not be recalled. I had to make a decision John . . . I had to do whatever was necessary to ensure that your father's interests were taken care of.'

'So you had Evelyn call me.'

Freiberg nodded. 'And then I spoke with Marcus directly, told him that in the absence of Edward I would stand as his representative, but that you were also here to ensure that your father's interests were correctly managed. For Marcus to disagree with such a proposal would have implicated him in the attempt on Edward's life. He had to agree. To have done anything else would have demonstrated that he never intended to keep his word in the first place.'

'And tomorrow?'

Cathy Hollander cleared her throat. 'Tomorrow Walt will meet with Ben Marcus and agree to the terms of the sale.'

'Which are?'

'Complete and unconditional surrender of all territorial partnerships, properties, resources, outstanding collections. Basically, everything that Edward owned, everything that was owed to him, becomes Marcus's property. Aside from some small bookmaker's traffic and a couple of loansharks owned by an Italian family, everything in this territory that belonged to Edward will belong to Ben Marcus.'

Harper nodded. He did not demonstrate any reaction to what he was being told. Inside his chest his heart thundered like a freight train. His hands were sweating, his pulse raced. 'And the price?'

There was silence in the room, just for a few seconds, but that silence was tangible and intense.

'The price,' Freiberg echoed, 'will be seven and a half million dollars.'

Harper looked up at Freiberg, his eyes wide, disbelieving. 'And this money . . . it comes from—'

'The actions we do on Christmas Eve,' Cathy Hollander said. 'That's where it will come from, and that's why we are working with Marcus's people for the first time.'

'You have to steal the buy-off money?'

Freiberg smiled. 'Ben Marcus doesn't have seven and a half million dollars, John. Nevertheless Ben Marcus has the contacts and resources necessary to take a lot more than seven and a half million dollars in one day.'

'And how many banks are you going to hit?'

Freiberg shook his head. 'That,' he said quietly, 'is a detail you don't need to know.' He paused. 'However, there is something you do need to know.' He glanced at Cathy. 'Ben Marcus is not a stupid man. Quite the contrary. A certain degree of license has been employed . . . creative license if you like. Ben Marcus has been told that you are a player of some influence.'

Harper looked up.

'He has been told that you have been employed in the same line of work as your father. He has been led to believe that there is a possibility that you might have your own crew down in Miami—'

Harper laughed suddenly, awkwardly. 'You've got to be kidding!'

'No, I'm not kidding. This was the only way he could be convinced to carry through with his agreement. He has been told, by inference, by lack of words rather than anything direct, that you have your own people down south, that you've come here to New York to make sure your father's territory isn't threatened. He thinks there's a chance you might take some direct action against him if things don't go the way your father intended.'

'Jesus Christ, I don't fucking believe this! You're setting me up . . . putting me in a situation where I have to pretend—'

Freiberg shook his head. 'You cannot *pretend* to be anything John, you have to *be* your father's son, nothing more nor less than that.'

Harper turned and looked at Cathy. Her expression was implacable.

'But, as I said, Ben Marcus is no fool. He will have made enquiries. He'll have asked his people to check up on you. Fact is . . . well, fact is that he may already have figured out that you're not who we've told him you are.'

'And where does that put me? He's going to find out I'm not what you've told him . . . Jesus Christ, Walt, he's gonna send someone over here to kill me—'

Freiberg didn't speak. He merely looked steadily back at Harper.

Harper could not look at Freiberg, or at Cathy Hollander. He tried not to think, tried not to show any emotion. He held a glass in his hand and swirled the whisky in it, looking down and watching as his own reflection was caught in a whirlpool and distorted. It seemed disconcertingly analogous to the situation in which he now found himself. Where was Miami, Florida? Where was Harry Ivens and the *Herald*? Where were the weather reports and small-time news stories about fishing trips and shark tournaments and hurricane warnings? Whatever life he'd imagined was his was gone. Nothing would ever be the same again. Nothing *could* be the same again no matter how hard he might try.

'John?'

Harper turned. Cathy was looking at him, her expression allowing some sense of concern.

He shook his head; he was not ready to speak.

A minute passed, perhaps two, and then Harper looked up at Freiberg. 'Okay,' he said quietly. 'You've put me in a situation where my life is now in serious fucking danger.'

He paused, looked at Cathy, then back at Freiberg. 'I want to know what's in it for me.'

FIFTY-FIVE

'Who?'

'Sonnenburg and Sampson.'

'Jesus fucking Christ,' Captain McLuhan said. He turned to the window, his head bowed, his hands on his hips.

'Sampson is sedated,' Sergeant Oates told him. 'Guy flipped out . . . you know Sonnenburg was due to be married?'

'Aw fuck, no . . . don't tell me that.' McLuhan walked back to his chair and seemed to fold down into it. 'They didn't have back-up?'

Oates raised an eyebrow and looked at McLuhan.

McLuhan raised his hand. 'Don't tell me . . . don't want you to answer that question. Jesus Christ, my ass is in a sling now.'

'They did call in for back-up but there was no-one available.'

'And what were they after?'

'Following up on the Jimmy Nestor thing.'

'What did they find?'

'Nestor's chop-shop and Nestor's cousin, a guy called Jesus Fernando. He was the one that shot Sonnenburg.'

'And he's dead?'

Oates nodded. 'Yeah, he's dead as well.'

'Who shot him?'

'As far as we can tell it was Sonnenburg . . . preliminary indications suggest they shot one another simultaneously.'

'And the girl?'

Oates frowned. 'What girl?'

'The fucking girl he was going to marry . . . what girl d'you think I mean?'

'Sampson told her . . . he called her and told her that Yale was killed.'

'And she's here?'

'No, she's not here, she's with her family.'

360

McLuhan inhaled deeply and leaned forward, elbows on the edge of the table, face in his hands. 'Thank Christ for small mercies . . . last thing I need down here is a hysterical Jewish police widow shrieking like a fire siren.'

'Whaddya want me to do now?' Oates asked.

'Was there anything significant down there? This chop-shop of Jimmy Nestor's?'

Oates shook his head. 'Doesn't seem to have been. We're checking it out. And we still don't really have anything significant from Jimmy Nestor's autopsy.'

'Go,' McLuhan said. 'Leave me alone for a little while. I have to think how the hell I'm going to answer up on this no back-up situation.'

'Hey, they turned down the money, Captain. There were guys willing to do the overtime but there was no money—'

McLuhan silenced Oates with a gesture. 'Sergeant, you're a great sergeant. I couldn't ask for a better duty sergeant. What you are not, however, is a public relations representative for the mayor's office. I get called to account on this thing, the last thing in the world anyone is going to want to hear is that it's down to the money they wouldn't give us. Fair it may not be, but nothing in this world seems fair to me right now. Let me sort this out myself. You get some people on the Nestor thing, see if there isn't something you can turn up at this shop of his. Follow up on the cousin . . . and get whoever is dealing with Jimmy Nestor's murder investigation to make some progress, eh? At least if I go there with something the heat will be less.'

'Sure thing, Captain.'

After a while she would become insensate and numb to all of it.

Evelyn Sawyer had forced herself to believe this.

The truth was different; very different indeed.

The truth? That was an irony and a contradiction in terms. Her life had been a lie, perhaps right from the beginning. Herself and Anne, herself and Garrett, herself and John Harper – the illegitimate nephew. And then there had been Edward, Walt Freiberg, the collection of criminals and thieves they had gathered around themselves; and all the while the threats, the broken promises, the words given which meant nothing at all. Everything had gone to shit. Wasn't that the truth?

And time, the great healer? The great charlatan perhaps . . .

Time had merely been the ground from which the darkest aspects of her own bitter anger and hate had grown. Her life could have been something. *Could* have been. Had she not forever been there behind Anne, beside Garrett, standing ahead of John Harper in an effort to soften the blows that the world landed on them.

How had she managed to fool herself for so long? How had she believed that she would keep him away from Edward Bernstein for ever? How stupid could she have been?

Mid-afternoon, the sky clear, the last stripes of snow still clinging to the edges of the sidewalk, the rims of storm drains, the eaves of buildings. Evelyn Sawyer stood at the bottom of the stairwell and looked up towards the landing.

A coolness seemed to fill the house, as if each room had been empty for years – maintained as it had been left, but nevertheless empty. Like the soul had gone.

She started up the stairs, paused on the third riser as if to catch her breath, as if the pressure she felt was almost too intense for her to walk through. She was still for some seconds, and then moved once again.

At the head of the stairs she turned left and stopped at the first door. This had been their room, herself and Garrett; had been their room from the point they took the house until Garrett left for the last time.

She opened the door slowly and stood there. She just looked; didn't move; didn't take a step inside.

'I need the gun,' she said. 'I need the gun for a while. I'm going to take the gun because there's something I have to do.'

'But—'

Evelyn shook her head. 'No questions . . . I don't want to answer any questions. I want you to give me the gun and then I'm going to leave. If I'm not back within a few hours then you'll have to figure out what to do by yourself.'

Evelyn extended her hand and waited until the gun was passed to her.

Her breathing was shallow, hesitant. She backed up and turned to the right, walked down the hallway to her own room.

Five, six minutes later, standing inside the front door, Evelyn Sawyer looked back towards the kitchen, the narrow hallway

362

alongside the stairs, the door to the right that took her through into the front room, the bay window that looked out onto Carmine. She looked at all the years of her life, the heartbreaks, the sorrows, the laughter, the anger and frustration, the emptiness, the tears . . . everything that had taken place within these four walls for the better part of four decades.

Everything of any worth was already gone.

She pulled her coat tight around her neck and opened the front door.

Once on the front steps she glanced over her shoulder, and then pulled the door shut.

She walked down to the corner, hands buried in her overcoat pockets, her face expressionless, inscrutable.

She didn't turn back; knew that if she did she might lose her will.

Harper walked three blocks before he found a callbox.

Once inside he dialled the number. Had almost memorized it. Never felt so scared in all his life. Had never doubted anything so much.

The phone rang twice before he felt the urge to hang up. He steeled himself, clenched his fist, felt his knuckles whiten as he gripped the receiver.

'Yes?' Unmistakably Duchaunak's voice.

'It's me.'

'Okay . . . you spoke with them?'

'Yes.'

'Where?'

'At the hotel.'

'Who came?'

'Freiberg and the girl.'

'And they're still there?'

'No, they left.'

'And where are you?'

Harper peered out through the glass of the callbox, rubbed a hole in the condensation. 'I can see the top of the Western Union Building . . . there's a store across the road called—'

'It doesn't matter. No-one followed you?'

'I don't think so.'

'You don't *think* so?'

'Fuck, I don't know. I'm doing what you asked me to do, okay? They came and saw me. I spoke with them. You said to call you . . . you asked me for my help and I'm fucking calling you okay?'

'Okay, okay . . . I'm sorry, Mr Harper. So tell me what happened?'

'Freiberg is going to meet with Ben Marcus tomorrow.'

'You what?'

'Ben Marcus . . . you know who Ben Marcus is, right?'

'Yes, sure. Of course I know who Ben Marcus is.'

'Right . . . so Walt Freiberg is going to see him tomorrow.'

'Christ almighty . . . they *are* working together, aren't they?'

'Seems that way. They're going to agree to something that was set up by my father. He was retiring. He was negotiating a deal with Ben Marcus before he was shot. Hell, it's complicated, Detective. Anyway, bottom line is Walt goes and speaks with Marcus tomorrow. He tells him that I'm standing in for my father, that I have the authority to approve whatever deal is going down, and I make everything kosher for the things they've planned for Christmas Eve.'

There was silence at the other end of the line, and then, 'Fuck! I knew it! I knew there was something. What is it? What are they planning?'

'They're going to pull several bank robberies simultaneously . . . several banks at the same time as far as I can figure.'

'Which ones?'

'I have no idea, not a clue.'

'We need to meet,' Duchaunak said. 'I need you to come and see my precinct Captain—'

'You must be outta your mind,' Harper said. 'You want to know what I think? I think someone's watching me right now . . . I think someone has an eye on me right now and is going to tell Walt Freiberg that I went out to a callbox and spoke with someone. Who the hell am I going to call, eh? Fucking ghostbusters, right? Maybe they'll think it's you. They're not going to tell me which banks. You want to know what else I think? I figure they might shoot me in the fucking head anyway. If they know I met with you and we went and spoke with your police captain then I can guarantee they're going to shoot me in the fucking head.'

'So what do you want to do, Mr Harper?'

'I'm going to go do nothing. I'm going to let Walt Freiberg tell Ben Marcus whatever the hell he wants, let them sort out whatever they have planned, and then I'm going to get the fuck out of New York as fast as I can and leave you guys to sort out Christmas Eve. That's what I'm going to do, Detective . . . unless, of course, you can think of anything better?'

Duchaunak was silent.

'So, Detective . . . any better ideas?'

'Call me if you get any word after the meeting tomorrow,' Duchaunak said. 'See if there's any way, *any way* at all to get some idea of where they're going to hit, and then call me after the meeting is over, okay?'

'And what are you going to do?'

'I don't know, Mr Harper, I don't know, but I have to do something, right?'

'I think that would be a good idea, Detective . . . think it would be a very good idea for you to do something.'

'Okay, we'll speak tomorrow. You call me and let me know what happens.'

'Detective?'

'Yeah?'

'The liquor store . . . the one where my father was shot. Where is it?'

'Why?'

'I want to know,' Harper said. 'I just want to know.'

'Up near where you are now . . . half a dozen blocks or so north. Corner of Hudson and Vestry.'

'Thanks,' Harper said.

'So call me tomorrow, okay?'

'I'll do my best.'

'Mr Harper—' Duchaunak said, but the line was already dead.

John Harper stepped out of the callbox and started walking, heading north, hands buried in his pockets, head bowed against the bitter wind that cut east from the river.

FIFTY-SIX

'Scariest bunch of motherfuckers . . . no . . . no, I take that back,' Neumann shouted. 'You lot are the *ugliest* bunch of motherfuckers I've ever seen! Jesus Christ, it should be illegal for more than two or three of you to congregate in a public place. You'd be scaring kids and frightening old people into a lifetime of fucking nightmares!'

The laughter was riotous, good-humored, anarchic. The battlefield of voices; all parties attempting to be heard over everyone else was almost deafening. Seventeen people crammed into a barroom beneath a club on Mulberry, itself a block and a half from the police headquarters building in Little Italy – cornered like a rat between SoHo, Bowery and Chinatown. They were all there: Ben Marcus, Sol Neumann, Walt Freiberg on down. Two families, joined at the hip in some way, and yet the faces still running confrontationals and threatening one another like sandbox psychopaths.

Walt Freiberg stood just inside the doorway. Even as he'd entered, the gathered crews were shouting at one another, throwing jibes and spiked words, all in that half-drunk, couldn't-give-a-fuck attitude that seemed requisite for such meetings. Maybe they were shouting at Cathy Hollander, the only female present: the way she looked it seemed that none present would have had the cojones to challenge her directly. Had John Harper seen her he would have believed her to be someone else. She had on black jeans, a black sweater, a leather jacket over; her hair was tied back and her face free of cosmetics. Perhaps it was the light, perhaps the angle of her high cheekbones, but it seemed for a moment that she was wearing the shadow of a bruise on the right side of her face. Perhaps not. All in all it didn't matter; no-one would ask, and even if they had they would not have received an answer.

Times were such a gathering could never have happened; times were that people like Ray Dietz and Joe Koenig could not have entered the same room without one of them leaving horizontally. But now things had changed; whatever words and wars and personal vendettas had existed in the past seemed irrelevant in the face of what was to occur. Change had come, and those present would go with that change or leave quietly. Everyone wanted something from this, whether money, reputation, or the credibility to move elsewhere and have folks pay attention to what they had to say. Perhaps this thing was a way of exorcising the ghosts of the past and starting over. A couple of those present knew that they either participated, or there'd come an evening when they'd open a door to unwelcome, but not wholly unexpected, visitors, and their fate would be expedited much the same as Johnnie Hoy, Micky Levin, Mouse Jackson and Jimmy Nestor.

This was a world, in and of itself its own thing, and it had a way of dealing its own cards, ranking its own orders and obligations; violation of such agreements carried with it not a sense of shame or self-abnegation, but a justice so swift and thoughtless it appeared too brutal to have been designed by human beings. To complicate this world, to attempt any real depth of understanding of it, was to miss the point entirely. Men such as these lived and died within a life that the vast majority of people could neither have comprehended nor suffered. It was that simple.

Ray Dietz, beside him Albert Reiff and Victor Klein; the drivers – Maurice Rydell and Henry Kossoff, beside them Karl Merrett and Lewis Parselle. At the head of their table was Ben Marcus, standing to his left Sol Neumann, ever the consigliere, ever the Devil's advocate. On the other side sat Joe Koenig and Charlie Beck, Larry Benedict, Leo Petri, and their drivers – Ricky Wheland and Ron Dearing.

Walt Freiberg and Cathy Hollander had been the last to arrive. Cathy hesitated just inside the doorway, and when Walt walked forward to greet Marcus she went with him, hanging a step and a half behind, almost a shadow.

'Walter, Walter, Walter,' Marcus chimed enthusiastically. 'This is a great day, a special day for all of us. This day, my friend, has been a long time coming.'

Freiberg was grinning from ear to ear, squeezing himself behind the seated man along the edge of the table and finally standing before Marcus at the head.

Freiberg held out his arms and the men hugged. After a moment Freiberg released Marcus and took a moment to shake hands vigorously with Sol Neumann.

'You look even better than last time I saw you, Sol,' Freiberg said, and then mock-punched him in the gut. 'You lose some weight, right? You lost a ton of fucking weight there, Sol . . . you look really good man, really fucking good.'

Neumann smiled like a cat, nodding his head. 'I did, Walt, I did. I got one of these exercise things, these little gym things you put in your house you know? My wife, she tells me I'm going to get a fucking heart attack if I don't do something, so what the fuck, eh? You have to make an effort, right?'

'Cathy, sweetheart,' Marcus said, and stepped aside to greet her.

Cathy Hollander smiled, took Marcus's outstretched hands, and stepped towards him. They paused there for some moments, and then Cathy said, 'You're doing good, Ben? You're taking care of yourself?'

Marcus laughed hoarsely. 'Taking care of myself? When did I ever take care of myself? Take care of everyone else more like it!' He shook his head. 'No, I'm good, I'm okay.' He looked away for a second. 'Hell, I know things were never great—'

Cathy Hollander smiled. 'Ben, it's okay . . . things move on, right?'

'Right,' he said. 'But I'm sorry about Edward . . . I am *so* sorry about Edward.' Marcus turned to Freiberg, his face sympathetic. 'Walt, I don't know what to say. This has been a tough time for everyone concerned. We have this thing tomorrow, right?'

Freiberg nodded. 'We'll meet tomorrow, Ben, we'll meet tomorrow and straighten out the details.'

'And the kid is good?'

Freiberg smiled. 'He's fine, Ben . . . don't you worry about him.'

Walt Freiberg looked directly at Marcus and said nothing for a second or two. Cathy Hollander felt a chill of unease across her skin, as if someone had opened a door and a cold breeze had crept in unawares.

'So be it,' Freiberg said, and then he smiled, and Marcus was smiling too, and then each of them turned to face the gathered crews. Marcus leaned towards Freiberg and asked him a question that Cathy Hollander didn't hear. Freiberg responded, and Marcus nodded at Sol Neumann. Neumann stepped forward. Marcus and Freiberg took seats behind him and to the left.

'Okay!' Neumann shouted above the noise. 'Okay, okay, okay . . . enough of the small talk and bullshit. We got a lot of things to talk about and we haven't got much time!'

The room fell silent. It was almost eerie, the sudden cessation of noise and commotion.

'Right then,' Neumann said. 'You all know each other too well already. Any of our people caught talking nice to any of the Bernstein crew is going to get fired!'

Laughter broke out in the far right-hand corner of the room and spread across both tables.

Cathy took a seat, on her left Joe Koenig. Ron Dearing handed over glasses, a bottle of Scotch, pushed an ashtray towards Cathy. The mood was more relaxed than Cathy had imagined it would be. Perhaps the calm before the storm.

Neumann remained standing. All eyes turned towards him, and for everyone present – regardless of their affiliation – Edward Bernstein was evident in his absence.

'So we have these things to do,' Neumann said. 'We have sixteen people and four teams. We've been through this over and over, but we're going to go through it again. Four teams of four, each team consists of the driver and three others. Two drivers from our people and two from Lenny's.' Neumann looked down at Freiberg. 'Walt Freiberg . . . he's here in Lenny's place. We're going to keep it simple. We've talked about this thing for long enough. Myself and Mr Marcus met with Lenny Bernstein on numerous occasions, and out of respect, out of acknowledgement for all that Lenny has done in this town, we're going to keep it as Lenny's family even though Lenny cannot be with us at the moment.'

Freiberg raised his hand and nodded. 'Lenny's family it has always been, Lenny's family it stays,' he said.

'Good, so we're agreed on this. We got two people from our crew, two people from Lenny's on each team. We got four hits.

West Twelfth, Bethune and Greenwich, West Ninth and Washington and West Broadway. You all know which teams you're in and who you're working with. You have the times and the locations, you got your vehicles, your artillery; we even have the names of those officials inside the banks that have access codes . . . you have everything you need, and the reason we're meeting this evening, the *only* reason we're meeting this evening is because this is the last time one crew is going to be in the same room as the other crew. All of you people will never be in the same place at the same time again. Ever.' Neumann paused and looked around the gathered faces, each of them intently looking back, each of them implacable, almost without expression. 'You get that? You understand that this meeting I'm talking about will never take place?'

There was a murmur of consent and acknowledgement from the men at the tables.

'You really understand what the fuck I'm saying here, people?'

A chorus of 'Yeses' came back and Neumann seemed satisfied.

'Right then,' he said. 'So – no words, no meetings, no high school reunions in Atlantic City for old time's sake. I hear any one of you getting back to someone from the other crew for any reason then I'm going to have a great deal to say about it, you get me?' Neumann looked at Freiberg. Freiberg rose and stepped forward.

'After Christmas Eve,' Freiberg said, 'none of you knows anyone else. The Bernstein crew will disappear. You guys from Ben Marcus's family are going to have a great deal more country to walk in. There will be no reason for any of you to speak with one another. That's the simplicity of it. Once this thing is done everyone goes home and never says another word.'

'Good, we're agreed,' Neumann said. 'Everyone is agreed, right?'

'Right,' Joe Koenig said, and others followed – emphatic and definite.

'So, we have a drink now,' Neumann said. 'We have a drink in recognition of what we are about to do, and then we go over the whys and wherefores, we iron out any little details that have been overlooked, and then we go home. Next time any of you see anyone else it's going to be Christmas Eve. We go out there,

370

we cause some trouble, and we have the best fucking Christmas we ever had!'

Riotous cheers, applause, raising of glasses; the room thick with smoke and the heady sweat of alcohol; sixteen men, one woman, between them a collective six centuries of violence and bloodshed, shootings and robberies, murders, beatings, grievous assaults and mayhem.

'To Christmas Eve!' Walt Freiberg shouted, and he too raised his glass, though his eyes never left Ben Marcus, seated there behind Sol Neumann and never saying a word.

For a long while Evelyn didn't breathe – a minute, a minute and a half.

She stood there in utter silence, perhaps aware of the eggshell-fragile tension of the situation. Her hands were buried in her overcoat pockets, her right clutching the .38, the metal now warmed to body temperature. She had gripped it tightly all the way to the hospital – determined, gritted teeth, purposeful, fully cognizant of what she was to do, of why, of how long it was overdue. Perhaps destiny had dictated that Edward Bernstein was to die, but she was not content to leave such a thing in destiny's hands. He had taken too much away from her, and she had steeled herself to set the balance straight.

But now she was there; now Evelyn Sawyer was there at St Vincent's, standing silent and breathless, looking through an eight-inch thick sheet of glass at Edward Bernstein, a window that would not have even delayed the bullet on its passage to his brain; the brain of an old man at death's door, an old man who should have been dead already but for some unknown reason was hanging on by a thread . . .

But now she was there, she no longer believed she could kill him.

For a time she cried; not so much cried as stood with tears filling her eyes, one of them tracking a lazy route down her cheek to the corner of her mouth. She remembered Anne as a little girl; she remembered Garrett as a young man, all of twenty-one or two, the way he laughed, the way he had the last word, *always* the last word; the way everything seemed like it would go in the right direction.

Never had; perhaps was never meant to. Wasn't that the way of the world?

Finally, with a sense of overwhelm and defeat in everything about her, she turned and made her way back towards the corridor that would take her away from Edward Bernstein, away from St Vincent's, all the way back to the house at 66 Carmine where everything had started, where everything was destined to end.

She wondered if she would ever summon the courage to tell John Harper the truth. Tell him the *whole* truth. The facts of Garrett and Anne, the events of that night when John Harper's mother had disappeared from the world.

She didn't know. Until the moment came she would never know. And until that moment there was nothing to do but wait and see what happened.

Perhaps God, in His infinite wisdom, would let Edward Bernstein die, and at least some of the difficulty would be solved.

Outside, standing on the hospital steps, Evelyn Sawyer looked up at the sky just as the snow returned.

She released her grip on the gun in her pocket and buttoned her overcoat.

She started walking back the way she'd come, hesitating at the junction and looking back as if having a second thought – as if, even now, she might turn and walk back, walk right in there with her .38 and shoot the man who'd killed her sister.

But she did not, and it was not for lack of courage, or determination, or any sense of imagined injustice she might perpetrate; it was because she believed the moment might come when John Harper needed the truth, and this was something only she and Edward Bernstein possessed. If Edward was dead then she would have to die too, and then John Harper would never find out.

She continued walking, the cold wind fighting her every step of the way.

FIFTY-SEVEN

It was a nothing place, could have missed it had he not been looking. When he found it he was surprised: surprised at its size, its insignificance, its apparent irrelevance in the face of everything else that was happening around it. Down the street a man argued with a taxicab driver; the man was drunk, the cab driver stretched to the limit of his patience, standing with his hands down by his sides, his fists clenched, everything twisted up inside him like the turns of a noose; a bag-lady wheeled a shopping trolley along the edge of the curb, her voice sharp, insistent, berating some invisible child for 'Goin' on and spoilin' everythin' again like y'always do'; the sound of cars, the sound of human passage, the rush of life as it came down Desbrosses and Canal, from Hudson and Vestry.

John Harper stood at a small junction of some other vast and consequential world, and yet it was here, here where nothing seemed important, that the most important event of his life had taken place.

Right here – in this awkward and senseless place – someone had shot his father.

After a few minutes, perhaps for no other reason than to step out of the increasing fall of snow, he walked to the door of the liquor store. A tattered dark green awning shielded him for a moment, and then – looking up – he realized that there were holes in the awning and it provided little if any cover.

Stepping back he was against the door, and before he had a chance to move someone opened it from within and he nearly fell backwards.

'What the fuck—' the person started, and then they were gone, hurrying away from the door clutching a brown sack filled with bottles.

Harper turned and stepped inside. The place smelled like

cigarette smoke and five-spice. There were aisles down the left and right of the store, a counter to the side, a Korean man reading a newspaper, a cigarette parked in the corner of his mouth. He looked up, looked down at the paper, and then shook his head momentarily and looked up once more.

'You!' he said suddenly, his tone sharp, almost accusatory. He tilted his head to one side and then frowned. 'No . . . I am sorry,' he said. 'I thought you were someone else.'

'My father?' Harper asked.

'Your father?'

'My father was shot here last week . . . Sunday night someone robbed your store and they shot my father.'

The Korean man looked suddenly concerned. 'Yes,' he said. 'I see your face, I think it is him! I am sorry. So sorry, yes. Yes, he was shot here . . . he tried to help us. He tried to stop this man and the man shot him and ran away. You are his son?' The man came out from behind the counter. He took the cigarette from his mouth. 'You are his son, yes?'

Harper nodded.

'He was shot here . . . he is okay?'

Harper shook his head, and then realized that he had not been to the hospital for . . . for how long? He couldn't even remember. He did not know how his father was.

'He's in the hospital,' Harper said.

'Right, yes, yes, yes,' the Korean man said. 'You must take him flowers from us or something.' He hurried back to the counter. He took a twenty-dollar bill from the cash register, and then hurried back. He pressed it into Harper's hand even though Harper was unwilling to take it. 'Please, please,' the man said. 'You must buy some flowers or something . . . your father, he tried to help us, he tried to stop the man from robbing us.'

'Did you speak to the police?' Harper asked.

'Yes,' the store owner said. 'I spoke to the police, but there is not much for me to say about this. I could not see the person who shot your father. I did not see his face, you know?'

Harper nodded. He looked down at the twenty-dollar bill in his hand and wondered if it represented the true value of Edward Bernstein's life.

'So you must tell him we are grateful for what he did,' the

owner said. 'Me and my wife . . . you must tell him that we are very thankful for what he tried to do. You will tell him, yes?'

'He came here?' Harper asked.

'Sunday, yes . . . he came here,' the owner replied.

'Regularly?'

The owner frowned. 'Just on Sundays.'

'Every Sunday?'

The owner nodded. 'Most Sunday, yes. He doesn't come one time, maybe two time in the last few month, but he always come the next week and tell us that he been away visiting friends or something. He was nice man, your father. He never say much, always friendly, and he would give me extra money than his purchases, sometimes ten dollar, twenty dollar. A good man, yes . . . a very nice man.'

'You have his wine?'

'Yes, yes . . . you want some for him. Help him get better perhaps?'

The store owner turned and hurried down the left-hand aisle to the end. He returned a moment later clutching a bottle which he gave to Harper.

Harper held it for a moment, and then looked down at the label. It was Cabernet Sauvignon, just as Walt Freiberg had told him.

Harper closed his eyes for a moment and gritted his teeth.

Nothing was ever as it first seemed. Perhaps Freiberg had been right. Perhaps Duchaunak had been taken in by the illusion created.

'You want another bottle for him?'

Harper shook his head and turned towards the door. 'No,' he muttered. 'No, no more.'

Once outside he handed the twenty-dollar bill to the woman with the shopping trolley.

She looked at him in amazement.

'For the child,' he said, and then he handed her the bottle of wine. 'And this is for you.'

She started laughing, a sound that was almost painful.

The sound of her strange and unfamiliar laughter followed him as he hurried back towards the corner, away from the scene of his father's shooting.

*

The meeting was concluded. The room was nothing more than empty chairs and tables.

The memory of voices hung like a ghost amidst the cloud of smoke that pressed against the ceiling.

Ben Marcus sat at the far end of the room furthest from the door, to his right Sol Neumann.

'So there's no word?' Marcus asked.

Neumann shook his head. 'No, nothing else.'

Marcus smiled. 'He's a face isn't he? Nothing more than a face.' He laughed drily, but there was little humor in the sound. 'Got to give Walt Freiberg some credit . . . acted fast, took the initiative didn't he? Got the kid up from Miami and made everyone think he was some kind of player.'

'He could be,' Neumann said. 'We don't know who the fuck he is. Word has come back. He's this, he's that . . . hell, no-one seems to know for sure.'

Marcus shook his head. 'He ain't nothing. He's Lenny's son, and that's all I'm prepared to believe right now. There's no crew down there. We'd have heard by now. We've had a week, all the people we have connections with and no-one has come back with anything substantial. Walt Freiberg has given us a ghost Sol, he's given us a ghost and we've bought it.'

'So what d'you want to do?'

Marcus leaned forward in his chair. He reached into his pocket and took out his cigarettes. Every movement he made seemed considered and decisive. 'You have someone who can take Freiberg's place on this thing?'

Neumann shrugged. 'Sure I have . . . I can always get someone in for something like this.'

'So make the call, eh? Get someone in and have Ray and Albert get them up to speed.'

Neumann nodded, didn't speak.

Marcus lit his cigarette and leaned back.

'So we're going through with the meeting tomorrow?' Neumann asked.

'Sure we are, Sol . . . we're going to meet with Walt Freiberg . . . but he's gonna bring the kid with him.'

Neumann smiled. 'Oh shit . . . this I gotta see.'

Marcus turned and nodded his head slowly. 'I'm going to give them the time of day, Sol, that much at least . . . and then I'm going to kill the fucking pair of them.'

FIFTY-EIGHT

Freiberg came early, a little after dawn. Cathy Hollander with him. Had Reception call Harper and wake him, told him to get dressed, they'd be up in minutes.

Harper let them in, stood there for a moment in his tee-shirt and his shorts.

'We need to talk,' Freiberg said, a cigarette in his hand. Absent-mindedly he stubbed it in the ashtray and then lit another one.

'Talk about what?' Harper asked.

'We need to talk about the meeting I have with Ben Marcus.'

Harper frowned. 'What about it?'

Freiberg sat down at the desk, seemed to hesitate for a moment, and then he rose to his feet and walked to the window.

'What?' Harper asked again. 'Will one of you tell me what the fuck is going on for Christ's sake?'

'The meeting,' Freiberg said once more. 'You're gonna need to come with me.'

'*What*?'

'You're coming with me,' Freiberg said.

Harper took a step back and sat on the bed. The weight of the world and all its gravity bore down on him. 'You've got to be out of your fucking mind ... Jesus, what d'you think this is, the fucking theater?'

Freiberg was on edge, the first time Harper had seen him anything other than calm and self-assured. He smoked in an agitated fashion, standing in front of the window, his back to the light. Made Harper's eyes hurt to look at him.

'No choice,' Freiberg said. 'You don't do this then we're all finished.'

'And when the hell did this happen?'

Freiberg looked at Cathy. She looked just as anxious. 'Late last night,' Freiberg said. He took a few steps forward and sat down at the desk again. 'Neumann called me very late last night . . . told me that the meeting would go ahead as planned but Ben Marcus wanted to meet you in person.'

'And you told him yes?'

'What the fuck choice did I have, John?' Freiberg extinguished his cigarette, stood up and put his hands in his overcoat pockets. 'Tell me that, eh? What the fuck choice did I have?'

Harper shook his head, tried to stand, couldn't, collapsed back again. 'No way, Walt, no fucking way—'

'You *have* to,' Cathy interjected. She walked towards Harper and sat beside him on the unmade bed. She reached out her hand to touch his arm but Harper withdrew.

'You have to do this, John . . . you don't do this and it's all over. It isn't something to fuck around with. This is serious John, deadly serious. You don't do this and everything your father created—'

Harper turned suddenly. 'Oh fuck off with that, will you? Everything my father created? Jesus, who in God's name do you think you're talking to?'

'Enough!' Freiberg snapped angrily. 'It is what it is. Get your shit together . . . we're going to meet Ben Marcus. You're going to do the best you can, that's all. Way this stands right now we're dead if we don't. If we do . . . well, if we do, then maybe we have a chance.'

'And if I refuse? If I just tell you to get the fuck out of here and I go back to Miami?'

Freiberg took a deep breath and slowly exhaled. He withdrew his right hand from his pocket. In it he held his lighter, nervously turned it over and over between his fingers. 'You have no concept of the lengths these people will go to to save face. Jesus Christ, John . . . you take off out of here and they will kill me, they'll kill Cathy, and then just for the hell of it they'll track you all the way to Miami and kill you as well.'

Harper sat motionless.

'Seriously, John,' Cathy said, and this time she reached out her hand again and touched Harper's shoulder. 'Seriously . . . this is the only hope we have right now.'

'The *only* one,' Freiberg echoed. 'Otherwise . . . well, I don't even want to consider—'

Harper raised his hand. 'Enough,' he said. He looked at Cathy. 'You're walking me to my own fucking death, aren't you?'

She shook her head, looked across at Freiberg. 'Either which way . . . hell, John, Walt is right. If we go we have a chance. We don't go we're *all* fucking dead.'

Nine minutes later, Harper's hands shaking too much to put on his tie, Cathy tied it for him.

They left together, the three of them. Harper paused to scrawl a note for Evelyn Harper. In it he said he was sorry, that was all; there was nothing else he could think of to say.

Aggressive.

A manner like the world was owned, and he owned the greater part.

Ben Marcus struck a discordant note with John Harper, and despite the apparent warmth of his greeting, despite the effusive compliments for Edward, what friends they were, how long they had known one another, the fact that the city had never seen, would *never* see, two people more bold and audacious in their ventures than himself and Edward Bernstein, the underlying tone was one of suspicion.

John Harper did not like Ben Marcus, and it took all he had to refrain from making his dislike apparent.

The room was on the third floor of a hotel near to where Varick became Seventh. He had been driven there by Charlie Beck; Walt Freiberg up front in the passenger seat, Cathy Hollander in back with him, the two of them talking a great deal but saying little of any consequence. She seemed relaxed and natural, as if this was the most normal kind of behavior in the world. John Harper wanted nothing more than some brief time alone with her, to speak of what he felt, to ask her whether she felt anything at all in return. But, in truth, he was aware of where he was going, of what might happen when he arrived. Perhaps for these people it was business as usual. For him it was a nerve-wracking step deeper into something he neither wished to understand nor be involved in.

A single thought kept him there, kept his hands steady, his mind centered. The thought that if he did not do this then people would die. People would die who had less to do with this life than himself. Not only Walt Freiberg and Cathy Hollander, but people like Lauren Sachs, others who had experienced the fallout and backlash of the world Ben Marcus and Lenny Bernstein had created.

'Sonny,' Walt kept reminding him. 'He will call you Sonny Bernstein. That's how he knows you, and that's the name you should respond to, okay?'

'Okay,' Harper had agreed, and asked no more questions. He sat silently in his impeccably tailored suit, his white shirt, his burgundy tie. He looked down at shoes that would have reflected his drawn face. He glanced at the watch that Walt had bought, but he did not register the time.

'It's going to be fine,' Cathy said a number of times, but Harper knew she was lying. She held his hand gently, almost tenderly, and each time she spoke she squeezed his hand for reassurance. At one point Harper turned and looked at her. His eyes searched for where she hid behind the front she presented, behind the words and gestures, behind the brave face she wore for the world, and after a while he believed there might have been nothing. Maybe the real Cathy Hollander had long since left with another of her alter-egos – Margaret Miller, perhaps Diane Sheridan, perhaps someone else.

Once inside the hotel they took the elevator to the third floor. Himself, Cathy Hollander, Walt Freiberg and Charlie Beck. No-one spoke until they stepped out into the deep-carpeted hallway, and then it was Walt who said, 'Won't be a long meeting . . . it's a formality more than anything else. We have to do this John, we have to do this to ensure that everything goes forward the way Edward wished.' There was something in Freiberg's tone that belied the reality of the meeting. If all Harper had heard of Ben Marcus was true then this meeting was a great deal more than a formality. This was where any step could be false. His heart raced. His palms were sweating. He wiped them against the legs of his pants. He did not want to shake hands with Ben Marcus and end the play before it had started.

Harper mumbled some acknowledgement, and then he was silent until Charlie Beck knocked on the hotel room door and someone asked them to enter. There was a moment's hesitation, and then Walt turned and nodded at both Beck and Cathy Hollander. They backed up without speaking, and Harper

381

watched both of them turn and walk down the corridor towards the elevator.

'They will wait in the car,' Walt said. 'They'll be there when we leave.'

Freiberg opened the door, Harper behind him, wondering if this would be the last room he would ever enter alive.

Marcus rose and came forward immediately. 'Sonny Bernstein!' he pronounced, his voice grand and deep and exuberant. 'Sonny Bernstein . . . Jesus Christ almighty, you look so much like your father it could be thirty years ago and I'm meeting him for the first time.'

Harper smiled. He held out his hand. He shook with Marcus. He said, 'Mr Ben Marcus. You have a name and a reputation that precedes you.'

'All of it bad, I trust?' Marcus joked.

'The worst, believe me Mr Marcus, the very worst.' Harper smiled. His face strained with the effort. He kept his eyes directly on Marcus. He attempted to show no fear. Inside he had already run from the building screaming.

Marcus laughed. 'That's good! I like that!' He turned to Walt Freiberg. 'He's a funny guy . . . I like him.'

From behind Marcus came two other men.

'My associates, Mr Neumann and Mr Reiff,' Marcus said.

Harper looked at them – heavy-set eyes, solid faces, like Burke and Hare.

'So come,' Marcus said. He turned and indicated two sofas, a group of chairs ahead of the window. 'We sit, we have a drink, some coffee perhaps, and we talk. We work out all these details for Edward and we make our final agreements before tomorrow.'

Everything he said was in the same tone – direct, but not direct with confidence, more like an aggressive and challenging undercurrent that defied anyone present to venture a word in opposition. It appeared to Harper that Ben Marcus wished to be in control of everyone and everything around him. Perhaps here an explanation for this meeting.

Everyone was seated. Reiff made a call and ordered coffee for five. Cigarettes were lit, ashtrays were positioned, Ben Marcus and Walt Freiberg seated beside one another in wing-backed leather armchairs. Harper chose a plain wooden chair with a straight back. He sat upright, his expression unreadable, his eyes directed first at Marcus, then at Freiberg, never once leaving them to look at Neumann and Reiff who seemed to haunt the edges of the gathering like dense shadows.

'It comes as a great surprise to discover Edward had a son,' Marcus said. 'All the years I have known him and never once a mention of your name.'

Think of the dead people, Harper thought. *Think of dead people in bank foyers.*

Harper shook his head, raised his hand and waved the comment aside. 'We cannot always know everything Mr Marcus.'

'True,' Marcus said, 'but it seems strange that a man of your reputation and connections would have no history at all.'

Harper shook his head. He tried to smile. 'No history?'

'Sure . . . people who know you. People who speak of you.'

'There are numerous people who know me, Mr Marcus.'

'I'm sure there are, Mr Bernstein, but it seems unusual to be unable to find any of them.'

'Depends how hard you look.'

'Indeed it does, indeed it does.' Marcus cleared his throat and leaned back. 'So tell me a little about yourself . . . I'm curious about the things you have been involved in down in Miami.'

'Miami?'

'Sure, Miami. Your own little territory, right?'

Harper shook his head, glanced at Freiberg. 'I didn't think the purpose of this meeting was to discuss my private business affairs, Mr Marcus.'

Marcus smiled, laughed a little. 'No, sure it isn't. It's just that when people do business together they like to know a little something about the people they're doing business with.'

'Depends.'

Marcus frowned, started to lean forward.

'I am not intending to be discourteous, Mr Marcus, quite the contrary, but my personal business matters seem entirely irrelevant in the face of what we are dealing with here. If you want to know something about me then you should have your people look a little harder.'

'I had my people take a look, Mr Bernstein.'

'And what did they find?'

Marcus shook his head. 'Very little of any substance, you

know? And that's what surprised me. You take me for example. Someone wants to find out something about me then there's no end of people who have an opinion, a viewpoint, something to say.'

'And you could find no-one who had something to say on the subject of Sonny Bernstein?'

'Certainly seems that way . . . which is why I wanted to meet you here today and give you a chance to present yourself.'

'And I have.'

'Yes, indeed, you have presented yourself . . . but you have presented a face with no man behind it.' Marcus leaned back in his chair. 'Sun Tzu says that it is the business of a general to be quiet and thus ensure secrecy . . . something which you have managed to do regarding your position and affairs in Miami.'

Harper looked once more at Freiberg.

Think of security guards with gunshot wounds.

Freiberg's expression gave nothing away. Harper wondered what he was feeling, if he was feeling anything at all.

Think of kids coming home from school to find out mom got killed while they were in Math class.

Harper smiled and shook his head. He leaned back also, assumed a pose of uncomplicated ease. 'My position and affairs are my business, Mr Marcus, as are yours. I can understand, considering the circumstances, why you have made enquiries as to my business.'

'Naturally,' Marcus replied.

'Then you will know that my position and affairs have as little to do with Miami as your own.'

Marcus frowned.

'I believe Sun Tzu also said that the skillful fighter puts himself into a position which makes defeat impossible. We create apparencies, do we not? We make-believe our position of power is one place when it is another entirely. Asking questions of me in Miami would serve no purpose . . . as much purpose as my asking questions about you in Boston.'

Marcus turned and looked at Freiberg. 'Walt here . . . he told me that you were from Miami.'

'We play games, Mr Marcus. Florida yes, Miami no. Like I said, my business in Miami is no more significant than your own.'

'Then you have people elsewhere?'

Harper smiled, shook his head. 'What I have and what I don't have are not the matter for discussion here.'

Marcus looked once more at Freiberg.

Freiberg smiled. 'We all carry a responsibility to protect our own people Ben. You know this. We're not here to discuss Sonny's place, what affairs he may control elsewhere. You, as well as anyone, understand that we take the precautions we have to, and that is the nature of our business. We're here to discuss the matter at hand, nothing more than that. All I can tell you is that Sonny will agree to acceptable terms, and he will do this for his father.'

Marcus hesitated for a moment, a flicker of something in his eyes. He looked once more at Harper. Harper returned his gaze unerringly. Ben Marcus turned to where Reiff and Neumann stood at the edge of the room. Almost imperceptible, but it was there. The slight shift of the head, the dismissal of whatever instructions Reiff and Neumann carried.

Marcus edged forward on his chair. 'You understand the mechanical aspects of this agreement of course,' he started.

'I understand that we are brokering a deal,' Harper said.

'Brokering a deal, yes,' Marcus replied. 'And from what I understand you are here to act as proxy for your father.'

'I am here to ensure that whatever proposal he made is executed to the letter. I am fully apprised of the terms of this sale, and I am determined to see it carried forward despite present circumstances.' Harper glanced at Freiberg. Freiberg nodded, his own almost unnoticeable tilt of his head. *You're doing fine Sonny*, that gesture said. *You're doing just fine.*

'Good,' Marcus said. 'I am obviously gravely concerned about Edward's welfare, and though I understand that his position is still critical and there is a possibility he may not make it through this thing, I also believe wholeheartedly that this is what he wished to have done.' Marcus looked at Freiberg. 'Walter I have known for many years, and though there have been differences between us I am still respectful of his position as your father's consigliere and confidant. However, considering the nature of this thing, the manner in which your father was so suddenly and brutally taken from this negotiation, I also respect Walter's wish that a representative of Edward's family be present to conclude this matter. This is a big thing we are speaking of, and it needs to be done right or not at all.'

Harper nodded. His mouth was dry, his throat tight. For a moment he believed he would lose his balance. He pressed his feet down on the floor, hard enough to feel the strain in his knees. He cleared his throat and started speaking. 'With the shooting of my father the control that he possessed of his own affairs was called into question. It would have been all too easy for someone to take away his interests and territory by force. An army loses its power when its leader is taken from the field. It creates confusion. Loyalties become all too easily subverted and transposed. My appearance here is to demonstrate nothing more than the consolidation of my father's interests, and to act on his behalf. I understand Walter's position, the fact that his authority might have been called into question, but let me assure you that I am in a position to act on my father's behalf and make this thing work.'

'And in the event of a failure to resolve this agreement satisfactorily?'

'Then I shall not be making any calls to Miami, Mr Marcus . . . Miami is the last place I will be calling.'

Marcus frowned. 'It is not a matter of threat or provocation, Mr Bernstein.'

'I never said it was.'

'But your implication—'

'Implication is neither threat nor provocation,' Harper said. 'Implication is the perception of one thing from the words of another. We are businessmen, Mr Marcus. I am here for my father, no other reason. This matter . . .' Harper waved his hand dismissively. 'This matter of territories in New York is of no great concern to me. My concern is for my father's name, the name of my family, and to see that whatever influence and capability I might possess be used judiciously to guarantee the name of that family. You will attend to your business with Mr Freiberg. Your people and my father's will work together tomorrow and conclude this agreement satisfactorily. When this agreement is settled I will see to my father, and then I will return to Florida. My understanding is that you will be left with both territories under your control. This is correct?'

'Yes, that is correct.'

'Then my advice to you, Mr Marcus, is to maintain your word, see this thing through to its settlement, and create no trouble that does not need to be created.' Harper leaned back and smiled. He felt assured, almost in control of himself. He knew it was a charade. He knew that the moment he left the room he would fall apart. He smiled graciously. 'That is all, Mr Marcus, no more nor less than that.'

'Which is good enough for me,' Marcus said.

'Then that is settled,' Freiberg interjected. 'For relinquishment of all concerns and interests, for the acquisition of all territory previously owned and controlled by Edward Bernstein, you agree to pay the sum of seven and a half million dollars, to be delivered in cash tomorrow evening at a location to be agreed now.'

Marcus was silent for a moment, surveying the faces of the people before him. 'Agreed,' he said.

Freiberg turned and looked at Harper. 'Sonny, you agree?'

Harper nodded. 'Yes,' he said. 'I agree.' His heart trip-hammered in his chest. He wanted to move, wanted to do anything but stay facing Ben Marcus. There was something terrifying about the man. The man was a consolidation of endless nightmares personified in human form. Such a man as Marcus would kill without reserve, without compunction, without consideration of consequence. Perhaps, Harper believed, that was what he had intended to do all along.

Marcus rose from his chair, Harper also. They met in the center of the room, for a moment each of them hesitant, and then they shook hands, held their grasp for some considerable time, each of them looking directly at the other.

Marcus stepped back. He seemed in his element. 'It is unfortunate, is it not, that you will not be accompanying us on our little adventure tomorrow. Perhaps we could have used some of your Florida crew, eh Sonny? I think West Twelfth—'

'No details,' Freiberg suddenly said. He rose from his chair. 'Sonny will not be with us on this thing, Ben. There is no need for him to be aware of anything that may compromise his objective position. He is here merely as a representative of his father, here to make sure that the agreement you made with Edward stands. Once this is done he will return to Florida and attend to his own business down there.'

387

Marcus smiled. 'Of course, of course,' he said. 'So now *our* business is concluded we should drink our coffee, speak of inconsequential pleasantries for a little while, and then away to prepare for Christmas, eh?'

'Indeed,' Harper said, believing that at no time in his life had he ever so desperately wished to be somewhere other than where he was.

Within minutes the gathering was disbanded. Marcus once again shook hands with both Freiberg and John Harper, and then walked them from the door of the room to the elevator. Marcus and his people waited while the lift was called, stood and watched as Harper and Freiberg stepped inside, Marcus never looking anywhere but directly at Harper, watching him even as the elevator door closed and started down. Harper and Freiberg remained motionless, each of them completely silent, until they reached the street below.

'You did good,' Freiberg said quietly, almost a whisper. 'Real fucking good. Edward . . . hell, John, Edward would've been proud of you.'

Harper, experiencing the greatest sense of turmoil, the greatest conflict and division of loyalties he had ever known, believed he would not make it to the car.

He did, for Walt Freiberg was beside him, holding him up all the way.

'I don't care,' Marcus said, his voice edgy, irritated.

Sol Neumann stood at the window, looking down into the street as Walt Freiberg and Sonny Bernstein came into view. He watched them as they made their way towards the car parked against the facing sidewalk.

'Let it go, Sol,' Marcus continued.

Neumann turned, stepped forward and took a seat.

'When this thing is finished . . . when Christmas Eve is done, then I'll find Walt Freiberg and kill him.'

'And Sonny Bernstein?' Neumann asked. 'Whoever the fuck this guy is . . . what are we going to do about him?'

Marcus smiled, waved his hand. 'Who the hell cares? He goes back wherever he came from. We get what we want out of this.'

'And Lenny?'

'Lenny is going to die. He isn't dead come Christmas Day then we're going to send someone in there and finish this thing for good.'

Neumann nodded, didn't speak.

'Whichever way it goes we wind up with New York,' Marcus said. 'Long time overdue . . . the way it always should have been.'

FIFTY-NINE

Later, close to eight, having left the hotel and walked four blocks west, Harper stopped at a callbox and dialled Duchaunak's cellphone number.

'I went to their meeting,' Harper said.

'You what?'

'The meeting with Freiberg and Marcus . . . last minute change. I had to go too.'

'Jesus Christ . . . what the fuck . . .'

'It's over now. Another story for another day. I gotta get back to the hotel.'

'So what happened?' Duchaunak asked.

'West Twelfth,' Harper said. 'That's all I know.'

'West Twelfth what?'

'How the fuck do I know? That's all that I could get. Marcus said that it was unfortunate I wouldn't be accompanying them on their little adventure tomorrow, and then he mentioned West Twelfth. Walt Freiberg stopped him saying anything further.'

'You think that's one of the places they're going to hit?' Duchaunak asked.

'Jesus Christ, you're the fucking detective. What do I think . . . oh fuck, I don't know, maybe they're all going to meet there and choose Christmas presents for the help.'

'Okay, okay,' Duchaunak said. 'I'm just thinking aloud, okay?'

'Go think aloud somewhere else. I really have to get back to the hotel.'

'Mr Harper?'

'What?'

'I appreciate your help.'

'It's as good as I've got . . . there isn't anything more after this.' He paused for a moment. 'One other thing.'

'What?'

'I agreed to do it for three hundred grand. That was the deal I made with Walter Freiberg. I would do what he asked and I'd walk away with three hundred grand.' Harper didn't wait for Duchaunak to respond; he hung up the phone and elbowed his way out of the callbox.

The snow came down thick and fast.

Tomorrow it would be Christmas Eve.

SIXTY

Eight-forty-two a.m.

'How many times has he called?' McLuhan asked.

'Counting this time . . . er, seven I think. Four calls last night and three this morning.'

'And what is he saying?'

'That he has to speak with you, something about Lenny Bernstein's son.'

McLuhan sat without moving. It was Christmas Eve. Last thing he needed was Duchaunak somewhere in New York City, out of control, beyond whatever dividing line existed between his sense and his obsessions.

'Call Faulkner . . . Faulkner will more than likely know what's going on.'

Oates nodded. 'I called him, landline and cell . . . left messages on both. He has family upstate, may have gone there for Christmas.'

'As we all should've done,' McLuhan said. 'How did he sound?'

'Duchaunak? God knows, Captain, how does he always sound? Manic?'

'Jesus Christ, this I do not need. He calls again put him through. Don't let him talk to anyone else, just put him straight through to me.'

'Sure thing,' Sergeant Oates said, and turned to leave the office.

'Oh, and one more thing.'

Oates turned.

'Don't say a word to anyone about Duchaunak. Not a fucking word, okay?'

'What . . . that he called, or that he's crazy?'

McLuhan scowled. 'That he called for God's sake. Don't mention to anyone that he called.'

'As you wish Captain,' Oates said, and disappeared down the corridor towards the elevator.

It took three attempts before the car started. Old car, an ancient Chrysler Plymouth station wagon, but Dr Kennet Wiltsey was determined to drive her until she died on the road. Wiltsey was a creature of habit, ignorant of fashion or trend, and regarded any attempt to revise his ways as both offensive and invidious. He was fifty-three years old, head of the Department of Anthropology and Religion at NYSU; graduated from Oxford University, England, with an honors degree in Religious Studies.

When it came to God, Kennet Wiltsey knew a thing or two. Cars, however, were a different thing, hence the Chrysler Plymouth station wagon and three attempts to start her after a night of heavy snow in New York. Christmas Eve the university was officially closed, but that afternoon – commemorating the season, acknowledging the acquisition of additional funding from a private benefactor that would permit the construction of an annexe to the university library – there was a luncheon scheduled. Dr Kennet Wiltsey had been asked not only to preside over the lunch, but to give the keynote speech. He had no family as such, and thus there would be no rowdy gathering of antecedents and progeny the following day. Others spoke of such gatherings and Wiltsey experienced nothing but relief. For Christmas dinner itself he had been invited – and had indeed accepted – by the university's deputy principal, Robert Bryan, and en route to this day's luncheon, Kennet Wiltsey had scheduled a stop at a small bookstore called The Reader's Rest. There, in the possession of a most pleasant young woman called Annie Parrish, waited a copy of James Fenimore Cooper's 1828 *Notions of the Americans*. Bryan was a Fenimore Cooper aficionado, and a first edition of *Notions* would not only surprise the man, it would damn near give him a coronary seizure. Such was Wiltsey's humor, such was his generosity, such his intention for that afternoon and the subsequent day.

He would indeed make his appointment at the bookstore, and there he would purchase the Fenimore Cooper. The luncheon he did not make, despite having prepared a most sardonic and

393

excellent speech, peppered with tasteful quips and wryly obscure references, for – as he entered the New York Providence Bank on West Ninth and Washington – he was shot in the face by a hooded man. It was nine-forty-two a.m. The bullet, a .45 caliber Glaser Safety slug, penetrated Wiltsey's head alongside the nose, perhaps three-quarters of an inch below the left eye; the proximity of the weapon, no more than eight or nine feet from the target, the simple fact that it was a handgun of significant power, and the nature of a Glaser Safety – designed to spread on impact and thereby reduce the possibility of passing through the intended target and hitting an innocent bystander – meant that Kennet Wiltsey, half the alphabet chasing his name, fifty-three years of age and of rare and inordinate intelligence, was dead before he hit the polished parquet floor.

Christmas Eve had started the way it intended to go on.

A black stripped-out Ford Econoline E-250 cargo van.

Sound of the engine was like something feral, hunched and waiting on the corner of Bethune and Greenwich. Driver was Henry Kossoff, thirty-nine years old, part of the Marcus crew for eleven years, three and a half of which he'd spent visiting friends at Altona and Sing Sing. Did his terms effortlessly, didn't remember much of it, never really gave it a second thought: it was part of the life.

Back of him, crouched, hooded, each back on his haunches, each clutching M-16s, were Walt Freiberg, Ray Dietz and Cathy Hollander. Van stank like a cheap bordello in summertime, and Kossoff had inched open the forward left window to get some air in there.

It was nine-o-seven a.m. American Investment & Loan was scheduled to open at nine-thirty. Time like that – cramped and armed and frightened, but at the same time experiencing the inimitable rush of anticipation that came with such a thing; looking to the right, ahead, back behind them, eyes the only thing visible in their faces, hearts running ahead of themselves, tension like a live thing in the base of the gut. Time like that, twenty-three minutes last as many hours as a week.

There was nothing they could do but wait.

So wait they did.

*

He had no number but Duchaunak's.

John Harper stood at the window, American Regent Hotel tenth floor, New York buried beneath him in a distant white-wash of snow. Glanced at his watch: nine-thirteen a.m. Had eaten no breakfast; no appetite; had slept little, restless and agitated all night.

All these people – Marcus and Freiberg, Cathy Hollander, the others that were part of this thing; they were all out there and he felt he had to tell someone.

Three times he'd started dialling Duchaunak's number, three times he'd hung up before the last digits registered. He was caught; he knew that; caught between darkness and its shadow.

Loyalty to his father? Is that what it was? In some way he felt such a thing could never have been possible, and yet he believed that that was what he was experiencing. Perhaps it was loyalty to Walt Freiberg, even to Cathy Hollander, a woman he'd hoped would mean a great deal more to him than an acquaintance, if only because he'd believed she understood something of what he was feeling. Hell no, it had been more than that. He knew it had meant more than that. She had let him walk a certain route, and when that route had taken him too close she had rejected him. It had made him mad but, perhaps more than that, it had served to highlight and intensify his sense of utter aloneness.

The hotel room was claustrophobic, his feeling of nervous anxiety pervasive and all-encompassing. He tried to smoke, but the cigarette made him nauseous. He paced, agitated and irritable, frustrated with himself for becoming involved in this nightmare, but at the same time aware of the slow-burn nature of what had happened. He had been drawn in, perhaps allowed himself to be drawn in, for hadn't there been something seductive and alluring about the lifestyle that was represented here? Walt Freiberg and Cathy Hollander had promised him something, something that had been so obviously missing from his own life. He had walked towards it, a moth to a flame, and now, only now – as he stood alone in the hotel room, aware that New York was at some point going to be subjected to whatever Freiberg and Marcus had orchestrated – was he *really* facing the truth of his father.

Edward Bernstein was a thief and a murderer. That was the truth. That was Harper's heritage, his ancestry, and that would be his legacy once the old man died. Yet there was something John Harper could not escape: a sense of allegiance. That was the only way he could describe it – a feeling that the old man was somehow due something from him, if only because he *was* his father; nothing, in truth, any more complex than genetics, but nevertheless *something*. Something where previously there had been nothing.

With no-one behind or ahead of you, no parents before, no children to follow, the world was some awful lonely place.

And if he called Duchaunak? What else could he tell him? He had told him everything he knew: the deal, the trade-off, West Twelfth, the three hundred grand he'd been promised for standing proxy for his father at the Marcus meeting. What else was there?

There was nothing.

And Freiberg, Cathy Hollander, the others involved? What of them? Was it right to have played one side against the other, to have made them believe they could trust him, only then to turn and speak to the police? As of this moment, what had they done? They had trusted John Harper, and he had betrayed them. Had they done anything directly and intentionally injurious to him? Truth? No, they hadn't.

Harper paced. He cursed, he sat down, stood up again. He closed his eyes and imagined that it had all been some insane, fractured nightmare, a throwback from his own imagination, what he'd remembered of Evelyn and Garrett and Walt and his mother . . .

'Aah, Jesus Christ!' he shouted, and with force sufficient to break it he hurled a heavy glass ashtray against the wall.

His mother had killed herself – and he didn't know why. To escape? Or to demonstrate that her loyalty to Edward Bernstein was greater than the value of her own life?

Harper did not know. Believed that if his father died he would never know.

And *if* his father died, then who? Evelyn? Harper believed that she knew only some of the truth, and what was to prevent her from continuing to lie? If not Evelyn, then . . . then Walt Freiberg?

Harper paused. He closed his eyes. Walt had answered every question he'd been asked. Until this point he had not lied to

396

Harper, at least not that Harper had been aware of. Not like Evelyn, who seemed to have lied about everything, and then once faced with the truth of her own lies had lied yet again to evade confrontation.

Perhaps Walter Freiberg was the only man alive who could really, *really* answer all of Harper's questions.

And where was Freiberg? Freiberg was on his way to wherever – possibly even West Twelfth – right into the line of fire that would be so ably and expediently provided by Duchaunak and the police.

Harper, hesitating for just a heartbeat, asked himself if warning Freiberg about Duchaunak was the right thing to do. The *right* thing?

John Harper believed that the right thing did not exist, and if it did then he was possibly the last person on earth who would recognize it.

He grabbed his jacket from the edge of the bed and hurried out of the room.

SIXTY-ONE

Nine-sixteen a.m.

Associated Union Finance on West Broadway.

Man called Richard Amundson leaves his car in the parking lot and walks around the corner of the building to the ATMs. There are queues. He glances at his watch, peers through into the bank and notices the lines for the internal machines are significantly smaller. He hurries along the sidewalk and enters the bank through the front door.

By this time it is nine-seventeen. Due at work at nine-thirty, Amundson is employed by the New York City Educational Board as an inspector for school catering facilities. This morning he is en route to St Mary Magdalene School on Lispenard Street.

He waits patiently in line. Ahead of him a large Hispanic woman is listening to something on a Walkman. Every once in a while she utters a single word in Spanish, and then nudges her hips to the right and left as if dancing with someone.

Amundson smiles. He is a man who often recognizes the simplicities of people, the way in which their idiosyncrasies and oddities are actually the things that make them human. Without such things there would not be a great deal left to like.

The Hispanic woman then destroys the effect by jamming the cash machine. A security guard is on hand; he speaks Spanish, fluently, and while he calms the over-emotional woman, while he tries to catch the attention of one of the bank assistants, Amundson steps to the plate glass window and looks down to the corner. The queues for the external machines, if anything, have merely doubled in his absence.

Amundson glances at his watch: nine-twenty-one. He turns and hurries to the counter.

Had he used the machines outside, had he been fractionally more patient, had he recognized that Murphy's Law dictated that whatever change he made to his position in one queue it would merely be replicated in the next, he would have driven out of the car lot behind the Associated Union Finance Bank on West Broadway at approximately nineteen minutes after nine.

At that precise moment he would have been turning right onto Duane and heading up Church towards the Lispenard junction.

But he wasn't.

At nine-twenty-two, Christmas Eve morning, as he steps to the counter with his bank card in his hand, three men burst through the front doors of the building and start screaming at the tops of their voices. Led by Charlie Beck, the other two are Lewis Parselle and Sol Neumann. Neumann carries an M-16 and a heavy cloth-wrapped metal pipe. He swings it like a baseball bat, takes one of the security guards down by bringing it around back of the man's knees. The guard goes down, Neumann sideswipes him with the butt of the assault rifle, and then stoops to remove the handgun from the man's holster. The man doesn't move, won't for a good eighteen minutes.

Four blocks east, on West Twelfth Street, a second black Ford Econoline, this time driven by Maurice Rydell and carrying Victor Klein, Larry Benedict and Leo Petri, swerves violently to avoid a red Berlinetta coming out of a sidestreet, and screeches to a halt outside the East Coast Mercantile and Savings Bank.

Victor Klein is not as young as he once was, but even as the doors of the Econoline open he is running across the sidewalk, M-16 in his hand, and comes through the front double doors of the bank like a tornado. He steps aside, holding the door open for Benedict and Petri, and before the security guards understand what is happening Klein has come up behind the other two men and taken a woman by the hair. Young woman, name is Trudi Mostyn, once did a stint at Bloomingdale's on the nail-care counter; today she is the primary hostage in a violent armed robbery. Three months' time she will sue the bank for damages, the cost of counselling to support her Post Traumatic Stress Disorder, but her case will fail. Twelve months from now she still won't go in a bank, no matter the time of day, no matter who is with her.

Nine-twenty-eight a.m., West Ninth and Washington. Three men – Joe Koenig, Albert Reiff and Karl Merrett – thunder across the foyer of the New York Providence Bank. They are dressed head-to-foot in black, all-in-one coveralls, heavy boots hammering a staccato on the marble flooring, the sound of labored breathing, faces closed up inside balaclavas, eyes wide and white, looking like a nightmare coming at sixty miles an hour. Each of them is armed, once again M-16s, and Karl Merrett, unstable at the best of times, figures that he's always wanted to shoot some motherfucker and today will be as good a time as any. Merrett is part of the Marcus crew, a wild card, a flying ace, and when he passes through the inner door and is confronted by one of the security staff he believes his time has come.

In his coveralls pocket he has a back-up piece, a snub-nosed .38. It is with this that he shoots the security guard through the left eye. The rush of blood that is jettisoned from the back of the man's head showers a white artificial Christmas tree standing behind the door.

People start screaming, screaming like fire sirens, and they keep on screaming until Joe Koenig releases a burst of rounds into the ceiling.

The bank is silent, deathly so.

'On the floor, motherfuckers!' Albert Reiff is shouting. 'On the floor. No sound. No movement. One down, plenty more to go!'

The people drop like bowling pins.

Somewhere, out of sight, a woman tries to calm a crying baby.

Nine-twenty-nine a.m.

McLuhan stands in the narrow toilet adjacent to his office when he hears the phone shrilling at him. In his hurry to zip up he pisses on his own shoes, the legs of his pants.

'Fuck, fuck, fuck,' he mutters as he hurries out of the toilet and across the corridor. He snatches the receiver from his desk. 'Yes?'

'It's him, Captain.'

'Well, for fuck's sake put him through.'

A second's silence, and then: *Captain McLuhan . . . been trying to get you since last night.*

'So I hear. What is going on with you now, Detective?'

Heists.

'You what?'

Heists Captain . . . several of them simultaneously.

'What in fuck's name are you talking about Duchaunak?'

Haven't got time to explain. Only one I know about for definite is on West Twelfth. It's going to be one of a number of armed robberies that Freiberg and Marcus are going to pull off at the same time. West Twelfth, that's all I know. I need as many people as you've got down there immediately.

'Right . . . you need as many people as I've got.'

Captain, this is no fucking joke. This is it . . . what I've been telling you about. Two, maybe three armed robberies simultaneously today . . . Christmas Eve—

'I know what day it is, Detective—'

You have to get some squad cars down there . . . SWAT, whatever the fuck you can lay your hands on.

'I don't *have* to do a fucking thing, Detective, not until you tell me exactly what you know and exactly how you came by this information.'

Harper.

'Who?'

John Harper.

'Bernstein's son?'

Yes, Bernstein's son. He went to a meeting yesterday with Freiberg and Marcus. Marcus is buying Bernstein's territory. That was the plan before Bernstein got hit. Freiberg needed Harper in New York to stand for his father at the meeting—

'Okay, enough already Duchaunak . . . this is just fucking Alice in Wonderland shit. You need to come in right now and see me. You need to get your ass in a fucking car and come down here right fucking now and tell me what the fuck is going on. I also need you to tell me where Faulkner is, because as God is my fucking witness when you pair are involved in anything together someone's going to get damaged.'

I can't come in, Captain . . . I can't come in. I have to do something to stop this going down. I need you to back me up on this Captain—

'Back you up? Fuck you! Who the fuck d'you think you're talking to—'

The line goes dead.

McLuhan frowns, shakes his head. 'Duchaunak?' he says to a disconnected receiver.

'Ah, fuck this,' he states emphatically. 'This is just too fucking much.' He sets the receiver down, comes out from behind his desk and steps into the corridor.

'Oates! Oates! Where the fuck are you?'

Sergeant Warren Oates appears at the end of the corridor.

'Get a black and white over to Duchaunak's place and see if he's there. And have another black and white go up to West Twelfth and see if anything's happening.'

'Anything?' Oates asks. 'Can you give me something more specific to go on?'

McLuhan, who is in the process of stepping back into his office, turns suddenly and glares at Oates. 'An armed robbery Sergeant, a fucking armed robbery! Have someone drive to West Twelfth, and if there happens to be an armed robbery going on down there then ask them if it wouldn't be too much fucking trouble to perhaps give me a call, okay?'

Oates doesn't speak; merely nods, turns, hurries down the corridor.

McLuhan walks to the office window and looks down into the street. Ten minutes before he'd been figuring out how to get his wife a Christmas present, something that would appear to have required a great deal of thought and consideration.

Now he is thinking about Frank Duchaunak running down West Twelfth with a handgun. He closes his eyes, bows his head. If there is no reward in Heaven he is going to be mightily pissed off.

SIXTY-TWO

Nine-thirty a.m.

Same moment that Frank Duchaunak finally gives up on trying to reach Faulkner, as he kneels beside his bed and drags out a shoebox within which is an ancient-looking .45, as he snatches a jacket from the back of a chair, as he hurries towards the front door of his apartment, as his heart kicks up into high-drive and he starts to feel the adrenaline pulling his stomach into his chest . . .

At that precise moment: same vehicle, Ford Econoline E-250, Henry Kossoff at the wheel, Ray Dietz hunched behind him, hands gripping the headrest of the passenger seat, back of him Walt Freiberg and Cathy Hollander, hooded faces, each of them unrecognizable, and on the floor between them handguns, M-16s, three heavy-duty kitbags, a tension like hot whipcord stretched to its limit . . .

Junction of Bethune and Greenwich, across the road the facade of the American Investment & Loan Bank, and as Kossoff eases his foot off the brake he doesn't so much as head for the front entrance, he aims the vehicle at it. Like some heat-seeking missile the Econoline hurtles across the road, cuts between moving cars with seemingly impossible inches to spare, and before the drivers even have a chance to lean on their horns the black van jumps the sidewalk, crosses the brief gap between the curb and the building, and ploughs right through a half-inch plate glass window into the foyer itself.

Inside the vehicle the three passengers are thrown against the seats, hands grabbing for anchor, shoulders undoubtedly bruised, muscles strained, but the sheer rush of the moment, the combination of fear and energy, makes such impacts and abrasions irrelevant. No-one feels a thing but the way the front window gives, and the skidding of the tires as they attempt to make purchase against the highly polished floor within.

Freiberg is out first, Dietz beside him, Hollander at the rear, each of them running across the foyer and through the internal doors.

Two security guards, one of them a good six and a half feet tall, each of them coping with shock, terror, the split-second hesitation that means the difference between reaction and overwhelm. Neither one is adequately trained to deal with such a scenario. The shorter one manages to withdraw his gun but he goes down beneath a terrific thundering blow from Ray Dietz. Ray Dietz is not a small man, and he just clothes-lines the guy, breaks his neck, and then keeps on running until he reaches the counter.

People are scattering now, and Freiberg makes it across the floor to the taller guard.

'Down!' he's screaming, and even as his voice breaks pitch the guard is falling like a tree. Face down, hands out before him, gun gathered up and emptied of shells. The shells are pocketed, and then Freiberg hurls the gun across the high-ceilinged entrance-way. It lands with a clatter somewhere out of sight.

Cathy Hollander is quick, quicker than both of the men, and by the time the guards have been disarmed she is already herding the customers against the back wall of the main concourse.

Dietz runs beside her, and then he turns left, suddenly, almost as an afterthought, and jumps up onto the counter that runs the length of the floor. Cashiers and assistants are screaming. People overturn desks and chairs in an effort to get as far away as they can.

Dietz releases a burst of gunfire into the ceiling and the screaming ceases, more from shock, the deafening roar that such a thing produces, than anything else.

'Cashiers back to the counter!' Dietz screams.

One of the customers steps from the gathered crowd against the wall. Cathy Hollander drives the butt of her M-16 into the man's lower gut. He goes down soundlessly.

'Cashiers . . . everyone on cash back to the counter!' Dietz repeats.

A single girl starts to edge forward.

Freiberg jumps up alongside Dietz, and then comes down on the other side. He hurries to the back of the enclosure, merely feet from the group of employees, and he grabs a young man by the collar of his shirt and pushes him down to the ground. He withdraws his handgun and presses it against the back of the man's head.

The young man is in shock, starts crying, heaving, eyes wide, face white with abject terror.

'Cashiers,' Freiberg shouts. 'All of you . . . everyone who has a cash desk position back to the counter. There are eight of you. Each of you back to the counter. All cash – fives, tens, fifties, hundreds – all of it up on the counter. No bullshit. No alarm buttons. No dye packs. Anything aside from taking money out of the drawers and placing it neatly on the counter . . .'

Freiberg pauses, leans down until his face is no more than six inches from the young man's. 'Name?' he asks.

The young man doesn't respond, doesn't seem capable of speech. A wide dark area has already grown from his crotch and spread across his pants.

Freiberg shakes his head, looks at a girl nearest him. 'His name?' Freiberg asks.

'Steve,' she says, her voice hesitant. 'His name is Steve Tyler.'

'Serious? His name is Steve Tyler?'

She nods.

'Okay, folks . . . co-operate like you never co-operated before or Mr fucking Aerosmith here loses the back of his head in a riot of color!'

The eight cashiers hurry forward, each of them to their stations, each of them immediately occupied with unloading cash drawers onto the counter. Dietz stands over them, walks back and forth along the counter, stepping over their hands as they hurry to empty all they can onto the surface.

Cathy Hollander stays back with the customers, never looking back at Freiberg and Dietz, scanning the faces of the people ahead of her, looking for the wiseass, the one who's going to try something – the retired cop, the off-duty security guard, the ju-jitsu nut who figures he can take three armed people with a rolled-up newspaper and a guardian spirit. Every few seconds she surveys the street, watching not only for people who might walk into the bank, but also any indication of police activity. There is nothing. Her heart thunders like a freight train. Her pulse has long since left the scale. She's never been so frightened in her life.

'Okay,' she hears Freiberg say. 'Where the fuck is Frederick Ross?'

Harper hails a cab.

Standing on the sidewalk, one foot in the gutter, raising his hand and waving like a maniac, it is nevertheless some minutes before a cab pulls up alongside him.

Once inside he leans forward.

'Where to?' the driver asks.

'West Twelfth,' Harper says. 'You know West Twelfth?'

The driver laughs. 'Know West Twelfth . . . Christ, I know the whole of New York like I know my own name.'

Harper leans back in the seat. He feels a sense of panic, something dark and close; he believes that whatever he may be able to do will not be enough.

Frank Duchaunak saw the commotion outside the East Coast Mercantile & Savings before he left the shadow of St Vincent's. He came from the east side – from Perry, crossing Bleecker, West Fourth, up onto Seventh Avenue.

At first he was uncertain, hurrying down past the hospital, glancing left at the facade and wondering whether Lenny Bernstein was still alive. He was uncertain why barriers had been erected, why there were black Hummers parked behind sawhorses, yellow and black crime scene tapes strung between them in an effort to keep people back. Uncertain because he'd heard nothing on the radio, nothing on the closed-channel police receiver in his car. Uncertain because nothing seemed to be making sense.

He believed he had coincidentally walked into something else entirely.

Down by the barriers he was stopped by an armed and helmeted police sergeant. Breast-badge gave his name as Mackey.

Duchaunak showed his ID. 'What we got down here?' he asked.

'Bankjob. East Coast Mercantile. Seems to be three men inside.'

'This was called in?' Duchaunak asked.

Mackey shook his head. 'We had forewarning.' He leaned a little closer to Duchaunak. 'Feds are here for Christ's sake.'

'Feds? What the fuck are Feds doing here?'

Sergeant Mackey shook his head. 'What the fuck exactly?'

'I can come through?'

Mackey shook his head. 'Not through this way. You got a car?'

Duchaunak nodded.

'Take it round the back, up to Fourteenth, head west and come down the Americas way. Think West Twelfth is open at the other end. What's your interest in this anyway?'

Duchaunak shrugged. 'Day off. Got bored. Figured I'd go stake out a bank robbery.'

'Fuck that,' Mackey said. 'Go get the kids some more toys, for God's sake.'

'I'll check out the other end of the street,' Duchaunak said. 'Then I'll go get some more toys.'

'Have a good 'un,' Mackey said, and raised his hand.

Duchaunak backed up, turned, and by the time he reached the facing sidewalk he was running.

SIXTY-THREE

Nine-forty-two a.m.

Kennet Wiltsey hits the ground.

Before his head even bounces off the parquet floor Reiff has him by the shirt collar and is dragging him across the floor. He leaves a wide, and ever widening, trail of blood as he goes. The color seems too bright, unnatural beneath the fluorescents, and when Reiff heaves the man's body up against the wall to the right of the main counters Joe Koenig knows that they have long since passed the point of no return.

There are now four dead.

The first was the security guard, shot in the eye by Karl Merrett. Second was some hero-of-the-moment bank employee; came up back of Koenig, figured he could floor him with a trashcan. Reiff was there, moved far faster than Koenig would have expected from such a big man. Trashcan hero neither saw nor felt what came. Reiff had him by the hair, jerked his head back with such force and at such an unnatural angle that his neck snapped like a greenstick. Man's body went limp and useless, rag-doll lifeless, and crumpled to the ground. Merrett realized what had happened, turned, looked down at the guy, and with a heavy boot stamped on the side of his face. His face sort of folded inwards like a watermelon. Lot of blood. More than Wiltsey.

Third hit was just an example. Joe Koenig was backed up against the counter. Tellers were frantically emptying cash drawers into canvas sacks. Karl Merrett was behind the main interview area hustling the bank manager out of his office and towards the vault. There was a lot of screaming. Things got confusing for a few moments. Reiff – standing near the front door watching for any external activity, making sure that he had a good view of the bank's interior – caught the reflection off a

408

side door. A man was pressed against the back of one of the internal pillars, no more than a few feet from where Merrett would appear once he cleared the rear offices.

Albert Reiff, a simple man, uncomplicated in both speech and manner, took three steps to the right, ducked beneath an overhanging pot-plant, and came up beside the man.

The man realized all too late that he'd been seen. He turned, looked right back at Albert Reiff, eyeball-to-eyeball in fact, and then opened his mouth to emit a sound like *Nyuuuuggghh* – an exhalation of excruciating depth and force – as Reiff drove a six-inch serrated combat knife through his lower gut. As the man went down Reiff caught him by his hair, held him suspended for a moment, and then cut his throat.

Six minutes later Kennet Wiltsey had entered the bank to cash a check.

At nine-forty-six Karl Merrett heard the first indication that things were not going strictly to plan.

The thing he heard was silence.

Beyond the plate glass front windows, out along West Ninth and across the corner of Washington, the traffic had ceased. It was a busy intersection; traffic ran through it twenty-four seven.

Silence was not good.

Joe Koenig, already aware of the fact that it was now an all-or-nothing gig, held his breath and closed his eyes. When he opened them Karl Merrett was standing beside him.

'Call Wheland in the van,' Koenig said. 'Tell him we're going to need to come out the back.'

Merrett nodded, took a heavy handset from his coveralls and switched on the transmitter.

Nine-fifty-one.

Harper's cab is stopped by the cops at the corner of Seventh and Greenwich. Two black and whites are angled nose-to-nose from one sidewalk to the other. Riot-suited officers crouch against storefronts, and from the rear window of the cab Harper can see uniformed men ushering lines of people from the back door of stores, from the mall facing him. A single spectator stands outside a record store on the left sidewalk, headphones on, in his hand a huge cup of Coke like he's at the drive-in.

'What the fuck is this?' the cab driver is saying. He winds down his window and hollers at one of the uniforms.

'Need to back up sir,' the uniform tells him. 'Back up the way you came and find some other way to your destination.'

'This is my freakin' destination,' the driver says.

The uniform smiles, shakes his head. 'Not any more it's not.'

The driver curses, winds up the window.

'Back up half a block and let me out,' Harper says.

'You what?'

'Back there . . . the corner down there.'

The driver shrugs, shifts gear, reverses the cab and turns.

A minute or so later John Harper is walking back towards the record store at the bottom of West Twelfth.

McLuhan snatches the receiver from his desk. 'Yes?'

He pauses. 'Who are you talking about? Who's not where?'

He shakes his head. 'Okay, okay. Jesus Christ. Let me know when you hear back from West Twelfth.'

McLuhan sets down the receiver and walks to the corridor. 'Oates!'

Sergeant Warren Oates appears at the end of the corridor.

'He's not home,' McLuhan says.

Oates frowns.

'Duchaunak . . . he's not home. Find out which car went over to West Twelfth and call them. I want to know what the fuck is going on.'

'I called,' Oates says. 'I was on my way up to see you.'

McLuhan says nothing.

'The whole area is sealed.'

'What?'

'West Twelfth, both ends. Sixth and Seventh. They have about thirty uniforms down there and a Federal crew.'

McLuhan is shaking his head, disbelieving. 'They have what?'

'Federal people . . . ATF, SWAT as well I think.'

'What the fuck are you talking about?'

'What I say,' Oates replies. 'There's something going on down there . . . down on West Twelfth, and we just had a report in from Despatch.' Oates pauses, like he's figuring the best way to say something he doesn't want to say.

'And?' McLuhan prompts.

'And it looks like West Twelfth isn't the only place.'

'Mr Ross isn't here this morning.'

Freiberg stands over the bank teller. Through the slits in his mask his eyes are small dark spaces, as if there is no light behind them, as if everything is switched off.

'Not here?' he asks. The intonation of his voice lifts at the end of his question. The sound is one of puzzlement, disbelief perhaps. 'Bullshit he's not here. Get him out here now!'

The teller starts to cry. Her name is Alice Dunnett. She is twenty-five years old and people constantly tell her how much like Helen Hunt she looks; younger, of course, but nevertheless so much like Helen Hunt. With mascara now smeared across her lower lids and the upper part of her cheeks she looks like someone kicked her six ways to Thanksgiving and home again for Christmas.

Freiberg turns and looks at Steve Tyler. 'Where the fuck is Frederick Ross?' he asks.

Tyler shakes his head. His face is white. His pants are soaked through. His eyes are red and swollen from crying. The man has almost nothing left of the person he was when he arrived for work. 'He's not here,' he says, and he steps forward, his right hand instinctively reaching towards Alice Dunnett in a gesture of camaraderie, of intended protection perhaps. 'He called in sick this morning . . . just called in sick.'

'You spoke to him?' Freiberg asks.

Tyler shakes his head. His voice is weak and strained. 'No, I didn't speak to him. There's a number for staff to call if they're sick. They speak to a nurse. If they're staying home we get a message through on our internal memorandum system.'

'And Ross called in sick?'

Tyler nods. 'Yes sir, he called in sick.' He looks down at the ground.

'So who's got the vault access code?'

Tyler shakes his head defeatedly. 'No-one has vault access until after lunch. We have an ancillary vault which Mr Youngman has access to, but until Mr Ross's replacement arrives we have no access to the central vault.'

'And where the fuck is Mr Youngman?'

'Here,' a voice says.

Freiberg turns, sees a middle-aged man in a dark suit rise to his feet.

'I'm Mr Youngman,' the dark suit says, but his voice – though clear and distinct – is lost in the sound of a helicopter overhead.

The East Coast Mercantile & Savings security guards, faced with a hostage situation, yielded to the demands of the three gunmen without question. They were relieved of their weapons, and once the first had taped the hands, feet and mouth of the second, Larry Benedict repeated the procedure on the first. They were then seated with their backs to a central pillar, invisible from the street if anyone were to look through the front door, and while Klein herded the bank's customers to a section of the lower floor, Leo Petri ran back of the tellers' positions and disabled the counter's alarm activation system. Without assistance he started filling bags with bundles of notes, one eye on what he was doing, another on the street. For some reason, neither apparent nor specific, he had woken that morning with a sense of uneasy premonition. He believed something had gone wrong. He said nothing, not to Walt Freiberg nor Larry Benedict. He didn't want to be the one who jinxed the operation, because he'd been there before. Did a four-year Fulton stretch on a jinx back in 1996. Back then, more than eight years before, he'd experienced the same feeling, the same sensation in his lower gut, all the while a dark thought at the back of his mind. Like an itch that could never be scratched, always out of reach.

He bagged the money; he watched the road; he did his best to ignore the negative vibe that had invaded his thoughts. Watched everyone and everything, eyes going two directions at once. Nervous, like a whipped cat.

SIXTY-FOUR

Nine-thirty-one a.m.; both John Harper and Frank Duchaunak are attempting to get as close to the scene of police activity as possible, Harper from the Seventh Avenue end of West Twelfth, Duchaunak from Sixth.

At nine-thirty-three both of them are aware of the sound of helicopters, and looking up they are witness to a black whisper-mode police chopper making its way past the roof of St Vincent's Hospital. Close behind it, no more than two hundred yards, is a TV station helicopter. Both Harper and Duchaunak are aware that whatever might have been planned is already falling apart.

Duchaunak thinks of Walter Freiberg, perhaps because he is the closest to Edward Bernstein, perhaps himself in some way an accessory to the murder of Lauren Sachs. He wonders why there is so much police activity when his call to Captain McLuhan seemed to produce nothing but rebuttal and protest.

John Harper, confused, uncertain of what part he might have played in bringing the same police presence so swiftly, thinks of Cathy Hollander. There is little else now that occupies his thoughts. He wonders if she will make it out of Christmas Eve alive.

At nine-forty-seven the fifth victim of what would later be known as 'The Christmas Eve Heists' was killed.

Associated Union Finance on West Broadway. Sol Neumann, Charlie Beck and Lewis Parselle had been inside the building for twenty-five minutes. They were already behind schedule. It had taken until nine-forty-one for the cashiers to empty the twenties, fifties and hundreds into holdalls – four bags in all, each approximately three feet in length, a foot deep, a foot wide. The dollar count for each holdall was unknown, but bank financial records would later estimate that somewhere in the region of two hundred and eighty-five thousand dollars had been stripped from eleven desks. As far as the original plan was concerned such an amount was merely a taster, an hors d'oeuvre before the main course. Each of the selected targets held considerably more than four million dollars within their respective vaults. It was the day before Christmas. The streets were jammed with people, the vast majority away from work, the vast majority engineering their way through the crowds in an effort to gather the last of their provisions and gifts for the following day. The banks had predicted that requests for cash would be high, much the same as every year, and thus the withdrawals anticipated by each crew were anticipated to be sufficient to cover the amount to complete all transactions between Ben Marcus and Walter Freiberg – and leave more than sufficient for the remaining members of Bernstein's outfit to start their own business elsewhere.

So, at nine-forty-seven, Charlie Beck hauled one of the assistant managers to his feet from the huddled staff and customer gathering at the back of the internal concourse and told him to point out Thomas Delaney, vice-president of the West Broadway branch of Associated Union Finance. Charlie Beck had seen the man's picture enough times, but the picture was small, a little grainy, and appearances in person were always significantly different from photographs.

The assistant manager, a remarkably punctual and reliable man called William Byrde, father of two, struggling to keep a somewhat awkward marriage together due to his wife's tendency to drastically overspend on a routine basis, told Charlie Beck that Mr Delaney was not in that morning.

Beck frowned, shook his head. 'Come again?'

'He's not here,' Byrde said. 'He's not well . . . he called in this morning and told me that he wouldn't be in until after the holiday period.'

Beck nodded, turned and looked at Neumann. 'So who has the vault access code?'

Byrde didn't speak for a moment.

Beck stepped forward, raised his handgun and pointed it directly at Byrde's chest. 'The vault access code . . . who has it in Delaney's absence?'

Byrde's eyes widened, more than seemed physically possible.

414

He started to shake his head, a reaction that seemed more apropos to his own disbelief rather than a response to Beck's question.

'Who?' Beck repeated.

'Deputy Vice-President Michael Roth,' Byrde said, his voice steady, but somehow reflecting his utter terror about the situation in which he had found himself.

'And where the fuck is he?'

Once again Byrde shook his head, slowly, metronomically, as if he believed such a gesture would perhaps alleviate the pressure he was feeling. 'He's on his way,' he said quietly.

'On his way?' Sol Neumann asked. He stepped forward. He raised the M-16, pointed it towards Byrde. 'On his way from where?'

Byrde looked at Neumann, back to Beck, at Neumann once again. 'If an access code holder is absent the code he possesses can only be relayed to another VP or manager.'

Beck was nodding. 'Right, right,' he said. 'Go on . . . get to the fucking point here.'

Byrde swallowed visibly. His skin was white, chalk-white, but glossed with sweat.

'The VP or manager has to come from another district though . . . a precaution against too many people in the same facility having the same codes.'

'And where the fuck is he coming from?' Neumann asked. He took yet another step forward, raised the gun a little higher.

Byrde started to shake his head more vigorously. His legs seemed weak, and for a moment it appeared that he would collapse right where he stood.

'Where the fuck is he coming from?' Beck shouted.

'Long Island City,' Byrde mumbled.

'Eh?'

'Long Island City . . . he's got to come from Long Island City.'

'You're full of shit!' Neumann barked, his temper already stretched. 'This is bullshit. For fuck's sake, this is just some goddamned bullshit fucking line . . . who the fuck d'you think we are?' He stepped forward, pushed the barrel of the M-16 into Byrde's chest. 'What the fuck do you think this is, mister? Some kind of party game? Tell me what the fucking access codes are!'

'Please,' Byrde started. 'Please, no . . .' His knees started to give.

He tried to stand but there was too little strength remaining. He dropped to his knees, his hands together like he was praying, his face red and sweating, his hair rat-tailed, dark stains beneath the shoulders of his suit jacket.

Neumann stepped back, aimed the muzzle of his rifle directly at Byrde's head.

'Jesus, no!' Byrde pleaded. 'I have a wife . . . have kids, two kids, mister . . . I have two kids and it's Christmas!'

'Shut the fuck up!' Beck snapped. He looked at Neumann, shook his head, and then turned to the gathered crowd of staff and customers huddled against the far wall.

'Hands up anyone who's first name begins with the letter A.'

Two people raised their hands, a young man, a middle-aged woman.

'Over here!' Beck snapped. Both of them hesitated. 'Now!' Beck hollered. 'Get the fuck over here now or this asshole is going to get shot in the fucking head!'

The young man and the woman moved fast, running across the floor towards where Beck stood with Neumann, Byrde on his knees between them.

'You!' Beck said, and pointed at the young man. 'What's your name?'

'A-Andrew,' the man stuttered.

'How old are you?'

'How old am I?'

'Yes, for Christ's sake how fucking old are you? It isn't a difficult fucking question!'

'Twen-twenty t-two,' the young man stammered.

'Married?'

Andrew shook his head.

'Kids?' Beck asked.

Again Andrew shook his head.

Beck turned and looked down at Byrde. 'The access code?' he asked.

Byrde looked up at Beck, his eyes wide and terrified. 'I don't . . . I don't know it . . . I don't have the access code.'

Beck nodded, raised his handgun, shot Andrew in the head. A wide arc of blood rushed from the wound and sprayed across the woman standing beside him.

For a moment the woman did nothing. Stunned horror didn't

even register on her face for a handful of seconds. She seemed to move her head then, in slow-motion, everything in slow-motion, her eyes wide, looking down at the mess of blood that covered her hands, her skirt, her legs, the side of her woollen jacket.

She opened her mouth to scream, but Byrde was there first, shouting at the top of his voice, a sound like a wounded animal, so whatever might have come from the woman's mouth was drowned.

Neumann stepped forward. He raised his hand and slapped Byrde viciously across the face. Byrde fell silent, the woman too.

'Access code?' Beck asked again.

Byrde started to shake his head.

At nine-forty-eight the sixth victim was killed. Her name was Anthea Hennessy. Anthea was forty-seven years of age, a nurse and a widow with no children; for the previous seven years she had devoted herself almost exclusively to the care of elderly terminal patients at St Vincent's hospital. She was a very close friend of Iris Piper, resident ward sister on the ICU wing, a woman who had spent the previous week monitoring the progress of a seventy-year-old gunshot victim called Edward Bernstein. Ironic, but nevertheless true.

The gunshot was loud, extraordinarily so, but somehow drowned beneath the sudden rush of a helicopter, accompanied by the first challenges from armed robbery negotiators across the street.

Beck looked at Neumann.

Neumann stood immobile for some seconds. Someone somewhere must have tripped a silent alarm. 'Get Parselle to radio Dearing,' he said. 'We're outta here.'

Words echoed by Victor Klein as he stood inside the entrance-way of the East Coast Mercantile and looked out into the street.

Leo Petri stood behind him, in each hand a canvas holdall.

'There's no time for anything else is there?' he asked Klein.

Klein didn't speak, merely shook his head.

'I'll get Benedict to call Rydell and tell him we're coming out early.'

'Out the back of the building,' Klein said, 'and we're taking a couple of people with us.'

417

Leo Petri nodded, turned, understood that there had in fact been a jinx somewhere, wondered when he would ever learn his lesson. Should've stayed home. Should've left New York when he had his premonition. Too fucking late now. Too late by far.

SIXTY-FIVE

'What d'you mean, inside?' McLuhan asks.

'Exactly as I mean. We have someone inside one of the banks.'

Seated across from McLuhan is a smartly dressed, perhaps *too* smartly dressed federal agent called Robert Hennessy. Everything about him seems smooth and polished, as if he has spent his life telling people that things are happening that they don't understand, but it's okay, they're not things that are meant to be understood.

McLuhan doesn't trust the man.

'It has been a very precise and detailed operation,' Hennessy says. 'Obviously there was a certain delicacy to the situation, considering the time and expense involved, and there was a particular reason we did not want to inform you of what was happening until it was absolutely necessary.'

'Absolutely necessary?' McLuhan asks. 'You call an hour after a bank robbery starts the point where it becomes *absolutely necessary*?'

Hennessy smiled ingratiatingly. 'This isn't about a bank robbery, Captain, it's about securing the arrest of Ben Marcus, Solomon Neumann, Walter Freiberg and a whole host of other unsocial elements that have been creating trouble in New York for a great many years.'

McLuhan is shaking his head. 'But you're federal. What the hell has this got to do with federal jurisdiction?'

'Bank robbery is a federal offence, Captain. Espionage, sabotage, kidnapping, drug trafficking, bank robbery—'

McLuhan stops him. 'Okay, okay, okay, enough already. So you're here to tell me what? That there's a bank robbery going on—'

'Four bank robberies,' Hennessy says. 'East Coast Mercantile on West Twelfth, American Investment & Loan on Bethune and

Greenwich, New York Providence on West Ninth and Washington, and Associated Union on West Broadway. Right now each bank is surrounded by both federal and police units, there are helicopters overhead, and the men within have not the slightest hope of escape.'

McLuhan is nodding, slightly disbelieving, and at the same time a little relieved that he does not have to handle a bank robbery all by himself. 'I appreciate your telling me what's going on,' he says, 'but why now? Why wait so long to let me know what's happening? This is my precinct, and one of those locations falls inside my jurisdiction.'

Hennessy smiles again, his manner condescending, as though McLuhan is five and must be scolded for drawing on the wall with a Crayola. 'Because, Captain McLuhan, you have a wild card in your hand.'

McLuhan nods. 'Duchaunak by any chance?'

'Frank Duchaunak, yes,' Hennessy says. 'You wouldn't happen to know where he is at this moment?'

McLuhan stands. He buries his hands in his pockets. He shakes his head and looks at Hennessy with an expression of concern. 'I think . . . I think that he might be right in the middle of this.'

'Where?' Hennessy asks. 'Where do you think he is?'

'West Twelfth. I spoke to him just before nine-thirty and I got the definite impression he was planning to go to West Twelfth. I sent a car to check at his house and he wasn't there, and the black and white I sent over to West Twelfth was stopped by one of the units down there.'

'You're sure of this?' Hennessy asks as he rises from his chair.

'Sure?' McLuhan echoes. 'With Frank Duchaunak, nothing – and I mean *nothing* – is ever sure.'

'Including his loyalties?' Hennessy asks.

By the time Walter Freiberg and Raymond Dietz have accessed the ancillary safe and removed the vast majority of its contents, it is obvious that the helicopter overhead has arrived for their benefit. Cathy Hollander, back behind one of the pillars nearest the front doors, has already witnessed the staggered deployment of at least four police units and what seems like a Federal Bureau of Investigation Negotiation Unit. On the roof of the building facing the bank sharpshooters have been stationed, each of them visible only by their weapons or the odd appearance of a reversed baseball cap above the parapet.

At nine-fifty-two a.m. Cathy Hollander, dressed head-to-toe in black, a balaclava, gloves, heavy boots, on her back a radio unit with a narrow wavelength transmitter, over her shoulder an M-16 assault rifle, at her hip a 9mm Glock, steps back from the pillar and runs across the open concourse to the rear of the floor.

'How many?' Freiberg asks her, he and Dietz cramming tied bundles of banknotes into further holdalls.

'Looks like four units of police, another Federal task force.'

'Fuck 'em,' he says, and though she cannot see his face she can tell from his eyes and the tone of his voice that he's smiling.

Freiberg is more than fifty years old; exactly how old she has never discovered, but his energy and stamina match that of a man half his age when he's at work.

'So?' she asks.

'So nothing . . . call Kossoff, tell him we're coming out the back, that he should come up from West to Washington and we'll meet him between the two. Tell him there's going to be some gunplay.'

Cathy nodded, unhooked her backpack and hurried back to the front of the bank. Behind the pillar she kneeled, undid the backpack, lifted out the handset and radioed Kossoff. She gave him instructions, aware even in that moment that the Federal unit out front would know that a transmission was occurring, some audio-geek in a van desperately trying to find the frequency before the message was relayed.

Kossoff acknowledged her, told her *Good luck*, to which Cathy Hollander replied, 'A pretty overrated commodity, right?' and then they broke off.

Cathy replaced the handset in her backpack, and then – almost as an afterthought – took off her balaclava. Sweating like a pig on barbecue day, her hair matted, the feeling of claustrophobia was almost too intense to bear. Perhaps, in the heat of the moment, a moment when sense and reason were relegated far below base survival, she figured that in escaping one should at least be able to see where one was going.

Nine-fifty-six, morning of Christmas Eve, Cathy Hollander, a.k.a. Margaret Miller a.k.a. Diane Sheridan, rises from a kneeling position on the concourse of American Investment & Loan on Bethune and Greenwich.

Outside it has begun snowing, and unbeknownst to her – unbeknownst to the vast majority of people in New York – the best plans of Ben Marcus and Walt Freiberg were even now falling apart at the seams. At each of the four locations – four banks that were due to be relieved of a combined sum approximating fifteen and a half million dollars, fifteen and a half million hard-earned Christmas dollars – police and FBI Units were deployed, rank and file, across the street, the facing junctions, the intersections, back doors, exits, entrances, underpasses and vantage points. Already news flashes have surfaced on KLMC, KMGV and Channel Nine. The scout helicopter for Channel Nine that both John Harper and Frank Duchaunak saw hovering above St Vincent's happened to be in the right place at the right time. That helicopter was the news station's equivalent of an ambulance-chasing personal litigation lawyer, the kind of lawyer that gave out business cards in hospital wards and doctors' waiting rooms. The pilot had seen the police chopper streaking across the horizon and had followed it. The fact that Channel Nine caught a bird's-eye view of the West Twelfth robbery as it happened was mere luck. Those pictures were syndicated across three more channels before ten a.m. New Yorkers, from the Lower East Side to Central Park, were transfixed by the events as they unfolded, all of them of the view that such a thing was occurring in *their* neighborhood.

But these things were unknown to Cathy Hollander as she set the radio down, as she half-turned to look at the street once more, as she came up from where she'd been kneeling and started back towards Freiberg and Dietz.

What was also unknown – even as Freiberg was shouting for her to hurry, that Dietz was in the exit to the car lot at the back of the building, that they had a straight run down to the rendezvous with Kossoff – was how easily she would go down when the bullet hit her.

She was lifted bodily when it struck. The sound was unfamiliar, new, not easily described, and the point of impact – the very center of her chest – was the kind of target accuracy that would be commented on when the shooter returned to his unit later that day. *Good call. Clean as a hound's tooth.* Such comments as these.

And when she hit the floor there was such finality, such an irreversible conclusion to her absolute lack of movement that Freiberg hesitated only a moment before cursing, turning, and running.

He never looked back.

Down at the entranceway to the bank's rear car lot Ray Dietz was waiting. There were two other people, both customers of the bank, each of them carrying two holdalls. These people would not only be couriers, but would also provide sufficient cover for Freiberg and Dietz to make it down to where Kossoff was waiting. Three blocks south-west the secondary cars waited, and this was their destination. Once in the secondary cars they had a prayer.

'Where is she?' Dietz asked.

Freiberg shook his head.

'Aw fuck,' Dietz said. 'She was cute.'

One minute past ten. Four people emerged from the rear of American Investment & Loan – Ray Dietz, Walt Freiberg, the two hostages. As soon as it was verified that there were no other gunmen inside the building, the front was stormed by a Federal Assault Unit. Inside, they found the security guard with a broken neck and the lifeless form of Cathy Hollander. Once the building was given the all-clear, fifty-three people were escorted from the foyer and into the street: thirty-one bank staff and twenty-two members of the public. All of them were shaken, some hysterical, but in all cases they had experienced a Christmas they would never forget. One of the Federal Agents stood over the prostrate body of Cathy Hollander, kicked the sole of her boot with the toe of his shoe.

'Nightmare,' he said to himself, his voice barely audible. 'What a fucking nightmare.'

SIXTY-SIX

It is three minutes after ten by the time John Harper realizes that there is no way he will get close enough to the East Coast Mercantile & Savings to understand what is happening, least of all to determine whether Cathy Hollander is inside. Police are everywhere, in sidestreets, along the roofs of the adjacent and facing buildings. Federal people in dark blue windcheaters run back and forth from one sidewalk to the other, and barriers are hastily erected to keep everyone away. Members of the public from nearby houses, apartment buildings and stores are swiftly evacuated and gathered at the end of the street, and when Harper tries to press forward, to make some progress towards the scene of activity, he finds that the closer he gets the more unrealistic it is to go any further.

Eventually he backs up and returns the way he's come. He finds a coffee shop on the corner of Greenwich Avenue. From a seat near the window he can see the front of St Vincent's Hospital. He is unaware of both irony and coincidence. He is distraught, afraid, apprehensive. He feels there is no adequate way to describe what he is experiencing and, had he been asked, he might have done nothing more than stare blankly and shake his head. He believes a life has opened up around him, a life he never knew he possessed, and just as he'd started to appreciate what might have been involved in such a life, it has imploded, folded backwards upon itself and crushed him within.

He thinks – just for a moment – that he should go over to the hospital and see what is happening with his father. He cannot remember when he was last there. He decides against it. He cannot face it.

Harper is then aware of the sound of voices behind him. He turns to see a small crowd gathering beneath an overhead TV in the corner of the bar. He makes his way across the room, stands

424

for a while, completely unable to focus his attention – but when he does, he realizes that he is watching reports of events unfolding at four different locations. West Twelfth is merely one of them. Something is happening in three other places, and he – John Harper – knows they all have something to do with him.

What he thinks, he is unable to believe; and what he believes he cannot bear to think.

After some minutes he turns and leaves the coffee shop. He starts walking, away from West Twelfth, away from St Vincent's. He doesn't look back. He is too frightened.

Joe Koenig, Albert Reiff and Karl Merrett leave the front of the New York Providence Bank on West Ninth and Washington in a hail of gunfire. The gunfire, targeted upwards, is merely designed to confuse and disorientate the police and Federal units that face them across the street. Using the same strategy as Freiberg and Dietz, they take with them four hostages, two girls, two men, and as they leave they are literally surrounded by uniforms. There is no opportunity for any clear strikes, except perhaps from overhead, and such an attempt would be considered far too risky. They intend to make it as far as East Ninth and Fifth where Ricky Wheland is waiting to take them west across the Village to the secondary vehicles.

The task force is set on standby. No clearance is given for any sharpshooters to attempt a strike. Enough innocent people have been killed already.

It is ten-o-seven by the time the awkward huddle of people reaches the rendezvous with Wheland. Only one hostage goes in the car with them, one hostage and something in the region of six hundred thousand dollars. Such scenes are replicated at two other locations – West Twelfth, as Victor Klein, Larry Benedict and Leo Petri make their way from the rear of East Coast Mercantile & Savings, again with hostages – three of them – and start running over Greenwich to the corner of Perry; also at West Broadway where Charlie Beck, Sol Neumann and Lewis Parselle start away from Associated Union Finance towards the corner of Spring and Thompson, five hostages gathered around them, where Ron Dearing waits patiently in the vehicle, his nerves taut, his mouth dry, his face drenched with sweat.

All four crews, carrying with them an estimated three million, two hundred and five thousand dollars, are expected back at the lock-up across from Pier 46 by twenty-two minutes after ten.

The West Broadway crew – Charlie Beck, Lewis Parselle, Sol Neumann, and Ron Dearing – are stopped dead in their tracks by a tirespike across Sullivan Street. In an attempt to run from the car, Sol Neumann is killed by a single shot to the head. Beck, Dearing and Parselle attempt to make it down MacDougal, but the weight of their burdens, the fact that their greed has outweighed their native instinct to survive, means that they get no more than two hundred yards before black and whites cut off the road and a dozen or more armed police officers stand between them and the way home.

They were last seen – all three of them – by another news station helicopter, this one from Channel Six, as they were spreadeagled on the road, faces down, hands out ahead of them, ankles crossed.

By the time Frank Duchaunak understood what was happening he knew that Walter Freiberg was not at the West Twelfth site. At ten-o-two he'd shown his ID to a stationed Federal Agent, a man called Liam Shaner, and Shaner had explained that they were covering four attempted robberies. Duchaunak had asked whether or not there was any indication that one of the four crews had a girl within its ranks. Shaner seemed surprised, smiled in a strange kind of way, and then said, 'She was the first one we took out.'

'Took out? Where?'

'Bethune and Greenwich, American Investment & Loan.'

Duchaunak did not respond. He merely thanked the agent for his help and turned away. He'd asked after Cathy Hollander because he felt certain that wherever she was, there he would find Freiberg.

He reached the junction at the end of the street and started running. Bethune was no more than five blocks away.

By the time the secondary rendezvous time had arrived only two crews remained. The West Ninth and Washington four – Joe Koenig, Albert Reiff, Ricky Wheland and Karl Merrett – had been roadblocked at the end of Cornelia Street by three black and whites. Joe Koenig and Albert Reiff were both shot, Reiff fatally,

Koenig merely wounded, as they ran from the abandoned vehicle.

Arriving at Pier 46 were the two remaining crews – those led by Klein and Freiberg respectively. Few words passed between them. They understood that nothing had succeeded the way it had been planned. From the moment they had invaded their target sites the game had been over. Between them they carried a little more than two point three million dollars. There were seven men in all – Klein, Freiberg, Maurice Rydell, Larry Benedict, Leo Petri, Henry Kossoff and Ray Dietz.

'The girl?' Klein asked Freiberg.

Freiberg raised his hand and drew his index finger across his neck.

'Shame,' Klein said, but there was no emotion in his voice.

'We use all four cars,' Freiberg said. 'Split the money. There's eight bags, put two in each car, everyone goes different ways, into the city, right into the middle of the city and gets lost like we planned. We'll speak and co-ordinate what the fuck we're going to do in a few days, okay?'

'Done,' Klein said.

Larry Benedict and Henry Kossoff divided the bags between the vehicles.

'We're gone,' Walt Freiberg said, and within moments, less than a minute perhaps, four bright yellow Medallion cabs hurtled away from Pier 46. Freiberg went alone, the others in twos – Klein and Kossoff, Benedict and Petri, Dietz and Rydell. They went different ways, out along West Street, hurtling away into silence as the first of the squad cars came from Perry and West Eleventh.

Behind them, standing in the road, terror-stricken, tear-streaked faces, hands shaking, nerves shredded, were the hostages they had taken – people who could never have imagined how this day was going to go. And now it had gone, all of it, and as uniforms surrounded them, as helicopters broke the sky into pieces over their heads, they wondered if such a thing as this could ever be let go of, or if such a thing would haunt them for the rest of their lives.

Better haunted than dead, one of them thought – a young woman of twenty-three called Faith Duggan. She'd been there

427

when Ray Dietz had broken a security guard's neck with no greater ceremony than a wishbone. Such things as this had always been part of other people's lives. Now, on Christmas Eve of all days, those people had included herself.

SIXTY-SEVEN

By the time Frank Duchaunak – breathless, drenched in sweat – reached Bethune and Greenwich the party was over.

He was immediately stopped by a Federal Agent who asked for his ID. When Duchaunak showed it the agent told him to stand right where he was, to not move, and then he took a radio from his belt and called someone.

'We have him,' the agent said, and Duchaunak – confused, unaware of what was happening – merely scanned the street for any kind of reference point.

The agent put away his radio. 'You are armed, Detective?' he asked.

Duchaunak nodded absent-mindedly.

'I must ask you to relinquish your weapon,' the agent said.

Duchaunak turned and looked at him.

'Your weapon sir . . . I need your weapon.'

'The fuck you do—' Duchaunak started, and then another man came hurrying towards him, an older man, dressed immaculately.

'Detective Duchaunak,' the second man said. 'My name is Robert Hennessy. I am responsible for co-ordination between the Federal presence here and the local police. I have spoken with Captain McLuhan—'

'He's here?' Duchaunak asked. The first agent stepped back, the weapon forgotten.

Hennessy shook his head and smiled. 'No Detective, he's not here.'

'What happened to the girl?' Duchaunak asked. 'I heard that the girl had been taken out.'

Hennessy frowned. 'Girl?'

'Hollander . . . Cathy Hollander . . . the girl who was with Freiberg—'

429

'Right, right, yes of course. Cathy Hollander.'

'She's dead? And Freiberg? Is he dead too?'

'Freiberg . . . no Detective, he's not dead. Right now we are still pursuing seven of the original felons.'

'But the girl . . . you got the girl?'

'Calm down, Detective. The girl is quite alright. She's being taken care of as we speak.'

'Alright?' Duchaunak shook his head. He was still looking down the street, over his shoulder, every once in a while upwards as the sound of a helicopter caught his attention. 'What d'you mean, she's alright? Someone shot her. One of your people took her out, didn't they?'

'Cathy Hollander is one of us, Detective. Her name isn't Cathy Hollander, never has been. She is a Federal Agent. It was she who provided all the information regarding the robberies that were planned today . . . she is the reason we were here, Detective—'

'What?' Duchaunak asked. 'She's what? What the fuck are you talking about? The girl has a police record going back fifteen years. She has aliases, names she's used in other states—'

Hennessy was smiling. 'She has a fabricated police record Detective. She has a fictional history. Cathy Holl— her name is actually Ruth Delaney, but as Cathy Hollander she was put inside the Marcus camp a long time ago to break the back of this New York situation.'

'But she was shot. One of your people told me she'd been shot.'

'She was shot intentionally, Detective. She made herself visible to one of our sharpshooters on purpose. She wore a bulletproof vest and she was shot with a rubber bullet. It was a simple procedure to have the remainder of her crew leave her behind. These people do not take their dead along with them, not when they could be carrying money instead.'

'I don't understand—'

'It's okay, Detective. Come with me. We're going back to see Captain McLuhan and there we can get you updated on what is happening with the remainder of the people involved.' Hennessy reached out his hand to guide Duchaunak away from the sidewalk and towards a waiting vehicle.

'And Freiberg?' Duchaunak asked as he walked.

'Who knows?' Hennessy said. 'He's out there somewhere,

doing his very best to evade capture. I'm sure we will have him in custody within the hour.'

Duchaunak stopped suddenly. 'And you know about John Harper?'

Hennessy smiled once more, an expression that made Duchaunak feel small and insignificant. 'Of course we know about John Harper. We've been keeping a very close eye on Mr Harper to ensure that he doesn't get himself into any serious difficulties. We even had people in Miami telling Marcus's people just enough to keep them wondering about him. We wanted to ensure that he did not become involved in what was happening today, at least not directly.'

'And now?' Duchaunak asked. 'Where is he now?'

Hennessy shook his head. 'He was last seen leaving the vicinity of West Twelfth. I would've had someone go after him but he was safe and we have no reason to upset him further. I'm sure he will make his way back to his hotel and we will speak with him later.'

'I need to see him,' Duchaunak said. 'I need to see John Harper.'

'Later,' Hennessy said. 'First we'll speak with Captain McLuhan, and then you can see Mr Harper.'

Duchaunak shook his head. 'No,' he said. 'I want to see him now. I'm going over to the hotel. I want to speak with him, and then I'll go and see McLuhan.'

Hennessy shook his head. 'I cannot force you, Detective. I would much prefer it if you would come with me and see Captain McLuhan—'

Duchaunak smiled at Hennessy. 'Look,' he said. 'The kid must be scared out of his fucking wits. He helped us, you know? He was the one who met with Ben Marcus. He told me about West Twelfth. That's the only reason I knew to come here. Let me go speak with him. Let me go give him some kind of an idea of what's happening here. Tell McLuhan I'll be at the precinct no later than noon.'

Hennessy hesitated.

'Am I under arrest for something?' Duchaunak asked. 'Jesus, I just want to go see the guy and make sure he's okay.'

'Okay,' Hennessy said. 'But go see your precinct Captain at noon like you said, okay?'

'I will, I will . . . don't worry.'

'And I'll have one of my people drive you over to see Harper.'

'Thank you,' Duchaunak said.

Eighteen minutes later Frank Duchaunak walked through the front door of the American Regent Hotel. He glanced over his shoulder at the Federal Agent seated in a car against the sidewalk. He hurried past the reception desk, along a corridor that ran adjacent to the restaurant, took a back stairway down to the lower kitchens and hurried between racks of pans and cooking utensils to the rear service doors. He flashed his ID at one of the staff and told her he needed to leave by the rear exit. The girl obliged, opened the door for Duchaunak, and then watched him as he hurried up the concrete incline of the delivery entrance towards the street behind the hotel.

Duchaunak knew that John Harper would not be in his hotel room. Truth be known he could have been anywhere in the city, but Duchaunak doubted it. He had an idea, just an idea, that John Harper might have gone home.

SIXTY-EIGHT

The man's hand was steady, remained so even when John Harper appeared in the kitchen doorway. The gun seemed too small to do any real damage, but nevertheless it was a .38, a caliber sufficient to keep Walt Freiberg right where he was.

Evelyn Sawyer smiled. 'John,' she said softly. 'It's good to see you.' She glanced towards the man standing in the corner of the room, the one who held the gun on Freiberg.

'I'd like you to meet someone,' she said. 'This is Thomas McCaffrey . . . he's been staying with me for a few days.'

Harper looked at McCaffrey, then turned and looked at Freiberg. Freiberg was seated in a straight-backed chair against the wall, his hands on his knees, at his feet two dark canvas bags.

'Sonny,' Walt said.

'Don't call me that, Walt,' Harper said. 'Please don't call me that any more.'

'Pay no mind to him, John,' Evelyn said. 'Walt has been busy this morning . . . busy doing the things that Walt does. Figured he could come over here and finish his outstanding business before he left New York for good. Right, Walter?' Evelyn smiled. 'He thought that he could come over here and charm me, didn't you Walter?'

Freiberg shook his head. 'Evelyn—'

'Don't say anything else,' Evelyn said. 'I've heard enough out of you for a lifetime. You don't have anything to say to me . . . it's John that you need to be explaining things to.' She turned and glanced at Harper. 'You come on in and sit by me and Thomas . . . come and listen to what Walter has to say.'

'I'm going to stay right where I am,' Harper said. 'I want to know what the hell is going on here. Who *is* this guy?'

'Thomas?' Evelyn said. 'Why, he's the man who shot your father—'

433

'What the fu—'

'Don't lose it on me now, John,' Evelyn said, her voice almost sympathetic. 'Thomas was paid a great deal of money to shoot your father. How much was it?'

'A hundred thousand dollars,' McCaffrey said.

'But Thomas only got half of that . . . half before and half after, that was the arrangement he made with Ben Marcus. Thomas did exactly what he was asked. He was there in the liquor store when your father arrived. He shot him. Meant to kill him, but hell, these things have a way of going wrong, eh?' Evelyn smiled, shook her head. 'But Thomas wasn't to know. He didn't know Edward was going to wind up in St Vincent's.'

'John, for God's sake—' Freiberg said.

'I'm talking now, Walter,' Evelyn said. 'You'll get more than enough chance shortly.' She looked at Harper, shook her head slowly. 'Thomas was hired to shoot Edward. He knew Raymond Dietz. He and Raymond did time together . . . where was that Thomas?'

'Attica,' McCaffrey said. 'We did time at Attica.'

'Right, Attica. And Ray and he got friends. Spend that much time in a room with someone and you're going to make friends with them, aren't you? It was Ray who gave Thomas the gun that he used to shoot Edward . . . and you know the irony of that? Gun was thirty something years old . . . same gun that was used in a robbery committed by Ray and Garrett back in 1974. That's amazing, don't you think, John? My husband's gun, a gun that ended up with Ray Dietz, was used to shoot Edward Bernstein.'

'I don't want to hear this—' Harper started.

'But you have to hear it—' Evelyn replied.

'She's a fucking lying, crazy bitch,' Freiberg said.

'Shut your mouth, Walter!' Evelyn snapped. 'Say another word and Thomas is going to shoot you in the face, right Thomas?'

'Sure as fuck I am . . . you keep your fucking mouth shut Walter.'

Evelyn smiled. 'I was hoping you'd come, John . . . hoping that you'd come and join us in a little game of Truth or Dare.'

Harper frowned.

'Evelyn here has her mind all twisted up in back of itself—' Freiberg started.

434

'Shut the hell up, Walt!' she snapped. 'My mind is as clear today as it was back then. I know what I know, there's no getting around that. You're going to let me finish what I have to say, and then you're going to have a chance to speak, okay?'

Freiberg said nothing.

Evelyn was quiet for a moment, gathering herself, calming down. She looked at Harper and there seemed to be a ghost of ironic humor in her eyes. 'So Thomas went to meet with Raymond Dietz after the shooting. Went to collect the other fifty thousand dollars he was owed. When he got there he figured something was wrong. He didn't see Raymond, saw someone else, and he knew that Ben Marcus was going to betray him. So what did he do? He thought about who might help him. He thought about the time he spent in Attica with Raymond Dietz, about everything they talked about. Raymond had told him all about Garrett, about me, about Edward Bernstein. He figured there was a chance I might not be too unhappy about Edward getting shot, so he took that chance. He came over here. We had a discussion, didn't we, Thomas?'

'We did, Evelyn, we did.'

'Discussion was a little tense to say the least. Thomas had a gun aimed at me the whole time, didn't you?'

'I did, Evelyn, yes . . . but I apologized for that.'

'Yes, you did, Thomas, you did apologize. So we had our discussion and we came to an arrangement. I would help Thomas. I would hide him here in the house, and he would protect me and you.'

Harper frowned. 'Protect me?'

Evelyn smiled. 'You were so naïve, John. You saw what you wanted to see. You had no idea who these people were . . . the kind of things these people could do. I agreed with Thomas that if anything happened to you he would find Walter Freiberg, Sol Neumann, Ben Marcus, whoever might have been responsible, and he would kill them for me.'

Harper looked at McCaffrey, standing back behind Evelyn, the gun in his hand aimed unerringly at Walt Freiberg. Walt Freiberg looked back at Evelyn with hatred blazing in his eyes.

'Walter?' Evelyn said. 'It's your turn to speak now. John's here, and you're going to tell him the truth about what happened

435

with Anne and Garrett, and then I'm going to have Thomas shoot you dead right where you're sitting.'

Walt smiled, almost laughed. 'She's a little fractious today,' he said.

McCaffrey edged forward.

Harper stepped out of the doorway and flattened himself against the right-hand wall.

'Evelyn?' Walt said. 'For God's sake Evelyn, tell him to put the thing away.'

'Shut up, Walter!' Evelyn barked. She shifted back in her chair, almost as if she was preparing to stand the recoil herself when McCaffrey pulled the trigger.

'Evelyn—' Harper said, his voice weak.

'It's okay, John,' Evelyn said, interrupting him. 'Walt was just about to share a few home truths with us . . . going to give us a few details about our family history, weren't you, Walter?'

Walt Freiberg shook his head. He turned to look at Harper, and Harper could see that the man was scared. Walt Freiberg was *never* scared. Evelyn had cornered him, and there was something he did not wish to face.

'So?' Evelyn prompted. 'Are you going to start with telling us how Garrett was there in the room when Anne took all those pills, Walter?'

'What?' Harper said. He stepped forward.

'Stand back where you were, John,' Evelyn said. 'You don't want to find yourself in the line of fire when Walter gets shot.'

Harper instinctively stepped back. He felt his knees weaken beneath him. He looked at Freiberg, perhaps expecting him to make some attempt to defend himself, but there was nothing. He just sat there, his hands on his knees, the canvas bags at his feet.

'You want me to carry on, Walter, or are you going to join in?'

Freiberg shook his head slowly. He closed his eyes and leaned his head back against the wall.

'So,' Evelyn said, 'as Walter was all set to tell us, Garrett was right there when Anne took those pills. She didn't want to take them, did she Walter? Didn't want to take them at all, but you and Edward decided she was a nuisance didn't you? Edward wanted to take John away from her but she wasn't going to allow that, right? You decided that she was in the way, and so you told

436

Garrett that if he didn't take care of Anne then he would lose his wife as well as his sister-in-law. You were going to kill us both, weren't you? You were going to kill me and Anne if Garrett didn't make sure Anne was—'

'John . . . you can't listen to her,' Freiberg said, and he raised his hand as if to emphasize something.

'Don't move your hands!' Evelyn snapped. 'Keep your hands exactly where they are.'

Freiberg returned his hands to his lap.

'You don't have to listen, John,' Evelyn said, 'but you wanted to know the truth, and here you're going to get it, pure and simple.'

Harper didn't say a word.

'Garrett was there that day,' she said, her voice cracking with emotion. 'He was right there in the room upstairs. He told Anne that if she stood in Edward's way then Edward was going to kill you. He would've done that. He's that kind of man. Edward Bernstein would have killed his own son rather than let him stay with his mother. She knew what kind of man he was, and she knew what kind of people he was surrounded by. She knew that Edward was going to kill her, or he was going to kill you. That was her choice John . . . that was your mother's choice. Give up her own life, or give up the life of her son.'

Evelyn turned and looked at Harper. Her eyes were filled with tears.

McCaffrey held the gun steady, never moving an inch from where it was aimed at Freiberg's head.

'So Garrett did what he was told. He sat there while she took those pills. He told me what happened. He told me how he lay her down and covered her with a blanket, and watched her as she went to sleep. He said she looked so peaceful, so content, like she knew in her heart of hearts that she'd done the right thing. He told me this, John . . . told me later. I said you were out with Garrett that day, but you weren't. You were over with Francine and Grace.' Evelyn paused. The atmosphere was unbearable. 'Last thing she ever said was to make sure no harm came to you. That's what she told Garrett, to make sure that no harm came to you. And then we had to protect you, protect you from your father, and because of what he'd done Garrett felt a duty to stop Edward taking you away. That's why Garrett was killed—'

'Killed?' Harper said, almost involuntarily. His mind was reeling.

'Killed,' Evelyn stated matter-of-factly. 'And we know who killed him, don't we Walter?'

Harper turned and looked at Freiberg.

'That's right,' Evelyn said. 'Our friend Uncle Walt, instructed by your father of course, took the situation in hand and murdered my husband. And then there was only me left . . . only me that stood between Edward Bernstein and his son. And that was the greatest irony of all.' Evelyn paused, smiled, started to laugh to herself. 'Two days after Garrett died your father was arrested and sent to prison. He was sent to prison for something else entirely, and he didn't come out until some time after you'd left for Florida. And he could have found you, he could have found you very easily—' Evelyn turned and looked at Harper. 'He could've found you so very easily, but you know what? He'd been away for that many years, and whatever had existed in his mind had long since faded away. He didn't want you any more. Two people had died, two people he'd believed had stood in his way, and it was almost like he reached a point where there was nothing stopping him from finding you, from speaking with you, from telling you who he was, and at that point, when it was right there for him to take, he didn't want it any more.'

Evelyn looked at Freiberg.

'And then Edward spoke to Ben Marcus, told him that he wanted to sell his territory. Ben Marcus figured he could take it with a lot less expense. He agreed with Edward, and as soon as Edward started paying his dues, letting people go . . . as soon as Ben Marcus figured that Edward was vulnerable, he paid Thomas to shoot him. When Edward was shot Walter's best-laid plans started to fall apart. He didn't know what was going to happen. Maybe he figured he should cover all bases and have you as close as possible, make you obvious . . . and to see that I said nothing to the police.'

Walt Freiberg shook his head. He turned towards Harper. 'John, none of this is true—'

'I told you to shut the hell up, Walter!' Evelyn snapped. 'You had your chance to speak and you didn't take it. Interrupt me again and—'

'John, believe me—'

'Believe you?' Evelyn said. 'Christ Walter, when was it ever the case that someone should believe you?'

'Believe me now,' Walt Freiberg said. 'Believe me now. Believe that I didn't have anything to do with your mother's death, and I sure as hell wasn't responsible for Garrett's murder—'

'Give me a reason,' Harper said.

Freiberg looked at him, frowned slightly.

'Give me one good reason . . . one good solid reason to believe you Walt.'

Freiberg hesitated.

'Where's Cathy?' Harper asked.

'Cathy?'

'Yes, you know? Cathy Hollander? Where is she, Walt?'

'She didn't make it John,' someone said from the hallway.

They all turned – Freiberg, John Harper, Evelyn, even Thomas McCaffrey. They all turned at the sound of another voice beyond the kitchen door, and before anyone could speak Frank Duchaunak appeared in the doorway, in his hand the .45, an expression on his face like everything was coming together, everything was tying up tight like shoelaces, and he was the one who'd done it.

'She was there at the bank, right Walter?' Duchaunak said.

'What the hell are you doing here?' Evelyn asked.

For a moment McCaffrey seemed unsure as to whether he should aim the gun at Duchaunak or keep it trained on Freiberg.

'Figured this is where John would come,' Duchaunak said. 'Figured it was time for a few lies and untruths to be dispelled.' He looked at Harper, at Freiberg, then at Thomas McCaffrey.

'We haven't been introduced,' Duchaunak said. 'You are?'

'This is Thomas McCaffrey,' Evelyn said. 'The man Ben Marcus paid to shoot Edward Bernstein.'

Duchaunak nodded. 'McCaffrey,' he said. 'You have a brother and a sister, right?'

McCaffrey frowned, started to look nervous. 'What about them?'

Duchaunak shook his head. 'They put in a Missing Persons on you,' he lied.

'We were just talking,' Evelyn said.

'Dispelling some little white lies, right?' Duchaunak said.

Evelyn smiled. 'We were doing *just* that,' she said. 'I was explaining to John how my husband killed Anne, and then Walter killed my husband . . . all because of Edward Bernstein.' She shook her head. 'It still amazes me that one man could have created so much hurt and pain and destruction in so many lives.'

'It doesn't surprise me,' Duchaunak said. He took another step into the room. He looked to his left, looked over at Freiberg who sat motionless, and then to his right at Harper.

'Go take a seat with your aunt,' he said. He waved his gun in the direction of the table.

Harper stepped across McCaffrey's line of fire and took a seat on the other side of the table.

'So here's another one for your collection Walter,' Duchaunak said. 'And maybe John will appreciate this.'

Harper looked up, first at Freiberg, then at Duchaunak.

'I told you a couple of things about Cathy Hollander,' Duchaunak said to Harper. 'Told you she wasn't only called Cathy Hollander, remember?'

Harper nodded.

'Right, sure you remember. Told you she went by the name of Margaret Miller and Diane Sheridan.' Duchaunak smiled knowingly. He looked at Freiberg. 'This one's for you Walter. Seems her real name is actually Ruth Delaney.'

Freiberg shook his head. 'You what? What the hell are you talking about?'

'Federal Agent Ruth Delaney, FBI Crime Task Force . . . she got your number Walt, Edward's too, and Ben Marcus and the whole sorry collection of wasters and assholes and fuckwits that you associate with. All of you, every single one of you is done for. We already have Beck and Parselle, Ron Dearing, Joe Koenig, though it's uncertain he'll make it, 'cause he got shot in the spine while he was trying to run away. We got Ricky Wheland and Karl Merrett—'

'Bullshit!' Freiberg snapped. 'You're just talking bullshit, Duchaunak.'

'Whatever you say Walt, whatever you say. Fact of the matter is that the whole house of cards you people built is crashing down around your fucking ears, and here you are, sat on a chair in Evelyn's kitchen and too fucking frightened to move.'

'I saw her shot,' Freiberg said, in his voice a tone of anger. 'I saw her get shot right there in the bank.'

'Sure you did,' Duchaunak replied. 'You saw exactly what you were supposed to see. You saw someone with a bulletproof vest get hit by a rubber bullet and go down.'

Freiberg was silent, his eyes blinking rapidly, looking at Evelyn, at McCaffrey, back to Duchaunak, across to Harper.

Maybe he was frightened; maybe he was just desperate; perhaps it was simply that Duchaunak had goaded him into responding. Whatever the reason Walt Freiberg moved, surprisingly quickly.

Regardless, he was not quick enough.

Evelyn Sawyer, incensed with anger, with guilt, with the tension of all that had happened, snatched the gun from McCaffrey and jerked the trigger back. The recoil almost knocked her from the chair; she was not used to firing a handgun, or any other type of gun for that matter. But her aim was sufficiently good, the range sufficiently close, and the bullet – a .38 caliber – hit Walter Freiberg in the throat and put him on the floor.

Harper and Duchaunak – deafened, stunned – didn't move.

Didn't even move when Evelyn turned and looked at Harper, when she shook her head and smiled, when she raised the very same gun and pressed it to her temple.

No, Harper mouthed. And then he voiced it. 'No, Evelyn! Nooo!' and his hand reached out towards her.

'I'm sorry, John,' she whispered. 'I'm so, so sorry . . .'

She pulled the trigger.

She was dead before Freiberg, but only by seconds, and perhaps Freiberg's frantic clutching, the way he clawed at his own neck in an attempt to take out the bullet, to tear the pain out of himself, to stem the rush of blood that jetted from the wound and spread quickly across the floor, filling the gaps between the ceramic tiles . . . perhaps his movements were nothing but involuntary nervous reactions, his brain fighting for survival even when survival had ceased to be an option.

Harper reacted; he lunged from his seat towards Evelyn, grabbing at her in some desperate attempt to stop her long after the point at which anything could have been done.

Duchaunak flattened himself against the wall, raised his .45

and aimed it directly at McCaffrey. McCaffrey – still stunned, speechless, his eyes wide – backed up and raised his hands.

Duchaunak kept the gun steady, but managed to grab Harper's jacket collar, held him back, almost fighting with him, dragging him away from where he kneeled on the floor.

'No!' he was shouting. 'John . . . no! No! Don't touch them! Don't touch anything!'

Eventually, unable to even register what had happened, unable to find words to describe, to define, to determine the consequence of such events, John Harper rose to his feet and stepped back against the wall.

'Don't do anything,' Duchaunak said. 'Don't touch them, don't move anything!'

Harper looked at Duchaunak; in his eyes a complete vacancy of emotion.

'You!' Duchaunak snapped at McCaffrey.

McCaffrey didn't move.

'Step over there to the right.'

McCaffrey did as he was told.

Duchaunak leaned forward and took the gun from Evelyn Sawyer's hand. He tucked it in his jacket pocket. He stood up, nodded to the two bags that had been at Freiberg's feet and told McCaffrey to pick them up.

McCaffrey complied, said nothing, merely stood there with an expression of horror on his face.

'You come with me,' he said to McCaffrey. McCaffrey nodded and took a step towards the kitchen door.

Duchaunak looked down at Harper. 'Get up, John,' he said quietly, his voice almost a whisper. 'Walter left a yellow cab out in the street.' He smiled. 'Smart people, huh? They had four of them . . . they were going to lose themselves in the taxi driver's parade in the city.' Duchaunak shook his head resignedly. 'Today they were not smart enough.'

Harper pushed himself away from the wall and started towards the door. He paused for a moment, daring himself to look back, to survey the devastation that had occurred within the narrow confines of a room so reminiscent of his childhood.

He couldn't do it. He held his breath for a moment, closed his eyes, and then stepped out into the hallway and made his way to the front door.

He believed, and was correct in his belief, that he was leaving the house on Carmine for the very last time.

Duchaunak motioned for McCaffrey to follow Harper.

The three of them moved quickly and quietly out of the kitchen, down the hallway, and left the house for the street.

Duchaunak had McCaffrey drive the yellow cab. Told him to drive to the American Regent. They dropped John Harper off at the front entrance. Duchaunak told Harper to go to his room, to wait there, that someone would come and speak with him. Said he was taking McCaffrey and the money to his precinct, to Captain McLuhan, that there was a Federal Agent waiting for him.

Once Harper was out of sight Frank Duchaunak told Thomas McCaffrey about his brother and sister. McCaffrey got hysterical. Duchaunak slapped him repeatedly, jammed Dietz's gun in his ribs and told him to 'quiet the fuck down'.

'Ben Marcus had them killed,' he told McCaffrey. 'He had two of his people go visit with them, wanted to see if they knew where you were. They didn't know a thing. When they were done asking questions Marcus's people killed them both.'

Then Duchaunak told McCaffrey to drive over to the warehouse on West and Bloomfield near Pier 53.

Duchaunak had McCaffrey park the car across the street. He pointed up towards the second floor. 'Ben Marcus is inside that building,' Duchaunak said, and then he took Ray Dietz's gun from his jacket pocket and gave it to McCaffrey.

'You should go in there and collect the fifty grand he owes you . . . and take whatever else you feel is adequate recompense for your brother and sister. I'll wait here for you, okay?'

McCaffrey frowned, shook his head. 'I don't—'

'You go see Ben Marcus,' Duchaunak said. 'You go tell him whatever's on your mind.'

McCaffrey hesitated for a moment, and then he reached for the door lever and stepped out.

'One other thing,' Duchaunak said.

McCaffrey turned.

'Give Ben Marcus a message for me would you? Tell him that Sonny Bernstein was a newspaper reporter . . . just that.'

McCaffrey frowned. 'Sonny Bernstein was a newspaper reporter? What the fuck does that mean?'

Duchaunak smiled and shook his head. 'It doesn't matter. Ben Marcus will understand what it means. Just tell him that would you? Tell him that from me.'

McCaffrey nodded. 'Sure I'll tell him . . . and you're going to wait here, right?'

'Sure I am,' Duchaunak replied, and smiled.

Frank Duchaunak did wait. He waited all of four or five minutes, and when he heard the first three shots in quick succession he started the engine and shifted gear.

When the fourth and fifth shot came he pulled away and depressed the accelerator.

He smiled at the irony. Ray Dietz's gun, a gun that had once belonged to Garrett Sawyer, had killed Walt Freiberg, Evelyn Sawyer, and now Ben Marcus.

If Edward Bernstein didn't make it . . . well, that would be the sharpest irony of all.

Frank Duchaunak glanced over his shoulder at the two canvas bags on the back seat, and then he reached forward and switched on the radio.

SIXTY-NINE

She came later, Cathy Hollander, Ruth Delaney, whatever her name was.

Came to the American Regent and sat with Harper in silence for some time.

She tried to explain who she was, what she did, how she had done her best to protect him from the violence of these people. She had done what she'd been capable of, nothing more nor less, for she believed in her purpose, and her purpose and duty dictated her actions. Not her emotions. Nor her humanity.

'And me?' he asked her.

She looked at him, her eyes wide, and then she shook her head.

'You don't have anything to say?'

'What do you want me to say?' she asked.

Harper laughed dismissively. Somewhere within him was the desire to make her feel bad. 'What do *I* want you to say? *I* don't want you to say anything.'

She stepped forward. 'I let you think that I—'

'You speak about emotions. Humanity. You think such things are the sole preserve of people like you? You let me think what you wanted me to think.' Harper glared at her. 'You led me on Cathy . . . aah, fuck, whatever the hell your name is now. You led me on. You let me think what you wanted me to think, and then when it became something altogether a little too real you just dismissed it. I have something to say about—'

'I know,' she interjected. 'And I'm sorry—'

'I don't want your apology.' Harper rose from his chair and took a step towards her. 'You wanna know what I want? I'll tell you, plain and fucking simple. I want my fucking life back, okay? If you can't give me that then I don't want anything.'

Ruth Delaney did not reply.

445

Harper smiled bitterly and sat down again. 'So tell me what happens now? Let's keep this strictly business . . . after all, that was all it ever was to you, right?'

She tried to apologize again, to attempt some explanation, but Harper cut her short.

'You don't want to hear anything that I have to say?' she asked.

'I want to hear how the fuck I get out of here and go home,' he said, his voice sharp and direct.

She nodded. 'Okay,' she replied. 'Okay.' She said that someone had called in regarding the house on Carmine. That the call was anonymous. There were people over there even now, people gathering the evidence needed for a clear understanding of what had happened.

'I know what happened,' Harper told her.

'You don't need to say anything now,' she said. 'There will be more than enough time to speak later.'

Of the crews, those who had undertaken the robberies that morning, she told him that they had all been arrested. All but two. Sol Neumann and Victor Klein were dead.

As was Edward Bernstein.

Passed away quietly, silently, at two-thirteen p.m., afternoon of Christmas Eve.

Harper said nothing. There was nothing to say.

After a while Harper asked her if she knew the truth of his mother, of Evelyn, Garrett, the things that had happened so many years before.

She shook her head. 'We think that Garrett assisted in your mother's suicide,' she told him. 'We aren't sure, but from the little I gleaned from Ben Marcus and your father it seemed to make sense—'

Harper raised his hand. 'Enough,' he said. 'I don't think I *want* to know any more.'

Ruth Delaney fell silent. As did Cathy Hollander, Margaret Miller, Diane Sheridan, perhaps several more.

There was silence in that room for quite a while.

Eventually she rose, stepped forward, reached out her hand and touched the side of John Harper's face.

'Go home,' she whispered. 'After you have said all you need to say you should go home . . . go back to Miami and put your life together.'

Harper looked up at her. He smiled, an expression of philosophical resignation. 'My life?' he asked. 'What life would that be?'

She smiled, withdrew her hand. 'I must go now,' she said.

'One question?'

She nodded.

'Did you really read my book?'

'Yes, I really did read your book,' she replied.

Harper raised his eyebrows.

'You should write another,' she said quietly. 'And another, and another . . . you have a gift, John Harper.'

She walked to the door, then paused with her fingers on the handle. 'A question for you,' she said.

Harper turned.

'Frank Duchaunak. He drove you here from your aunt's on Carmine Street?'

Harper nodded.

'And did he say where he was going?'

'To see his Captain,' Harper said. 'He said I was to wait here, that someone would come and see me. He said that he'd tell them what happened at the Carmine Street house, and that he had to go and see his Captain. Why?'

She smiled, shook her head. 'No reason,' she said.

Harper said nothing.

'I'll call you,' she said. 'I'll call to see you're okay.'

'Whatever,' Harper said, his tone disinterested.

'Do you want someone to talk to about this . . . I mean, apart from everything that happened . . . do you want someone to speak to about your father, about Evelyn?'

Harper turned and looked at her, an expression of disbelief on his face. 'Talk to someone? What d'you mean?'

'We have people who are trained to—'

'To help me deal with this? Is that what you're saying? You have people who are trained to deal with this shit?' He shook his head. 'Get out of here. Just get the fuck out of here, will you?'

She paused by the door, paused for just a moment, and then she was gone.

Harper didn't move for a while, and then he rose slowly,

447

walked to the window, and leaning his hands against the glass he looked out through the spaces between his fingers.

New York, he thought. Sinatra's town. He tried to imagine such a place being his home. It didn't work. He bowed his head; he closed his eyes.

It was a long time before he moved.

EPILOGUE

Perhaps it is to here that I have been travelling all my life.

He feels no pain, no emptiness. He feels nothing that demands any attention.

Above and beneath everything there is no guilt; this more than anything.

Standing there, looking out towards the keys of Fish Hawk and Snipe, beyond that Johnston and Sawyer, the name in and of itself a small and quiet irony, John Harper believes that everything has in some way turned full circle.

He took the Greyhound Bus; made eight stops between Miami and Key West. Down through Islamorada, Key Largo, Marathon and Grassy Key; two routes – one from the Florida Turnpike which wound up in Homestead, the other along I-95 which became US 1 at the southern end of Miami. Both roads made it to the Overseas Highway, but this time he'd kept on going.

And there was something about this place – all thirty-one punctuations of limestone, the eight hundred uninhabited islands that surrounded them – that forever gripped his imagination. Here, on this awkward peninsula of hope, he believed himself a million miles from the memory of New York.

South and east was the Atlantic, west was the Gulf of Mexico; forty-two bridges, dozens of causeways; gingerbread verandas, widow's walks, wrought-iron balconies; John Pennekamp Coral Reef State Park with its starfish and lobsters, its sponges and sea cucumbers, its stingrays, barracuda, crabs and angel fish.

And then there was Key Largo, shoals of blackfin tuna, overhead the waves of frigate birds that told you when the fish were running. And the smell, the once-in-a-lifetime smell of salt, seaweed, fish and marsh, mangrove swamps and rocks, the memory of pirates and Ponce de Leon, the Dry Tortugas, the footprints of turtles, the reefs, the clear water, the citrus, the coconut . . .

All these things a hundred and fifty miles from where he'd once sat in a small backroom office in the *Miami Herald* complex.

And all these things were now his home.

John Harper understood that to feel no guilt was not a crime.

He understood that time would pass, and as it did a certain vague and indefinable shadow would close over the past, and the past would become a representation of what he once had been, not what he would become.

He did not stay in New York.

He answered as many questions as he could bear – questions from Federal people, from Captain Michael McLuhan, others whose names he could not now recall. He asked for Frank Duchaunak, for Cathy Hollander, but neither of them appeared. He told them of Thomas McCaffrey, of the final minutes in the house on Carmine. They acted like Thomas McCaffrey didn't exist, and they forwarded no details of his whereabouts.

They went over Duchaunak's final words to him; exactly what had been said, how Duchaunak had looked, every nuance and possibility. Harper told them what he could remember, which was not very much at all.

Harper attended no funerals, paid no respects. He felt that such a gesture would have been as much a lie as those he'd been told.

He left New York on the twenty-seventh of December.

He believed – in his black and broken heart – that he would never go back.

John Harper no longer works for the *Herald*. He no longer speaks to Harry Ivens, or any of the others who populated the life he lived before New York.

He never spoke to Cathy Hollander again, for she never called, and Harper believed that such an omission was perhaps a good thing.

Harper believes now that the muse has come home; he finds his dry narrative and his succinct prose, and he sits before a battered typewriter, ahead of him the doors open, beyond them the plankboard veranda . . .

He moved all the way south to the end of the peninsula, and he writes.

Because that was, and still is, what he was supposed to do:

Passionate, impassioned, bruised, forgotten, lost; grabbing at life in handfuls too broad to be carried. And staggering now, heart empty, folding beneath the vast weight of loss like an origami bird crushed within a fist. An angry fist, white-knuckled and pained. Sweating, wide-awake, the dawn was cold, brutally cold, and I longed for morning if only to know another day had started, and thus be certain – irrevocably certain – that a day such as this would end. But this day, of all days, I lost my father. In a moment of brutality that was some ironic reflection of his own life, he was subjected to truth and reality. And it was the truth – above and beyond all else – that finally killed him. Another light. Silently, almost unnoticed . . . another light went out in New York.

Come nightfall John Harper walks out onto the beach. He knows that Hemingway and Williams, John Hersey, James Merrill, Tom McGuane and Phil Caputo . . . knows that all of them once stood right where he stands, and they too looked out towards the Keys of Fish Hawk, Halfmoon and Little Truman. He hesitates in the footprints of giants, and there – at the southernmost point of the continental United States – John Michael Harper, he of the dry and bitter humor, he of the lost loves and lonely nights, he of clenched fists and once-silent typewriter, he of burgeoning promise and unfulfilled potential, knows that he has come home.

Home, perhaps, is not where the heart is, but where – at last – you find it.

He had been there a month, perhaps a little more, when the package came.

He'd rented a place, nothing more than a plankboard shack truth be known, but the roof was sufficient, and the wood was strong, and he felt safe and detached and hopeful. He had a little money, nothing to speak of, and he knew that at some point such an absence of provision would demand his attention. For

451

the meanwhile it seemed unimportant, irrelevant, a responsibility that was awkward and unharmonious.

So the package came by hand; a mailman walked down the sand road at the top of the beach, and he smiled as he gave Harper the package and said his good day. The package was wrapped in brown paper, the size of a large shoebox, and when Harper opened it, tentative, curious, he took a moment to inspect the careful script with which the address was written. It seemed to be a disguised hand, as if someone had not wished their writing to be identified.

The package had made its way from somewhere to the *Miami Herald*, where someone had forwarded it to Harper's previous address, and from there someone had impelled it to find him come what may. And find him it had.

Inside the box, stacked neatly, bound tight with rubber bands, was three hundred thousand dollars in used fifty-dollar bills.

There was something else, wrapped in newspaper, wedged in the corner, and when Harper opened it he started laughing.

A baseball.

A beat-to-shit baseball with someone's name scrawled along the line of stitching.

Harper put the money back in the box. He hid the box beneath the floor. He told no-one.

The baseball he kept on his desk, right beside his typewriter, and every once in a while he would hold it and think of Norma Jean.

He never heard word of the sender, and it seemed that no-one else did. Harper believed he was out there somewhere, out there living his own kind of crazy, and the world had swallowed him silently and allowed him to disappear.

Standing now, looking out towards Key Sawyer as the sun rises, as it bravely escapes the line of horizon, Harper is reminded of Roth and Auster, Selby, Styron, all those before him that had written of New York. For it was the center of everything; a microcosm which represented all that was senseless and beautiful about the world.

And once more he felt no shame, no guilt, no desire to question the method or motive of his own existence. For a while, a short while perhaps, he would simply be himself, and in being himself he would experience all that such a thing entailed.

The wind picks up. The sun breaks the surface of the water and lights the sky quietly. The smell of the sea fills his nostrils. He is reminded of Styron in that moment, and how he had so eloquently paraphrased Emily Dickinson. He thinks of Sophie, Styron's heroine, how she had been forced by life to make her decision, a decision much the same as his own mother.

It was her choice, a choice so difficult, and yet so brutally simple.

And then Harper smiles and does not think of such things. For to think of such things brings darkness and pain, and these things he believes he has owned enough.

He knows now that this is not judgement day – only morning.

Morning: excellent and fair.